The Steep Side of the Marble

The Steep Side of the Marble

A Novel

Jones Deady

Rand-Smith Publishing

THE STEEP SIDE OF THE MARBLE
Copyright 2020 Jones Deady
All rights reserved
Print ISBN: 978-1-950544-20-2
Digital ISBN: 978-1-950544-22-6
Registered with the Library of Congress
Author photo by Andrew Cate Photography
 Rand-Smith Publishing
www.Rand-Smith.com
Ashland, VA
Printed in the USA

CONTENTS

1 | Baby Shoes 2

2 | A Home Painted Baby Blue 7

3 | The Unwritten Rules 14

4 | Burrowing into a New Horizon 19

5 | Prep Work 26

6 | A Week In 29

7 | Reeling Toward What's Known 37

8 | The Smell and Taste of Change 43

9 | Like Swallowing a Tiny Frog 47

10 | Bones 53

11 | The Windward Side 60

12 | The Tick of Old Roads 64

13 | Ghosts and Sparrows 71

CONTENTS

14 | The Still Air of Summer's Heart **73**

15 | Greetings **76**

16 | To Each His Own Will **83**

17 | Bracing **91**

18 | Covert Blooms **97**

19 | Truths that Hurt **100**

20 | Untethered **108**

21 | House Birds **117**

22 | Stretching Hope **122**

23 | Interred for Life **128**

24 | It Is Why We Fish **136**

25 | Fire **144**

26 | Crossed Fingers **151**

27 | Second Half **156**

28 | The Ghost of Them All **165**

29 | Pulling Off the Cloth **173**

30 | Room Temp Jell-O Molds **175**

CONTENTS

31 | Morning Glory 182

32 | Bliss in Old Ruins 187

33 | Salt in Our Wounds 194

34 | Crossing 198

35 | The Writer's Bloody Sword 208

36 | Beauty and Dead Eyes 218

37 | Threads to Darkness 227

38 | Sleight of Hand 231

39 | Back on the Front Lines 236

40 | Home 242

41 | A Glass Half Empty 248

42 | A Hard Change of Venue 251

43 | Our Unfaithful Minds 255

44 | The Pith of Summer 262

45 | The Tricky Prism of Health and Nostalgia 267

46 | Where Parallel Tracks Really End 274

CONTENTS

47 ▌ Looking to the Heart of the Marble **279**

48 ▌ Bird of Prey **281**

49 ▌ After the Rains, Into the Sparkle **290**

50 ▌ The Edge of the Marble **295**

51 ▌ Letting Go of the Handlebars **299**

52 ▌ Evoking Truth **303**

53 ▌ Behold a Piece of Paper **306**

54 ▌ In the Cold Nest **311**

55 ▌ The Tempest **318**

56 ▌ Bigbee's Last Night at the Party **324**

57 ▌ The Finest Hour **327**

Acknowledgments

This book is dedicated to my beautiful wife Laura, always the equilibrium in my life, always the one to remind me of the importance of my dreams. Her softness, balance, and also stalwart manner is a gift I will forever be trying to replicate. To my daughter, Tucker, and son, Dakota, who have grown up watching me within the highs and lows of writing, lending their cheering and support all the way. You are my heart and soul.

To the wonderful writer, Suzanne Kingsbury, for being the reader of my first draft and for believing in me.

Baby Shoes

Dar braced as the water hit her chest. Cold showers were not her custom, but the day ahead required a soldier's preparedness. Selling her daughter, Lily, on their new home would be a task, not unlike being called out of the trenches to face a hail of lead.

Turning to let the icy water fall over her shoulders, back, and legs, Dar felt remote to even the best of her senses and qualities. She breathed in and out, clenching and unclenching her fingers in the same rhythm. Her divorce, now a year past, had pretty much governed every conversation in some form or another. Even the narrowest roads of dialogue found their way to that man. Last night, it had been the steamed broccoli, or more so, the lemon. That was the way *he* liked it. Dar had abstained squeezing on that innocuous juice, and Lily had accused her of being "a big fat martyr," as her mother loved lemon in everything. Dar had laughed and told Lily she was being extreme. Adding that she did not plan on being sacrificed for being a purest, by just using salt. Squinting sharply, Lily had squeezed the whole lemon on her broccoli, saying that she and her father were alike in every subtle manner, and by damned, Dar better get used to looking in her eye and seeing her ex. There they were, stirring the same pot of fault, pain, melancholy, and their undeniable mother-daughter bond. How something so flawless as all that became riddled with holes flummoxed Dar. The inflexible truth—his affair—stood in such contradiction to the magnitude and depth of his goodness. He was a wonderful man, his flaws beguiling.

And there lay the pain of their shared loss. Dar reached to turn off the frigid water but took a deep breath and left it on.

An unconscious squeak exited Dar's chest. The sound coming off the shambles of her life, she told herself. Months of being single and afraid had turned her into a mess, she mused, shivering. Barely able to hold a job, or at least find one where promise, money, and satisfaction met and shook hands as friends. She was, by God, so unfairly lonely. Dar slapped the tile wall of the shower she would soon leave behind forever. A shower she had shared a million times with a man she had loved. Communed in this space, skin on skin, with a heart so full of sweetness and certainty that the image of it being over swamped her now with something that felt deadly and insidious. Marriage had faked its smile while conspiring against her.

She knew what it was like to be lost in a Bolivian jungle. That is how Dar had described the divorce to her psychiatrist, a woman she divorced when, after the third session, she accused Dar of looking for excuses to blame her ex for everything. Dar ran her rigid fingers through her wet hair and wanted to scream. Lowering her hands, she turned them palms up. The skin was shading blue and several strands of her auburn hair clung.

"I am even losing my goddamned hair," she said, the shrill of her voice echoing beyond the fall of water. Dar prayed Lily, in her bedroom down the hall, had not heard her. Lily must see her as strong this day, a tower making hard but necessary decisions for both.

Dar soaped up and told herself that she and Lily must begin to practice what the future might look like. They must look back at their prior family as an island they once lived upon. The unspoiled beauty of that time must be replaced by logic. The soap slipped from Dar's hand and fell with a clatter. Dar sighed, as Lily would never move offshore with her in whole. Lily was still plugged in to this house and its memories, clutching them as her old, raggedy stuffed animals. Lily missed her father, and anything Dar wanted to imagine to the contrary was an illusion. Yes, this was going to be a hellish day.

A week prior, in preparation for crossing over to a new life with Lily, Dar had mistakenly announced the divorce as having been a necessary arrangement for them to find goodness in their lives. She had patched that over, penning a different angle, with words not so clinical and unfair. She had commended their never-ending shared journey and things about new chapters.

That did not sit well with Lily, nor did the news falling out of Dar's mouth in tandem, that they might have to downsize from this big house and lower their expectations for a while. Lily's eyes glazed over, her chest stiffening to the image of her childhood fleeing. Dar cursed the ambition of her words to have a mind of their own. "We're broke, Lily," she added.

Lily struck back at this fiction. "Semantics," Lily said, adding, "Bet you have to look that word up." Both fell into hard silence, staring each other down and jerking their eyes away. The fact hanging over the room was that Lily's granny, Virginia, would line them up with whatever they needed if her ham-handed mother kicked the pride mantra. After their bout of silence, Lily accused Dar of being the most pedestrian mother in the world. "It is your albatross," Lily added. Dar told Lily to go her room, and Lily said she was leaving anyway.

Turning back, Lily apprised Dar with the most doubting look she could summon. "The downsizing idea, Mother, is like a tiny dot of light in a long dark tunnel that I will not be traveling through. I will move in with Granny."

"I am the adult here, like it or not," Dar responded. Now, Dar balanced that scene with how Lily would react today.

She turned off the shower and stood, dripping and cold, recalling the moment when Lily was told that she and her father were divorcing. Lily had put her hands over her ears and began to hum. Then, lowering her taut arms, she looked Dar in the eye more like a junkyard dog than a sweet and thin girl of fourteen. "Never," Lily said, and ran away for three days to her granny Virginia's house across town. The divorce should not have been a surprise for her, Dar thought, as she stepped out of the shower. After all, Lily had been awakened by their yelling the night Dar confronted her husband about his affair.

Dar grabbed a towel and dried off. She looked at the luxurious bathroom and told herself to remain strong. Today was the day they would split off from the tangible connections to her ex-husband and this once-happy abode forever. Lily would view their new house as the enemy and she as a traitor. Dar was then stricken by another reality. The family reunion was just weeks away. The thought of the Hooper family gathering conjured emotions of nostalgia, but also of gut-wrenching challenges. Of battles oiled up with liquor and spit, Dar mused, seeing the worst angle of that time. The wayward antics of her mother's sister, Bev, bore down on her psyche. The other sister, Sarah's method of riding the gathering out in a stupor, exposed and pale as Bev's puppet, made Dar's gut go hard. The toll on Virginia would be hard to watch. And if that weren't enough, there was Lily's ironclad hatred of her male cousins. "God damn those boys," Dar hissed, shivering and pulling the towel about her.

And then there was Lily's "maturity," as Dar liked to call what others called precocious. The fact was, though her body had not followed as yet, Lily's psyche had ripened. The girl could tear apart and reassemble a situation and the person holding it before two breaths were taken. Bev was coming down the pike on the wrong side of the road like a runaway semi. Lily had lost all filters with the divorce. She had become candid with the world, sometimes to a fault. She would meet Bev and the whole gang head on. Bev said Lily's developed side had bad traits. Dar argued it was just plain wit and intelligence. Nonetheless oil was to hit water, at the same time a lit match fell into dry tinder.

Taking a deep breath, Dar tried to escape the wreckage of the reunion by imagining a better view. The wide and graceful river outside that family estate offered her solace. She thought about sunsets, Lily fishing, and long walks along the shore. And that grand house, Dar thought, blessing her mother for keeping it intact. Dar then watched that image vaporize into another. A caustic and recurring theme every year: the morning where Dar would come down the stairs in that grand old house and find on the table at the bottom a pair of golden baby shoes. In her mind's eye, they were as perfect in every detail as they were heart wrenching. Thirty years later and still the pain ran deep. Her brother had barely passed out of those shoes into bigger ones before he died. And someone thought it an important tradition to put them in the open on the anniversary of his death. Like belladonna for an already toxic stew.

2

A Home Painted Baby Blue

The cicadas were as loud as pounding rain on a tin roof, Lily thought standing by the curb. The hot car engine crackled behind as she watched her mother, Dar, sashay behind the car. The Georgia June heat, near ninety and not even noon, hoarded every inch of air. Yes, Lily mused, all was devious beside the determination of her mother to make this day go her way. Lily felt like a square peg being crammed into a round hole. She curled her bare toes, gripping the hot strip of grass.

It had been a good day to start, birds singing, a free summer advertised across thin clouds, and mowed grass wafting sweetness through her open bedroom window. All that had been squelched the moment she had gone downstairs. Her mother faced her with arms crossed, trying to appear casual in announcing plans for the day. "House browsing," she announced, sipping sweet tea.

Divorce continued to deliver, Lily thought, looking about for her dog, Bo. For the clatter of his claws seeking her out, for his happy face and wagging tail. A move to another home was a move to another planet, Lily mused, like cheating on the one that had gripped her since birth. Her mother's tidying voice set back in. "Not set in concrete. Just something to ponder, honey. Well, seriously, anyway." They were out the door within an hour.

This was a day of turncoats, a grand scheme, Lily thought, watching her mother hopping the curb like she was meeting friends. Her mother was pretending not to notice the heat, though her neck was blotched red and beaded with moisture.

Dar crossed the uneven sidewalk and aimed for the steps going up.

With hands shoved hard into her shorts, pinching bits of dirt and lint, Lily wondered if she would be able stand her ground. Hang where she was by the car for starters and let her mother frolic up the walk to their prospective new home alone. Thus far, Lily had refused to look at the house, but she now let her eyes fall upon it. The place was unkempt and shabby, sitting in weeds like someone hiding for a smoke. And was the color of a thumb-sucking boy's blanket. Baby blue.

With her insides squirming, Lily was not prepared to let a house just be any other. Surely, she thought, taking in this squat dwelling, her mother imagined the same thing. A step down from their old place was not progress.

"Dammit to hell," Dar screeched, her poise gone as she stubbed her toe on the last concrete step. She took off her right sandal, the toe strap broken along with her nail. She turned and looked back at Lily for a hint of sympathy, or maybe just acceptance without a battle. As, what's done is done. Meeting Lily's unsympathetic gaze, Dar shot a hard look into her daughter. Yes. The ink has just about dried on this deal. Lily smirked as Dar attempted to unnecessarily balance on one leg. Under Lily's simpering gaze, Dar stomped her foot. She was in charge, by God, the adult in the room. Dar looked at the house and then back at Lily, adjusting her expression to show the hard chore of having to make these decisions.

"Once every seventeen years, the scourge of insect. And so, our undoing begins," Lily stated, pointing to the home. By the puzzled look on her mother's face, Lily knew she did not understand the cyclical appearance of cicadas. She frowned and ambled forward, scraping her bare feet across the sidewalk.

"Forget the bugs. What do you think of the house?" Dar asked, trying to rise above the throbbing in her toe.

"It's a dump," Lily answered. "Looks abandoned."

"Better be," Dar said, grinning. "What's really wrong with it?"

"It's too rectangular, for one," Lily answered. "And so low it looks like it's crouching to hide in those crummy shrubs, like it's ashamed to be called a house."

"So, shape's a problem?" Dar asked. "It's two stories in the back." She stiffened to challenge Lily.

Lily swiped a hand over the back of her hot neck. "Think of the palace we would have been moving into if you had accepted Granny's offer for that nicer place," Lily quipped.

"Two dormers and a garage does not make a place a palace," Dar responded.

"We could have stayed where we were," Lily snapped back.

"Your father inherited that house from his parents. Could have moved back in himself, but he's at least decent in some regards. Knows I need the money, and he volunteered to sell it. Besides, you know things will look up when we get away from all those memories," Dar said, immediately wishing she had not said that last part. Lily looked like a stake had been driven through her.

"Sweet, Mother," dribbled from Lily's lips.

"I'm sorry," Dar muttered. She turned sideways and took in the yard and house. Her cocked her head with her right hand settled over her mouth, envisioning she and Lily scampering about to make this neglected place shine.

Ten feet separated them. Lily did not offer to close the gap. Just then, the high-pitched drone of cicadas ebbed. Lily sighed with relief at the sudden quiet. But then the cloud which had given them a moment's relief passed. Sunlight exposed everything Lily did not like about this place, and the heat bore into her neck like hot matchsticks. Her mother, with poor stealth, was taking her in out of the corner of her eye, at the same time posturing sophistication and righteousness. Lily looked down to hide her smile. Her beautiful mother was such a spaz.

Dar was tall, almost five feet ten, and carried, what Lily termed, awkward elegance. It was, Lily thought, grinning inwardly, as if she had a golden retriever bouncing inside all that grace. Lily chuckled as she recalled the prior September when her mother, turning thirty-five, blew and missed every candle on her cake.

Dar heard her quiet laughter. "Ah-ha, there's my funny girl," she said, pointing. She looked striking to Lily, her red hair blazing under the hot lamp of the sun. Her eyes were crying out the color of blue that made people pause. Sapphire. Yes, worked up as today, unproven or not, and left stranded by her husband, her mother was beautiful from end to end.

"It must be a taxing job to convince the world that here stands a pearl," Lily said and flicked her wrist toward the house. She then scrunched up her nose. "I feel for you. Wouldn't want to be in that single shoe of yours." Wild-eyed, her mother took her in. Lily felt satisfied.

Dar took a deep breath. "One person's trash is another's...um...peach," Dar said.

Lily laughed. She sputtered through her lips and spun her hand toward the ground like a crashing plane. She moved off the grass and toward the steps.

Dar took measure of her fifteen-year-old daughter. Lanky, flat chested, and already tan as a blackberry. About to sprout into loveliness, even if that shine was far off Lily's radar. Her "little piece of magnificence," Dar called her on occasion, though Lily cringed at such, saying once that "hyperbole should be reserved for better analogies. For maybe looking at amoebas through a microscope, or for the awe over the world's best shooting marble." Dar had to look up the meaning of hyperbole. Right then, she had the temptation to voice the magnificence bit. Tight-lipped, she watched as Lily, coming forward, drew a hand through her dark hair.

In salutation to the coming of her favorite season, summer, Lily had cropped her dark hair. "I like your hair like that. Like it long too, but it'll be cooler in the heat," Dar announced.

Just past the last step, Lily held firm and did not respond.

Always effortless in finding her tomboy, Dar thought, looking at her daughter's trim and fit body. "Just finding my monkey," Lily had said that day, defending her haircut as Dar repaired Lily's hasty transformation with real scissors, not the kindergarten cutters she had used.

"Such beautiful thick hair," Dar said. "Like your father's," dribbled out and lost volume. Lily did not appear to have heard, was instead looking past Dar at the house. Her hard squint did not show indignation, nor curiosity.

With a new home and the arrival of summer, Lily's healing will take hold, Dar thought. Already, despite the upcoming reunions predictable failings, Lily was buoyant envisioning the fairy-tale parts. She had shared that. The ancient smell of the house, the chortling river. Of course, reading, her national pastime. She even joked about sneaking a beer, talked about her turreted room on the third floor, about her cousin Tish, and the bamboo pole stored under the porch. Dar's insides brightened. They would move in here and then break away to breathe in the goodness of River Oaks. Together they would swallow down the malice with maturity. Team Lily and Dar. Despite her sharp-edged teen cloak today, from eyes to elbows Lily seemed ready to spring into action, to challenge summer and its wall of heat. Lily, Dar mused, was pretty much indestructible. With that notion, Dar emboldened herself to make Lily feel like this decision was both of theirs, while relaying that options were off the table.

Just then, Lily was balancing on the edge of her right foot while bringing the left up off the walk below. With hand raised and her eyes focused, she struck down with a hard slap to her bare knee. "Got it," Lily yelped, flashing her palm to show the squashed and bloody mosquito. Wiping the dead insect on her shorts, Lily added, "Our blood, Mom." Her voice sticky sweet, her bright green eyes radiating smartness.

"What a jester," Dar said, waving for Lily to join her. Lily shrugged and came forward.

"A change and four walls are all we need right now," Dar said, hoping to impart the transitory nature of this necessary step. Lily looked to the walkway and did not respond.

Dar hoped to finish whatever was to transpire on a positive note. "You know, the houses in this neighborhood were military housing before the old base closed. All built to last. Strong as soldiers," she added then regretted that obvious analogy. Dar cursed herself as never being one for words. Lily's mind had just about absorbed the entire vocabulary of mankind, and as per usual, Dar felt Lily's dismay drill into her.

Yes, the house was as Lily described. Dar's first impression had been similar. The house was squat, dated, dressed like a man-boy that lived with his mother. Dar thought of the home that, without her stubborn pride, they could have owned. But then, Dar was employed like the tides, flush in one moment and down to dirt the next. Even though her mother, Virginia, would buy them a respectable place, Dar needed to prove whatever her gut told her needed proving. Lily had said her pride made her oblivious to reality, comparing that affliction to grabbing the handle of a red-hot skillet and blaming the pan. Maybe she was right. But Lily was just too young to understand the goodness of doing things on your own. Lily had seen life from the world of the Hooper clan. With them, there had never been issues with curbside appeal. Wealthy was what they were from their very beginning on the plantation. They were fruit dipped in chocolate and champagne on the wrap-around porch. Lily was coming from a home that was beautiful and spacious. She had seen the old plantation and had spent many a summer day at River Oaks.

Dar stiffened as Lily was looking up at the roof and frowning. It was the pitch, Dar knew. Almost not one at all. Lily killed time at their present home by throwing a tennis ball onto their high roof, chasing it, and guessing where it would fall to catch it. Speed was everything.

"The backyard has a picket fence. And an alley," Dar said.

"It's baby blue," Lily moaned, ignoring that and affirming the worst attribute of all.

"Makes the place feel cooler in the hot summer," Dar defended.

They looked at the front door at the same time. Bright red with "Welcome" painted on it.

"Oh, we can paint over that," Dar said, and then, in silence, each took in the entire structure. The home had wide-board siding in need of bleaching. Blotches of grayish-green mildew shown up to the eaves. Leading to the front door were cracked-brick steps that ended on a pitched concrete slab. That stoop was hemmed by rusted wrought iron that Dar found attractive and was about to say so when Lily spoke.

"That's where I will get lockjaw," Lily said of the rusty metal.

"You've had your tetanus shot. And I think lockjaw has gone the way of dinosaurs."

Lily moved closer with her arms crossed. Her wide, bony shoulders were cockeyed, her flat chest pushed out. Lily glanced up at the sun, shielding her eyes. "High noon," she announced. "Time for the gun-fight," she added, and then moved to face her mother. Dar closed the gap and stood face to face with her. Lily then felt the force of tears moving into her throat. She did not relish ending this way and bit down on her tongue.

Dar reached and mussed Lily's hair. "Come on. Let's go inside," she said, turning.

"We should have brought surgical masks and gloves," Lily said.

"I bet it's not as bad as that," Dar said, reaching back for, but not expecting, Lily's hand.

Lily caught her mother's eye and looked up at the roof again. "A ball could never get a good fast roll off of that."

3

The Unwritten Rules

Dar and Lily entered the house and looked about from the tiny foyer. Both minds were on the same thing, though Dar had seen this view already. She held her breath. Lily's silence behind her said everything. The bullet plunge of a fair ride was in the air, and then Lily gasped. A pained hum followed. Before them was a small dilapidated living room. The paneled oak veneer walls were dull and scuffed. There was a starved outline where a couch had sat up against one wall.

"You can choose the color," Dar said, and as Lily looked at her with suspicion, added, "If we buy the place, of course."

Aghast, Lily pointed toward the floor.

"I know, I know. I told them to leave it. They had it cleaned. It's very cushy," Dar said, without looking Lily in the eye.

"Orange shag," Lily affirmed. "No question about that."

"It has a little white in it. Here, let me show you," Dar said, reaching for the switch to the overhead light. Flipping it once, twice, then a third time.

"What's dead is dead, mother," Lily said, coming off the small raised landing onto the carpet. She dug her toes in, frowned, and then slumped away to look out the window toward the street. Overgrown camellias pressed into the glass, placing the room in shadows. Lily stood on her toes, emphasizing this and more.

"It's a good thing we are in the twentieth century," Dar sang. "Most anything can be fixed."

Lily stood in the center of the room with her hands in her front pockets. She faced an arched opening leading into a kitchen. Framed within that: hospital-green, speckled Formica, and a derelict black-and-white checkered floor. The room made a low grinding noise that Lily identified as coming from the refrigerator.

"It is just impossible to see the goodness of a room without light and furniture," Dar announced, following her daughter's eyes. She came over and encircled Lily's shoulders with her arm. "You and I being so modern, we could have this place looking at the future." Dar's enthusiasm was real. She turned Lily away from the kitchen and pointed back toward the glass facing the yard and street. "And there will be light," she said with a weak cackle.

After a quick tour of the kitchen, Lily stood perplexed. Her stomach tightened. She already missed her old house, its bright rooms, sun porch, and a kitchen fixed to their liking over ten solid years of life she could recall. Her mother's next words rang with irritating resonance.

"Anything, with the right eyes seeing it, can be made into a world of wonder."

"We are nomads moving through a decrepit land," Lily countered and went to a closed door. Opening it, Lily shook one hand forward and pinched her nose. Facing her was a moldy pink-tiled half-bath with iron stains in the sink and a toilet without a lid.

Dar did not flinch. She flicked on and off the light and backed out. "Well, good. That's a light we won't have to fix," she said.

Lily watched as her mother held her assured pose. She must have her doubts, Lily thought. Lily hated shenanigans, what she termed, "happy-squirrel mothering." Lily felt her resolute stance going nowhere besides bouncing off her mother. Supermom, indifferent to everything besides frugality. Over the past months she had survived by stoicism. No job. Stoicism. TV dinners. Stoicism. No handouts for help. Stoicism. Fairy-tale grit bound her mother from heel to head. With this house, her mother's vision had slumped. Lily looked sideways at her, imagining a hundred wires holding her up.

Dar was humming. She did that when the weight of the day got too heavy. She moved toward the stairway. Lily followed. Dar's long legs took the steps. Her movements were slow, as she held the rail and looked up as if frightened. A wary praying mantis, Lily thought, with a foot paused on the first tread.

Dar was in throes over the probability that Lily would be disappointed in her prospective room. Her current bedroom was a pearl. From the first scratch of her entering the world, her doting father had bequeathed his own mother's favorite room to Lily. The princess suite, he called it, and put a sign on the door. That memory drove a lump into Dar's throat.

"You know, Mother, I don't have to see more of the same."

Dar shrugged and leaned into the wall, looking as though she just might remain there. Lily squinted, blurring her, calculating the chore facing this brave woman. She squeezed her sight to imagine she was not her mother. One part of her subject was meek against the waves of change, the other could never be knocked down. Dar did not budge for what felt like minutes to Lily. She resembled a swan, Lily thought; the male gone, the nest all but dismantled. But still the grace remained, and Lily felt suddenly proud of her.

Dar threw her head back and took a deep breath. "It is what it is," she said and ran her stiff hands down the sides of her cream-yellow dress. The light from the stairwell streamed down through faded sunflowers sprouting up from the shift's hem. Lily wanted her to be as happy as that light-filled shift.

Dar looked down at her taut hands and then relaxed them. She ran a finger over where her wedding band had been. She had promised Lily to have two rings by summer's end. One opal for Lily, a sapphire for her—their birthstones. The day she announced that, she hid behind flashing, unreliable eyes, knowing the sapphire was beyond her means. Her hours at work had been cut to near nothing. Virginia was spiriting them through with a flow of cash as Dar searched for a job with some promise.

Dar refused to look Lily's way. Instead, she stood in that field of flowers and spirited hope forward, alone. If there was such a thing as a superhuman, it is my mother, Lily thought. Dar then spoke. "You're right, we've seen what there is to see."

Back outside, Lily stood on the stoop, sighting the blazing sun and lamenting that there were no trees for shade. Behind, her mother held that look of finality. It is what it is, she had confirmed, after all. Dar touched Lily's arm. Her pithy and strong daughter would be fine. She just had to take it in. She would need some time alone. Lily called those moments her "nighttime driveway." In her present home, the driveway was Lily's oasis. "It's where I get my news," Lily said. Looking through her telescope, dinner over, homework done, and all routines in order. Dar had not understood the literal translation of what news Lily received from those stars, but she always came back in glowing, telling her father and Dar she was fuller of the universe than of dinner. That her father had found another woman had shot Lily out into those stars. When she came down, the divorce knocked Lily into the ground like a fence post. Lily had thrown her telescope, and her fantastical hopes of them all visiting other planets as a family, to the curb.

Watching her daughter's frustration, Dar laid out her vision for crepe myrtles, a magnolia, and a hedge of azaleas. "Things grow a foot a second," she announced, running down the steps and pacing across the bare front yard. She turned in a circle, squared her fingers and hands, and panned her sight through them. "Yes, perfect," Dar chirped.

"That's a tough sell," said Lily, rolling her eyes and coming into the yard. "Not sure our kind of dreams would grow here."

Dar squinted at Lily. Folding her hands together, she looked back at the house and then at Lily, sending her a definitive look. Lily's gaze went blank. She swallowed hard and felt she was about to cry but hadn't in many months. She would not today. It was not just the yard and the squat rectangular house, but the whole transaction. Her parents' flame had been snuffed out by the pincers of their own vapid love. Her father's affair was a consequence of that and lived in her mother's eyes right as guilt at this moment. Fault went everywhere. Still, Lily understood why her mother wanted to leave all that behind, to abandon the bad memories formed in once-happy rooms. But how could they make a new life in a place that would never understand all that?

"Lily, it's time to understand the truth, as that cannot be recast, but only weakly challenged," Dar had said as her father drove away, his face blotted with tears. Then, as now, her mother had spoken hard love and then soft love, like a wizard moving a hand.

Lily felt the resolve to fight leave her. They were in this together, she knew. And were both tired from just about everything.

"We must deal, Lily. It is how things are, and it will end up fine. You'll see." Lily turned and moved closer to the house, shading her eyes. Dar spread her hands on her hips and watched as Lily, with a bare foot, pitched up a little dirt skirting the foundation. She then patted the earth back down.

Lily turned and spoke. "The paperwork has all been signed, hasn't it?"

"We can move in anytime," Dar said.

4

Burrowing into a New Horizon

Virginia, under her coiffed crown of silver hair, smiled and then brought up the reunion. Glib chatter over deviled ham sandwiches had ruled the discourse until the June gathering was brought up. The three of them sat in huge stuffed chairs, sunlight pouring into Virginia's big Victorian living room. A ceiling fan stories above pulled blood hot air through the screens.

"To hell with the heat, I just love these good old sultry summer days. Makes excuses for not moving a trifling waist," Virginia smiled and said, taking a minuscule bite off the little triangle sandwich in her pink hand. Placing the rest down, she then clasped her hands, saying she was pleased as could be that they would soon all be gathering under the roof of River Oaks. That said with a tiny quiver of trepidation in her throat. Her comment was followed by her heavy silence.

"I, myself, am as excited as a summer bee to get there, Granny," Lily said. "Fishing, sunburns, and all that food, my God," she added, then apologized for the "God" word.

Dar looked on, knowing about when this anxiety in Virginia had begun. For ten years she had been alone. The first time in her life. Her housekeeper, Bigbee, had left, and with Bobby gone, her mother seemed minuscule in this massive home. And, of course, Dar mused, the coming reunion would set even the most stalwart on guard. Virginia was just prepping, Dar thought, as she herself was doing. As Lily, in her own way. Dar followed her mother's gaze. In her best guess, Virginia stared at a picture of her deceased husband, Bobby. Why a picture of such a reprobate was still there was a mystery.

Virginia spoke up after taking a long drink of her iced tea. "Plantation tea is still the best, though we are running low," she said with concern then diverted back to the reunion. "Yes, Lily, this year's assembly is going to be the best ever." Her lips pursed, she moaned with frail delight. Virginia went on to describe her enthusiasm. Lily recognized none of the things Virginia tried to describe—children's somersaults, parlor games, and a house teeming with helpful hands.

Dar chimed in. "This year, we are going to up the ante on all of that threefold. Yep, I'll tell you what, Lily and I are as excited for the reunion as we have ever been. It's all we talk about." Dar watched as Lily sharpened her sight on that little lie.

"Let's just say we'll give it our best," Virginia said. "You know how I adore that place as much, if not more, than my father did."

"How much liquor should we bring?" Dar asked, and then could have kicked herself for such a self-exposing question.

Virginia retorted, "Bring everything, and more, as usual." She smiled and sat up straight. "Bev called this afternoon to say that I should tailor my clothes this year so as not to clash with hers. Then she had the nerve to ask me to accept the verdict that I am just no cook at all. That I should just let others steer that part of the gathering." She paused, adding, "Bev cannot resist the temptation to be shameless. Virginia clucked. "Sarah, of course, the moment she smells the mothballed air of River Oaks, will fall backward. She doesn't have a lick of courage anymore unless she's handing out food at the shelter." Virginia clamped her mouth. "Sorry. Don't mean to complain before it all starts."

Dar steered them back to even ground by bringing up the endless venue of delicious food they always had there. Lily chimed in as Dar mentioned her favorites. An hour later, they left. Gripping the wheel with both hands, Dar accelerated. They were on a long straightaway, the car, in fact, eating up half the center line. Lily caught her mother's eye in the mirror. Dar's brow was furrowed, her eyes glassy. Lily was curious.

Over the past days, she had seen that same look. It couldn't be just the reunion. Maybe it was the transition, Lily mused. After all, her father's moving boxes looked like packed up monuments in their old home. The past was moving out. Lily pointed to the front of the car. With a tiny gasp and muted apology, Dar whipped the car back into her lane.

Dar looked over at Lily, her right hand picking at the fabric. "A deer painted fluorescent in hunting season, that's what the reunion is going to be." Dar tried to smile with the comment.

"Wow," Lily said. "That's an image. Are things going to be that bad? In that case, I will remain behind in our new little military bomb shelter."

"Trying to make it on your own is not an excuse to toss out common sense," Dar whined, exposing the reality of who had invaded her mind. She had repeated that line at least three times in the past two days, her venom toward packing boxes becoming a crescendo of obscenity. Aunt Bev had planted those words, lamenting Dar's purchase of a home beneath that which fit her pedigree.

Lily wanted to retort that for once Bev had spoken well, but today she would not. Still, Bev was like fruitcake Lily wanted nothing to do with. Lily's stomach now soured over the thought of having to cross words with her at the upcoming reunion. They would just have to immerse themselves in the glory of River Oaks. That would balance out the trickiness.

"We can swim and fish the whole time. Eat meals after all the others are done. Sleep in the car, if it suits the situation," Lily said, trying to insert humor into the catastrophic scene playing in not just her mother's head, but hers now.

Dar reached and flipped on a static-y radio station, something about sin, God, trust, and sacrifice, then about a spike driven through a hand. All in one sentence, and the voice was out of breath but still managed to cry out, "Praise be." It was meaningless distraction for her mother, and that was good. Lily dug a nail into her palm, wondering how painful it would be if she could push it through to the other side. "Ow," she hissed, and withdrew her finger.

The hardships of the reunion were an inevitable reality, and Lily pondered survival without sacrifice. She was struck by a perfect idea; one she had begun to experiment with over the last year; the murky water of Hooper secrets. It was as obvious as car sickness that there was something going on. She had heard things she was not supposed to.

Lily looked over at her mother. Her hazy sight was glued on a road that might or might not be there. Lily wondered what she knew and was not sharing. She thought back to lunch, to Virginia's retreat into worry, maybe even fear. As far back as Lily's mind had allowed her to grasp substance over just joy, days before they all gathered, something came over her granny's demeanor. She always began with druggy minutes of nostalgia, but then those brightly painted images were rolled back over with dark strokes. The mood sank.

Yes, Lily mused, this Hooper family was one hard nut to crack. They are bound by that old name, by their prestige, by the past, by being one of the few owners of a real live southern plantation going by the wayside. "By what else?" Lily wondered. Lily had heard stories that led her to believe the sisters were one cagey and sneaky bunch back then. She had heard whispers in rooms gone to silence when she walked in. Yes, Lily thought, looking over at her mother with suspicion, there are untold vanities and secrets in the Hooper name.

Lily looked sideways at her mother, suspicious that her comrade was a traitor, not telling her things. Something was at play here. More than just a look, more than just the bickering of old matriarchs cloistered in the grand space of River Oaks. Something dark plied against the old girls. If Lily brought up her suspicions of something sinister, as she had before, her mother would claim it was Lily's "lucrative imagination." That is what she said last year. Lily had retorted that there was nothing profitable in an imagination without truth as a reward. Dar had just laughed and said, "See what I mean about that imagination of yours?"

Just then, Dar narrowed her gaze back over the seat and frowned. "Let's keep it simple this year. Gonna be hard enough as it is," she said. When Lily looked back, blameless in her wide expression, Dar countered. "Poker's not your game. If you got something up your sleeve, let's have it. I know that face, and it tells me you have sneaky ideas traveling through that big brain of yours." Lily drew her fingers over her lips, zipping them shut. "Right. I wonder how long that's gonna be the case," she said and smirked.

They pulled into the driveway. Dar shifted to park but let the car keep running. Both looked forward, each distilling what they would miss the most. Dar felt her throat constricting. Everything about the house was beautiful, but its center seemed to stare back, as pained inside as she. The story here at ended. Lily was staring sideways at her. "Just wondering how you are going to keep busy this summer," Dar lied. "You are getting to that age after all."

"Ooh, that age," Lily said. "The 'what are you going to do with the whole fish of summer?' speech. Job included." Lily reached for the door. Her mother's hand fell on her shoulder. Dar tried to look confident. Part of Lily wanted to pat her mother on the head. Part wanted to rebel.

"You have been talking to the country club moms, haven't you? Those not around enough to keep tabs on their budding daughters?" Lily asked.

"I may have had lunch there last week. On Virginia's tab, of course. But I hardly pay attention to those ladies. They have things in mind that I would be remiss in grasping."

"Just because those mothers want to force their daughters into minimum wage bondage doesn't mean you have to make the same mistake. I'm in no danger of falling into bad habits. Yep, no need to keep me busy," Lily said, then paused. "And, you know most of the summer will be filled piling leaves into our new nest."

Dar gave her daughter a conciliatory smile. She knew Lily understood the specter of the reunion and would handle things. But Dar was reluctant to find the moment to discuss the subject that was paramount to her mind of late. There had been big changes in her life, railroad switches throwing her onto new tracks. She would find the right time. Maybe next week.

"Lily, I'm not talking about serious summer work. Maybe mowing a lawn or two in the new neighborhood," Dar said, with a hand waving all of that away. She then pointed a finger at her own head. "Lily...in there. Are you set? Been a long, hard year."

"Set?" Lily asked. "You mean, am I crazy? Still a virgin? Yes, to both."

A minute passed, and Lily shifted into a Buddha squat and widened her eyes. With palms up on each thigh, her head tilted back, an impish smile grew on Lily's face.

Dar started right back in. "I mean that summer break has just begun, and you appear a little distracted. You seem to be traveling a little farther out on your bike than normal. Well, you know. Are you all right with this big change in our lives? Feeling rebellious or anything like that?" Dar asked, looking sideways at Lily.

"Just gathering my troops, greasing my gears–and my dog Bo's–for a major summer romp," Lily responded. "Though I suppose I will have to start all over with friends and stuff, as we have moved...it seems. I wonder what kind of mess the new neighborhood is in?"

"We will be only half a song from our old place and your friends, honey," Dar stated.

"By car," Lily murmured, then added, "You have a bike, Lily," knowing her mother was forming that retort. Dar flinched. Lily studied her. Her left arm lay sprawled out the door, her fingernails tapping a nervous ditty on the chrome of the outside mirror. She squinted and then scraped at a white spot there with her finger. It came off wet under her nail. "Oh my God, bird shit!" she yelled. Drawing back her hand, Dar looked about for something to clean her finger. Seeing nothing, she slumped and rested her hand over the wheel.

Lily laughed. "It is an anomaly," she said, looking her mother up and down, "that one of such constant beauty cannot hide her queerness."

Dar started and shot a hard expression back.

Lily shrugged and placed her two feet on the dash. "P.S., I am not a country club girl on the skids. Gotta have buds first," Lily said and pointed down at her unimproved chest. "'Not even a champagne glass full,' as Great Aunt Bev said last summer. Though, she meant that to be more funny than cruel, I think," Lily added, and watched her mother's look go sour.

"She said that?" Dar's lips moved, sharp and silent. "Bitch. Why do things have to be so complicated?" she said, looking at her filthy nail then at the radio. Though she had turned it down, the preacher continued to rant. "I hate those 'God' people coming into my car. Trying to strike fear and guilt into people out for a nice drive," she said. "Not working, you bastard," Dar snapped, flipping her index finger at the dramatic voice coming over the air and turning off the radio. "We can still have a good time, Lily." Dar flashed a pacifying smile, knowing Lily understood she was speaking of Bev and the reunion. "Damn them all," Dar said and hunched over the steering wheel. "We can take them."

Lily pushed back against the seat. She had an image of her mother driving some unwieldy beast. Dar held the look of never wanting to leave the safety of this car, but that also she would drive right through the heartland of those who got in the way. White-knuckled on the reins, they would drive all night, pick up the good along the way, and escape those who chased them: the fickle, the malicious, the insecure, and those with impulsive appetites to maim the indefensible. Those, her mother called last year halfway through the reunion, "love in its rudest awakening."

5

Prep Work

In her once-upon-a-time princess room, staring at her throwaway pile on the rug, Lily heard the kitchen door creak, then car keys clank onto the table. It was not a complacent tone. Her mother had returned from "a drive," a term that meant her mission was of a personal nature. Dar chewed on things in this manner, one time taking off and heading east until she hit the coast, chatting up the voiceless rider beside her. Lily had learned this out of forewarned confession.

Lily leaned to pick up Old Yeller, a stuffed dog with a broken back she had owned since she was four. She kissed the dog on its shiny black nose and tossed it onto her bed. The ceiling light brightened his yellow eyes. His stitched smile promised what it always had. Loyalty. At her feet, her real dog, Bo, thumped his tail twice on the carpet. Lily had just come back from dodgeball practice and had begun the process of eliminating the nonessentials. Her mother had folded that term into breakfast, saying it was time to pare down. "Yep," Lily had retorted, "there is only so much you can squeeze into dire circumstances." Dar had left shortly thereafter.

When Lily walked into the kitchen, she found Dar staring at their disassembled life. Boxes stacked high, furniture separated into claimed piles, empty shelves for someone else's belongings. Her mother had a look on her face like she wanted a drink but knew it was too early in the day. Her eyes were searching for maybe a cure for reality, her heart limping not far behind. Lily and Bo came to stand before her.

"Hard to prepare for the unknown," Dar said. "Hard to know what you're getting into when you're a novice."

Something in that statement, but more so in its tone, told Lily this had nothing to do with the schematic of their present lives. Moving or the reunion were stacked upon something more personal. Her mother was cagey beyond the scope of family dysfunction that had no remedy but to hold one's breath until it passed. Lily tried to catch her mother's eye, but she looked away.

"Are you hungry?" Dar asked. When Lily held up the sandwich she was finishing, Dar stared. "Of course," she snapped, threw up her arms, and left to go stand in the rain that had begun to lightly fall.

"Shit," Lily said, feeling the escalating force of helplessness. She looked about the cluttered rooms, confirming that there was no reverse to this situation.

Days before, Lily had noted the thin array of dinged-up furniture moving with them. Since their new house was not particularly clever, spartan would do, her mother had said. Lily had not known if the comment was condescending, an admittance of not giving a damn, or further proof of her mother's stoicism. "Pride is spit," Lily had announced, deciding on the latter and embroiling them in a bad mother-daughter yelling fest from one room to another.

The real reason Dar had decided to give all the nice furniture to Lily's father became clear the next day. Lily had walked into an argument over the cozy chairs and couches. Her father was standing there, bludgeoned by the cold force of Dar's declaration that she did not want to sit on anything that once provided vows of adoration. That comment had sucked the air out of a thousand moments of laughter and smiles still clinging about the house. For Lily this had been the low point. She told her mother to never again burn her personal garbage in her ears. Dar had taken that to heart and moved to voice her regret, but she knew a scar had already formed.

Lily shook her head from those bad hours as Dar came back in, her hair wet and matted to her ears, her white dress shirt clinging to reveal the paisley bra beneath. Dar began to pace between the divvied pile of boxes, her father's and theirs. Her sad look confirmed that she had learned nothing in the rain, or the drive for that matter.

6

A Week In

They moved into their new house in a whirlwind. Dar said the frenzy of it would make crossing from one house to another less painful. Lily was sitting at the kitchen table reading. She was a voracious reader, fast, consuming books with her whole being. Tonight, she was tearing through *The Stranger* in a humid, poorly ventilated kitchen, skin sweaty as she pined for the dry heat of Algiers. Placing a finger on her place on the page, she looked up at her mother.

Dar was puttering around the kitchen, the energy of her first assault on the unfamiliar house exhausted. She had been unpacking a single box of dishes for the past hour. Tiptoeing, but around what? Far off in expression and holding a plate, she drew a rag back and forth over the dish's surface. Dar lifted her gaze to Lily, her mouth triggered to purge. "Jump," Lily said under her breath. Dar slapped the rag in her hand down hard on the top of the box. Lily pressed her eyes back into her book. The phone rang. Startled, Lily shot a glance to the far wall.

Her mother dropped the dish on the counter, let out a little "whoop," and pranced across the kitchen to the receiver. "Praise be," she said. "Service at last."

The song of the old beige phone had drawn Dar out of her melancholy in an instant. Her eyes, Lily mused, expressed pleasure well beyond what a phone call should offer. In a matter of seconds, her expression changed. "Oh, thank you. We're not interested in brooms." Dar hung up the phone in slow motion and flicked back her hair. With eyes wide and blinking, her expression said, "Dammit to hell," her words something else. "Not what I thought. Just a solicitor. With a speech problem."

Lily was aghast. "Mother, those people sold us brooms at our old place. They are handicapped, and they make those brooms to support themselves. You should be ashamed."

"I know, I know. Hey, who's the parent here? I was just expecting..." Dar turned and nervously took back up her rag and dish.

Lily quickly asked, "Expecting what?" but her mother ignored the question. She appeared to be working from many competing angles. And maybe secrets, Lily thought, insulted and sure.

"Hey Lily, how'd the dodgeball game go this week? It's been so hectic, I forgot to ask. Bad mothering, I suppose you think."

Lily felt she was getting a plate full of nothing. Without doubt, there was a new angle to her mother's anxieties. Lily decided to answer her question with her own secret of late. If she gave up some dirt, her mother might. Bright-eyed, she sat up in her chair.

"Well, of course, we won the dodgeball tournament. The losers were dumbfounded by the agility of the reedy girl running circles and yelping alone among them." Lily brushed her chest with the knuckles of her right hand.

Dar cocked her head, breaking out in smile. Lily was known as the Queen of the Court. The adrenaline of winning and being the last one standing was her goal in life.

"Thanks for asking," Lily added. "This was the big one, the last match before the heat of summer brings on family moves and reckless reunions. If you had been there, you would have seen me do my victory dance. I pretty much set the place on fire." Lily got up from her chair to pose and then demonstrate.

Wide-eyed, Dar watched as Lily's tomboy gears flipped to something more seductive and feminine. Right, then left, heel to toe, her legs pumped in slow motion. Synchronized, her willowy arms swam and turned over her head while her hips gyrated wildly. Dar had witnessed a toned-down version of this two years prior at another game. At Lily's age then, all had been forgiven. Now, with more attitude, her scanty uniform, some curves and a good tan, Dar was sure her antics must have turned some parents' heads. Dar splayed her palm and fingers over her mouth and eyelids.

Out of breath, Lily sat back down. "So, after my dance, Billy Fontaine—one of my teammates—and I ended up shoulder to shoulder. Our sweat was kind of co-mingling. I think it was on purpose, and we just held there until it was uncomfortable. Then we had some excited discussion about going to get root beer floats. Then a dare to sneak around old Mr. Wiley's house to scare him. But I think, Mother, that I wanted something more. Something beyond tame, done-that ideas. With Billy so close and our win chiming in me, my body felt electric. My mind misbehaving. Lordy, I was surprised, Mother, as until then, Billy had acted unattainable."

"You mean you had tried before?" Dar asked, worried about where this was headed.

Lily ignored her. "Well, there was no looking back or forward into consequences, as we spotted our bikes lined up. Like outlaws' ponies. Five of us had ridden over together. Two of us left together." Lily blushed. "We crossed Curtis Boulevard and went way past the tracks." Lily let this sink in.

"You know that is a rough place and forbidden by all parents. Including me."

Lily continued. "Billy bought me an orange soda in the little store from a very old, nice black man. He got a grape for himself. They were floating in ice and soooo cold."

"Just cut to the chase so I can punish you."

"We entered a park of sorts. At least that is what we would have called it in our neck of the woods, except there the grass was deep and the place unkempt. Litter, you know, a mangy dog, a guy sleeping it off in the shrubs. The trees, though, were just as big as the ones around our prior home, the shade under them old and welcoming. We sat, hung out, and talked about the game. Then, I leaned over and took Billy's face in both my hands and kissed him for what felt like a fortune of time. When we released, Billy sat dumbfounded and red as a wagon. For me, it felt dangerous like I'd wanted it to. By the magic of minutes, small talk, and Billy pacing, the situation went most of the way back to normal. At least, enough to remount and ride back home in silence."

Dar said nothing, her face bending through an escalating scale of awe and concern.

"Don't look at me that way. I know that area of town is off-limits. In hindsight, well, in a parent's way of seeing, I suppose we made a mistake. Well, part anyway," Lily said and laughed. She waited for Dar to respond. Nothing. "What, already feeling scandalized in your brand-new neighborhood? Like in your kitchen sits the new neighborhood tramp?" Lily slapped the table.

"You think you're joking, Lily, but you're good-looking, you know. Boys will...you have those gorgeous eyes of your father's," Dar said. "And all else that could corrupt a boy's mind."

Lily narrowed her gaze on her mother, whose posture had gone the way of a dying flower. Dar then let out a slow breath. "Don't leave yourself so wide open to be taken advantage of, Lily. Men are just...well, I thought your father was gold in the bottom of a pan of silt. Instead, he was a panhandler."

"He's a father I love, by the way," Lily responded with ire. "The days have gone where you can get by with insulting him. Own it, Mother. You're concerned about your daughter's reputation and how that affects you the most."

"I'm worried about my daughter. Every part of her," Dar answered, blinking hard.

"Or are you jealous that I am the only one in this house having any luck with men?" Lily asked. With her comment, Dar stammered. If ever there was a nerve exposed, Lily had witnessed it. Her remark had only been meant as a parlay in defending her father.

"Don't try to sway me against him," Lily added. "I will remain in the middle." She did not wait for her mother to tell her to go to her room.

She jumped up from the table and waltzed away. *The Stranger* stuck up from the back of her pants.

Dar started to follow but stopped, placing a hand atop the table. She felt light-headed, spewing. "Dirty dancing around boys and their God-forsaken hormones is plain dumb. Yeah, go to your room," she added, unsure.

Lily paused at the bottom of the stairs. Not turning to look back at her mother, she called out. "Proof. Over-protectiveness is as dry as a stick. It is how wildfires start."

"Well..." Dar said, leaning full on the table.

Lily raised her eyebrows, smiled, and left without a word.

Dar spent the next half-hour pacing, unpacking, and mulling over some manner of punishment for Lily crossing the tracks: Take her bike for a week, though that would be a burden on her, as Lily would need driving everywhere. Not allow her to have Bo in her room. The dog had done nothing wrong Lily would say and be right. She smiled with the thought of making Lily dress in a brittle wool smock, until the image upset her. Giving up, Dar opened the cabinet and fixed herself dinner: a can of sardines, crackers, and half a block of New York cheddar cheese, extra sharp. She put Tabasco on everything and stood at the counter eating. Her tongue burned, dry and salty. Out the window, she saw Lily's bike leaning against the picket fence, looking rusted in the orange hue of the alley streetlight. That was the first thing Lily did, put that bike there. Once, it had been too big for a child. Now, it was just fast and taking her away.

Lily lay on her unmade bed and tried to erase the clamor in her mind from the incident. She thought about the river at the old family house, River Oaks. Lily got butterflies. The film of tepid iron water was enough to cleanse anything, Lily thought. She remembered the first time she broke that water's surface at eight years old. It had rained. The river was swollen, muddy, and roiling to take her with it. Beforehand, she had sat on the grassy bank, stalling: frightened of what might be lurking in the dark water, but desperate to keep her mean cousins from knowing she was afraid. Her mother appeared behind her and put a hand on her shoulder.

"Don't worry," Dar said. "It will be special the first time you choose, today or tomorrow. And then it will be with you forever. In there," she pointed, "people don't matter." Dar had stood back. Let Lily face the sheer bounty of that river alone.

Her mother had been right. That water was indelible as a tattoo. Lily recalled the warm, thick rush as she succumbed to letting her legs release from the gravity of sodden earth. The dangerous feeling from that first strong pull. Her mother, on shore, crossed her arms, braced with this rite of passage but still managing to smile. "It is only hard-hearted for a second, then never again," she called out. With that memory, Lily thought the reunion ahead might not be so tough. Lily considered her rush to kiss Billy Fontaine. It was, as that first swim in the river, a ceremonious experiment of life. And then with her forever.

Her mother, Lily thought, is afraid of the dark, the places in me or across the track that might spoil everything. Just as she knew that roiling river had things to offer, Lily needed to tell her there was nothing lurking within her that she needed to be afraid of. "I am not Bev, or Sarah, or my male cousins," Lily would tell her. Lily rose from her bed and eased open the door. Downstairs, she heard her mother rooting through boxes. Lily came down the stairs. She watched Dar unwrap a glass and drop the newspaper on the floor. "Is there an open-door policy to my cell?" Lily asked, and Dar turned. Her eyes lit up, and she nodded. "The bourbon is under the sink," Lily said. "You're out of gin."

"Are you keeping bar now, too?"

"We grow up fast these days," Lily answered with a big grin.

Dar shook her head and smiled. Lily followed her into the kitchen. As Lily picked at the crumbs left behind from her mother's cheese and cracker feast, Dar poured herself a Hooper family drink: ice to the top of the glass, drowned in as much liquor as could fit.

"You're grounded," Dar announced, stirring her drink with a finger. "For a couple of days." Dar licked her finger and seemed pleased all the way around. "You start tomorrow."

"Saturday? That's overboard for a kiss."

Dar was moving toward the living room. "It's not for the kiss, but you know that." Dar wiped the cold glass over her forehead. Loosened by the bourbon and ebbing in her anger, she added, "Lily, my burgeoning kissing bandit, tell me about this Billy." Dar sat in one chair, Lily in the only other.

"Five ten at least, and with a polo shirt and haircut he should have outgrown three years ago. He made my move easy." Lily's tone was matter of fact.

"Wow," Dar said, leaning back into the air.

"On my terms, like you always said. And I think I carried myself like an expert. As for Billy, by his performance, I doubt he was much more than a novice. Pillow practice and all that, you know."

Dar touched the top button of her blouse, blew out a long stream of air, and took a deep pull of her drink. Rubbing her knees and rising, Dar walked to the window facing the street and squinted over the high shrubs into the darkening sky. Reaching into her apron pocket, she brought out a pack of cigarettes. She fumbled into a bureau drawer already filled with junk and took out her silver lighter. She struck the flint twice.

Watching the little yellow sparks, Lily prayed it would not light. She hated to see her mother smoke. Dar leaned and sniffed the fumes of the lighter. That disgusting habit, where her eyes closed in exhilaration, was the mark where there was no turning back her "essentials," a word her mother used to describe the tools for surviving moments as these. On the third strike, a blue flame erupted. Dar lit the cigarette dangling from her lips. Like sacrament, Lily thought, watching her face relax.

"Lily, I think when you return to school, you should join the Christmas play," Dar announced turning from the window. "Since you are so hell-bent on dragging people about in a fantasy world." She let it sink in, watching Lily's shock. Dar then bellowed, laughing in the special way she reserved when she thought she had landed a zinger.

Lily sank down into the cushions and watched her mother's cigarette hand tremor in delight. Her left arm was tucked under her breast. Smoke drifted out of a chimney formed in the corner of her mouth. Despite the cigarette, her mother looked magnanimous.

Dar stabbed out the cigarette in one of Virginia's ornate gold-rimmed ashtrays. She crossed in front of Lily. Her magnolia perfume weighted the air. Her look down said *don't judge me*. Going to the refrigerator, Dar pulled out a bottle of white wine and poured it over the highball's thin slurry of liquored ice.

7

Reeling Toward What's Known

It was Saturday morning, and Lily couldn't stand another minute of fighting for a decent dream. She got up and flicked on all the lights. She paced, exercised, rubbed Bo's belly, and watched the rain sweep over the yard. As the clouds at last cleared and the sun baked down, she cut the lights off one by one. The sun was bright, the street steaming, and the trees wet and sparkling, the kind of day the kids in her old neighborhood were wallowing in.

The house was quiet, her mother maybe sleeping in or sipping coffee at the kitchen table. She had come up to Lily's room the night before. "It has been a thirty-six-hour day," her mother had announced, poking her head in. As Lily responded, "Twenty-four to be precise," Bo pranced in between Dar's legs. "He's peed, so you're good until morning, precious," Dar confirmed. Tipsy, she pressed Lily into giving some thought to the upcoming reunion. "Maybe start packing. Just the pretty things we know you won't be wearing until then." Her mother had not blown her usual kiss goodnight. The way she shut her door, with a snap versus a gentle click, confirmed that despite being precious, Lily was still jailed. But maybe it was something more.

Beyond filling a suitcase, Lily had no idea how to prepare for the gathering at River Oaks. How could she brace herself for the scrutiny of her aunts? She would bring her favorite clothes no matter. Yep, Lily mused, sheer clothing will be my armor. The pretty dresses her mother spoke of, her olive branch. Packing could wait, Lily mused, wiping sweat from her brow.

Stretched on her bed, twirling her pen, Lily sought inspiration. Her diary lay beside her. She considered writing about her kiss with Billy Fontaine. Lily tossed the pen several times in the air, catching it each time. The image of the sweetness of kissing Billy was killed as her male cousins assaulted her senses–their Marine buzzcuts, tinny voices, malicious air, and unbrushed teeth. Perverts, Lily added to that list, her stomach tensing to that truth. Their kinship could never dispel her disgust. Lily then had the brilliant notion of getting a dodgeball game going at River Oaks. Imagined the massacre of Marcel and Jessie, bloody lips, raspberries, maybe a permanent injury.

Lying back on her bed, Lily jotted down her thoughts. *In this small chamber of needless punishment,* she began, *I am ready to soar. I take inspiration from all writers who languished in prison before me. In the end, as I lay with the lacerations of worldwide rebuke as a cynical and now promiscuous teen, I doubt I will mean anything substantial to anyone but her. Except, of course, my father.*

With those words, Lily was overcome with a sense of protectiveness for her mother and sadness that her father appeared to live in constant self-reproach over his mistake. She viewed his small house across town as a hovel to endure a world he thought his error had created. The last time she saw him, two weeks ago, he had put the basket on the front of her bike. She had draped her arms about his neck and reminded him that there were two sides. And just as she had expressed to Dar tonight, she told him she would remain in the middle.

Lily now pondered her mother's mental thinness of late, of her reaction to Lily's remark about having no luck with men. That had seemed to knock her down. Lily dipped her pen to the page before her. *I am the holder of her frayed rope. Divorce, paper-thin attempts at a date once or twice, threats to quit every job.* And even life once, Lily recalled. Thinking the mason jar of Windex on the kitchen counter was a glass of water, Dar had taken a big swallow. Lily grinned thinking of how that tragedy turned to laughter after coming back from the hospital.

Lily again pushed her pen to paper. *I have seen her cry. I have seen her coil in anger. I have seen her reminisce on just the bad. After those spells, she puts on her silk PJs, sprays her wrists and soft throat with magnolia perfume, and stares into her bath mirror. Those radiant and rare eyes, like jewels in that glass, I am sure, give her hope.*

Lily cleared her head and looked down at Bo. His face was flattened on the carpet, sad and missing their skullduggery this weekend. Lily let out a little squeak, watching his ears lift and then settle. Bo's eyes rounded, the scalloped whites lifting Lily's spirits.

Hours later, cross-legged on the carpet, Lily peered out the window and sighed. The happy light of Saturday had vanished, the neighborhood voices and mowers quelled. Her mother had come, taken Bo and returned him, with the affectations of a true guard. Or so Lily told her. Orange hues of dusk sprayed her room and the fringe of white lace curtains transported from her old bedroom to this one. She rose crablike from behind a fragile table in the making, a two-foot square paper cube of plaster, newsprint, and the covers of her least favorite books. Romantic novels. Select passages were displayed beside each book cover, glued and pickled in white. Over the sides, lust-stricken faces from an imaginary era stared out.

Virginia's sister, Bev, had gifted these books to Lily over the entire stretch of her fourteenth year. The year Lily's father had the notion of greener grass. "These might fill the vacuum left in your pretty little head from such a surprising divorce," Great Aunt Bev said to the baffled girl before her. Lily found the books trashy. Wanted to tell Bev she would not choose that colorless wasteland of literature. "I find them inspiring," Bev had said and winked. Insinuating far more than filling empty spaces left in a young girl's head.

Dar, playing missionary, had nudged Lily in the side to see good intention in the gift. All Lily saw was the ridiculous cover: a man engulfing a woman like fire on some castle turret, the woman enjoying being burned by lips brushing her neck and pretending to put it out by throwing her own fuel back on. Bev had hovered, smelling of the wintergreen mints she was addicted to between drinks. Lily had given up her best smile and thanked Bev.

"Thank you so much, Bev," Dar chimed in. "Lily will love it. You know how she reads."

Pulled in by that first book's comical cover, Lily, that night, had read the first chapter. As hinted by the cover, the duos' passion came out of the gate like a racehorse. Even at that age, Lily understood by decency and common sense that those human desires portrayed in that book should have been slow, generous, and sweeping. She had seen her parents' tenderness. They had never been so desperate. Saddened by that memory, Lily read on. Where she wanted to see a vista, the lust invaded her space and made her feel queasy. When she wanted eloquence, the character's stuttered, forgetting the fine breeding their clothes expressed. In the following books bequeathed by Bev, new couples, fleeing beings caught by their husbands, found objects, from ships rails to altars, to press against in getting at the other's lips and clothing. It was a recipe creating boredom and gave Lily pause in considering anything beyond owning a dog.

Staring at the cube now, Lily's heart plunged. She thought of her father again. Why was his tryst not discovered when the first match was struck, when maybe it could have been repaired? Did he pause in the attraction, or did he go blind from the start, as the figure bent over the rail of a ship in the book cover before her? Lily felt angry and saw Bev's insensitivity in gifting these books as just a dig at her broken family.

"Piss on that, Bev," Lily said, wishing Bev could witness the mutilation of her books. Lily pushed away, feeling dizzy from the fumes. She sprung up, opened her bedroom window, and turned on the fan. Not long after, her mother knocked on the door frame. She was dolled up and held a plate of cut carrot sticks surrounding a can of Vienna sausages.

"Weird," Lily said, taking in the offering.

"There's a thawed chicken pot pie you can put in the oven for dinner later."

"Thanks, warden." Lily said, scanning her mother's attire. "You're going out, aren't you?"

Dar nodded and averted her eyes, her cheeks flushing. She leaned against the door frame, a girlish pose that meant tonight was special. Dar did not normally glow like this when she went out. She had had a couple of dates months before at the old house—salesman types, smelling of talc, and with teeth too bright to look at. Lily had met each at the door, her entire system rejecting that this could be happening on the stoop her father had crossed a million times. As Dar came up from behind, each man had eyed her gorgeous mother, not the special person she was, but like something to eat.

After those flop dates, a hiatus followed. Two weeks later, Dar, placing a second Gibson down with five pearl onions in the bottom, had compared finding the right man to parallel train tracks. She spread her two elegant arms and brought them into a slow V, her extended fingers not quite touching. She then let those index fingers, braced on that far horizon, touch, and made a popping sound with her mouth. "The death of hope and love," she had said with that noise, dropping her arms to her sides. The scene had depressed Lily for days.

Now, noting the care her mother had taken this evening and the way she and the wall behind seemed complicit, Lily knew something big had been caught. Dar was embracing the evening before it happened. This man must be different. Dark, with longish hair and a soft laugh, Lily imagined. Maybe with some imperfection not whited out by pretense. And a sense of humor just a bit sardonic. That would be fine. "Who's the Don Juan?" Lily asked.

"What is that...box?" asked Dar, reddening and pushing off the wall.

"Love as does not occur on earth," Lily answered with robotic tempo. "You saw me making it this afternoon when you came to get my prison uniform to wash. Duh."

"I guess I didn't really take it in."

"If it were a snake it would have bitten you, Mother Dearest."

A second later, they were on the floor together admiring Lily's creation. Lily pushed down a drying corner and looked sideways at her tranquil mother. Lily felt a smile come into her heart. On hands and knees, they took in the sagging plaster table. Lily let it feel like they had constructed it together. They both, after all, knew the donor of those books.

Lily watched her mother's mouth lift into a mischievous smile. Dar began reading aloud the sultry passages Lily had arranged beside those love-tossed faces.

"Oh, this is hateful," Dar said. "Just hateful. If Bev knew…" Dar kicked off her high heels.

Taking in those spikes, Lily wondered how she made it up the stairs. "I swear to God, I will never wear such things," Lily said.

Dar winked. "Of course, you will." Standing, Dar posed for Lily. "How do I look?"

"Like you're excited, for once."

Dar swung about and left. Lily followed, trying to mimic the way her lithe figure carved the steps going down. Dar looked back and grinned. She appeared hopeful. Her sapphire eyes would be an enviable pairing to a happy evening out, Lily thought. Dar glanced in the glass of a crooked picture on the stairwell wall and fixed her hair. Lily sashayed down to her.

"You are a funny one," Dar said, then turned toward Lily and spread her arms, as if presenting herself as a new person. "Ta dahhhh," she said.

At the bottom of the stairs, Dar confirmed that Lily could come out of jail after a good night's sleep. Back in her room, Lily thought she might stay put Sunday morning. With books to read and her journal itching, she would just leave the cell door open. Thirty minutes later, Lily listened as the Chevy II started, and her mother backed out of the drive. Lily wondered what it meant that her date was not picking her up.

8

The Smell and Taste of Change

Sleep had come hard for Lily. A possum in the trash out back, Bo in a frenzy clawing at the window, and a sit-up-straight-in-bed nightmare had covered her first hours. Her mother had come home in the early morning, her tipsy body brushing along the wall at the bottom of the stairs. She was singing. The song sounded made up, but the melody was high and sweet. An all-right combo, Lily thought in the dark as she listened to her mother fade down the hallway below.

Lily was thrilled when the yellow light of morning filled her room. Getting dressed, she went downstairs to let Bo out and then came back up. Her mother was still asleep.

"A lot of good you have done me," Lily hissed an hour later, deriding the crystal ball sitting atop the chest at the foot of her bed. Having dug it out of an unpacked box, she had spent the early part of morning asking it for a vision of her mother's future. When the ball had not answered, Lily asked for something else—how to escape her male cousins. Blot them out, erase their names. Silence prevailed. History, as always, left them intact. Lily then asked for a glimpse of how her body would look in another year. Nada.

From around her head she uncoiled the tie-dyed T-shirt she had formed into a turban. Sighing, Lily tossed it over the glass ball and the curved reflection of her hawkish glare. The globe had been a Christmas gift from her mother, who gloated on finding something so obscure. She had gone to the next town over, where Mother Maria was telling fortunes at the county fair. Dar saw this as a logical maneuver to procure such an unusual gift. At first, Maria had chastised her for making a mockery of serious business, treating such spiritual wares as a trinket. Then, taking her hand, she gave Dar a glimpse at her future. Dar frowned as Maria told her she would be divorced and struggle to find a job. Those things having already occurred, she would have the globe the next day for a good price.

Lily, having a flare for the bizarre was beside herself upon receiving the crystal ball. Later that day they went to Bev's house for Christmas lunch. While the rest of the family gorged themselves, Dar told the story of finding the ball, which all agreed was an extremely unusual present. Lily's cousin Marcel had used the news as ammunition, mocking Lily and calling her "spook." The final assault came from her other male cousin, Jessie. "The Trojan Horse of space cadets," he cackled, spitting a bit of food onto the table.

Lily glared back. "So?" Lily asked, taking in Marcel and Jessie. "Which one of you wants to be the first to see in my crystal ball how they look with a black eye?"

Lily frowned, looking at the covered globe, at the large cartoonish drawings of magic mushrooms and gargantuan flowers on the back of her mother's 60's T-shirt. Grabbing *Swiss Family Robinson* from the top of her bureau, she went downstairs. Later she heard her mother drawing a bath. Then listened as her humming turned into a Crosby, Stills, Nash and Young song, a shrill version of "Our House."

After dinner, the darkened sky and driving rain gave the kitchen a sense of hominess, Lily was thinking. Next to her at the table, Dar had been quiet, playing with her fork. Lily tried to coerce conversation, asking if she had ever owned a dog at the plantation. Dar looked up, clearly unaware of what Lily asked. She eyed the full glass of milk sitting before Lily's empty plate. "When did you decide you don't like milk?" she fumbled to ask. Knowing that her mother would come to her senses and recall she hated milk, Lily picked up her book and began to read. Dar leaned across the table and guided the book back down.

"Yeah, I don't know why I poured that for you," Dar said in a strained voice. She then shook the limp wrist in her hand, closed her eyes, took in an exorbitant amount of air into her mouth, blew it out, and reopening her eyes, spoke. "Lily, a mother's greatest fear comes from the mere thought that she might outlive her children. It brings on a loathsomeness that you just cannot understand." She shifted in her creaky chair. "The next worst thing is those children watching their parents get old and lonely." Dar swirled her highball glass of white wine but did not drink.

"Wow. Am I dying?" Lily asked.

"No," Dar half-shrieked, flicking a hand toward Lily's head, which was wrapped once again with her makeshift tie-dyed turban. "By the way, you can't wear that at the reunion."

"So, morbid woman, what's on your mind?" Lily asked, rubbing Bo's belly with her foot.

Dar looked down at the dog and back at Lily, wringing her hands. "Okay, here we go," Dar began. "I have realized that I am a lesbian. There, I said it."

Lily didn't know how to respond. She searched her mother's face, then grinned waiting for her to explode into laughter. Dar's expression held firm. And then Lily's belly constricted. The divorce, this squalid place, which her mother had just yesterday called their own little piece of America, and now this new unwavering truth.

Dar rose and went behind Lily. She placed her hands on her shoulders. Lily stiffened. "I'll give you a minute to think, then we can talk. Only if you want," Dar said and left the room.

The rain against the window lost its romance, and the room shrank. The fluorescent ceiling fixture shone bright and intensely into Lily's eyes as she stared at her food-smeared plate. Life had made another hard turn. Lily tried to shake off the abstraction in her mind created by her mother's news, the shape of two female bodies touching. She then saw the face of her father and knew he was really gone.

Lily took in the speckles in the Formica top and thought of the days she and her mother had sat side by side here adjusting to their new lives. Those had been the best moments, with just small talk and serious dialogue forbidden, though that had never been discussed. She could not have imagined any subject as tonight's ever coming to pass. Lily pushed away her plate and let gravity take her head down to the table. She pressed her humid cheek to the surface, the smell of gravy from her soiled dish fouling her senses. Lily told herself, over and over, things were not so dire. Her mother had not changed skin, heart, or soul with the news. They were still an unstoppable team. They had made it to this home with just a little help, planted trees, counted stars from their own stoop, and granted tours by consent only.

Lily heard her mother's soft footsteps and then her breath as she stood close behind. Lily erased the distress from her face and tuned her head up from the table. She saw in her mother's expression a whirlwind of emotion and pleading. In those bright, praying eyes, the past year was compiled upon a wholly new transition, one that Dar prayed Lily could fathom. She placed her hand on Lily's neck. Lily pushed back into it.

"Okay." Lily sighed. Dar rubbed a bit more then drifted away.

Minutes later, Lily sat up straight in her chair and looked to where Dar stood before the sink. She was smiling impishly. A particle of indisputable joy, but also confusion, shot out of her sparking eyes, waiting for Lily.

"How long?" Lily asked.

"We had a go about three months ago. Then a big pause as I needed some time to know what had happened. A few more times over the course of me getting familiar with the idea. One-hour stand, a little stuff in her car. That was it. Lost track, then she called. We had a date, then another, and well...."

"Okay," Lily expressed, her tone shutting down any more details.

9

Like Swallowing a Tiny Frog

Even as Lily owned little judgment toward her mother's appetites, besides her smoking and maybe her reach for that final unnecessary drink, she awoke with her sensibilities shaken by Dar's admission. This was piled upon minutes later by her mother's sleepy-eyed confession downstairs. Lily was eating toast when Dar came into the kitchen wearing the same dress as the night before, albeit now badly wrinkled. Eyeing Lily with her hands on her hips, Dar began as if last night's sentences had just been placed on pause. "Experimenting in my teens seemed just that. It was innocent, maybe even frivolous, as it could be blamed on the many different hazards of those hormonal years. It can no longer be called that. My test is out of the lab and gone mainstream," she said and tried to smile.

As Lily stared back, stupefied, Dar put her hand up. "Lily, let this second piece sit awhile. I don't want you to think I just placed the needle on the record without having been familiar with, and maybe even liking, the song." With an impish smile, Dar shaded red. Lily looked past her mother into nothingness, seeking understanding to this string of tangential statements. Dar continued. "It is a single truth in my life, and you will have yours, though I suspect differently," she said and then left for a temp job.

Dar's newest admission and its casualness set Lily off in many directions. First, it made Dar's marriage to Lily's father seem like an insincere way station for this inevitable truth. Her mother was preset to prefer being with a woman than the greatest guy in the world. Lily always thought they might have worked it out, but now she wondered if that were not her dream alone. Disseminating this, Lily felt the same surging heat in her body as she had when her father walked out the door. Panic at learning your world was not yours, and that what you thought belonged to you, did not. One cannot own a father for life. Nor now understand a mother's need to share the building blocks to her sexuality in such cold narrative.

Lily got up, paced, and stared at the back door as if the last hours were imagined. She could open it and let illusory out and then close the door and seal them into a mere two days past. When news was old. Lily scrambled for logic. Perhaps, the most severe form of loneliness, like lightning, had struck her mother. Maybe this woman just kind of fell in her mother's lap, Lily thought. Like a cute dog when one is at her wit's end with everything in life. As that, Dar might have thought this woman just plain irresistible. "Hell, what have I got to lose?" Lily could hear her mother's weakened, probably inebriated, gears turning. That's it, Lily mused. This unnamed woman had liquored up her fragile, divorce-recovering mother. She had maneuvered her passion as it was unspent and longing. Lily imagined her mother hurrying back to tell her that she had been mistaken. She then felt selfish for feeling that hope, as support was their shared weapon against these times.

Lily recalled the date Dar had confessed her "unrestrained years" to Lily, calling them "transformative." Listening back then, right out of the horse's mouth, Lily thought she had learned it all. Her mother's honesty made her feel grown up. How fantastical it had sounded to her ears. It had been on Lily's fourteenth birthday, right before divorce would ride through like some headless apparition. It seems her mother had been a free-spirited youth, had protested the Vietnam war, marched topless protesting male sexism, smoked maybe a few joints, and had lined up enough boyfriends to fill two VW vans. When Lily looked aghast at that last admission, Dar had explained to Lily that the glory of those times was set to beat away inhibitions. To emphasize this, Dar said she would forever be unapologetic, nor did she have any regrets. She then tempered all her past sexuality by saying that Lily's father had been the best of the bunch and that he was the one. Recalling these admissions, a pit went into Lily's gut seeing life and transformation as an ever-changing act.

Lily grew offended, realizing that for months she had been left in the dark, pining away for the things she missed while her mother was laying down fresh turf and playing with her new girlfriend. Her face grew hot.

The next morning, Lily came right out with it. Dar was scurrying about her bedroom getting ready for a job interview. "You were dallying for months with this chick while I was viewing the split of my parents as problem number one. You could have come right out with it. Saved me wasting all that hope." Lily paused and took in her mother's sinking face taking this beating. "I could have helped you," Lily said. "Must have been a hard decision."

Dar took in Lily, her athletic daughter now just a mess of slumped and gangly angles. She looked like she had lost her best friend. "The pile of baggage already on your lap left little space for adding any more. Besides, it's not a decision. It's a transformation, like coming out of that...that sacky thing Luna moths come out of. Think of me as having been already on my way."

"Chrysalis, Mother," Lily said. "And that just sounds cold. Like Daddy was just...."

"It's been a confusing time for me. You know, opening my eyes, then my wings." Dar said. She was having trouble stepping into her dress, tripping over the hem. She turned for Lily to zip her up. "Lily, my coming out, as they call it, and its effect on me is not the issue...really. You are the other half of this family, and I am most worried how me being a lesbian has touched you," Dar said. She turned back after Lily instinctively pulled up the zipper.

The last comment put a burden on Lily and kind of offended her. "Is half better than the third I once was?" she asked. "Boy that changes family math as we know it. Like seeing my father once every two weeks. Or moving from that big, beautiful house into this palace. Mother, I am not frightened by your lesbianism." Lily's tone had become one hundred percent sarcastic. "I am only fraught," she drawled, "over my worry that your new friend might have a temper, track mud in our house, or hate dogs."

Confounded, Dar stared back. "You know what I mean, smart mouth. And I am wholly concerned about you. I have laid it on us, I know. Anyway, we can get back to this later. Gotta go get that job," Dar said, grabbed her keys and shook her fist in the air. "Wish me luck."

Dar came home late in the day. Though still with no job, she had a smitten glow on her face that said she had met up with her new friend. "So, what's the young lady's name?" Lily asked.

"Chantelle." Dar braced for Lily's comment.

Lily chuckled. "Good lord, does she arrange funeral flowers, do hair, or...does she have a nightclub act? Maybe we should just ask her parents what they intended her to be, because growing into that name would be a nightmare."

"Wow. That's not even a bit narrow-minded," Dar said. "Sit," she said pointing to the kitchen table. "Kind questions only. And let's keep it appropriate."

Lily fired off a grocery list of topics and then waited for Dar to respond. She asked about Chantelle's hobbies, body shape, clothes style, whether she was a happy drinker like her father or a mean one like Bev, had she ever been with a man, and at last, whether she liked dogs.

"She likes bowling, if that's a hobby," Dar said. "Maybe darts, as she has a board hanging in her garage." Lily pronounced these as lame drinking games. And said they showed she liked to throw things and that Dar might want to be wary. Dar revealed what she knew about the rest, bypassing mentioning Lily's father in any way. "And we have not broached things as personal as her experience with men, as she just broke up with a woman a month before." Lily raised her eyebrows to this bit of info, letting Dar guess what she was thinking. Dar's neck reddened when Lily asked what it felt like to share a bed with a woman.

"Softer bodies and less hair. Yet I can't say no snoring, so far," Dar answered and for shock value added, "And we have only shared a car seat and a couch."

"How cute," Lily responded and blushed.

"Watch out for what you wish to be answered," Dar responded, as Lily went to the cupboard, opened a pack of fig newtons, took one out and began nibbling around the outside. Lily's questions brought on dread for Dar as to the reunion. She was determined to let her mother know, for sure. She saw Virginia, the one who hates loud noise, brace with hearing the news, then accept the verdict with no skin lost. Dar then saw the manifestation of the others, the smirks and judgment, the way they would look her up and down, like evidence of her tryst was physically smeared on her. Yet Dar, in a manner, relished telling them. "For just the expressions on their faces," Dar crooned, bringing to life those thoughts.

Lily got it. "Oh, wow. You are going to tell them? There will be carnage, Mother. Could be plain beautiful, though," she said with a grin. Lily's eyes lit up. She shot up from the table, groping for Dar's hand. With her mother in tow, they arrived sink side. With her left hand, Lily threw open a kitchen drawer and fumbled around until she pulled out a filet knife.

Dar did not even protest as Lily took her index finger, held it over the sink, and squeezing blood into its tip, made a tiny cut across it. "Ough, ough, ough," Dar squealed.

Lily then cut her own finger without a whimper. They froze, watching the warm, red blood drip and turn into pink rivulets on the wet porcelain below. Grasping her mother's finger, Lily pressed their cuts together. She looked Dar in the eye and counted aloud to seven. Dar's lucky number. Then to three. Hers.

"Lily, that's about the sweetest thing anyone has ever done for me. I cannot imagine having a better friend. And my daughter to boot." Dar paused, holding up her cut finger. "Who do you suppose ever thought of something like this? Leprechauns?"

"Indians, you goof. The ones who used to own the land this house is on. Just think, a cool tee-pee might have sat right here," Lily said. "Wanna cut another finger? For fun?"

"No. We're on the road now," Dar said, whisking her hands away from Lily. Dizzy from the sight of blood, Dar slid down the kitchen cabinets to the floor. Lily plopped down beside her. Bo got up and raced over, licking Dar's face then Lily's. He then lapped up a couple drops of blood from the floor.

Sucking on her right finger, Dar then withdrew it. She looked at Lily, reached, and touched the tip of her nose with her left. "Lily, honey, I want you to know I'm proud of you. You should be proud, too. I mean, handling all this. Boy, have I ever put it on you this year!"

They leaned side by side against the cabinets and looked across the kitchen, through the arch leading to the living room with its floor of thick, orange shag carpet. Dar let out a little laugh. "To shag carpet and the fleas in it, to the reunion and whatever it hides and springs on us. To today, yesterday, to the future, in fact. Lily, we're gonna go all in with confidence. And charm, 'cuz we got it, blood sister."

Tucking her hair behind her right ear and watching blood trickle down her wrist, Dar continued. "But just in case, bring what you have on the dodgeball court to River Oaks. My news, the divorce, and our sweet little rectangular house will be targets. No need for swords and shields. Well, maybe the shield," Dar said and then smiled. "If you handle it all with grace there, we will have a long walk. I know you have more questions about Chantelle. Maybe I'll know more by then. And, yes, she had a dog." Dar added and frowned.

"Had?" Lily asked.

"Liked to sleep under tires in the driveway," Dar said.

Lily dragged Bo across the floor, tucking him between her legs. "And I suppose your chick had a habit of knowing that info about where the dog slept? I hate you for not lying. You could have said it was a cat."

"Even if you don't like them, Lily, cats are people too."

10

Bones

Lily rolled her bike across the face of the white picket fence. From the kitchen window, Dar thought she looked like a champion readying for a race. So graceful yet taut in profile, so filled with anticipation, maybe even butterflies for the summer ahead. She smiled. Lily, it seemed, had been to the Salvation Army. Below the crisp sheen of her happy Saturday morning face, she wore red slip-on shoes with blue-and-white striped socks running halfway up her ankles. Her tight shorts were the color of spring grass. She wore a clean white tank top with pale blue bra straps showing. Her waves of dark hair were beginning to grow back and fell to her tan shoulders. Dar knew the horizon she was seeing, indescribable by anything but the teenage heart. She remembered those mysteries. They were like alien worlds. But first, Lily was taking care of business. One last spin around their old homestead, a farewell to her father who was there cleaning the garage out, before they packed up the car and headed to River Oaks.

Watching her daughter, a nervous pang spread from her chest to her belly. A lot had been shoved into the package of the stoic girl out there. As much as she had expressed to Lily her sorrow for that, it offered no remedies for how she was to deal with it. She had taken it for granted that Lily would pop out the other side of the divorce licking her wounds, no worse for the wear and only smarter. It is a mother's delusion that is her best friend, Dar now thought, knowing that things were not so simple. Number one, Lily did not lick wounds. She drove right through pain. Maybe that was good, but then maybe Lily would just stack them up until one day all life's struggles came down and buried whatever world she had simulated for herself. She would pull herself out of that rubble and move on.

Lily looked over everything in the huge metal basket hanging from the handlebars of her bike. Finding a basket that big had been one more fated thing. That had been on the good luck side of life. By the side of the road, with a "take me" sign on it, Lily could not believe that no one had snatched up such a rare beauty. Taking it, she had ridden over to her father's house with it hanging by a rope off the frame. "Wow," he had exclaimed seeing it, "a grocery cart." An hour later, he had it mounted. Afterward, sprawled on the lawn drinking lemonade and sharing a bag of boiled peanuts, they reviewed the new wares.

"Those are nice digs you have there, Lily," her father said.

"Yep, it'll handle quite a bounty," Lily responded, as her father wrapped his arm about her, pulling her to his chest. Lily's heart swelled. These moments used to be regular and now felt constrained, like a jail visit.

"I'm sorry," he said, and both knew what he meant. He had then stood and smiled, walked into the one-car garage of his tiny rented house. A minute later, he presented a cardboard box of his own nostalgic pickings. Fumbling through it, he brought out clumps of Spanish moss taken from the resting Hooper tea plantation. "Like that place, this plant is just waiting for the right partner," her father said helping her spread the dry clumps out on the bottom of the wire basket.

Lily viewed that gray bromeliad as a charm, with her basket, pointing the way to goodness around the bend. As an afterthought, Lily's father had attached to the front of her basket a crude peace sign cut out of the top of a five-pound baked bean can. "Made that after I met your mom. Had it on the front of my VW van," he told Lily.

Imagining his face, Lily swallowed hard and scanned the inventory in the basket. *The Hobbit* was there in a plastic bag. A hummingbird feather, sure as sin, sat tucked into the first page. Tiny, blue, green, and translucent, it made a perfect bookmark. At a rare Sunday dinner

Dar had orchestrated "to keep the family inspired to be one," Lily had bragged to Bev and Sarah about owning such a thing. They laughed. "Yes, it's like finding a fairy wing," Lily had confirmed, saying, of course, she owned one of those also. Lily had enjoyed the faltering reactions of the old gals that night. "Like shuffling turtles poked on their shells," Lily had told her mother in the kitchen later that night.

Lily's gaze now fell on the bones tied in blue ribbon in the corner of the basket. She picked them up and smiled. Billy Fontaine had laughed at those. "A harmonica, bird feathers, who rides with this stuff? Creepy bones tied in blue ribbon. They look real, like human," Billy exclaimed, pushing at the small bundle with the tip of a finger. "And what's this?" Billy asked, lifting a perfume bottle out of the basket. He inspected the contents through the old glass. "You collect dirt. Weird, there's something else in there," he said then laughed.

Lily took back the bottle. "Found it in my granny's trash. Who knows?" Lily said and shrugged. "Life's full of cool stuff." A bleached bird's skull in Lily's basket had set Billy off on a tangent. "It's a treasure if you keep it," Lily had retorted and wheeled away.

Lily had collected the bones from the grounds of the Hooper plantation, in an area of old fallen shacks. It was one of two summers they were cleaning up around the place years after Virginia had abandoned it. The shacks were off-limits because of rusty nails, snakes, and such, or so she was told. Lily had always snooped around the area, finding old spoons, metal buttons, and yes, she had seen a couple of big rat snakes, but they were harmless. Reviewing some of Lily's finds one day, Dar whispered that the place was, in a sense, spiritual, though she meant haunted, Lily suspected. "Some parts of history are meant to be forgotten and remembered at the same time," her mother said, when Lily pried.

"Slave quarters for sure," Lily had said to Bev and Sara over dessert that same Sunday. She had pulled the bundle of bones from her shorts pocket and held them for all to see. Before Bev or anyone else could object, Lily had quickly described where the bones belonged on the human body, holding up her left hand and pointing. Dar's eyes across the table warned Lily.

Sara and Bev had lit up toward Lily's suggestion of a correlation between the plantation and slavery. Lily had come back hard. "Yep, finger bones most definitely from slaves," she said and clacked the bones together. Lily then traced their unnatural curvature with her dessert spoon. "Bent from being overworked."

That comment had set a fire under Bev. "Father did not even inherit the place until the twenties. His own hard work was what made that place. Those are old chicken coops and tobacco storage sheds," Sarah added.

"Those bones are from pigs we slaughtered," Bev said.

"Silly me," Lily said. "Your father did inherit it from his parents. When did you say my great-grandfather was there?" She let the insinuation linger. Bev picked up her plate and stormed away. Recalling that, Lily fingered the white bones, nodded and shoved them in her pocket. Lily placed a foot in the stirrup of her metal bike and swung aboard. In moments, she was swept into the alleyway, the incline beyond, and down the avenue of wide and tall oaks and fading dogwoods. She shot away into the congregation of hums emanating from the neighborhood. A mower, the peak of children's voices, the bark of a dog.

Lily came home and tucked her bike away from bad weather. She went into the kitchen and took out a Popsicle from the freezer. Dar was in her bedroom with a layer of Noxzema absorbing into her face. The phone rang. Dar and Lily picked up at the same time. Dar spoke first, though she did not know Lily was listening in. "Hooper residence." Dar had dropped her married name and returned to her own.

"Dar, honey, it's Bev. Got a minute?" Here we go, Dar thought. Lily clenched and wanted to hang up but decided a bit of sleuthing would do no harm. Dar could not get through a syllable of answering before Bev interrupted. "Don'tchewknow, I am just thrilled to no end about the reunion. House full of kids, all those gourmet meals, and of course our sparkling personalities."

Dar was cordial but braced out of familiarity with Bev's sugarcoated sword. "It's all that's on our minds," Dar answered, hoping in some way Bev picked up the sarcasm. "You're lucky you caught us. We're just about to leave."

"How'd dear Lily end up in school? Grades improving?" Bev asked.

A terse snort followed. Dar buried the receiver into her breasts and hissed, "Lily," knowing that she was listening in. "Her grades?" Dar asked, cramming the phone back to her ear. "Not perfect, not bad, but all this transition, you know. We have not received them yet. Could this wait?" Lily cringed.

"So, I hear there will be perfect weather for the week. Hot, of course," Bev continued. "Oh, you know, that makes me wonder—knowing that sweet, precocious daughter of yours—will she be wearing appropriate clothing? I mean clothes." Laughter from Bev pierced the phone. Lily could hear her mother's measured breathing, counting, as she did, to avoid snapping.

At last, Dar answered. "I think, because it will be so hot, that Lily will dress accordingly."

"Can you see that she behaves? You know, not interjecting herself into adult business. And there is that discourteous little mouth she carries around. She is expected to be mature."

Lily was proud of her mother's prowess at handling snakes. Though she knew Dar probably wanted to spit through four miles of phone line into Bev's ear, she remained silent. Lily listened for anything that ensured Bev was jilted by the silence. Bev clucked once. "Dar, honey, I know it's been a hard year for y'all—you know, with your divorce lingering in your mind and having to set up in a lesser house than you're used to. Well, do you think Lily is ready to come into the fold with her male cousins? Lily is a little tenderfoot, you know. She just does not understand how to be gracious, when in families that's just what we do."

Lily was sure Bev's question had been rehearsed while pacing her tiny mothball-scented living room. She knew Bev was tormented with the idea of her great niece's scantily clad body parading about River Oaks. And the gall of Lily shirking the cousins for an entire week.

"Number one, Bev, teens cannot be expected to act as adult as you, dressing accordingly and all. And as for that other issue, girls and boys of that age don't always come into the fold at the same time." Lily sensed Dar was biting her lip, maybe smiling. "Girls, you well know, Bev, mature earlier than boys. Lily, and probably Tish, by now, are thinking of broader issues. Like, how to make the world a better place. And, of boys. The kind with their ducks in a row."

"Well, I can see we are getting nowhere here. Maybe this is not the best time for you, Dar, honey. Remember, you are visiting, so keep Lily in line."

"Families don't visit, they reunion, Bev. Sure am glad my mother has kept that place up and running. And I can't watch Lily all day. No telling what limits those little male nitro sticks will push her and Tish to. But I guess you'll be having this same talk with their father, right?"

Bev ignored Dar's suggestion of who owned what. She would get to that at the gathering. "No need to. Mickey's a good father. Better parent than that wife of his, who will be skippin' out again this year. Says it conflicts with plans already made."

Dar muttered, "Maybe she's just smarter than us."

"Dar honey, the real reason I called was to make sure you got the list of groceries you will need to contribute. Left it tacked to your front door yesterday. Sorry if that's hard on the budget, but you're getting a free stay at an original river estate house. Not many of those left in the old families. Those homes are just falling apart."

"Right," Dar quipped. She had found the grocery list and thrown it in the trash.

"All right then. It's all settled. All's left now is to get there and start drinking," Bev said.

"Amen to that," Dar said, wondering by the silence if Bev was still on the line.

"Bitch," Dar heard Lily hiss into the phone. A click and then the phone went dead.

"Lily Hooper Smith," Dar snapped coming into the kitchen. "You know better than to listen in."

"I'm a girl on a tear and not a novice. Bev has no clue," Lily yelled. "And I'm going to dress down so far and show so much skin...You just wait."

"Bev just says what she says to get wherever she's going. Kind middle words or gracious goodbyes don't matter. But Lily, I hope Bev had hung up when you called her a bitch. We don't need that burr in her side. And I will never hear you call her or anyone in this family that again," Dar added. "Let's get out of here, sassafras."

Seeing the July reunion in full color, the danger, and most important, the mysteries to be uncovered, Lily had prepared. She would bring her own arsenal. She would bring her relentless curiosity and sleuth's eye. She would bring tenacity as sharp as any knife. And of course, she would bring the bones in her pocket.

11

The Windward Side

Virginia crossed the room and stopped. River Oaks loomed around and above her, quiet and cavernous. She remembered three years before, when Lily, then twelve, had climbed up and stood on the shoulders of her father to run a finger over the surface of the ten-foot ceiling. From there she had howled, waited, and then claimed something had called back in a whisper. And then pouted so sweetly, until her father cocked his head listening. "Yes, yes, there it is."

Virginia angled her ears to the house, certain of the presence of her mother, Sage. She had promised to spend part of her afterlife between here and the plantation on the coast. That assertion was made after dinner on the plantation porch, dusk dropping its curtain of gray and orange across the land. Having walked the dunes that day, she was in a pensive mood. She had begun dinner telling all she had for an hour watched a gator eat a badly wounded pelican. "The bird offered itself to the gator, walked right up and lay itself right over its wide-open jaws." Sage said that thing of beauty gave her solace that when her time came, she would do the same. "Metaphorically," she added when her three daughters gasped and protested. Virginia's father, Winfield, had gone off to the kitchen to fill his pipe. Sage lowered her learnt eyes, taking in all three of them at once, demanding attention without a word. Her daughters, dead still, listened.

Sage's voice was tender but as consuming as the humidity on that porch. "Goes without saying that you will never be rid of me," she had begun. There would be no argument or myth to these facts, Virginia recalled thinking of her tone. "You will keep River Oaks and the tea plantation intact. I will swim between them and make my presence known. I am sure some of you, maybe all, as you are bound so tight in your faults, will need my skills for a long time to come." The ease with which she spoke of her death startled the three of them, more so when she added, "You know girls, death is man-made, a plot to make paradise look better than earth. How can there be more?" she said, spreading her arms to display the radiant land before them. When you know these things, one can plan in unity with the place as it was meant to be. "This, my sweet angels, is what comes before, grows in the middle, and what is forever after. Heaven is a business plan, no different than trying to grow tea," she said taking a long pull from her drink. Winfield had come back, smiling at Sage's last statement. Sage continued. "That's eternal, and I am wagering on what I can see, touch, and taste. Girls, I will advise you to do the same. It'll make life a lot more fun. Don't be spooked by the kitchen staff telling you that the devil is in our cellar eating beets, as that is nonsense. That bad man is too busy plotting to sit around in that cold place. And there might be a God, but not the one you suppose. Look no further than your father standing there, the gators in the dunes, the angels of pelicans soaring through the pinholes of waves. Or the luck that got us all here at once together."

Looking to the pine floor, Virginia smiled, imagining her mother's travels from that old house on the coast, through the lowlands and hot onion fields, to the room right here where she stood. Virginia counted on Sage being here this week. She would need her quiet resolve, her philosophy of fairness, and her backbone to get through it all.

Virginia wanted to believe that goodness would prevail this year. Over the past few summers the atmosphere had gone from prickly to combative. For more than one hundred years, River Oaks had been blessed with voices of joy. If rancor existed, it was swept away as trivial. River Oaks had an aura of having been nurtured and loved. When family entered, every element rushed to greet them. And that gracious host remained after they left. Sage had always said that River Oaks was a "she" and that she could hear the swish of her billowing dress against the walls coming forward. Winfield said the river beyond was the gentleman constantly courting that unattainable beauty. Both would agree with Virginia now, that condescending voices hung from the past few summers. She imagined that hostess now braced with Sage patting her on the back.

Virginia told herself she would tamp down Bev's vigor this year. Yet Bev's conscience did not run as designed by either God or parent. She was an undertaking. Straight iron tracks from her wild, untidy youth to the present, where Bev assumed that she was absolved of any sin. Virginia suspected it had taken some form of insanity to get her there. Bev seemed to delight in letting those things they should never talk about hang a thin hint away like fruit to be plucked and thrown about the room. Virginia had plotted to stay resolute in contending with Bev's new ploy against River Oaks and the plantation. She wondered who Bev cajoled to join her drumbeat of selling all and putting the money to better use. Bev had never owned a compass for being homesick or nostalgic, nor wistful for the heart of anything. The fact was Bev did not own a conscience.

Virginia wondered how Sarah would be this time around. She had forever been a ticker tape to Bev's parade. In fact, she had sided with Bev in her new foray against the properties but backed off when Virginia reminded them both what they already knew. That she owned everything. Bev said that was a technicality usurped by common sense. And believed it.

Enough of this, Virginia thought, and moved about with a dust rag. She threw the sheets off the massive table then looking about, stilled, seeing on a side table, a black-and-white photo. The picture was taken ten years ago in Virginia's house in town. Bev, in the foreground, must have placed it there before she left last summer. Retaliation for Virginia claiming to make the decisions for this house. The message was in the background, a can of Falstaff on Virginia's old Victrola and Bigbee's heavy black hand resting on the wood, Sage's maid and then Virginia's until a week after that transforming day.

She stiffened. That photo recorded a date, a freeze shot of heartache and anxiety. The day her second husband, Bobby, died in the bathtub. Falstaff was his beer, and that was the last one he ever had. Virginia looked at the black hand and shook her head. "Oh lord, why?" Virginia listened to her voice, and all that was in it, echo about. She took the small, framed photo and shoved it in the pocket of her dress. Bev, of course, knew that is what she would do.

Virginia turned away. She tried to smell the cooking that evening, hear bits of laughter, and hear the chortle of the river from her bedroom window when all went to bed. The tide headed that way took over. The oak leaves on the lawn blew in a swirl. Sage slunk back between the batten boards. "Bad times are dying with the years," she whispered, and Virginia tried to take hold of that for support. She felt an urgency for the house to be full and for night to rush in and pass. She saw Bobby's pale bloated body. "Go to hell, Bobby. Get away from me."

Hurrying, Virginia began to open the windows of the great room. Things would not be so stifling once the air filled the house and steeped into the furniture, curtains, and bed sheets. The scent of flowers filled her nostrils. Somewhere, charcoal was burning, and laughter echoed from down river. She thought of Lily coming to savor it all. And of Tish, thank Jesus for her. Virginia then frowned. The boy cousins would fill the world with their noise and unsavory antics. They gulped without tasting and lacked the sweetness of Lily and Tish, the kind that made flowers push up through hard clay to sip the sun and air. Dar had said the boys, like Bev, had been born without oxygen. Then there was their father Mickey, Bev's yes man. Virginia felt pity for him. Pretending so poorly to be wise and even, Mickey lacked muster to repair the ruins of conflict around him and disrespect toward him. Looking about, Virginia felt anxious for the survival of this old home. When she was gone, would they bulldoze this palace? Would they pick their teeth with it and her splintered bones?

12

The Tick of Old Roads

They were headed down the highway bound for the reunion. Dar was puckering her lips at the rear-view mirror and applying red lipstick. "I can already feel things falling off of me," she said. "Hey, let's just let worry seem obsessive and unnecessary. We are there to have fun. Hooper reunion, here we come," she cheered, and glanced at Lily in the back-seat.

Lily nodded with enthusiasm, though she knew all their wishes would soon meet the ways of others. Her mother's declaration of being a lesbian would land like spit on a hot iron. Bev was already riled up that she, Lily Hooper Smith, dared even to breathe.

"Yep, obsessive and unnecessary," Lily said. "Who, me? Worry?"

"I mean it, Lily. We are there to have fun. And to act like family, even if acting is all we've got." Dar stuck a cigarette in her mouth, flicked her lighter to light it, and hunched up with confidence. She reached and turned on the radio, rolling through the prospects. The car was filled with static. "Got to adjust that coat hanger," Dar said, taking the smoke out of her mouth and frowning at the bent piece of wire jiggling in the wind.

"Yep," Lily, bored, called out minutes later and slapped the seat beside her. "There is enough room back here for whatever two people want to do. But I suppose you already know that, as you and Chantelle had a date in a car one night. What is it with cars? Boy, I'm itching to find out." Dar stared straight ahead, refusing to jump at the bait, and Lily pushed the seat back with the balls of her feet.

Dar snuck a look at Lily's wild, unruly hair, her eyes flashing the same. "Firecracker," she muttered and then waved to a prisoner picking up trash along the road. In the process, ashes from her cigarette dropped onto the seat between her legs. She beat and brushed the ashes to the floorboard. "Dammit to hell, that's the fiftieth burn hole."

Lily was amused. "That should be telling you something," Lily said. Stretching out, she hung her leg out the window. "Harmful, just as the surgeon general said in 1970."

"My little encyclopedia," Dar said. Her eyes then flashed between the mirror and Lily's legs out the window. "Lily. Telephone poles, car mirrors, anything could take off that leg."

"Doesn't matter. We're already half squished into the pages of a scary book—a new neighborhood of possible molesters, a yard of medical waste I'm sure, and a probable Grimm's fairy tale ending at the reunion to finish us off," Lily announced. Rolling her eyes, she pulled her leg back in and placed the flat of her bare foot onto the ceiling.

Dar squinted, wondering of Lily's fidgeting and contentious behavior. "This fairy tale is just a trail of little crumbs," Dar said. "We can follow to the end. Or just run away and tuck inside our cozy little home."

Lily's muffled voice carried over the seat. "Seems like the fairies are really angry."

"God knows when they rest," Dar answered and looked back again. Lily had vanished somewhere within her haven. Dar sighed, knowing Lily was going through a lot of late.

To make matters worse, they had received Lily's school grades right before they left. They were abysmal, even though Lily's IQ test put her at her top of the scale. And Bev asking about her scores an hour before the mail arrived was an ominous sign for her. Also were Lily's God-awful male cousins, both of whom Dar had ten years ago considered smothering in their sleep for their creepy shenanigans. Mickey had made them visit a prison to thwart their primitive notions of fun. That had done little to grind down the razor's edge of his sons. Dar hated how their very presence sent Lily straight down. And now, there was Chantelle to stir the pot. My God, Dar thought, no wonder Lily's mood is so off. Grinding out her smoke in the overflowing ashtray, Dar thought of something reassuring to say. Lily was looking out the window. Her eyes had sharpened into shrewdness. Plotting against her foes, Dar thought. "Buyer beware," Dar muttered with confidence and faced back toward the old familiar road.

Thirty minutes passed. At last, Lily's bright and perky face popped up over the seat. She then frowned, looking out. "Where are we?" she asked. "What a sad-looking town."

"Even steel can break, Lily," Dar said, as they passed boarded-up storefronts and a landscape of shimmering broken glass and litter. "And this place was just that, once." Both stared at an old black man with a skinny white dog. Neither bothered to take in the only car on the road. The man fed a cooking fire in a barrel with bits of a broken pallet. The dog circled the drum and lifted its leg to pee, but nothing came out. Lily's heart felt broken. "Bo," she whispered. They rolled past a busted up Dairy Queen sitting between two big oaks. The oaks were green and thriving like conquerors over the seedy thing they grew over. A hundred feet farther was a paint store with blue graffiti across its bricks. "Bang 'em up," it said.

Dar slowed, taking in the awful message. "Be thankful for what we have. God, we are so lucky, Lily."

Lily pulled her legs up onto the seat and hugged them. Dar lit up again. They came to a stop sign. With her arms over the steering wheel, Dar blustered through her lips. "Think of the good memories here. Someone still has them. I'm going to hold onto that," Dar said. "Yes, someone will bring them back. Just like we are going to do at River Oaks. Make the good things push the bad away."

"You know, looking out at all this, it's hard to see River Oaks as real."

"It's not, to many," Dar said. "Some take the whole place for granted. Not seeing that it could all be gone in a flash. Just like a life. Or a good marriage."

Though Lily wanted to retort to the last part of that, she kept to the message her mother was trying to impart. And then, Lily saw that Dar had teared up. She drew her arm across her eyes and rolled through a stop sign. She had picked up a smear of mascara over the top of her hand. "Sorry, must be my period," Dar lied. She then lifted her head and expelled a blue cloud of smoke across the ceiling, then frantically waved the smoke away. Her jerky motion and clown-painted eyes reminded Lily of a jack-in-the-box. Dar looked at herself in the mirror and laughed. She was back to beautiful and slipshod, Lily thought, smiling.

"I'm all good now," Dar said. The car moved onward, now through dark swampland and thick trees hanging over the road. On and on the engine stabbed at getting to sunlight and at last found it in rolling pastureland speckled with cattle and horses. A heavy scent of sweet blossoms blew in. Dar and Lily inhaled at the same moment and nodded; ecstasy shared in their looks. "Thank God for little things," Dar called out and Lily began to get butterflies, excited for all she loved about River Oaks.

"Let's go have some fun," Lily whooped, and Dar nodded, "A beautiful hour more."

Lily leaned forward, draping her arms over the front seat. She squinted at the center line of the narrow road. There was a choice to go on forever, and Lily looked forward to the day she was behind that steering wheel. The day she could come to River Oaks alone, or just with Dar. Or Tish and a bucketful of worms. Or boys, she smiled, thinking. Just then a billboard blew into and out of view: "Best Boiled P'nuts in the World. One mile ahead." Lily kneed the back of the seat, but Dar was already slowing down.

Eating boiled nuts and tossing shells out the window was the best there was. Her mother was humming under her breath. All was back, Lily thought. Watching the tick-tick of trees by the side of the road, Lily felt how close they were to River Oaks. She began to plot how to get the old sisters to spice things up with stories about when they were young.

If that didn't turn into an argument, it would be fun and possibly give up some dirt.

"Lily," Dar blurted out. "This week, some will want us to remember our places in the order of the family tree. There is no order. Just as pecans in an old tree, we all belong. Also, Lily, you do not have to follow others' rules." Dar winked. "You are almost an adult, well, in the sense that those three gals, by the time they were ten, were pretty much pushing up through the concrete. Thinking the world couldn't wait to see them. As you know it will be a drunken ordeal. I will be part of that party, but that is strictly for my own protection."

"Let's get 'em really loosened up," Lily said and leaned forward again. "I wanna hear the guts. They must be hiding a ton of stuff. Sick of hearing about the larks of three entitled girls. The juicy stuff is missing," Lily said. "I have overheard things, you know."

Dar considered what Lily conveyed. She decided to not answer, and put a peanut, shell and all, in her mouth, suck on it for a bit, then crack down on it. Leaning over, she spat the shell into the wind, scattering it amongst a dead possum and two babies strewn about her in the road. Lily swiveled to watch the carnage through the back window. "Wow, what got them there in the sweet spot at the same time, to be met so evenly with a random swipe of a tire? Seems unfair. Yet beautiful in a creepy way."

"Fate, and of course loyalty," Dar answered. "Others would say just darn bad timing."

"Like Bev, Sarah, and Granny," Lily said. "The loyalty thing, I mean."

Dar smiled. "Virginia would not have followed them into the road. Though there is strong loyalty there, it is not as when they were young...when she might have. They have changed over the last dozen years or so. Have in fact become quite irritable. I think that's typical with age. I suspect it must be hard for them realizing their beauty and energy have faded." Dar then sighed. "I hope mother survives this week. Unlike those possums, fate is still sorting itself out with them. I think they bamboozled their good story by running too hard in life. Some of them forgot what to appreciate. And I suspect that once it is sorted out, there will be some hard punishment. On Bev in particular, from what we have seen of her act."

"I just know I am not following those girls into any road," Lily said and nodded.

"Whew," Dar said. "Don't even want to go there. Makes them sound dangerous."

"That's what I think I'm talking about," Lily answered, and sank back to consider that. This all pointed to what Lily, in her thoughts, referred to as The Great Mystery. That name underlined twice in her journal the summer before. "*Intrigue. Mildew on the family tree,*" she had written. The elder sisters, their ragdoll souls, their club, was guided by a conspiracy, she was sure. "*Maybe something as big as an affair with the Pope.*"

Lily's suspicion had begun with words overheard in Virginia's kitchen two years before: "Let it go, Sarah. Bigbee has moved on. Are you trying to imagine it as unnecessary?" Bev hissed. Sarah moaned back, "We were never as taciturn over wrongs as you, Bev."

In a tired voice, Bev sniped back, "A bad dog's a bad dog, Sarah." Virginia's silence lay as hard as the floor, as Lily, having eavesdropped, entered. The word "wrongs" hung over the room, telling her this was big.

"Sounds like someone shot a dog. That is never right," Lily said to them.

Bev put on a face that no other could achieve and told Lily they were arguing about the tea plantation, the upkeep necessary, and of the old maid there, Bigbee, who had kept it bright, cheery, and in order. "Well, Lily, the place just became too much," she added with a flair of sadness that for her was never real.

"Oh, dear lord, what are we gonna do, Miss Virginia? Bigbee's done worn out with those cutting shears, and the tea bushes are attacking the house," Lily had called out, smacking her cheeks. Bev was aghast.

"Please, Lily," Virginia had pleaded in the same second Bev said, "What a queer child."

Dar's voice snapped Lily out of her reverie. "What you see, Lily, is nothing more than accumulated damage. They were three wild, beautiful girls with few roadblocks beyond Sage to slow them down. Now, there is just death itself to stop them."

Lily half-heard this as she was plotting her mission with the old girls. Her prying at the last reunion had revealed nothing. Maybe this year, her granny would let down her barrier. She was the most sensitive and affected by the hard parts of the reunion. Last summer, by the end, she resembled a sweet mouse portending a long winter. When Lily made that analogy, Dar had called her state "war trauma."

13

Ghosts and Sparrows

Virginia sniffed the air. From somewhere came a hint of potpourri; orange peel and clove. She had left that there last year and still it blessed the air. She looked toward the portrait of her father above the fireplace and stood on her tiptoes to see the reflection of her face mingled next to his. From the depths of his portrait, clouds then formed, the faces of her inseparable teen sisters demanding their space beside him. Bev's look, pushing forward, was full of mischievous and stringent delight. Sarah, heeding the hard nudge from her, waited her turn.

"You fools, we were blessed," Virginia said and continued to prepare. From a bureau, she took out the dining room table runner and spread it out. She then placed her mother, Sage's, two ornate candlesticks on the huge mahogany dining table. In the middle, she put her favorite item, a large and beautiful silver pheasant. She heard Bev's voice saying that someday those would be hers. Virginia became anxious and looked back to her father for support. She thought of setting up the dining room table, thought about the silver pheasant, and looking, realized she already had. Virginia squeezed the rag in her hand in anger, and then relaxed by pressing her fingers into the spongy upholstery of a chair back. These sensations had begun a year ago, the last time about three months prior. Virginia told herself she could stop them with a drink. Something scraped outside. She then heard the flutter of wings on shutters and tin. Just a swallow. She put a hand to her chest. The clamoring bird quieted, nesting.

Virginia ran her shoe over the oriental carpet. She watched the light straining in over the furniture. Her pulse was racing, her stomach fluttering. Virginia went to the front door and opened it. She stuck her face out to breathe the hot and humid air. Leaving the door open she turned back. A waft of oak and grass and river filled the air about her. She wished her father were here to put his arm over her shoulder. He would tell her she had absolution from Bobby, from Bigbee, and that there was a God to sort everything out. He would return her son to sit on her lap. Her mother would drift by in her tolerance of all things. Her calm view of the world would quiet Virginia's racing mind. Sarah's soft hazel eyes came into focus, telling Virginia that there were greater things in the world to worry about.

Virginia heard the crunch of gravel down the long drive. She moved as fast as she could, pulling sheets off the last of the furniture and furling them over her shoulder. They smelled of burned dust and of her age. She prayed for her first drink, only hours away now, to be strong. She could almost taste the fumes, felt them finding and opening a place of solace. Of absolution.

Virginia turned as she heard her driver's heavy steps on the boards and then the thump of her first bags onto the porch. She had hired the man, no longer trusting herself to stay awake on the long drive. Virginia grabbed her vase of fresh flowers, spruced them up, and moved to the base of the stairs to place them in her room. Her eyes followed the stair runner as it went above into a gray corner, into the mist of colored light coming through the stained-glass window. The rug's pattern was gutted and smooth, the happy and sad traffic of a long life.

For a moment she imagined the day had ended. The initial battles were over. The frenzy of catapulting adolescents fighting their demons and sunburns had quieted. She imagined her drunken form bow into the chair before her vanity. There she would swab off her makeup, lying that not a tear had run through it all day. Grasping the newel, Virginia pulled herself up, telling herself she was as prepared as she was going to be.

14

The Still Air of Summer's Heart

Dar and Lily closed out the drive singing Beach Boys tunes, those songs pumping them up for their days in the sun ahead. Lily lay in the back on an oasis of pillows, the hot wind lashing her hair, writing in her scribble journal; the one she carried for bumpy car rides and tenuous ideas. She sat up straight as they passed Dogwood Drive. In a few hundred yards they would come to the painted and chipped sign announcing their arrival at River Oaks.

Pulling in the long drive, Dar stopped the car. Over the tick of the engine, the air hissed with insects. Dar sighed, relieved to have her foot free of the pedal, glad to be surrounded by lolling oaks and tall grass. Turning off the engine, she took a sip of steamy air.

"Boy, I love it here. Listen to that quiet, will ya?" Dar announced. They sat in silence, sensing, smelling, breathing. With a loud sigh, Dar restarted the car.

Dar pulled under the same lolling limbs they parked under each summer. Standing outside the car, they stretched, both grinning, the thrill of being on these beautiful grounds hitting them. Lily moved her bare feet in the hot, sandy soil. Draping an arm over Lily, Dar swung her about to face the massive house and its countless angles of roof and darkened windows.

"It is always something to behold," Dar said. "Like the face of a king," she added.

Nodding, Lily swooped her body out from under her mother's arm and faced her. Lily raised a hand as if taking an oath. "Mother dear, I,

Lily Hooper....Smith, hereby swear to do my best to have a good time this week."

"Since when was I raising a Girl Scout?" Lily watched her mother's eyes twinkle. "This week will not be easy," Dar added.

"We will face it together...with a Girl Scout's rigor," Lily commanded.

Dar eyed the girl before her. "Where on earth did you come from?"

"You know the answer to that."

Dar and Lily watched as Virginia's driver came off the front porch and waved to them. Dar turned and opened the trunk to begin unloading. "Just leave my stuff where it is. I'll get it in a minute," Lily announced and raced away. Her mind was on tradition; a single loop around the house, a dash to the river's edge, finished with a skip of her first stone.

Dropping her bag, Dar hurried to follow Lily.

Lily let her mother catch up and then took her hand. Once, twice, they raced around the house, their shrill voices filling the yard. In minutes, they were at the river's edge. Dar gasped for a full breath beside Lily, who smiled sideways at her. "Gonna quit smoking one of these days," Lily said, repeating what she had heard a hundred times before. Lily then jumped down the steep bank with Dar sidestepping to follow.

Dar watched Lily, scampering right then left on her long gazelle legs, her eyes scanning the bank and narrow shore. Leaning with her tan arms down, she readied to lunge at the perfect skipping stone. "Hah!" Dar exclaimed, looking down to see at her feet the silver dollar of all rocks. Dar held up the stone between thumb and index finger and moved her arm in pitching motion.

"Make it good...you'll kick yourself if you blow it with that one," Lily said. Licking her lips, Dar went to the river's edge. Setting up, she then released the stone. It hit the surface flat and true.

Lily counted. "One, two, three, four, five....eight. Wow, first throw of the summer, and a real sweet one." Lily looked about for a perfect match.

From her bedroom window, Virginia watched as Dar and Lily arrived. She glowed inside as they looked up at the grand old house, their faces awed by luck and fortune. Nothing could cross over to shadow their spirit, Virginia mused. Beware, she thought, to those who might attempt to assuage Lily and Dar to foolish ideals. Those two had long ago made their pact with the heart and lungs of this place. Right now, they looked like grinning magpies taking in River Oaks. Yes, Virginia thought, feeling giddy. "Go," she mouthed as, in ritual, Lily raced to complete the first great house loop. Dar caught up and took her hand. Virginia could hear their yelps. Make tradition your stronghold, you two, Virginia thought, wringing one hand into the other. Virginia knew the rest. They would not enter until they had visited the river. Where worry and trepidation had embroiled her earlier, Virginia now garnered hope.

Having dressed as the queen of River Oaks and sprucing up her makeup before the vanity, Virginia stood to make her charge below. The last thing she did was to pin on Sage's favorite brooch. It was a peculiar piece of jewelry, a Celtic knot with an alligator across the center. Its tail became part of the interwoven roping to the piece, a continuum of life, Sage had said. The gator's eyes were two tiny garnets, her mother's favorite stone. The alligators leathery back bore pelican wings. Sage had it made, saying that it promised her resolve in the afterlife.

15

Greetings

The family arrived, the elders trudging in first. Bev marched in with fierce determination, her hard shoes snapping at the pine flooring. Sarah followed in her soft soles. She looked about as an acolyte in frightened reverence of the great room before settling her gaze on anything else. It was like she already wanted to apologize, Virginia thought, watching. Marcel and Jessie exploded in, throwing what little they had helped carry onto the floor. They spun around, their feet spasming on the polished wood, and shot back out the door.

"Aren't you a sight for sore eyes," Bev called out to her sister Sarah, who stood swiping her brow with a handkerchief. Bev's son, Mickey, came in sweating, dropped two bags, leaned in to kiss Sarah on the cheek and missed it. Tish sauntered through the door, a fluid and graceful stream among these pillars of sweat and affectation. She hooted, Tish's call of delight. Dropping her load, she swung about through that bramble of voices, unnoticed.

Virginia stood across the room in the spot she had promised herself, staying away from the initial hurricane of activity. They will settle by the third day, she thought. Everyone was here but Dar and Lily, who were still down by the river. Like Tish, they will bring relief, she knew. Leaning against the mantle, she felt her father's wisdom over her shoulder. She glanced back. The painting had captured his discerning gaze, and his eyes appeared to roam the room.

They had made it another year, Virginia thought, testing positivity. Maybe this year the voices will be quieter, the tones gentler and less confrontational. Virginia convinced herself that the excitement on the landing sounded poetic, the words full of grace and civility. Still, Virginia was impatient for silence to come over them, for all at once to look about in awe at where they were. They will find solidarity, Virginia told herself, and called out without thinking, "By God, look at us all, not a laggard in the bunch."

There was a momentary pause on the landing. Bev shot Virginia a conciliatory smile and went right on showing Sarah a new ring, holding it up before her eyes. Sarah bounced an excited hand toward Virginia, and Mickey, at the door, shrieked for his boys out in the yard to "get with the program."

A minute later, Marcel and Jessie charged through the front door again. Pretending to be stallions, they stampeded into the main room making circles around the dining room table. The silver pheasant shuddered as Marcel cantered into the table's edge. Empty handed, they galloped in place at the bottom of the stairs. Marcel, then Jessie, began making buzzing sounds, and they vanished like hornets up the stairs. Virginia had stepped forward to greet them, but they were oblivious to their host. Their sister, Tish, came in again. She turned and smiled to Virginia with a small curtsy of thanks. She then raced up the stairs yelling at her brothers about which room was hers.

Just then, Dar stood in the doorway in a negligible white tank top, the daylight exposing the shape of her breasts and point of her nipples. Lily floated in behind, her eyes glazed over from the harsh light of the river behind and the bounty she found staring about the massive room. She wore an Indian weave shirt of turquoise and yellow. It fell to just above her cutoff shorts, exposing her navel. She gripped her mother's hand. Their glow, the ease by which they found their sanguine posture, gave Virginia hope.

"Travel clothes," Dar announced, noting Sarah and Bev looking them up and down.

"I have seen more cover on a newborn's scalp," Sarah replied, and Bev cackled.

"If that was not so funny, I would think you were offended, Sarah," Dar retorted. Sarah reddened, pursing her lips and smoothing the lapel of her white linen dress. Dropping her frail hand, she fingered the silver cross on her neck, then held it out, as to view it.

Bev had drifted off from the pack and stood rifling through a drawer of a bureau by the door. Dar watched her grasp something inside. Bev then turned back, looking pleased with herself. She paraded over to greet Dar and Lily. "Well, well, what a little menagerie we have here," she announced, at the same time flashing a greeting to Virginia across the room.

Lily felt tension flood her. All the hope she carried was mangled by Bev's crooked smile and divisive tone. Please don't spoil this beautiful space, she wanted to call out. Lily opened her mouth to speak, but her mother's hand clamped down on her shoulder. "Try," Dar whispered, as Bev faced them full force.

Noting Lily's intense focus upon her, Bev raised her brows and threw her shoulders back to convey forewarning. She gleaned Dar and Lily's attire. Her gaze was efficient and amused. "Aren't you two just so fun? Dar honey, I guess I wasted my phone call."

"Oh, that," Dar said smiling, her free hand pawing at the air between them, shushing all that nonsense. She set her eyes on Bev's hand, clutching whatever she had taken from the drawer.

"This belonged to my father," Bev said. Within her palm was a small carved horse. "'Cuz it meant so much to me, he wanted me to have this. I remembered on the way here where I had put it three years ago. He knew how much I loved my ponies."

Virginia, hearing, tapped her foot hard on the pine floor. Bev shot a glance her way. Virginia's eyes were narrow, her mouth firm.

"All our ponies," Sarah muttered, and Virginia nodded.

Sliding the carved horse into the jacket of her sky-blue pants suit, Bev pressed Lily's right hand between both of hers. Lily froze, as Bev's translucent blue eyes settled into hers. Bev stilled, letting her eyes be revered. Dar stood over and behind Lily, looking through that shiny cerulean glaze to where Bev's saccharine and contempt played. Dar held back her own scorn, a smirk pushed back down. Never was there a gaze as that, those radical globes of blown glass lying to deeper troubles. Bev then smiled to Lily like they were best friends. Dar patted Lily on the back, breaking what Bev pretended was her spell.

"It is so good to see you, Lily...whether it be too much of you or not," she said, looking down at Lily's scant shorts. "I am sure your father would have disapproved, but we girls can get by with things when the house is empty." Throughout, Bev's expression remained innocent.

Lily felt hot over her condescending slight. Greeting Bev with grace, as she had promised her mother, was out of the question now. And the way Bev let the hard candy in her mouth clatter against her teeth added to what was already unnerving.

"Let's keep my divorce out of things this trip," Dar said. "Lily and I are fine," she added. Dar could have kicked herself for this defensive remark. Bev was already working to get under her skin. She could not let that happen. In that moment, Lily's voice came alive.

"My father bought these shorts for me at a mall in Atlanta," she said and hooked her thumbs under the front waistband. A big positive kiss of a smile was planted on her face.

Bev shrugged. "Yes. Let's move on. We're here to have fun. I suppose you are loaded to the hilt on those fantasy novels for the holidays. Hope you saved room for clothes. Remember, we dress for dinner."

"My suit of armor," said Lily.

"Enough," Dar announced.

Lily met her mother's gaze and slumped to express she was exhausted already. The little quiver in her stomach said coping would not be easy. Bev appeared unencumbered with a notion that this was a bad start. In fact, her confidence seemed to expunge any suggestion that she was not already on the top. Bev brushed her hands together. "Well, let's get this show going."

Dar turned back to the melee of greeting which had fallen to small talk. Even reserved Sarah seemed lithe and happy, talking to Mickey. "Hey there, all," Dar said, sashaying forward.

Lily looked to where her granny, Virginia, stood nonplussed to the activity by the door. She would let all greet, then make her way over. The lady of the house. Right now, she had the presence of having been here for days, fiddling with a pot of flowers on the mantle with her back to the world. Virginia was burrowing in. She looked sharp in her bright green dress, her fingers precise, pushing the flowers to where they looked best. Daylight was always best for her, Lily knew. Dusk on would test her. Bev, by then in her cups, would take combative to a higher level. Sarah would have moved up and down the scale of intensity, gloom, and drama ten times. Leaving her sweet granny, treading water for bed and holding on for dear life to her highball.

Last year, by the end of the second night, a contentious evening by all standards, the sisters had dug their trenches. They had become combative, thrilled in self-illusion, or in the case of Virginia, had put out her flag of surrender. All were pushing down the drinks hard. "Granny's a moth hitting the porchlight," Lily had mused aloud to Dar. Virginia was clinging to the table's edge, unable to sit and afraid to stand. Mickey had passed out at the table. Bev was pacing around like she had cold-cocked everyone there with her smart talk. "And the good shall fade at the feet of the wicked," Dar, also inebriated, retorted, and having gotten a kick out the religious tonality of her statement, and that a true God had nothing to do with this place, laughed aloud.

Lily began to see the future, drinks flying about the sisters like swallows, and prayed she could rescue her mother when the time came. Virginia turned and saw Lily. She raised her hand awkwardly but with a broad smile, nonetheless. Lily waved and moved to greet her.

Just then, Bev's shrill voice filled the room. "Just like people, Mickey, an old house knows when it's on its last legs." Lily felt her neck turn hot and looked at her granny.

Virginia's face was rigid and hurt. "God dammit," she muttered.

"A big yawn to that," Lily called out over her shoulder toward Bev. She had forgotten how this grand room took a tiny voice and threw it out for all to judge. Yet, hearing Bev's loud cluck in response, she smiled.

Virginia spread her arms wide to Lily who wriggled over, hugged her just so, then pulled away. Lily wished she could overcome her inability to fall into those heartfelt wings. She loved Granny with all her heart, would protect her in battle, but could not overcome an unfortunate crossing in their lives. The incident had occurred when she was young and had punched a hole in Lily's psyche. She had, for reasons unknown, been unable to fill it back in. The adult world that night was crude and frightening. With maturity, a child's confusion had grown to judgment. Virginia, even as she surely felt Lily's awkwardness, might have grown unaware of the incident. Holding Lily by the shoulders, she said, "We'll all get the kinks out once Bev settles down."

"I suppose you're right, Granny." Lily pecked her on the cheek and sniffed the air. "I smell watermelon." Lily knew her voice shook just so.

Virginia pointed to the table, to a platter under a wire mesh dome. "Sliced up and waiting."

"I am so excited to be here, Granny. Like, sunny-side-up happy." In that moment, Lily was determined to find a method to heal this impasse between them. She left, grabbed a slice of watermelon and a napkin, and shook the dripping piece back at Virginia in thanks. She went and leaned against the bookshelves to take measure of things and eat. Jessie and Marcel came down the stairs, shredded the room with their voices, and raced out.

Lily pushed aside the shudder in her core. She turned her attention to her mother, chatting with Bev with professional courtesy. Sarah slid into the fold, her awkwardness like a short leg, Lily thought. Bev was all smiles and wobbly pirouette, showing off her new outfit. Dar spread her fingers over her mouth. Such skill in expressing awe at the great deal Bev had gotten. "Glamour for peanuts," Bev's bullhorn voice wailed. Sarah, consoled by invisible means, nodded dreamily at something Dar said. Lily squinted, wondering when she had slipped off to imbibe some relief. She had witnessed this transition before. Sarah was water dribbled over a sugar cube already beginning to melt.

Bev looked past Dar, finding Lily. Bev nodded. Lily smiled back. Bev's red lipstick was elongated at the edges of her mouth, which she had once expressed added a certain elegance. Lily mused it was era long gone. Bev's expression warmed, and she winked. An attempt to parlay. Lily couldn't think what she had to offer in trade that would not include her dying on the spot. She grinned as she considered throwing herself on the floor, maybe pretending she had choked on watermelon. She could hold her breath until they thought her dead and then spring up when Bev had hopefully broken down, sobbing into her mother's shoulder. Lily shuddered thinking what that would do to her mother.

Bev's son Mickey had come back in, breathing heavily under another load of bags. Dar sprang to help him. What a teammate, Lily thought, watching her dance around him. Her supple mouth moving, stretched with kind words, chewing her exuberance, like there was more where that came from, false or not, her eyes lit, thrilled to no end in receiving the family.

Bev slid forward with Sarah tagging along. Bev draped a loving arm over Dar's shoulders at the same time telling Mickey to get the gifts off the backseat of her car. Oh God, here come the bribes, Lily thought. The re-gifting queen had a thing for passing along what she did not want. Dar once claimed Bev was a klepto, even stealing from her own family a few times. "Pie plates, Melrose patterns. Like a crow if the thing is shiny."

"You better get in that kitchen and see what else I brought. Peanut butter pie," Virginia announced, looking over at Lily. She then lowered her voice. "Don't wear yourself out in speculation of the future. It's too early," she said from ten steps away. Smiling, Lily headed off to get a slice of pie before Marcel and Jessie.

16

To Each His Own Will

It was late in the afternoon, the unpacking done, and the spread of luncheon meats devoured. The boys were determined to be the first in the river. They attempted to sneak down, only to find Lily, Tish, and Dar waiting on the sprawling lawn, reasoning to be kind and not go without them. Dar counted to ten, and Lily, Tish, Marcel, and Jessie raced over the grass. Lily let everyone win, even taking the hard chiding by the loud boys for being so slow. She could have beaten them wearing chains. Dar went along as lifeguard for all and as moral support for Lily.

Lily tried to join in. At least with Tish. She was a few years older and had physically matured well past most girls her age. Lily thought her a goddess. They had been close in their younger years, but in different schools and things brought about by age, they drifted apart. Holidays and the reunion were where they found each other again. Lily jumped in the river alongside her cousins, only to be noticed, at best, as floating debris by Marcel and Jessie. Each grunted something disapproving, sneering at her thin body. Though it did not feel good, Lily let this slide. Tish mouthed her apologies, eyeing her brothers with disdain.

Sitting on the bank, Dar was proud of Lily's attempt at inclusion and at her patience when that failed. Lily would be hard pressed to break into her male cousins' superfluous world. And understood why she might never choose that as an option. When they scurried out of the water, huddled and shivering in the wrap of their own skinny arms, Dar sighted each with scorn.

"This is a reunion, time to get to know the finer parts of those you rarely see," Dar snapped, glad they had forgotten their towels and happy for the breeze against their wet skin.

Tish dunked under the brown water, rose up, and stepped onto the shore with the care and grace of a swan. She turned back toward Lily, who stood in waist-high water. "Coming?" Lily flashed Tish a look of sisterhood and a thumbs up.

Dar watched as Tish climbed the bank to get her towel. The last year she had taken to flourishing. At seventeen, she had reached five foot eight and might add another inch or so. Yes, it was the equanimity of Tish's spirit that set her as whole in Dar's mind. Her long blond hair, olive skin, and bright hazel eyes buttoned her up. And the fact she seemed always delighted by the smallest things. Right now, she apprised the far side of the river and seemed astounded, the bank and trees there lit up.

Lily was alike in her appraisal. Not because her cousin's body was near perfect, and thus bode well for her own chances. But because she was just so normal and would remain so. Right then, Tish was grinning back at Lily, throwing rays of emphasis on how great it was to see her again. "Aren't you a sight," she said, throwing her hands on her hips. Then squealed to express her excitement for the days ahead. Lily answered with a loud hoot that echoed across the river on the tail of Tish's yelp.

The two converged at the water's edge. Dar watched as they poked at each other, grinning, two dopey girls. They were a handsome pair. Dar was impressed by the ease with which they reunited, having not seen each other in months. Without a word between them they began to move their arms and upper torsos doing "the swim," a dance they had learned when they were little. The flash of the moment used up its time and became awkward. Each positioned themselves, posing in their bikinis for a world that was not watching. They would, Dar mused, own different tactics to the fray here, but on the last day would walk away like electricity returning home through the same wire.

"Here we are, day one," Dar called out, her chirping voice playing over the water.

Just then, Tish yawned and covered her mouth, smiled with those puppy eyes. Lily caught the contagion and followed suit. They both laughed. Marcel and Jessie, forgotten, were on the grass above Dar, still mocking Tish and Lily's dance. Tish rolled her eyes, tucking her hair over her right ear. "Sorry for the losers. I didn't get to choose them."

Hearing that, Marcel and Jessie looked with scorn upon Lily. She was pulling their sister against them. Marcel whistled to Lily to get her attention. He swiped his palms together, intimating the fact that her chest was flat. Jessie followed suit, mocking the crude gesture. They then turned and raced away. Tish whisked up the bank and across the lawn, up the steps, and into the house, following her brothers. There would be a price to pay for them, Dar was sure.

Dar took in Lily. Glistening wet in her blue bikini, she stared down at the water with her arms crossed over her chest. No words necessary. Lily fell back, disappearing beneath the flowing surface. Even as Dar knew the unnatural capacity of Lily's lungs and spirit, Lily remained invisible far too long. Dar rose. A minute later, Lily popped up, her look washed of prior hurt.

Cocktail hour and dinner had seen just one spat, noteworthy only by its silliness and longevity. Bev's red velvet cake was supposed to be center stage, as it was each year this night but remained untouched. The argument was over a conflict five decades before between Bev and Sarah. Virginia had abstained from getting involved, even as she knew the winner of the truth. Something about a man who was not a gentleman and which of them had received his blessing with a certain piece of jewelry and which of them had stolen it from the other. Having had enough, Sarah snapped. "Oh, just forget it. We know the truth."

Bev hissed back, "His lower parts were worthless junk, but you would not have discovered that, Sarah."

"Whoa," Lily said to that confession. Tish giggled. Dar, who all night had been getting up the nerve to declare herself, moaned with disgust. Mickey rushed to hush his mother, waving his arms as if he could erase her words. Bev leaned back and called him a "goose."

Hours later, Virginia pulled herself up two steps to the first landing. They had gotten on well, overall, she thought. The festive nature eventually groomed the vinegary center out of Bev, and thus her early transgressions were forgiven. Everyone was exhausted and retired to their rooms by ten. And then Bev had made sure to make her wicked mark.

Bev had approached Virginia as she switched off the kitchen lights. She congratulated herself on her contribution to dinner, and for the first time noted Sage's alligator brooch pinned to Virginia's dress. "No sense in mixing the Irish and the South," she said. "What a silly piece. Last time you wore that was the night Bobby died. Did it make you fearless, then? Maybe cunning," she added and laughed. "And why tonight?" she added and sneered. Virginia remained silent. "Oh sister, love you, but you were never good at subtlety," Bev said and stumbled away.

"And you sister, have a memory for only what suits you," Virginia said to the closing door. Virginia fingered the jewelry over her heart, thinking of Sage.

Virginia lingered to say goodnight to the house and to recompose herself after that interlude, topping it off with a final bourbon while sitting in her father's favorite chair.

Now, holding tight to the stair rail, Virginia took in the shimmer of her green silk sleeve. The tiny wrinkled hand sticking out could not be hers, she thought. She looked down the front of her dress at a small food stain across one wide, tawny-colored, cushioned button. Sage would have said she was "a point shaped for bed." Virginia recalled where that comment had arisen. The first time sneaking in past curfew. Sage had carried Virginia's shoes up the stairs so her father would not find out. Sage's comment had made them both laugh, waking him anyway.

Dar came up beside Virginia on the landing. Virginia started. Dar had been to the river. "Didn't hear you coming. You are a quiet one," Virginia said. "The river? Imagine just flowing as that...and never knowing a lick of guilt or sadness."

"You've had a blessed life, mother."

With Dar's hand on her waist, leading her up, Virginia took a breath and continued. "My mind's not the same. Couldn't even remember where my cane was tonight, until I realized I don't have one," she added and chuckled.

"Nonsense," Dar said. "It's the booze."

Virginia changed the subject. "This reunion is about the younger ones, really. Lily, Tish, even those brat boys."

"You will survive with those beautiful thoughts, Mother," Dar said. "And you are not old and ailing. Pessimism sounds funny coming from you." Dar leaned into her.

Virginia perked up. Dar's voice reminded her of her own once. Slow in cadence. One did that in thoughtfulness. The smell of grass, fresh air, and mud wafted from Dar's skin. Virginia reached and touched the ends of Dar's damp hair. She sniffed it and smiled.

"Hooper women in their prime," Virginia said with a knowing look. "Long swims in dark ponds...where each wished she were being watched," she said with a cackle. "All else is fairy tale," Virginia added, gripping Dar for stability. "Maybe I'll go skinny dipping one night."

At her bedroom door, Dar kissed her mother's forehead and said goodnight. In her room, unsettled, Dar paced. Soon she would declare herself a lesbian to a household of sneers. Dar leaned and pressed her face into the window screen. The warm metallic air offered no solace. The soothing chime of the river was stolen by the agitating hum of mosquitoes. Dar slapped the screen. She crossed the room and fiddled with a stuck drawer in the mahogany chest. With enough noise to wake the house, she at last wriggled it free, picked up the sundress she would wear the next day and threw it back in. She looked at the door and left. It was time to practice what was hanging on her lips.

Virginia sat before her vanity expelling an exhausted breath. She had changed into her silk nightgown, yet still wore her pearls. She looked back just so and waved a hand over her shoulder. Dar reached over her, took Virginia's hairbrush and, in what felt luxurious for both, combed through her thinning gray hair. A gentle breeze blew through the screen. Fireflies spotted the darkness beyond.

When Virginia spoke, her voice sounded small and far away. "Will we survive intact with the visage of God, and not the devil on our faces when we land at last in our coffins?"

"Goodness, Mother. That is a thought for people who have done something truly horrible. You've done nothing but see yourself get all the way here. Can't we just enjoy this moment?"

Dar suspected Virginia had been reminiscing about her two bad marriages. Drinking always invited that back. Dar was angry that those men could still prey on her. Bobby's death, though imminent by his god-awful behavior and bad health, had hung about Virginia like a harness. The image of Bobby led back her first husband, Dar's father, another reprobate and scoundrel. He liked the sound of his own sorrow more than healing Virginia's when they both took on their ultimate loss. Losing a child is an impossible journey. Losing a brother, hard, but not the same, Dar mused. Her father had left, too weak to be a man.

"Some men are dying more than living," Dar said. "Bobby was a pariah in your marriage. Someone was watching over you when he died. I know that's cruel. But life can take away and give in the same moment. Like erasing words with your right hand and writing better ones with the left." Dar watched Virginia' s reaction, her taut lips saying she did not want to hear his name.

"Just hold on to the beautiful memory of those who mattered," Dar added, and winked. "Give yourself permission to know that finding a moment's pleasure was not adultery but a reckoning to give you what you deserved."

Virginia reached back and patted her daughter's hand, which came to rest on her shoulder. "You're right," Virginia said. "It's just that others won't let things go. And what purpose does it serve for my sisters, mostly Bev, to punish me for not relinquishing everything I have to them?"

Dar looked down at her, tried to catch her eyes in the mirror. "Bev's accountable for every bit of bad in her life. She knows that," Dar said. "People like that, those at war with their failures, need blood from the veins of the good—yours."

Virginia exhaled. "You're right, by God. Let's move on. At least the children will be graced with the fortune of being a Hooper and all that brings them."

Once more, Dar began to brush her mother's hair. She tried to think of something easy to talk about, before moving into her news. "I—"

Virginia's voice cut in. "You know, the real worry of this summer should be on Bev's insistence that this beautiful old home is falling apart. You heard her start today, jabbering on about seeing some rot on a northern eave—Mickey nodding, like some red-eyed prep school snot. By God, I have paid the bills for fifteen years on both places, and Bev thinks things are hers to dispense with. They sold their shares to me and spent what they got down to bone. I have kept them floating all these years. Now, Sarah's on board. You know, more to go around if the houses are sold, and that some of that could well serve a charity or two. Mickey, I think, is champing at the bit, seeing this land as a better alternative to selling whatever he sells. Maybe sees a bunch of well-healed bungalows over the whole swath of green lawn. I will not have it."

"No, we will not," Dar said, feeling despair at the notion. She squeezed her mother's bony shoulders. "This summer house and the tea plantation will stand and thrive—down to the last chortle of our voices," Dar exclaimed.

Straightening in her chair, Virginia looked up. "Will you tuck me in like I used to you?"

"As long as we don't pray before you hear what I have to tell you," Dar said.

In bed, with the white cotton blanket up to her chin, Virginia remained silent. Dar sat on the edge of the bed with her back straight and her hands in her lap. "First, I want to tell you that you have not failed in bringing me up. You have allowed me to see the fullness of this world.

It is big, and so therefore are the possibilities." Dar paused and watched her mother's eyes. Under the covers, Virginia's hands rested on her belly.

"Mother, after much trial and so many errors, I have come to realize something. I have been rescued. One part of my anxiety has found a reason to go away." Virginia's mouth had become flaccid, her gaze up now impatient. "Okay, I have found a partner, a lover, and thus my true self. Her name is Chantelle. Not the best name, but she is a wonderful and quiet person. Though, Lily would not say that. But that's another story." Dar then bit her lip. "Gay, yes, I am a lesbian, in fact attracted to the idea. And to her." Dar was now gasping through her dialogue.

"A quiet person," Virginia said, rolling her smiling eyes. "What does that mean? If you mean unobtrusive like the opposite of so many in this family, then I am on board with this woman with the bad name. Does she have a middle name we could use instead?"

Dar was stunned by her mother's reaction to the news and wondered if it was the liquor. "That is all wonderful, my dear," Virginia added, with drooping eyes. "I look forward to meeting her. You're happy, I am happy. Now, I need to sleep. Out there, lines are being drawn to close down our happy show."

17

Bracing

Swimming to the middle of the river, Dar turned against the current and pulled into the roiling water. She swam until her lungs felt like they would burst. Dar cursed her smoking. Dizzy, she flipped onto her back, spread her arms and let the river take her naked body.

Dar coursed through the long bend. The water slowed, and Dar let her legs fall. Drifting and moving her arms over the silky surface, she breathed in the luscious smell of earth and mineral. She thought of the night before and of combing her mother's hair. It had been a flawless moment, mother and daughter in a vacuum, locked and safe. The grace her mother provided upon hearing her confession was nothing she expected.

Taking in the cerulean sky and filling her lungs, Dar pushed her body down through layers of warm and cold until her feet sank into the muddy bottom. She pushed harder into the muck. She had performed this ritual since youth. The first time, at ten, was frightening. The second, her fear gone, she knew she touched the very essence of creation. Thereafter, in the sanctity of such a void, she felt illuminated. Special. The ultimate definition of isolation, no helping hands here, Dar now thought, the slime gripping her ankles. Just the fine edge between life and the unknown, Dar thought, tightening her lungs to keep on.

Beyond the pressure in her ears, she swore there was a voice. Like Winfield said, "the gentleman." Here she was in a place where she had two simple choices. Naked at the edge of life, it was stay or go, and the first was a temptation she always had. She was not suicidal and was sure that thought would cross the mind of anyone. It was just so peaceful. Dar heard the crackling in her head telling her she was on the brink of the mystery being revealed. Twisting out of the mud, she rose and surfaced, gasping. She was ready. Today or tonight, she would announce her relationship with Chantelle to the family.

Virginia stood on the lawn in the cool shadows of the house. She had watched as Dar disappeared down the grassy bank. On the horizon, a puffy white cloud stalked Dar. Floating on her back, her naked torso shown bright against the brown water. She disappeared around the bend. Virginia was not frightened for her. She had taught Dar this ritual of leaving civilization, of meeting the surreal world of the river bottom, where gripping the outer edge would separate her from the self that keeps us bound up. There she would maintain her courage against of men on earth. Virginia closed her eyes and drew in the mingled odors of sweet grass and metallic river water. She blinked her eyes open as Dar came up and over the bank, her clothes damp from being thrown over her wet body. With a smile on her face, Dar greeted a neighbor's bloodhound that came bounding to her through the shrubs. The dog veered off with its nose to the ground. Dar waved to Virginia who came to meet her.

"The river received and gave," Dar said, smiling and squeezing water from her hair.

"Always there for the bold and honest," Virginia responded.

Lily had yet to go downstairs to begin the first full day of the reunion. She lingered to counter a gut of worry that across the barrier of her door snapping jaws waited. Lily looked for optimism and found it as sunlight filled her room. The night before had, she told herself, ended on a positive note. Feeling upbeat, she sprang up and hurried to the window. Through the limbs of the giant oak outside, the sky was the deepest blue on record, she was sure.

Below, her mother was crossing the light-speckled lawn. She held a small handful of flowers. Her peaceful stroll seemed irrevocable. Another sign. Her mother's hair looked damp. Dar had made her ritual plunge to the river bottom. Lily surmised with that tradition her mother had armed herself and was preparing to make her big announcement.

The prior night, Lily had seen her mother's face, watched her glass-filled hand in constant motion priming the pump to speak, then biting her lip. Lily thought her mother should have sprung it on them then, as all were on "first night behavior." Lily had remained prepped, ready to throw herself over her mother's body and cover her ears to the on-slaught. The first lesbian in the Hooper family tree. Well...that white lies can't cover, anyway.

Below, Virginia stepped into the shadows. Dar passed her, spoke, squeezed her hair, and headed toward the back door. Virginia followed. Excited, Lily raced to get dressed.

Coming into the kitchen, Virginia saw the swinging door opposite swoosh shut. Wet footprints crossed the black-and-white checkered floor. Sarah stood stove side, waiting for water to boil for tea. Bev and Mickey leaned against the counter and looked ready to drop the curtain on fun. "What a glorious day. Everything, just as I had dreamed it would be," Virginia crooned.

Bev and Mickey locked eyes. "Nostalgia is never the truth," Bev said, pointing her chin at Virginia. Mickey shifted and crossed his arms as Bev reached to the counter behind her and picked up a Bloody Mary. Raising the glass, she toasted Virginia. Bev's morning preparation for challenging her. Here we come, Virginia thought.

"Good morning, Virginia," Sarah said tapping the kettle with a spoon. Her look solicited with guilt. Virginia clung to the goodness of the house behind these voices. This nonsense did not matter. River Oaks was here to stay.

"The smell of the house, the yard, the river," Virginia sang, holding an expression of defiant wonder. Sarah turned and parted lips to agree but was silenced by Bev clearing her voice.

Virginia took in Mickey and hoped he would show a little backbone, maybe admit he liked it here. His lumbering presence and sleepy-eyed agreeability to his mother made Virginia sick. Tucking his fat hands into his pockets, Mickey left by the screen door. As it sprang shut, he muttered about getting things out of the car. Virginia smiled, took a biscuit from a bowl on the counter, and left to savor more of the morning outside.

"We'll get to this another day," Bev called out, as Virginia pushed open the screen.

"Or more likely, not at all," Virginia called back.

After a few hardy breaths, Virginia tried to give Bev the benefit of the doubt. She had little to celebrate in her present life. She clung to war stories and to her victories, for the most part involving men way back in the tunnel of the past. Her short-lived marriage had provided her Mickey and not much else, besides aggravation as she liked to say to his face and anyone else that was not tired hearing it. She lived in her routines and woke up with a hangover. Bev maintained her fear of dying and peculiarly called herself the bravest one in that regard. She was superstitious to a fault, and some form of madness skewed her common sense. Virginia tried to push back the sting of their culpability. Since birth, they had all been in this together.

Virginia sighed and told herself that she was strong enough to handle anything surrounded with all the positive beauty. In fact, when the sun's arc reached the massive oak on the river, she would drag out a chair. She knew the exact spot each month of summer where the glow would float and then wither on the water. She would clap her hands when the sun was just a sliver on the horizon. She would finish a fat drink, then go into battle if required.

Three stories above the others, deciding what to wear, Lily thought of her mother's needs. She would want Lily to present well today. Lily reached for a white sundress then cursed the very idea of starting a day in such perky attire. She must consider the hours ahead and what she and her mother had to endure if last night turned false. Lily pulled her nightgown over her head and began to thumb through the arsenal in her still-unpacked suitcase. She picked up a bra and threw it back down. Useless, she thought. The mode today would be to stay loose. Her mother, she prayed, would play a bit on the wild side with her.

Lily giggled, thinking she must nurture the wild child reaching into her. Her clothing must be a little provocative. "Triumph is not always achieved with subtlety," Lily said, practicing what her mother had said last summer when Lily tried on her new skimpy bikini. She chose blue cotton shorts to match the sky. They had a hole in the front showing through to a button of tanned skin on her inner thigh. She then pulled a light-yellow linen shirt over her naked upper torso. The material clung just enough for speculation. She would wear her athletic body with pride. Knock her male cousins' teeth out if they even looked her way.

Opening the door, Lily heard, far below, her mother shriek. A call of godliness, of sweet morning contentedness to the ear of someone, Lily hoped. Another sound made Lily reconsider the prosperity and hope for the morning. A derogatory snipe had flown up the well of stairs. She prayed for her mother, as she had just secured from the river her wares for going forward. Yet, her mother had always been good at the architecture of her dreams, terrible when the sticks started to fall. Lily hurried to get to her.

Dar had come back into the kitchen from changing, praising the day and full of glee. The sisters were arguing. Bev was pushing her angle that the house and the plantation were going to ruins and that the upkeep was eating up Virginia's money. "Thought that might have sunk in after another year of bills on these places," she said, snorting.

That had not set well with Virginia, who had reentered the kitchen from her respite outdoors right before Dar entered. "It's my money, and I will spend it as I please. I also spend it on you. Maybe I shouldn't," Virginia threatened.

As if Dar were not there, Bev made a curious insinuation. "Well, well, who's to say who has the bigger bank. With one big deposit in it." Dar watched Bev's eyes go uneven as she forged on with this destructive bent, even as Sarah was hissing at her to shut up. "What do you suppose Bigbee has in that account?" Bev asked.

To which Virginia snarled, "Your name comes to mind."

Racing down, skipping steps, Lily landed on the pine floor. Hearing the bitter gaggle of voices coming from the kitchen, Lily slowed. She had heard the beautiful sound of her mother singing of the day ahead. Then the antique lungs of Virginia speaking in rancor and Bev's in cocky retaliation. A sharp retort back from Virginia. Dar's voice, just then, ticked in a sharp and precise manner, a recital of new rules.

"We will not have this nonsense this year. I don't even care," Dar said. "Don't want to know. As for Bigbee, I feel awful for whatever mess you got that wonderful woman into. I do know that's probably why she left, and you should be ashamed."

"Yes. She left because she had enough of the same nonsense we are having here," Virginia said, her voice quivering. "And, she had to witness a second death in her time with us," she muttered quietly and looked like she would sink onto the floor in desperation and sadness.

"Let's not let this game carry this reunion. So, stop. Especially you, Bev. I don't see what you are gaining by dangling subjects that no one wants to talk about. That's the weakest stab at power I've ever seen," Dar yelled and wrapped an arm around Virginia.

This, Lily knew, was more than laws being rendered. There followed a silence that was tragic. Like a cat stare down, Lily thought, now nervous for the day ahead.

18

Covert Blooms

The tension lifted, but still Lily was not prepared to move. She could not discern what existed in silence that could have healed such a throw-down. After a bit of loud clattering about the kitchen, maybe a dish breaking in the sink, the conversation grew normal. Lily then heard Mickey's voice and the screen door shut. "Who is gonna have the best football team this year, Alabama or Georgia?" he asked. When no answer came, Lily tiptoed forward. Taking a deep breath, she pushed open the swinging door and entered.

Dar looked over Lily, smiled, and threw a nervous hand over her waist. "You are looking like my wild child there, Lily," Dar whispered. "What about the sundress?"

"Triumph is not always achieved with subtlety," Lily said, sharpening her eyes and trying to look around her. Dar stepped closer, as if to block the entirety of the Hooper stock gathered behind. "Dressing like a once-upon-a-time sorority chick works only in a pack," Lily added, eyeing Dar's outfit. "Fancy tailgate attire at a battle, that's rich." Dar kissed her on the forehead. Lily placed scorn on her features. "Traitor," she said.

Dar turned and vanished out the door. Lily went to the stove and picked at remnant pieces of bacon. Behind her, Sarah raced to make a pitcher of Bloody Mary's while Bev cut celery so hard that Lily thought the knife would break. Virginia was in the pantry. "It's like riding in the car on a hated Sunday drive in here," Lily called out.

Dar came back ten minutes later, an eternity for Lily in that voiceless room. Dar had changed into a petite emerald-green shift. She entered out of breath and painting her nails. Dar shook her fingers to dry them, then ran a hand over her attire for Lily to appraise.

"Right as summer rain," Lily said, and Dar slid in beside her. "We're not done here," Lily whispered to inform her that she wanted to know in private what the hell was going on.

Sarah placed her drink down and took a tray of bacon out of the oven. "Keeping it warm for y'all," she said, then grabbed her drink and backed away.

Dar and Lily each took a piece of bacon, raising their eyes in ecstasy as they ate. Dar began cracking eggs into a grease-filled skillet. A minute later she flipped eggs onto two plates, topping them with another round of bacon. "Quick and as beautiful as the day," she said.

The glamour of bacon and fried eggs died, as from across the room, Bev's voice rang out. The tone was conciliatory, though Dar knew that would not last. "I remember those times here when we were young, down for a solo swim," she began, with her sight on Dar. "Only thing to worry about, if your man of the day, or night, as was always my case, was gonna show," she added with a cackle. Her face then contorted into concern. "Dar, dear, I think it's great that you're free here to not worry about things as that. Nothing wrong with a little hiatus from men....and how, lord, do you piece together so many small jobs and make it work? Must just eat at you, not knowing what's next. At least you and Lily have something small over your heads to keep the bugs away," she added.

The big Bloody Mary had set in, and Bev's eyes were bloated. Dar winked at Lily and whispered they would not be robbed. Mickey went to stand next to Sarah. Virginia was still in the cupboard, rearranging shelves and fuming. Bev looked around the kitchen with disgust. "Where's the right side of things when you need them in this family?" she snipped.

"Do you have a script you follow, same as always? Is it necessary, like cocktails?" Dar asked her. Raising a hand to her cheek, she strummed the skin with her painted nails, in consideration of the three faces lined up across from her. "Y'all look like a bad club there, a sharp peach pit sticking out of a bruising hangover. How do you do it, Bev? Find the energy to assault your bloodline, when that's pretty much it in your cul-de-sac? Your inquiry about my job, Bev, is as shallow as shallow can be. Thanks for your pity party, but Lily and I have a plan."

Dar swung about and looked at Lily. She then touched the tip of her nose, their shared signal for one or the other needing to go to pee.

Lily, though thrilled with her mother's performance, grew anxious over her departure. Bev's mouth stood empty of retaliation, but in her eyes was a fire stoked. This, Lily thought, on such a significant morning; the first whole day was outside screaming GLORIOUS. Lily felt Bev's gaze running all over her, freezing on Lily's tiny, ragged shorts.

Bev looked across at the cupboard and lowered her voice. "Lily, you could wear a trench coat and still be viewed as some kind of teenage femme fatale. Sex is in your eyes." Those words hung over the kitchen alongside Lily's disbelief. Sarah turned away. Mickey might have choked on the apple slice he was eating. His expression pleaded with Lily to know he would never agree to that comment. His mouth moved to stymie his mother, when Lily spoke up.

"I think it might be illegal to make sexual comments to minors, Aunt Bev," Lily said, and shoved a whole piece of bacon in her mouth as Dar came in and read the air.

"I can't even piss without you starting trouble," Dar said to Bev. Taking Lily's arm, she nudged her out the door.

19

Truths that Hurt

Dar and Lily strolled hand in hand down the shore of the wide curving river. "You okay, honey?" Dar asked, feeling the quiet intensity of her daughter. Dar threw off her shift. Underneath, she had on a worn-out cotton tank top with blue bikini bottoms.

"Genes do not always provide on equal terms," Lily said, admiring her figure.

"Yes," Dar said, missing the drive of Lily's comment. "Bev's just an unwashed pickle jar. Nothing left but the sharp residue of vinegar. Yet mother turned out so well."

"No," Lily said and kicked a small stick on the shore out into the water. "The gene thing. That is what Bev—always ogling at my body—might as well say every time she looks at me. And then she says it. You don't want to know what you missed. But I might tell you, if you pony up what I missed in your steaming powwow before I got there," Lily said.

Dar looked at Lily. "I got what you got," she said, though she hated lying. "Sorry for whatever Bev said. The thing in the kitchen is nothing. Just me trying to stomp out things before they start, like I promised in the car." She then remained silent for whatever venting, or quiet, Lily required. Lily's sharp eyes looked inward. Her fingertips curled into her palms.

By God, Dar thought, they had prepared for this week. "We are too good to scrap like dogs," Dar said, looking out over the water.

"I am just glad Granny did not hear what Bev said to me. That would not be fair...IN HER HOUSE, BY GOD."

Dar put her arm around Lily, then let it slide off as she did not respond. "Lily Hooper, your cool back there was admirable."

"We are helpless here, being normal." Her mother lifted her eyes to that truth. Lily leaned to pick up a perfect skipping stone. "Thirty seconds in the door with hope, and now I'm left with worrying what's going to hurt next." Lily released the rock over the water. It bounced once, twice, and sputtered. Lily's green eyes took on fire.

"Go on," Dar said.

"Is there something you know that might take the edge off around here? For me at least. It's like having a hair stuck in my throat." Her mother stared, baffled. Lily continued. "I learned in the kitchen that we might be stuck hanging onto worry with white knuckles. The tip of the iceberg is always sticking up in this family. And what I can't see, Mother, makes me worry."

Lily screwed her eyes into Dar. Her mother's gaze shot around looking confused. Lily was sure that was all an act. "Your eyes get smaller when you lie. And you bite your bottom lip."

"I do not," Dar exclaimed. "Lily, let's be thankful and just worry about what matters. Dinner on the table, gas in the car, schoolwork. Things that move you forward."

Lily eyed her mother. "Schoolwork? That's kind of like third-grade lame, like when you are told to keep your cursive in between the lines—or perish some awful unspoken death. Just like those big whispers and hissing in the kitchen. Keep your secrets between the blue lines but make sure to taunt the fifteen-year-old femme fatale."

Dar slowed touching Lily's arm. "Following all that would take a map," Dar added. "Wait. Femme fatale, where'd you get that? Oh God, that's not what Bev said." Dar clenched.

"Yes, besides the sexual part that might land her in prison," Lily said and turned to Dar. "I see your point on worrying about announcing this lesbian stuff to a cell full of thugs."

Dar crossed and uncrossed her arms. "What the hell are you getting at, Lily?"

Lily smirked and then shook her arms before her. "What is the deal here? Who slept with the Pope? What the heck has turned privileged blue heads into a rat's nest of bad actors?"

"I'm telling you once again, Lily, I know nothing. There's no act there. Now, can I be cleared of all charges?" Dar slowed and looked hard at Lily.

"I'll consider whether to take that as a fair and honest answer," Lily said.

"Lily, honey, a daughter dropping out of high school because she's pregnant, a man falling apart after the war, those things are really bad, because they really smack you in the mouth," Dar added. "There is nothing I have seen here that compares."

Lily sighed. "Are my genes going to make me like them? Make my life shady and tragic?"

"There is some shadiness, I'll grant you that. But I think you're safe, Lily. As for tragic, this family is only that in terms of some's personality." Dar paused and looked out to the water. "There has been heartbreak," Dar said, thinking of her brother, Marshall. She felt Lily's gaze grind into her with that statement. Dar wondered how to ground herself and sum this up. "Lily, Vietnam was tragedy. I remember," Dar said, walking several feet in front of Lily, her arms crossed. "I'm glad you are not a boy." Lily caught up, rounded her, and walking backwards held her arms out pleading. Dar did not look Lily in the eye. She didn't know if she was ready to talk about Marshall. "You know, you were conceived while I was protesting the Vietnam war." Dar tried to sound chipper with this news.

Lily stopped. "With witnesses? In the middle of the street, holding a banner? I hope you put it over you. I hope my father was your co-protester. What the shit?"

"Watch your mouth, Lily. In a VW van. We were empowered."

Lily blushing from this news, contemplated her mother. "Wow, that's got to sink in. Let's move on. So, I keep hearing Bigbee mentioned. She seems to be like a hero or maybe the Hooper house dictator of reason and logic. But no one can be just be that. Heroes get dirt under their nails too. Where is she?"

Dar squinted. "Long gone. I suppose home, to her island off the coast. She was something, all right. She could cover ten miles of this family in a day and still have a breath left."

"And?" Lily asked, prodding her to continue.

Contemplating Lily, Dar continued. "First, since they are center stage, I will tell you what I know about the sisters. Might explain what you think you see. You know, there are a lot of stories dragging them down. Like veterans of many wars. But theirs was a privileged conflict. Dramatic in scale, as you can surmise. The old gals have made a shrine of sorts around their pasts. Some are weirdly proud of the more scandalous parts. People were hurt, and they might tell you in all circumstances their pain was justified." Dar saw Lily's eyes go up, curious to know more. "Maybe Virginia will fill you in on their antics someday. I can just tell you I think lots of money and privilege snared them early on. They have secrets I'm sure, Lily, but none that involve sleeping with even one Pope. Virginia would have told me. Well, I think. They do, after all, have the loyalty of a pack of wolves."

Dar turned to face Lily. "We must bear witness to what unfolds in our families. Even accept what we do not know, though that sounds impossible. You do not want to be thinking ill of them when they are dying. We get some horrible magic in life sometimes—reaching down from above to make you question life's purpose." Dar paused to take Lily's arm. "That hand can be really cruel, Lily. I know."

Lily slowed with the hardness of that last statement. Dar pulled her along and continued. "Lily, I can only speak for myself and your granny. I was really young when I got my first awakening to the hardness weaved into life. My mother had it worse. Downright unfair," Dar said looking at Lily, contemplating going on or maybe not. "This is hard stuff, Lily, things I don't share. I will make you a deal. Well, not really a deal you have a say in. You can never bring this up to your granny. It will always hurt her." Lily nodded, and Dar continued.

"I had a brother once. He died," Dar said, pausing to let Lily take this news in. "Just listen," she added, as Lily opened her mouth. Lily's face was many things at once—a kaleidoscope of dismay, hurt, and fear. Then every inch of her body tensed, and she just stared.

"I'm sorry I never told you. Some things you just want to close away, and you can almost. But then you carry the moment you heard the news, and forever you see that the world is cruel and not lying to you," Dar said, weaving her arm through Lily's.

"He was a beautiful boy. Young. And died, horribly, but dying young is always horrible for those left living. Nothing ethical about God in that deal, if he's what you believe in. You, Lily, were how I managed to escape it. Took me that long. That loss set your granny back and dulled her for things ahead," Dar said. She waited until Lily took that in.

"We were at the plantation. Marshall and I were playing in the yard with a stray kitten. It was a Tuesday. The rest I heard or gathered as time went along. My father, by lunch, had driven off in his truck after another of his speeches to Virginia, stomping about and kicking up dust about how much he hated the place. Virginia was on the porch having tea with a friend and planning a party. Marshall walked away from the yard in search of enlightenment. An hour later and two thousand feet away, he discovered the ruins of the area's first and last sugar mill. He wandered about the old rotten boards; wood desperate to fall. Marshall fell through to twisted metal a story below ground. Ensconced and broken on the ruins, he became part of the town's worst history. The site was bulldozed, and vegetation was left to do the rest."

"I am so sorry," Lily said. "It's not fair," she added, her vision blurry. "I get why you haven't told me."

"Marshall's death was pure devastation for Virginia. My grieving made little sense to me, thinking at first that of course Marshall was just away. For years, I held only dreams and images of my brother, kind of like a row of pictures that never shuffled." Dar said. "Then he was as a closet inside the house of me with the door shut. Until you."

"As I said, my mother was caught in the fires of hell. I still do not know how she survived with her mind intact. A piece of her burned away. She lost forever the part that makes a smile complete. As that indescribable terror raged through her, I shook only inches away from her not understanding or knowing what to do. In time, it was like we were both pulled away from a long drowning, and the hand that pulled us out was invisible. We fused forever. I will forever protect her. There is a spot in her eye that is Marshall. You can see it, if you look closely. I have been wondering lately if his death is what slows her mind at times. And I wonder if there is a bit of peace from that."

Lily skirted in front of Dar and embraced her. For the first time since her father left, she cried. A shiver curled up from her gut to her shoulders. Dar cinched her closer. Lily wiped her eyes and pulled away.

"Bev and Sarah were amazing throughout that period. They moved back to the plantation for six months, did everything, each taking turns as sentry over their sister and over me," Dar said. "Yep, they were wonderful. Are, I still think, beneath their bitterness at being once wealthy and now surviving on the tit of their sister, Virginia."

Dar looked out and watched a kingfisher snap at the water. "Bigbee returned from a trip the day after Marshall's death—yes, she was there then. She walked into the driving black rains of a home in utter dismay and loss. Marshall had by then driven himself into her heart. He just had that way. His big easy smile, his puppy dog manner that never gave any of us peace. Her spirit was crushed, her visual of the wild boy she rocked every night flailed and separated from the old oak rocking chair. All as thick as an everlasting nightmare. With that sweet boy's impression molded into her, Bigbee grew beyond mournful." Dar looked at Lily's ashen face. Lily moved her mouth and waved away with both hands any hope to express her sorrow.

"Bigbee became consumed by guilt. She blamed herself for not being there to keep Marshall from wandering off. Blamed my father, saying he should have been there to raise his son. The fool told her she held no position to speak in his house as such. I was there on the floor in the corner of the kitchen. Any brightness Bigbee might have owned left her face then and there. It was like she saw a ghost in my father's shallow words. Grayness formed, maybe a bit of madness. 'Marshall was my bridge,' she said to him, and later, cradling me and my tears in the yard afterward, she repeated that. She hardly spoke again, unless it was to me, Virginia, or to herself in an undefined plain. Virginia told me Bigbee met the voices of her past in that place. None in her past were there to share her sorrow, Virginia said of those invisible souls."

"I wish I had gotten to meet Bigbee, well, had been old enough to remember her," Lily said, watching as pure sadness took over her mother's form. A shadow seemed to move in and stall, dulling Dar's eyes.

"The months moved on," Dar at last continued. "Emotions moved loud and clumsy within every plantation worker and family member. As I said, the sisters came and went as interns for their ailing sister. Bev and Sarah at their best. A woman knows. Even if she is not the one having lost a child. Even if she is not wholly decent by nature."

"And then there was nothing to be done. The gloom that set over the house made the plantation feel abandoned and ill. A vibrant hall gone silent. Bigbee was as a cauldron in the center, throwing out food and duty, despite—or maybe because of—her misery. I was just a child, but to this day I have never seen such true and silent pain. Bigbee's look expressed that there would never be healing. As Virginia later said, there was only the hard record written in her eyes that in both her worlds, Bigbee had failed. In Marshall's death was a mirror of both losses. If Virginia knows anything about Bigbee's past, she has never divulged it. I do know that Bigbee was glued to your granny until she saw the need to leave."

"What about your father? Did he ever come to terms with Marshall's death?" Lily asked.

"Anger was his deal. And I later learned about his indecency, his vanity, and how poor a family man he was. Boy, Virginia could pick them.

My father one day came to say there was no more time. He burned his and Marshall's baseball gloves, the memories, all with killing tears and anger. Any attempt I made to reach him was slapped down. And in his presence, my mother became that old mill with timid floors. In his gaze was his truth. She had taken their son. He walked away into oblivion, as far as we knew then." Dar shook her head.

"About ten years ago, Virginia spoke of him to me for the first time since he left. She had come across his picture, stuck into an old book. Her words were strange for a man she had once known so well. A man predictable in his dislikes only and in tolerance of his own faults only, she said, shaking the picture and dropping it in the waste bin."

Lily searched over Dar, the sky, the ground, the river for pieces of her mother she had not known were missing. They stood in silence for a few minutes and then turned back. Lily hooked her arm in her mother's. They came back to where they could see over the bank to the backyard. Lily's face fell. Dar saw what caused her consternation.

Bev stood secure in the huge shadow thrown down by the house. Her two arms were gesticulating to Mickey. Virginia was walking away, her strides showing things were not well.

Lily's gaze ran back along the shore from whence they had come.

"A yellow jacket toward an unfinished fire," Dar muttered.

"It must torture her to move so much. Don't you suppose she wants some relief?" Lily asked.

"She wouldn't know where to start. Mad dogs can never atone for who they have bitten. Becomes habitual. Everybody else is wrong. But Lily, remember these people are your family," Dar said, her tone unconvincing and her gaze leery on going forward.

Lily pointed past Dar. Her face was tightened in disgust. A hundred feet down the beautiful curve of river, Marcel and Jessie stood, their pants down about their thighs and their pee shooting into a burrow hole in the bank.

20

Untethered

"A fabulous dinner, Virginia," Bev said. Her voice dripped with cynicism and surprise.

"I reeaally mean it, Virginia," she added, and looked across the table. Not at her sister, but at Dar, who raised a weary eyebrow. "You pulled it off... the menu, the planning. And the cooking...well?" she added, the stab obvious, as Bev had in the last minute pushed Virginia aside to toss in a handful of salt and herbs. "Now it won't be so bland," she had said.

Next to Bev, Sarah continued to scribble on a scrap of paper on the table before her. She might have been oblivious to Bev's cynical intrusion or just cold to it. In reality, Sarah had not even heard.

Lily leaned back, watching Sarah's mechanical strokes of pen to paper. Never an inkling of defense for Virginia. Bev's pithiness rules again. "You're weak candy, Sarah," Lily mused concentrating on sending in thought waves...butterscotch. Sarah stopped writing and looked Lily's way. Whoa, Lily thought, ducking down but keeping a single eye on her. Looking right then left, like someone readying to cross traffic, Sarah hunched back down over her paper.

Sadness fell over Lily, seeing that spindle of a woman. Sarah, for sure, was living under some scar. Lily liked her when she was happy, as she had been when Lily was little, bringing her funny and weird gifts. Once a bleached turtle shell, flipping it over to say it was a great place to hide secrets. Another time a square gold coin she left to Lily's imagination. Pirate loot set into Lily and Sarah had laughed. Virginia had said that Sarah was once a fireball. Now she looked frightened of stepping into any sort of limelight, unless it was for her charities. When Sarah was sober, Lily mused, she could be kind of brainy, but that took time to work itself free from the fog. Sarah was just stuck. As a live fly to flypaper, she needed a little flick to be free.

Just then, Lily felt a nudge on her shoulder. She turned. Her mother was looking past her toward Sarah. "Sarah is a Hallmark card that just needs to be put in the envelope and sent away from Bev," Dar said.

"Wow, this is one clairvoyant night," Lily retorted. Her mother, looking sunburned and worn, for sure tipsy, pushed back her chair, nodded toward the bathroom, and left.

Lily's gaze shifted to her granny. At the head of the table, though Lily knew she had the ability, she did not appear to have the energy to defend herself. She appeared marooned. Her jawbones were clinched, her mouth mollifying something sour, Lily thought. Virginia watched Sarah. Lily imagined what she thought. That Sarah did not have a bird's worth of backbone either. Wherever Sarah left her happiness, Lily suspected her granny knew.

Lily recalled, in the haze of her single-digit years, Sarah waltzing arm-in-arm with Virginia. Sarah had taken a man's name in that dance in Virginia's backyard. Lily remembered giggling until she fell backward onto the grass. The sisters fell into one another, laughing like there was not a time ahead they would not. Now, Sarah's body and mouth moved with Bev's hand shoved up her jellied spine. Sarah had become blind to the beautiful things around her. Why?

A light went on in Lily's mind. She sat up straight in her chair. Perhaps the sisters fell together at the same time and are handling it in different ways. Lily's thoughts were racing to find a point in time when all this began, when Dar came back and leaned over her. Following Lily's gaze to the end of the table, she said, "Their youth was not supposed to die. That's all."

Lily swiveled to face her. "Stop getting in my head," she said and smiled. Her mother's gaze was loopy. Lily knew she was prepping, had gone to the bathroom to practice her speech.

Just then Sarah lifted her eyes. "Bev, dear, which charity did you tell me was run by charlatans?" Bev, talking to Virginia, had not heard a word or chose to ignore her. Sarah's stony voice was almost eerie and reflective of Lily's angst.

Dar's mouth was near Lily's ear. She giggled and then whispered. "In the afterlife, Sarah will be a statue in a park no one will recall. The saying on the bottom will say 'she was a good soul' and pigeons will shit over it." Dar reached for her wine glass.

"Mother, that is scary. And amazing," Lily said, facing her. "And though I am not holding you to know it, the writing on her statue is called an epigraph. Learned that when we had to make small plaster statues of our favorite heroes." Dar was not listening. "My hero was Scarlett O'Hara, because, like Bev, she was so darn smart," Lily added in sarcasm, then leaned into her mother so their shoulders touched. "You can do it, Mother. We can take 'em." Lily locked her eyes into Dar's until Dar smiled and nodded.

Down the way, Bev was grumbling. "Jesus, sister, we might as well have brought Lily's dog with us for what we are getting out of you tonight," Bev said to Sarah. She then cackled in delight with herself. Her voice was loud. "You know, I've—well, Mickey also—been thinking. The plantation needs a real man's hand on it, like our father's. Mickey's maybe. We could pay him to run it like our daddy did. Virginia, you are just not interested enough. And you should not have to be. It is too much, and it has become a jungle." With that, Bev's eyes roamed the big room about her. "Both places have merit," she added, looking at the ceiling. "And great value, if spruced up. If not, in both places, the value is in the land."

Virginia's sharp gaze said she was calculating a response. Mickey pretended to be busy talking with Marcel, though his eye kept wandering to Bev and back. He then took a quick swig of beer, the can popping under his wired grip.

"Daddy, I'm gonna go write some postcards if that's okay," Tish said and then stayed put with a pleading look from her father.

"Oh, pshaw," Virginia blurted at last. "We will not be going there, my dear younger sister. I have everything under control," she added, slurring. "There's no jungle there. You know I've got tenants. They are shaping the place up fine," she added, though she did not know that to be true. Bev opened her mouth to retort. Virginia cut her right hand through the air, silencing her.

"Sarah," Bev called, demanding her support.

Sarah looked up then back down, her lips pursed. "It's just something to consider," she said just above a whisper.

"That is just plain pitiful, Sarah," Virginia called out. "If you're going to back something, make it believable. Where the hell is my old sister?"

"You know," Bev answered.

Sarah began to move her lips without sound. She held her pen like a tool one would stab with and looked like she might be losing control. Her hand snaked over the table toward her tiny black sequined purse. Lily could see the palpitation of her frayed nerves.

"Just a Hallmark card until I know more," Lily demanded, turning to her mother. "What the hell." Dar was fiddling with her fork. Lily whispered. "This is one crazy place. You know, it has dawned on me that these old girls are not really that old."

"Alcohol since their teens drove them here fast. Socializing can wear you out," Dar said, avoiding Lily's insinuating gaze upon her full glass of wine. Dar released her grip from the stem.

"Oh, Dar," Bev bellowed, "Virginia tells me that you and Lily went through that decrepit old town on the way here. Makes you feel lucky where you were born," she added. "I take the bypass around it. Never know what might get hold of you there," Bev added, shaking her head.

"Yes, Bev, we did. Place is not what it used to be," Dar said and made to end the conversation by turning to Lily to speak.

"I won't say what they now call it," Bev said to Sarah. Beside her, Marcel's eyes shot up. "What, what, what do they call it? I think I know." Bev's eyes shot up mischievously, and she crunched down on a sliver of ice. "It's as dark as molasses," Bev hinted.

"It rhymes with...," Marcel began, and Mickey reached behind Jessie and cuffed him on the ear. Beside him, Tish then knuckle-rapped him on the back of the head. "Little racist," she said.

"Mother, please, no," Mickey pleaded.

Dar turned toward Bev. "I will never hear you speak like that again, or I will pull your old yellow feet up to your insides," Dar said. "The rest of the family is better than that. Always one throwback in a crowd," she added and made to stand but paused, reeling in anger,

Lily leaned back, flabbergasted. Bev pointed a crooked and threatening finger at Dar. She stood, huffed to the bar, and poured bourbon halfway up her glass. "That would be a trick, Dar," Bev said with her back turned. "It's just what they call the place. Every town has got to have an appropriate name," she added and snickered.

Dar pushed back against her rage. "Poor Bev," she said, getting up. "I really have to go this time," she said to Lily.

"Catch your breath and charge back in," Lily called to her. She then followed the ruins of the table to Sarah, playing with her purse, opening and snapping the pearl clasp. She rubbed her eyes and when Dar returned, snatched it and shuffled off. Dar and Lily eyed one another.

With a blind hand, Dar stabbed at her wine glass on the table, almost knocking it over. Swallowing, she then sucked in a lungful of air. It tasted of turkey, alcohol, and smoke.

Lily leaned way out with her elbows on the table and met her mother's wistful look. Lily grinned. "I think it's time," she said. Dar looked back. Lily's face was as bright as a noon ocean, prodding her forward. Dar gently took her elbow and led her back down to her chair.

"I'm getting there," Dar hissed, and Lily slumped back.

A moment later, Lily began to wriggle up and down. "Oh, by the by, news alert. My red vireo is back. Same nest as last year, in a notch of that big old oak fifteen feet below my window. I can see the chicks, their sweet mother, Nessie, feeding them fat little worms and everything."

"Wow, that is news," Dar exclaimed. "I'll have a look later."

Sarah had come back. With the help of the chair she sat down, looking pacified. Just like a baby the second its mouth leaves the nipple, Dar thought. This is ridiculous, she thought and placed one hand on either side of her plate.

"I'm ready. It's time." Dar turned her gaze and fixed on Virginia. She cleared her throat, bringing Virginia, Bev, Sarah, Tish, and Mickey to attention. Virginia held firm; a proud sentinel ready to protect her daughter. The male cousins were lost in whatever small board game they had brought to the table.

Dar began. "Since you are all my family, and we are here to support one another, I would like to share a bit of news. It appears that I am not a hundred-carat heterosexual." Dar let that sink it for a few seconds. "Yep, homo, lesbian, gay...maybe bi. Take your choice. Though, I am still one hundred percent me. Isn't that funny how that works? Her name is Chantelle."

The silence was broken with the sound of Virginia's gentle clapping hands. In unison, Bev, Sarah, and Mickey turned slack faced to her. Then back to Dar. Tish and Lily were smiling. Tish's brothers looked back and forth. Two dopes, with their crewcuts, big red ears, and eyes dull as a fish two hours dead, Lily thought. She braced to retaliate upon any judgment from their hanging mouths. They begged their father to tell them what they had missed.

"Dear mother of God," Bev said from near the bar. Her voice was metallic, tragic.

Under the table, Lily took her mother's hand and squeezed. Bolstered, Dar straightened. Her head spun in a glorious fog of wine.

"That was no shot across the bow," Lily said. "That was a direct hit."

Dar ignored Bev, instead watching the distillation of her news upon Mickey and Sarah. She waited for some loud expletive from Mickey, for a mention of God from Sarah who had praying hands on the table and stared at her lap. Dar did not know this would feel so good. Reaching up, she mussed her hair. Lily laughed. Bev moved toward the table. Dar and Lily took in the drama of her loud movements as Bev licked her fingers, stared at Dar, and pinched out the wick of the candle in front of her. All watched the single trail of smoke.

Leaning sideways against Lily's shoulder, Dar smiled and let her eyes roll up Bev's thirty-year-old grasshopper-green dress. Bev brushed a crumb from her breast. Her nose up just so, she shook the multitude of bracelets on her right wrist. Every bit of Bev was showcasing her disgust. Her piquant gaze wandered over Dar.

"A spoiled row in a once productive field of Hoopers," she announced with sorrow.

Dar hooked her elbow into Lily's. "Look how well I have added to the orchard," she said, refusing to let this moment turn to anger.

"Cool as milk," Lily announced, watching her mother's face glow with heat and strength.

Hunching up, Bev said, "You've got to be shitting me. But I suppose we can count our blessings you had Lily before you made this U-turn," she added with venom.

"Gee, thanks Aunt Bev, didn't know you felt that way about me," Lily responded.

Dar took a long drink from Lily's water glass. G-a-y, she spelled in her head, wanted to burn it into the tablecloth with her cigarette. "Gay as a parade," she affirmed aloud. "Love is love, Bev." Dar smiled, letting her mouth go full, knowing how beautiful her smile could be.

Just then, Mickey, nervous, was making the rounds filling up the glasses of those drinking wine. Dar half turned in her chair holding up her glass to take the offer. Mickey paused above Dar. He was about to speak, then looked away. Whatever snide remark was on his mind turned him beet red.

"Yep, Mickey, don't want to be caught with your pants down sounding like a fool," Dar said. Leaving the half full bottle beside Dar, Mickey left. Dar fumbled for her cigarette case and lighter.

Mickey's children were seething, begging to know what they had missed. Tish stood behind, refusing to tell them. Marcel and Jessie looked in unison to Bev. As downy-haired soldiers would look to the front lines, Lily mused, disgusted.

Bev eyed her son and jerked her head. "Tell them, you dumb galoot," she snapped.

Mickey glowered at Bev and plunged a threatening finger toward her. "Don't count on me always supporting you, Mother," he said.

"I don't believe that for a second," Bev retorted and threw her shoulders back.

Lily was impressed. Maybe there was something in big goofy Mickey, some earnest desire to show some backbone. Dar just then reached in front of Lily for the bottle of wine Mickey had abandoned. Smiling, she wriggled the bottle toward him. "This is what we drink, and just about everything else," she called out.

Mickey nodded back. He seemed renewed to have at last had his say with Bev. "I have had enough. Bed for me," Mickey said.

Tish left with a pile of dishes. "Dinner cleanup for me," she said, and let out a hoot.

Dar filled her glass to the brim and watched as Lily leaned and drank off the top. "Lily Hooper," Dar said, with little annoyance.

"It is for your own safety," Lily said.

Stiff in her walk and tipsy, Virginia tottered to where Bev and Sarah, fresh drinks in hand, milled before the bar.

"Bev Hooper," Virginia demanded. "Come on now. I'm a little shocked that such contemporary news would shake up your world. You were contemporary once, if I recall."

Bev half turned and sharpened her gaze. "You mind your business, sister."

"I have always minded my business, and yours also, when you needed tending to," Virginia retorted. "You, dear sister, have lived your life to suit you, and have expected to be surrounded by love and understanding no matter what you got yourself into. Well that has its limits." Bev half turned. Her tongue knotted. Beside her, Sarah's face was ashen, her gauzy eyes reaching for the stars. Virginia looked at Sarah and frowned. "Oh Sarah," she said with pity. "You've gone there again."

"I expect respect in this house," Virginia announced to the room. "Period."

"Granny's house, her rules," Lily called out. Dar placed her hand over Lily's to still her.

Bev glared at Lily and then Virginia. "Well, we will have to see about that," Bev said.

"Give them strength," Dar said, smiling so hard it almost hurt. Lily got up, picked up as much as she could carry and left to help Tish with the dishes.

21

House Birds

"Dar, you started purring for boys on your way out of the womb. And by the time you were twelve you had that look in your eye that embarrasses grown ones," Bev said. It was the morning after Dar's revelation. Virginia stood at the stove stirring Welsh rarebit for later.

"Comfort food is what we need," Virginia announced, her gaze meeting Dar's.

"Kitchens are supposed to bring out the best in all," Dar said. She had slept well and upon waking had hoped for the best. Her staid tone did not convey the rancor in her chest. Outside, rain was coming down in iron sheets. Dar wanted to throw herself into it.

"So now you've gone man-less and have a girl?" Bev continued, ignoring all but her task.

Dar zeroed in on Bev with a hard look, searching for something to say to put her in her place. Should she comment on her nearly bald eyebrows, how she slumped, or how she had failed to cover her hangover with smeared highlights of rouge and powder? Virginia crossed over to put the tomato aspic Bev had made in the refrigerator. "Tomato aspic," Dar slurred. "A dish held firm by being cold and uninteresting," Dar said and smiled. Bev stared back, confused.

"I have a woman, Bev, not a girl, because that would be creepy."

"What is it you see, or don't for that matter?" Bev retorted. "A man has got real picnic equipment. A woman's got...Lord, I can't even think about...well, of anybody, you know what she's got."

Dar pondered Bev's ignorance. "You think that's all it's about? Well, Bev, the mind's an organ too. And there's spirit, decency, and how about just loveliness without the nether parts. Did those things ever mean anything to you?"

Bev shrugged away and began digging into Virginia's cheesy snack with chunks of torn Wonder bread. Virginia shook her head toward her, sighed, and flung the bag of bread to the other side of the counter. Virginia hissed sideways. "Your rudeness is insatiable, Bev. Be careful, sister," Virginia warned her, and Bev sneered.

Behind, Dar was incensed that Bev showed not an ounce of remorse for creating such a scene. "This situation is beyond reproach, but I am prepared to make it worse."

Bev looked back, her gummy jowls moving as she chewed. "Dar, honey, I've...we've been no angels in our time, but I can never conceive what your generation is up to. And forget about me figuring out Lily's. You turn queer as easy as flipping pancakes. Hell, maybe next year your daughter will walk in with a midget." Bev's high-pitched laugh filled the room. She glanced at Virginia to see if she had joined her jocularity.

"Please," Virginia said, rubbing an age spot on the back of her hand. "What is it about you, Bev, that you cannot recall your own liabilities?" Virginia gripped the dripping ladle in Bev's right hand. "Alden Carter mean anything to you?"

Bev let go of the ladle. She carried a look of pure fright. Then dismay and rancor, as Virginia had with certainty broken an old pact.

Dar stared out at the driving rain. "Let's just knock this hornet nest down." Dar sighed, longing to throw herself out into the downpour. "Who is Alden Carter?" she called over her shoulder. "Another casualty in the closet, I suppose. Oh God, what did Bev do to that mystery boy?" Bev remained silent. Dar took a quick look. Stymied, Bev might have been glued down.

Virginia slid over next to Dar, whose hands were now spread on either side of the screen. "One of the best views in the house," Virginia said.

"Need to count potatoes," Sarah muttered, coming in from the living room. Her voice was reticent and tired, potatoes maybe just a whim or a craving.

Dar turned. She wanted to place her hand's on Sarah's shoulders and tell her everything would be all right. Tell her to run from Bev. The lavish God of whom Sarah so often spoke was being stingy in offering up solutions for her, cruel in just handing out what worked a couple of hours at a time. Dar felt bad seeing her fear so evident. "Forget potatoes, let's get some tea," Dar said, and led Sarah to the stove. Virginia remained staring out at the rain.

"Mickey, you are a dear," Bev called out, though he was not present. Her head was in the freezer, her voice quivering. Mickey's task was to keep the ice trays full. Bev came out with a metal tray, pulled up the lever, cracking the ice. "Sweet," she said, avoiding looking about.

Handing Sarah a hot mug of black tea and receiving a slow and thankful nod, Dar went back to Virginia. Placing her arm around Virginia's waist, she had a vision of them being here alone. The house silent, her mother in her favorite chair humming her favorite songs. Lily reading with Bo at her feet and Tish thumbing through magazines. Of herself drinking a gimlet with some secure love beside her. Maybe Sarah on the couch, breaking the quiet with a belly laugh over some fiery memory when plantations were fun.

Virginia took in a lungful of muggy air. It was now just misting, the yellow sun coloring the thinning clouds. "Sweet Jesus, that's why I'm here," Virginia said and pushed open the door.

Mickey, coming in, brushed past Virginia. Soaked, he looked a bit lost and frothy, had a towel over his shoulders. He had been fishing, had drunk too much beer already, and been caught in the storm. He scowled at Dar while drying off. "That daughter of yours is like a rolling ball of barbed wire," Mickey exclaimed.

Dar braced and faced him. "Mickey, we were almost on the same team last night. What's got you so wound up?"

Mickey shoved his hands in his pockets. "Your sweet daughter. She used my ice chest to collect turtles. Left my beers in a fish net in the river. Beer is warm and the cans smell muddy."

Dar laughed. "Ahh, how sweet and considerate of her. Keeping everything cool."

"Mickey, you lazy dolt, you look like you're going to die of skin disorder, all blotchy and red. Why don't you go lie down on the couch in the living room? That should please you," Bev said. She laughed, looking sideways at Dar, her expression oblivious to any prior issues. She looked satisfied and regal. Dar realized that Bev was insane.

Lily entered in a single burst of energy. Mickey started. Every face fell on her. With a gentle, albeit pleading smile from her mother, Lily wondered what had transpired. "What is it with this room? Too small to be jinxed by witches and smells too good for everyone at once to have a mood swing," Lily asked, grinning.

Mickey leaned beside Sarah near the fridge. Dar came over and whispered in Lily's ear. She then took her by the shoulders to face Mickey.

"I am sorry, Mickey, that I used your ice chest. I thought since the beers were just bobbing in dirty water that the river would be okay. I considered putting them in the fridge, but it is full of leftovers." Lily finished her apology with a gentle nod and stoop.

"It is Uncle Mickey, Lily. You are not old enough to just use my first name."

Lily feigned curiosity. "Well then, if we have a calendar around here, could you mark down the day that I can begin calling you Mickey, Uncle Mickey?" Lily asked. Her tone was full of glee, her hands clasped before her as a schoolgirl. From behind, Dar tugged hard on her shirt. Turning, Lily grabbed two slices of bread and left with the intention to read in a chair on the lawn above the river. Dar followed her out.

"Mickey, get yourself together and make some more ice," Bev snapped.

"Yes, Mother," Mickey said with a certain amount of relief.

On the porch, Virginia was savoring the humid air and listening to the pops and cracks of the wet roof and gutters hit by the heat. Dar and Lily came out.

"You know," Virginia said as they came forward, "I was my father's favorite. He loved those two also," she said nodding back toward the house, "but grew tired at times of their swank and antics—at the hurt they threw out into the world he loved. I was no perfect angel, but what I got myself into, he said was tolerable. He used to call me 'sky blue' when those two in there were caught fraternizing with their more depraved sides." Virginia gave an impish smile. "At least, most of the time I was not that wild. Remind me, Lily, to share some stories with you. It's about time, and you are old enough."

"I'm holding you to it," Lily called back, as Dar dragged her away and down the steps.

Sarah came out as Dar and Lily sprinted out over the lawn toward the river. "Let's get our bathing caps and go for a swim, sister," Virginia said. "We can call it our Baptismal and forgive ourselves, if that is allowed." Virginia looped her arm in Sarah's. Sarah smiled.

"Remember, Sarah, we are bound like knotty pine and its hardened sap. Sage said that, if you recall. 'Culpability will never lay in strict closure upon just one of you,'" Virginia quoted. "Those words came as a man had died as a result of Bev's reprisals. Bev cannot leave us alone. Sage supposed, in one way or another, we would always remain involved. Our webs were pretty tangled, sis." Virginia touched Sarah's arm. "Sarah, whatever prospects, whatever future we have left, we must remain dignified over our mistakes. And never divulge it all."

22

Stretching Hope

Lily ran a finger along the inside of the near-empty pot of leftover mashed potatoes. Dar opened a large cardboard box on the kitchen counter. Virginia was in the cupboard searching for her mother's old teacups. The back door opened, and Sarah came in. Dar and Lily stopped what they were doing and turned.

Sarah drifted by; all her features pressed to wax. "Gonna go lie down," she uttered, her lips just surviving those words.

Lily squinted at Dar. "That was odd," she said. "The middle sister is already tanked?"

Dar looked at Lily. "No. She just appears to be moving her way off-shore. It's that time."

Virginia came out of the cupboard with six dainty teacups hung on her fingers, three to a hand. "Two more in the cupboard," Virginia said, nodding down at her full hands.

Taking three cups from Virginia and getting one more from the cupboard, as Sarah would not be joining them, Dar began to imagine the next days. They were at a predictable junction. Her mother was wounded but holding up, and today she looked to throw optimism into the mix. Sarah had drawn down quicker than the prior summer, and Dar was sad about that. Bev, as always, was the nemesis to all. She never faltered, standing like one of those damned statues in a Savannah fountain, a false hero betrayed by lies and yet fostered in history by the same.

Mickey stood behind the family lined in chairs above the riverbank. "That was one hell of a feed bag," he said, rubbing the pouch of his belly.

Bev looked at Lily, who walked up balancing teacups on a tray. "Thank you, Lily, for your help in orchestrating another famous Hooper feast." Her appreciation was genuine. "Where is that sis of mine?" she asked, and Lily shrugged.

Virginia and Dar arrived. Dar, with hot pads, was toting the ten-cup coffee urn Bev and Mickey had brought and left in the box until today. "Tea is ready," Dar announced. Lily helped set up pot and cups on a small Chippendale table. A breeze ruffled the white lace tablecloth.

"Tea?" Mickey blurted, just as Bev exclaimed, "You made tea in our coffeepot?"

"Worked like a charm. It's what we are," Dar said. "Tea people. Remember?"

"And what we shall remain. Tea planters," Virginia added with vigor.

"Are those Sage's cups?" Bev asked. "Virginia, those are too fragile to bring outdoors."

"You say they are too fragile indoors," Virginia said, smiling. She then began to fill the cups and pass out the tea.

"Too hot for tea," Bev said and began to fan herself. "What are y'all thinking?"

"Bev, if you think hard, you'll know why," Virginia said. "It's our father's birthday. We are going to celebrate with Hooper plantation orange peel black tea to honor him. His favorite."

"Oh my, I guess you're right," Bev said, and smiled. "Where is Sarah?"

"She left to go lie down," Dar answered. "Said she was not feeling well."

A minute later, each held a cup. Even Marcel and Jessie, though Tish had to draw a welt on Marcel's neck with her nails to get him to take his. Virginia spoke of Winfield's hard work but in particular how much he loved Sage. She raised her cup, and all toasted him and then Sage. "To what we never achieved in love," she added. "You'd think in light of their fine example that we would have found the same." Her expression flickered to sadness.

"We pretty much all took the lust path." Bev joked, adding, "Good thing sister Sarah's not around to hear that. Though she was a busy little minx back then."

"Hush, Mother," Mickey said.

Virginia, ignoring Bev, looked toward the water. "Our father stood in awe of this river. Sage, too, but more so the sea with her," she said, walking to the edge of the bank. "To the gentleman," she said. Rearing back, she tossed the cup into the river.

"Oh, dear lord, what are you doing?" Bev protested. Virginia eyed her and nodded for Bev to do the same. Bev frowned, struggled to rise, and came beside Virginia. "To Winfield," Bev said and threw her cup. Marcel and Jessie yelped to follow. Mickey told them to stay put.

With a lull in the conversation, Mickey moved to stand behind his two boys who were seated but wriggling their lawn chairs. "Well guys, your mother would have been proud of you today." He looked at Lily and nodded his approval. "You really chipped in. All of you pulled together as one happy tribe in the kitchen and in playing together. That speaks of maturity."

"Yes," Lily said, matching Mickey's hearty smile back. "They made a rich effort, and we had a dandy time." She turned in her chair and looked at Marcel and Jessie. The two were shined up for the midday meal and glowing under their father's pitch. When Mickey looked away, Marcel mouthed Lily's words right back at her. Lily shook her head. Half the day those two had spent throwing rocks at frogs and herons, or sticky missiles of cloves from the ham at her when no one was looking at the dinner table.

"Daddy, Lily's a really good badminton player. She and Tish almost beat us." Jessie said, looking up at the smiling face of his father. Jessie's sunburned face lit up.

"We did beat you, two out of three, remember?" Lily said back. She was proud.

"Just let them think they won, Jessie," Marcel said.

Tish crossed her legs. "Daddy knows the truth," she said, looking up with endearment.

Lily was hit by a sense of jealousy she did not know she owned. A rush of heat ran through her. She would have liked to be in Tish's place, with nothing being wasted in just wishing. Watch her words fall into the soft mitt of her own father's face. A lump filled her throat. Mickey was here in blood and flesh. His sons adored him. And the way Tish looked up to him, her love shining.

Missing her father, Lily curled her toes until they hurt. Hunched over, she looked sideways at her mother and then away. She thought of Dar's responsibility in that failed marriage, making Lily feel worse. Her father might, with his affair, have driven the stake in, but her mother had held it. The fact that Dar refused to see her faults ate at Lily. Dar had become obsessive against her father's cool and casual, something she said drew her to him in the first place. She became the rule maker against his way of taking each hour at a time. She chided him as lazy, even as she said she did not mean that after their arguments faded. Pinching grass blades between her toes, Lily tore them from the earth.

During their separation, he confided in Lily that Dar was frustrated that her life had become mundane. "Everything seems dull once plantation blood gets into you and you are yanked away," he said. The frustration over that beautiful place sitting without a Hooper became harder once Dar lost her job after eight years. Every day, the reality of returning to the coast got further away. "Just like tea bushes, dreams get weeded over with too much time sitting idle," he said. The contradiction of Dar's berating his free spirit was in how much she cherished him. At times, she could not keep her hands off him. Embarrassed in those moments, Lily also bubbled over with joy. But soon her mother fell right back into critiquing him, pushing the oil around like she could change the painting. Candy Stripe volunteering at the hospital and taking flower arranging classes while unemployed did little to quell Dar's frustration. She blamed him, saying they were trapped because of his job and his God damned adherence to the status quo and trying to pretend he was still a child of the sixties.

In the end, Lily had told Dar that maybe his affair was a way of crying out. "Plain and simple," Lily had yelled, "I watched as your love toward my father became uninspired. I'm not saying what he has done is right, but you lost your compass to keep him. And he is a keeper."

Now Lily looked down the shore, a vision of her father standing in his favorite casting spot. Not so far out was the mother lode of sweet fish, he said. That had remained unproven. Lily smiled. She saw him outlined by the light of the river, his laugh echoing over it as he made a joke. Her mother was sprawled out on the grass, slapping her knee in spasms of giggles. In that era when their love seemed inspired, Dar said he was and always would remain THE ONE. Now, the frog in Lily's throat became something sharp. She and her father loved to wish upon a star, fish when the river was perfect, raging, or even boiling hot. Now, he turned and drew up a smile for Lily. Easy as sipping air.

Dar followed Lily's moony gaze. "Nice gathering," she said, hoping to draw Lily out of this queer change of mood. "Maybe we should take our winnings and flee," she added when Lily did not respond.

Lily looked deep into her mother's eyes and tightened her mouth to hold back the things she might say that no longer mattered. Dar touched her nose, asking if Lily had to pee. Lily shook her head, no. Dar looked confused.

"It's four," Lily drawled, gulping, changing the trajectory. "Time to fish."

"Right as sunshine," Tish replied. "Daddy, is that ok?"

Mickey smiling, shrugged. "Whatever makes you happy, sweet pea."

Anticipating his approval, Tish had already started sprinting across the yard toward the house to change out of her dress. Lily stood to check the hooks on the bamboo poles lining the bank. In minutes, Tish returned in tight cutoffs and a T-shirt tied off under her round breasts.

THE STEEP SIDE OF THE MARBLE

She held a big bowl of fruit and spooned a piece of honeydew into her mouth. Lily watched her slow chewing. Soulful, gleeful, like the melon might have been the best on earth. Holding up the empty spoon in mock dismay, Tish grinned. *Yes, I get it. She's the bee's knees,* Lily thought.

Dar leaned over the bank above Lily. "Well, I suppose I must go empty this bladder."

"Sure. Good," Lily said, with her back to her. Dar did not move. Lily felt bad. Her mother did not deserve this. Dar left, and Lily continued to prepare the poles.

Mickey paced along the line of chairs. His empty teacup was still pinched between his thumb and forefinger. He looked edgy. Lonely. Lily wanted to tell him he was doing fine. Then tell the boys how lucky they were to have him. Marcel and Jessie stood up. "Can we be excused?" With a nod from their father, they bolted.

Mickey called out. "Don't gig or stone any more frogs today. Oh God, what about your clothes? Your mother..."

"Be on your mind about snakes and dark men," Bev said, as they hurdled away.

"Oh, God help us," Dar having returned, said to Bev's racist comment. "And things were looking smart around here for a second."

"Bev," Lily said, "I wish more than many things that you would not speak like that. It is difficult to imagine how beautiful you might have once been when you talk like a bigot."

"Amen," Virginia called out.

Lily scanned the broad river looking for circles in the water. Mickey announced he was going to get a beer. Bev's eyes, Lily wanted to think, expressed sorrow, though she was not sure Bev felt things as that.

Tish came toward Lily. "Smells fishy out there," she said. She then leaned to pick up a pole and with great care made her way down the slick bank.

23

Interred for Life

Lily and Tish caught two catfish, cleaned them, and placed them in the freezer. Sneaking one of Mickey's beers, they hid in the cupboard to share it. Before opening it, Lily and Tish took turns rolling the cold can over their burned foreheads, noses, and shoulders. Then, as each downed half the beer, they prophesized, by evidence of all things, that there was a hard path ahead for the remainder of the reunion. They shook hands, agreeing to stand firm together.

Dinner that night was light: ham, canned cranberries, and pie. Throughout, Bev bemoaned that Dar had not purchased the expensive honey baked ham she had requested. Beyond that, most had been congenial. Tish was in another world daydreaming with a playful smile. Her brothers leaned on the table with their bony elbows and argued about who would kill the biggest deer in the fall. They used the words "fool" and "idiot" a lot. Mickey seemed sated and had to keep shaking himself awake. Next to Lily, Dar was in a world of her own, smoking and drinking.

Lily interrupted her mother and told her that everyone looked really bored. Dar laughed, saying, "That's because no one is being defiled in the middle of the table." Lily turned red after imagining such a scene and wondering who the victim would be. "The fact that you say such things and that they seem plausible makes me know I will be in therapy by the time I am eighteen." Lily said, and then Dar mussed up her hair.

"Sorry," Dar said. "By the way, what got into you out there today? You went from fine to bed. Looked like you had seen a ghost and were mad at it."

"Thinking it might have been the hope of things going better than they have," Lily lied.

"I thought all went pretty darn well," Dar said, and tapped her glass for luck. "And besides being bored, you seem no worse for the wear now. Pretty as a peach, too. I like that dress." Dar picked up her glass, slinging it toward her like a device for resuscitation.

Lily concentrated on Virginia, thanking her in silence for her colossal effort by the river. Her granny, even with her nervous hands playing on the table, looked hopeful. She had distanced herself from whatever Bev and Sarah were talking about. Something about sets of silver. Watching Virginia's fidgety hands, Lily had an image of her family as tangled fishing line. Who the hell has the kind of patience to get that nest undone? Granny was trying to do that, every day trying to be the matriarch of this unruly bunch. Her tiny hands working, pinching, pulling to find the path. Lily fishing today had to cut her line and throw away the knot. She gazed around the table wondering which knot in this family would need to be cut out to save the rest. She saw an obvious candidate, another caught up by association, as both their voices escalated in rancor.

Dar looked sideways at Lily. Squinting, she tried to read her thoughts. "Duh," Lily, said, waving a hand toward the others. "Tangled up, lost, crazy from the start."

Amused, Dar nodded. "Nothing to do but hold on for a few more days."

"Watching Granny try so hard is the most painful thing for me," Lily said.

Cigarette dangling from her mouth, Dar took Lily's shoulder and worked the tense muscles there. "Tight," she said and dug in harder. Lily's head lolled back, her mouth falling wide open toward the ceiling in a silent scream. "I am so sorry, honey bunch," Dar said. "Your sunburn. I am such a moron. I'll go get a cold cloth."

Bev and Sarah were huddled, forgiven, and now whispering. *I'll never solve any crimes here*, she thought, feeling time slipping away. She looked over at Tish, who was filing her nails with a look of contentedness. Why can't I be like Tish? She is happy not knowing what she does not know. Lily moaned and lowered her head into her hands.

Just then, Lily heard the squeaky voices of Marcel and Jessie. Their tinny cries of pleasure made Lily feel vulnerable. The boys had been excused from the table and sounded like rats heading up the stairs. Lily squeezed her hands into tight balls.

Dar came back and draped a cold cloth over Lily's neck, but Lily's angst was already on its way up. "Let's bake Marcel and Jessie in a pie with twenty-one blackbirds," Lily hissed. Tish had just come up to Lily's side. "Oh Lily, let's keep things peaceful tonight," Dar said.

"Headed up. The sun has zapped me. Going to write a postcard to a guy friend," Tish said and winked. As Lily locked pinkies with her, Bev leaned hard into the table, knocking the silver off her plate. Palms flat, Bev steadied herself. The room quieted. Bev's glare confirmed she had overheard Lily's comment.

Tish lifted her dress and fled. Lily covered her mouth, saying, "Whoops" through her fingers.

"What the hell has gotten into you? That's a deranged thing to say. If your cousins were here, I would take you by the ear and make you apologize," Bev said.

"If they were here, they would be pinching either Tish or me on the ass," Lily said.

"You insipid child," Bev shouted. "You've got no class whatsoever. You and your mother will be poor white trash all rolled into one soon enough," Bev said, glaring.

Mickey moaned, asking for peace. Virginia tossed down her dessert fork. "Please."

Dar gripped Lily's sunburned arm below the elbow. It was a knee-jerk reaction, her hand in white anger on Bev's throat. "*My* daughter. Not yours," Dar shrieked to Bev. Releasing Lily, she pushed away from the chair. Dar grabbed the damp cloth which had fallen to the table, dunked it in her iced tea and placed it back on Lily's burned neck.

Bev, drunk, pitched just so to the right, then steadied herself. "You two have fallen off the family tree," she said pointing. "Embarrassing white trash," she slurred.

Lily picked up a butter knife. "*My* daughter, not yours," she said, then muttered, "blue-eyed witch." She pushed her chair back and plopped both legs atop the table. Her short dress rose up to just below her buttocks. Dar reached and tugged it down but did not suggest Lily remove her legs. "And to think I once complemented you on how good you look for your age," Lily uttered, adding, "First, your bigotry. Then your queer hating. All that makes beauty just plain ugly. Well, Bev, I'm queer too, and think an all-white society would stink."

"Let's tone it down a bit, sassafras," Dar muttered to Lily out of the side of her mouth. "Drink some water. In fact, a lot."

Bev looked down the table at a spot somewhere between Dar and Lily. Her face shaded almost purple. Her expression said she had registered little of what Lily had gone on about.

"What did you call me? Bitch?" Bev demanded.

Lily opened her mouth to correct her but relented with just an impish smile.

"Slut," Bev yelled, and threw her glass down the table in the direction of Dar and Lily. It landed, shattering the serving platter, the highball, and sending the ham bone onto the floor. Mickey almost fell out of his chair getting away. Sarah buried her head in her hands.

Virginia remained silent, though her small face seemed dangerous. "Bev Hooper, not in my house. Not to my daughter or my granddaughter," she snapped and got up. Standing on the oriental carpet, she spread her arms wide. "Yes, *my* house. Not yours, not Sarah's, not Mickey's."

Bev stood with her mouth crooked and aghast. She ran her hands down the sides of her billowy dress and took a deep breath. "We will see about that." Bev then sharpened her eyes on Mickey. "I can't be expected to carry this alone. You agreed to help."

"Virginia," Mickey sputtered. "We think it takes too much work for you to keep this house afloat. And it is only used maybe a month a year."

"Mickey, you know nothing. You can barely keep a car going," Dar said. "Enough." Mickey turned redder than his UGA game shirt and sat hard into his chair.

During this melee, Lily had risen to stand by her mother. In her hand, her arm cocked, was an empty wine glass, and she readied to hurl it at Bev. Dar grimaced. "Wow, that would not be a good thing, Lily," Dar said, prying the glass from Lily's fingers. They stood in silence as Bev stormed out. Mickey stood, and with striking similarity in his walk, followed his mother. Sarah was still in her trench of denial, drink, and possibly medications. She struggled to rise, frowned at Virginia, and made her way upstairs.

Virginia tottered to her oasis chair by the fireplace and with a loud grunt slumped down into it. Dar and Lily sat back down. No one spoke. Lily grabbed a half glass of deserted wine.

"Go for it," Dar said.

Swiveling sideways, with her elbow on the chair back, Lily watched Virginia and sipped. Distressed by the pain on Virginia's tired face, Lily said quietly, "I will never abandon you." Virginia's eyes twinkled back. Lily lowered her chin onto the back of the chair and waited for her granny to flap her little wings and rebound. The corners of Virginia's mouth lifted. Then she sighed, exhausted.

Lily drank down the wine. She leveled out, and her mood soon turned to sensibility. She loved the sudden quiet. She was able to push aside Bev and Mickey, as, like hornets, they were gone. She imagined the cousins stuck in the honey of their nest getting fat and ugly. Still, the collage of the evening left a pit in her belly. Something at every junction was off-color here.

Just then Dar muttered, "We are the closest we can get to being in-bred and not be." Dar looked over at her mother. They were at least now hunkered down and safe. Still, because of Bev's maniacal behavior, Virginia seemed to drift in sorrow, a bird wrapped in some big fleshy hand sunk down in those cushions. Her eyes were pleading. She looked culpable of things where she should not. "Just a few more days. Guilt and age are God's worst inventions," Dar mumbled, reaching, finding her glass empty. Dar lit a cigarette. Her head went back, her lips pursed below a trail of blue smoke.

Beside her, Lily felt safe, tucked under the wings of her mother, this stormy and powerful creature. She just wished her father was here, but those days were gone. She must support a new lover, she mused, but did not know Chantelle enough to make that promise. Just then, Dar's gaze went from dumbed down to wild, and Lily waited.

Dar was calculating whether victory or catastrophe had set them in this sudden quiet. A little smirk rose in Dar's profile. "Victory. We have gone to war and won," Dar announced, smiling down at the ham bone between their chairs. Reaching, her hand maneuvered around glasses and plates. She pinched and dragged forward a Charleston fashion magazine she had brought down before dinner. She contemplated the cover, touched the cleavage of the beguiling woman there while wriggling her fingers toward a half bottle of wine farther out. Grasping it, she looked down at the ruins of dinner. "Damn, they left this all for us to clean up," she said, filling her glass and swirling it over the deserted table. "Hell, it's worth it for a moment of peace." She lifted the magazine, shaking off a piece of glass.

Her long fingers peeled back the slick cover. She curled back page after page. Thumping one picture after another with moans of delight, she froze, pointing at the photo of a redhead who she resembled. Curious, Lily leaned in and nodded.

"Except I don't own a red dress. All redheads should own a red dress. I am going to get one," Dar said. She ran a gentle hand over Lily's cheek and then lowered her finger into the alluring face of the redhead. "You know, honey, you would not know it by looking back upon this evening, but there is a refined beauty in southern women. Short, tall, heavy, or thin as a firecracker," Dar said. "Dudn't matter," she slurred with a flick of her wrist. "We all got it. Even blue-eyed witches. We can at least find a little pride in that."

Lily spoke and smiled. "Is vanity a quality in all that refinement?"

Dar again tapped the picture of the model. "A strictly southern gene is not so easily understood by outsiders," she confirmed, looking proud. "How it came to be is a secret nobody really knows. Some say it was done by a spell. I think it possibly that and the heat. Yes, despite their present condition, Bev and Sarah were once standouts. Our Virginia, over there, a real zinger." With that, Dar slammed shut the magazine. "Lily, that beauty, as you've seen, comes with trickiness. Men don't know what they'll get when a southern woman asks them to pick a card out of their deck. That trickiness is endearing, mesmerizing to any man. Or to another woman," Dar added and blushed.

Lily remained transfixed. She liked her mother like this, only less drunk. Dar pointed at Lily. "Southern girls, in voice, in confidence, and in poise, well...something is dropped into their little beaks in youth. No...long before that," she added. "When God, crying, was about to shed his last and most generous womanly trait upon the world, he found the South. From there, it's history."

Lily grinned. "That was pure poetry, Mother Dearest," she said, rolling her eyes.

"One cannot move here and own such," Dar continued with a chuckle. Her childish grin went to a drunk's frown. "That southern trance can be dangerous, Lily. There is venom laced in when a woman needs it. But Lily, that venom should be only used to pluck out a bad splinter. And some men, and women for that matter, carry those like quills on a possum."

"Porcupine, Mother," Lily interjected, and Dar nodded and continued.

"Though some do, you can't use venom just for fun. Bev has broken that rule. For fun, I think. Maybe more so insanity, but neither should excuse her. Yep, the South can be as plain frightening as it can be beautiful. Look at how Bev has bruised that bright magnolia over there," Dar said and pointed at Virginia, who was dozing. "That's just wrong. Sisters are meant to be something better."

Lily grinned. "I want what God, crying, gave up," she said.

"That is already baked in," Dar answered, gently pinching Lily on the cheek. Her eyes then narrowed, and Lily could see a white dot of anger building in her big blue eyes.

"Yes, Bev has broken the rules." Dar did not care that her voice carried. She slapped the magazine. "The South and God has left her. She is an angry drifting gypsy thrown out of her camp looking for a new home. A junkyard dog serving nothing but rust and thin hopes. An old southern gal on the skids, that's what she is."

"Wow," Lily responded. "Is this the venom thing you were talking about?" Lily hoped a little humor might bring her mother back.

Ignoring her, Dar's mouth drooped. "The sad thing is that we are part of this by heredity. The entire family displayed in a permanent ink-lined tree. All our years combed like hair to something simple and sparse. Our lives artless. Our beauty common."

"Dear lord, Mother. You went from the South winning the entire country contest to low awful fast. Nothing is that bad. It's only ink, and we can white-out who we don't like on the tree." Behind them, fabric shuffled.

Virginia's arms were up encompassing the whole house. Her gaze settled on Dar. "What if the whole tree is dying?"

"Then we stand apart and maybe flee to start a new one," Dar said and pointed to the rooms above. "But until then, we must show ourselves as stronger, beat back the devil and all that, and put a smile back on that ugly man's face." Virginia, with much effort, lifted her right hand and crossed herself.

"Granny, Mother—we are thriving," Lily announced.

"And sultry until the blood dries," Dar added.

24

It Is Why We Fish

It was the next day, the river muddy and placid under the fat belly of a massive cloud. Dar and Lily strolled down the shore to Lily's favorite spot to fish. There was long pause after Lily asked Dar to describe Chantelle. Long enough for Lily to hook a worm and hum two parts of a nameless song stuck in her head. Her mother, at breakfast, had seemed primed for these questions. Daydreaming, twirling her eggs in circles, she had appeared homesick.

With two fingers rubbing up and down the skin between the cups of her bathing suit top, Dar, with a perplexed expression, contemplated Lily's request to describe her girlfriend.

"Is Chantelle a fork or a dead end?" Lily asked, changing tact, waiting for a response.

"Well, she is neither. It's too early. We're on a straightaway at this stage."

With pole poised and the hooked worm dangling just above the grass, Lily shrugged. "Okay. Her looks first, her personality and state of mind next. And I am curious but do not want to hear much about anything personal, if you know what I mean." Lily reared back and swung the pole out. The worm flew off the hook. "Mother of Jesus," she mumbled.

"You know Chantelle is fresh from a sudden breakup." Dar was sitting on a tuft of grass behind Lily. "And fifty percent of rebounds end in failure. We have joked about those lousy odds together," she added, half-smiling. "That's just how open we are." Dar reached into the leaf-filled teacup, took a worm out, and shook it for Lily to take.

"Two points," Lily stated, turning to take the worm. With the long pole leaning against her shoulder, she threaded the line through her hand and took the hook. "One, Chantelle is a seasoned lesbian. Two, you are not. Thus, she is probably more concerned about your end of the deal. You're from different tribes and all. And you know, Mother, you are a green shoot coming out of your own little torrid breakup," Lily added. Pausing, she put the fresh worm alongside the piece remaining and cast out.

"Not a tribe, Lily," Dar said, wiping her slimy hands on the grass. "That's not proper." Dar paused. "Okay, looks first. Dark hair with a hint of auburn," Dar said pinching and displaying her own hair. "Tall-ish, like me, slightly Romanesque nose, and a mouth, I will tell you, that's right out of a glamour magazine. You know, full, pouty, and the color of a red rose. Skin still smooth, and unlike mine, able to catch a good tan. Talks fast because she thinks fast."

Lily looked back. "Is that an admirable trait or something to concern us?" Dar glared back but did not respond. "Detached ears or aristocratic?" Lily asked watching her red bobber in the pulling water.

Dar squinted her dissatisfaction that Lily was making light of this moment. "She is very smart. A legal assistant, wants to be a lawyer."

"So," Lily said, then jerked the line just so, as the bobber had shimmied. "Darn baby fish, always on the front lines to protect the big cheese." Lifting the pole, she smiled to see the worm still hooked. "So, she has a kissable smacker, and she will one day be handling divorces," Lily said, unable to resist the plug. "Tell me something else, like how this highly unusual spark ignited in you and, besides the gender thing, how it's different than the last round. Am I hearing the sucking sound of a vacuum being filled or the flow of water into an empty pond?"

"My goodness, Lily, I shouldn't have expected this to be simple. You know, where I divulge these hard things and you nod sweetly back. You are acting..."

As Dar searched for the right word, Lily chimed in, "Contentious, or maybe bitchy, and I'm sorry. This is all so new."

Swallowing, Dar continued. "Well, Chantelle described our first meeting the best. Said it felt like a prophecy when our eyes first met. Boy, she hit it."

Lily brought the line back in and watched her mother's dreamy expression. Without being asked, Dar handed her a new worm. "Needs freshening up," she said and Lily, impressed, nodded in agreement. Lily cast back out. Twenty feet out the bobber pulled away in the current. "Nice throw," Dar said. She was bent forward, her arms draped over her knees.

"It is called a cast."

"Right," Dar said. "Lily, Chantelle is, well, just different. Kind of like when you go to the beach and breathe that air for the first time in a long while. And when your feet feel just so alive in the sand and the cool wash of waves over your ankles feels like heaven. And you can just walk and walk because there is no one to tell you to turn around. And you really don't have to, because she and I can talk about anything and forget the world exists."

Lily eyed the river and then her mother. "That was really nice. I kind of get it," she said. Dar's gaze went up to meet Lily's, her hand reaching to brush Lily's leg. Lily reviewed the hard issue at play here. The struggle for her mother to set herself apart from a judgmental world, be proud, and show confidence. She thought of Bev's violent hand the night before. Sarah's dopey world. And Virginia, braced against her own bloodline. With the old gals at their tattered ends, her mother must be wondering what her own future would look like. She did not want to be lonely and cantankerous. Lily looked back. Her mother's goofy, satisfied gaze in finding her heartfelt description of her lover was still present.

Dar shook a finger toward Lily's bobber, which was going down. Lily gave it a tug and frowned as the bobber popped back to the surface. Laying down the pole, Lily went over, got on her knees, and hugged her mother. Pulling back, Lily stared into her smiling eyes. "Now, tell me what you bring to this romance. What does she like about you?" Dar looked perplexed. "I think I know," Lily added, as Dar squinted. Lily squiggled on her knees closer, and with wide eager eyes hinted that Dar knew the answer. "You got bucket loads of it," Lily hinted.

"Hope," Dar answered.

"No, you big bass," Lily retorted, slumping back. "Infectious grace," Lily answered. "Even when sloppy. That is what Chantelle likes...can't resist," Lily added. "My bastard father—remember him—you called him that in front of me, once said you were like custard on a spoon. Irresistible, he said, while pulling one out of the garbage disposal. The second utensil you had sacrificed that week, and he had still not lost sight of that which he described in his heart."

"He said that," Dar drawled sweetly.

Lily rose and pulled in her line. "Let's come back at dusk and try again," she said, pulling up her mother.

"I really have grace?" Dar asked.

"Like a polished stone."

Lunch was a free-for-all. Lily raided the refrigerator, Dar jumped in to challenge her in creating the best sandwich. "Not the biggest, Lily, the best." Ten minutes later, Dar determined Lily to be the winner. "Leftover fried goose liver with cranberry and mayo," Dar exclaimed. "Not for everyone, but creative wins against my meat loaf, butter, and pickles," she said, just as Bev splattered hot gravy for the evening's pork dinner on her apron.

With wide, irate eyes, Bev spewed a litany of charges. "Too many things at once, too many dishes, too many people in the kitchen." And to Sarah, who was fingering a salad to make it presentable before eating it, "Too many damned people on earth." Sarah had just finished her preaching about starving sub-Saharan people.

Dar and Lily stood up against the screen door, grappling with their big sandwiches and chewing. They tried to ignore Bev as she continued to sputter on. They began discussing the cool changes to making their tiny kitchen at home more contemporary. "A shiny and bigger fridge would be a start," Lily said.

Dar sputtered through her lips, "Let's think smaller to begin with."

Virginia came in, greeted all and moved to the center where there was no congestion. Bev eyed her and spoke. "Yes, Lily, listen to your mother. Your lives are suited for smaller things now. We all must come to terms with what is behind us. The truth sometimes is lost in wanting more than we can afford." Bev eyed their sandwiches, smirked, and continued. "This very house should seem too big. Yes, the plantation days, the good days, are behind us."

Lily took the last third of her sandwich and with the help of two fingers pushed the whole thing in her mouth. She smiled, showing her teeth.

"That's disgusting," Bev said, and though Dar agreed she kept quiet.

"You know, Bev, your dreams for the two properties are just different from the person holding the keys, the driver's license, the glove compartment, and title," Dar said.

"Virginia owns the whole damned rusty car," Virginia called out.

"The glove compartment?" Lily whispered sideways to Dar.

Dar nodded, "It was symbolic."

"My dreams are for fairness," Bev snapped. "We should all be able to go forward on equal financial standing. Sage said our strongest trait was our bond in making decisions as one."

"Sage lied to keep you from making them on your own. But you did that anyway," Virginia answered. She then looked to Sarah. "What do you think, third sis?"

"Sarah and I think as one," Bev cut in. "You're the missing party."

Virginia clucked and then laughed, riling Bev up. "The plantation has gone to hell in a hand basket," Bev quipped. "The clock is ticking," she added, applying those words to Virginia by looking at her with pity. "Which one of us will be going first, do you think?"

That sent Dar to a sallow place. Bev did not care about the living. She was attuned to Virginia's inevitable demise. Her only worry was she might beat Virginia to that gate. Dar stomped her foot. "Are we ever going to get this Ferris wheel going? Or are we just gonna stay put in this lightning storm?" She did need or want an answer. Bev's mouth went lax.

Lily pondered Virginia. Her quirky yet succinct statement about owning the whole rusted car made Lily smile. Her white hair, done up that morning, seemed as a blue crown under the fluorescent light. The queen, Lily thought, though she wished she would not slump when Bev attacked. Her entire being was taking up a single square of black linoleum. Pawn like.

"Going be a sweet day out there," Virginia said, stepping off the square and smiling to Lily. "Hot as a field melon. Live for the day, I say."

Dar and Lily took a quarter of a blueberry pie out into the yard. "Today, Bev is in fragile control over her raging bipolarity," Dar said to Lily, as the screen banged shut behind.

Lily plopped the pie on the grass and sat down next to it. "Today? Any day she could ruin a rotten egg. I was still hungry, now I am just mad. Again." Dar, sad, sat cross-legged beside her.

Within a few seconds, Lily regrouped to console her mother. "You know, only halfway in, and we are already beating Bev in this cat-and-mouse stuff." Dar showed no reaction. Lily then remembered the bones she found at the plantation and had brought with her. *It is time*, she thought, *to stir things up*. Maybe in the ensuing spasm Bev and Sarah would have over Lily's charges of slavery, one or the other would become unhinged enough for Lily to pry further. "Who killed the Pope?" Lily muttered. Dar shrugged that she did not know. Lily nodded back toward the house. "We could, though, just about fit our whole house in that dining room. Drop that tiny hovel on the wicked witch. Can't you just see Bev's ugly pink stockings twitching out from under that mess?"

With that, they rolled back on the lawn in tears of laughter until the cousins came to stand over them. Marcel and Jessie shrugged and went on their way. "Let's get Tish, put on our smallest bikinis, and go swimming," Dar said, springing up.

Twenty feet away, Tish, reading in the depths of an iron butterfly chair, said, "I'm hot as Jesus during our pastor's sermons. Let's go."

Midday, Lily walked through the dining room in her wet suit. Sarah and Bev were sipping quinine by the bar, as they claimed it helped with leg cramps in hot weather. As Lily went by and started up the stairs, the two rambled on about not wearing wet clothes in the house. The neighbor's bloodhound, seeking Lily, came through with a stick in his mouth.

"Dear Jesus, is this a barn or what?" Bev yelled. "Get that dog out of my house."

"Come, Singer, come," Lily called. Dropping the stick, the dog bounded toward Lily. Thinking of Bev's statement of ownership, Lily placed a winning-ticket smile on her face. The dog panted beside her. "I believe we have established several times that this is Virginia's humble home." She knew the statement was dangerous. She had no one to defend her if Bev started throwing things. Bev and Sarah stammered.

Bev at last muttered, "Such continual disrespect."

Sarah looked down and touched her pearl cross. "Dammit, to hell, Lily," trickled out of Sarah's small mouth. In that noise was pleading. In her gaze was anguish, but not for what Lily said.

Lily leaned to stroke the drooling bloodhound. "You have nothing to fear from me but my thirst for truth," Lily said to cut off Bev, who seemed to be about to speak again. "And as my dear mother says, we are family. Until the last dog is called in and all lights are out. She said that's from a song." Lily turned, the bloodhound following.

Bev called up after her. "Poor Lily, always on the cusp of having a rear-ender. In those, you know who is always at fault," she stuttered. "You need to pay attention, young gypsy," Bev added to cover that nonsensical insult. Lily had vanished.

"How dare you not watch the road, Lily?" Dar said, standing in the kitchen doorway and glaring at Bev. Dar crossed the room in her dripping bathing suit and went up the stairs. Tish followed with her pink mouth spread in apology. In squeaking flip-flops, she made it across the carpet to the steps in three long strides.

"Sister," Bev said. "This has gotten out of hand. We have our work cut out to get this back on track." Bev and Sarah lost the opportunity to make good on their wishes that particular day. Two hours later, the perfect harmony of dusk, the sweet smell of ham hocks and collards, and slow sputter of roasting pork was shattered by the shrill voice of Tish as she crashed into the crowded kitchen.

25

Fire

"Fire," Tish screamed. The red and liquored faces of Sarah, Bev, and Virginia turned in unison. Mickey, to his credit, recognizing and trusting the panic on his daughter's face, was the first to react. "The shed is on fire!" Tish yelled at him as he passed her.

Dar and Lily dropped their playing cards on the dining room table with the worst visions in tow. Dar was the first to the phone on the small table at the bottom of the stairs. Lily continued straight into the kitchen, out the back door, and into the yard. Not twenty feet from the grand old house, the back wall of the garden shed was engulfed in high orange, blue, and yellow flames. Thick black smoke curled thirty feet into the air, obscuring the window of Lily's room.

Mickey raced by Lily and uncoiled the garden hose from the side of the house, the whole while calling for Marcel and Jessie. They were nowhere to be seen. Virginia was the second one out the door, in her hands a two-quart pot of water, which Dar, racing by, grabbed and went to throw on the fire. Sarah, then Bev, startled and ashen, came out of the kitchen and stood frozen on the back porch. Each held a pot of water. In the distance sirens could be heard.

Fifteen feet out from the side of the burning shed, Mickey, holding his thumb over the end of the hose and shaking it up and down, did all he could to coax the weak stream into the high flames. His face was beet red, his sweat smoking. An eternity and seconds later, the fire department arrived. They had the fire under control in a matter of fifteen minutes.

Out in the yard, the entire family was lined up. Fifty feet behind them, weaved in and out of a hedge of shrubs, ten or so neighbors watched. In the middle of that bunch, Marcel and Jessie stood aghast and began to argue. The bloodhound sat on his haunches in front of all.

It was in that moment, when most of the family turned to register the arguing voices of the male cousins, that Lily walked away and stood below the old twisted oak and its arching limbs. The tree was between the house and the burned-out shed, its trunk and upper limbs blackened, its leaves curled, browned, dead, and some falling. Lily's arms went up as if by pulleys and she began to cry out. "Nessie! The babies!"

Dar came up beside her, turned and wrapped her arms around her daughter. Their wide eyes turned up in unison to see, in the notch of the tree, the burned-out nest. Wound into the reeds and twigs of the blackened nest hung a yellow ribbon. It swam back and forth in a breeze and dripped water, its end melted and smoldering.

Jessie came forward and whimpered, "We didn't mean to." Marcel's voice followed, and although he tried to say it low, all heard his words, "Shut up, Jessie."

An hour later the firemen left, expressing how lucky the family was. "That old house would have gone up in a flash. Heart-of-pine floors inside. That stuff's like gas," one said to Virginia, who stood in the yard, shaken. The captain, having lectured the male cousins with two big hands on their thin shoulders, wandered away last. He looked up at the tree and down at Lily.

"I'm sorry about your birds, but I am sure they got away," he said.

"The babies couldn't fly yet," Lily uttered, unable to lift her face.

The story went that Marcel and Jessie were in the shed. "Looking for things to do," Jessie said.

Marcel, in telling their side, kept to the speech that it was just bad luck. "We were trying to rid the place of varmints," he said, shaking, but so stoic in his attempted man voice that Lily, next to Tish in the circle of adults around the boys, thought she might explode right into him. Feeling that anger, Dar dug her hand into Lily's collarbone.

Marcel then added, "We poured some old motor oil on their nest of old newspaper and twine."

"And lit it," Jessie said, "to smoke 'em out. Didn't know motor oil burned...well, like that."

"What planet are you from?" Dar snapped.

"Lucky I took out the mower gas before it could catch," Marcel bragged, looking around like someone was going to pat him on the back. Moments later, Mickey stood over both his sons in the yard as they did pushups. The sun had just set, the house glowing red. Lily and Tish stood cross-armed in the yard, watching. Dar and the sisters had gone in to rescue dinner, thankful that someone had turned off the oven.

"Ten, eleven, get your skinny knees off the ground, Marcel. Jessie, I believe you are stronger than your brother now. No matter, though, as it will be the belt for y'all upstairs when we are done here. Then we'll see who's stronger."

With that, Tish and Lily turned to each other, smiled and bumped their hips together. Turning, they went inside. "I'm sorry about your birdies, Lily," Tish said, patting her wrist.

Dinner, for the most part, was a humble affair. The mood was gloomy and redolent, the smell of wet, charred wood wafting through the screens. After gulping her dinner down, Lily decided that for tonight, enough was enough. She was tired and emotional over the loss of her birds and the image of just how fragile things could be.

Virginia crossed the room sighing and aiming for seclusion. Lily watched her sit. Her body, as last night, small and fragile. Down, down into the depths of that cushioned chair, her granny appeared to give in to the water folding around her. Or so, Lily pondered with a lump in her throat. Then something told her that there was a far greater force of fear within her granny.

"I just don't know what I would have done if I had lost this house to fire," Virginia trilled, taking in the big room with tiny, sorrowful eyes.

With Virginia's nostalgic plea, never inclusive of any of her sister's having a single stake in the possible loss, Bev picked up her lipstick-covered napkin and tossed it down. Lily looked her way. She just wanted to cuddle up and read.

Dar came back from the kitchen and took in an eyeful of her daughter. Knew the signs when she had enough. She leaned and kissed Lily on the temple. "It's been a hard day, I know, and we did not catch any fish either. That was probably an omen. The fish were hiding with their insight of our upcoming day of tragedy," she added, tapping Lily's shoulder to get her to smile.

Lily did not respond. She watched, as across the table, Mickey looked pensive and unsettled. Could neither sit nor stand. He felt her gaze, flashed a smile, nodded, and took a tiny a sip of his beer. His boys were quarantined in their room with plates of food. In Lily's view, Mickey looked to be exploring the possibilities, maybe wondering how he had handled things. Mickey, Lily mused, was always waiting for the old days to come roaring back. It explained his fidgeting. His boredom and frustration swallowed in beers, pacing, and jittery hand movements. Lily took in his ruddy face, his small eyes swallowed in puffy eyelids. Maybe hoping that someone would come stumbling in from the dark to drink with him. Lily wanted that.

As Dar nudged her, Lily took her eyes off Mickey. Dar, with a load of dishes, headed to the kitchen. Lily followed, grabbing water glasses, relieved that she would soon escape to her room up in the high breezes.

"I'm sorry if you didn't like the flowered shirt that I gave you when I arrived, Lily," Bev called out from the bar. "We can exchange it." Her tone was sincere, and Lily stopped to take her in. She had the sense that even for Bev the day had been hard. Balancing glasses, Lily curtsied, though it felt awkward. Bev secured her feet and ran an ice cube over her forehead before dropping it into a fresh glass. She looked Lily up and down and smiled with a look of pride, then glanced at Tish, who was sitting at the table doodling with a pen on paper, her long shiny blond hair falling over her tan shoulder to her breast. Bev appeared to glow in the view of them both.

Placing the dishes back down, Lily thought of the chocolates Bev had given to her along with the flowered shirt. They were Lily's favored chocolates, dark. That had been thoughtful, even as Lily had in prior admonishment thought her as the original re-gifter. Here, Bev was admiring her as on equal standing with beautiful Tish. Under that focus, Lily folded her hands over her thin waist. She liked the feel of the silk dress. Never her first choice by nature, but pulling it over her body at dusk, Lily had mused to the mirror that she just might be pretty.

"God has certainly blessed us," Bev announced.

"I'm sorry, Aunt Bev. The shirt is really nice, and I meant to wear it today. In fact, I love it," Lily said. She really meant it. "And I am savoring the chocolates." Lily rolled her eyes in delight, almost relishing the flavor on the spot.

"I'm glad you liked them, dearie," Bev retorted, adding, "My mother once told us young gals that we would look good even in burlap sacks. You and Tish have inherited that," she said. She then raised her glass to Lily and Tish who, lifting her head, flashed an embarrassed smile.

Dar listening from the kitchen door, stood silent. Mickey and Sarah were admiring the house and talking of how lucky they were. Dar, beaming, walked up to Lily. She surveyed the faces about, thinking of a room of cats, the sisters licking their coats, digesting dinner and fires. It might have been a painting, Dar thought. The lamps gave off warm, yellow light. The expensive rugs underfoot, rich and spoiled in the glory of something out of Americana. Lily nudged her and eyed the upper stories.

"I will be up shortly," Dar said, as Lily left. Clasping one hand into the other, Dar took in Bev's profile. Wished this lapse into civility would take hold. Bev raised her chin and smiled.

Mickey, Bev, and Sarah seemed a real family in convivial conversation at the bar. With a wave of a freshly lit cigarette, Dar let her head linger in the smoke. A sense of relief filled her. They had made it through another day, an unusual and almost tragic one at that. She took one more drag and squashed out the butt, the last one tonight.

Sarah poured more coffee, usurping Bev's motion for her to join her in one more drink.

"Come on, sis. One more. We almost lost the house today," Bev said.

Sarah chirped back in her small sparrow voice, making a funny gesture with her thin hands. "No, or you will find me on the floor." Bev, smiling, reached and poured bourbon in Sarah's coffee.

Dar turned as Virginia slurred something unintelligible. No others had noted the sound. Virginia seemed to be pushing down on the arms of the chair, her fingers curled and maybe digging. Her gaze was befuddled, almost alarmed. Her mouth funny. Her face was the color of the pearls on her neck. Dar came over and stood before her. Virginia's mouth drooped as she tilted her head sideways. She struggled with up-turned eyes to look upon Dar. In the next moment, Virginia expelled a lungful of air. Color returned to her face and her grasp on the chair arms relaxed. She gazed up at Dar with an impish smile.

"Mother," Dar whispered, "Are you all right?"

"Of course, silly," Virginia answered. "These days, I get real bad indigestion with wine. Would you mind getting me a glass of milk?"

Partly satisfied that her mother was telling the truth, Dar went to get her milk. When she came back in from the kitchen, Virginia had come alive. She had made some comment, which had her sisters giggling like wily foxes. Their words continued in garbled clarity. Sister-speak, Dar thought. Happy squirrels, she imagined, headed for their little hole in a tree. A place where, for a while anyway, their pact of love forgot any bad chirping that had passed before. Dar brought the milk over to Virginia who folded the glass in her two pink hands and smiled. "Thank you, sweetie."

Dar looked around and was convinced that when she left, consoling tones would rule this room. In the exhaustion that comes from hard truth, the sisters seemed in need of one another. The fact that the mood might be temporary did not matter. Despite that, they would have a couple of more drinks, tell each other how lovely they still were, and admit to having loved the same boys. They would not argue. When they headed up to bed, each would announce that they would return in the morning, renewed, and fed by wonderful dreams.

26

Crossed Fingers

Lily began the morning with a feeling that yesterday's near tragic event had set a new tone or maybe at least softened some edges. Perhaps Bev's bad rhetoric and glass-throwing impulse was quelled. Lily crossed her fingers and kissed them.

In the yard below her window, Singer, looking for his new playmates, barked. Lily had the urge to go to the window, but she had been unable to look down to where Nessie and her chicks had lived once upon a time. She let her mind cross back into hopeful visions, thinking a little exercise might put positivity on firm ground.

On the twenty-fifth and final push-up, Lily smiled, thinking of how her mother had opened her heart about Chantelle. Lily flipped over and started sit-ups. When she got to thirty, she heard Singer barking again. As she got to fifty, the barking was Bev, who yelled, "Shut the hell up, you filthy mongrel!" The dog quieted, probably skedaddling back through the shrubs. Lily slapped the floor alongside her body.

"Always look for the good," her father said, and Lily tried for that now. He had advised that right after the divorce, his sad drive-by days, after his fling mate had vanished. He had lost the single greatest story in his life, his family. That was what he said, which almost crumpled Lily right there on the curb. "It is at the height of emotion when one can see the clearest," he said, near tears. "There, people see reason, fault, and good and hope others can see it, too," he said, looking at the house. He was sitting in his car, Lily leaning in the window.

"Look for the good works," Lily said, standing and gulping away the sadness of that afternoon. When she went downstairs, she saw Mickey perched in front of the bookshelves as if waiting for something. Sarah sat with a cup of tea, tapping a pencil on an open newspaper. Bev's voice came from the kitchen, complaining that someone had refrigerated the butter. First Mickey, then Sarah glanced toward the kitchen and frowned. Both looked tired. Lily wanted to tell them that everything needed to be averaged. And that despite the smell of charred wood in the air, things were looking up. It was another spectacular day outside.

Mickey turned and took in Lily. He smiled. Maybe Lily had some reserve to share with him. He shrugged toward the bookshelf. "Nothing here but old romance novels."

"I suppose some good might even be found in those," Lily said, and Mickey looked back confused. "I am near starved, Mickey," Lily chirped, and headed to the kitchen. Mickey smiled and followed.

Sarah looked up at Lily. "That's unlikely dear. Let me tell you about real people who are," she said, but Lily had already entered the kitchen.

Bev stood before the refrigerator. "Who put the damn tomatoes in the icebox? Tomatoes and butter never go there." Outside the kitchen window, Lily saw the black corpse of the shed, Virginia circling it in wonder. After grabbing a cold hard-boiled egg with Durkee sauce on it, Lily went out to greet her.

"An entire era of dreams and hard work almost gone," she said as Lily walked up, shoving the last of egg into her mouth. And then, as if to punctuate her own sentiments, Bev came out onto the deck, leaned, and pushed a finger into a rotten piece of trim. "Just as well you worry, lookie here," she said.

Lily headed to the river. She welcomed moving about unhindered. That image, a walk along the river, and later a perfect lunch of pimento cheese sandwiches with garlic and jalapenos, built up her hopes. The weak could remain weak. She did not have to follow.

At the peak of heat, Lily put on her new white-and-blue polka dot bikini. Crossing the wide green lawn, she felt free and dazzling. Moments later, she was made to feel naked under the glare of Marcel and Jessie as they ceased splashing in the river to watch her come down the bank. Her stomach turned, remembering just how awful they could be.

Setting herself on the riverbank next to Tish, Lily traced the water with a fallen branch from the willow above her. "Tish, do you have to work really hard to be civilized to your brothers? I think there must be an art to that, considering what we know."

Tish looked at Lily with sorrow and remembering, slumped onto her back. Shading her eyes, she answered. "Oh, it's not so bad. I just think of them as little bitty bugs. Pitiful. Squashable. And remember, I have had years and years of practice. My brothers are simpletons who will never close in on anything resembling smart. I choose to pull one leg off at a time, like real slow," she added, and giggled.

Lily laughed. "I think I would do that in a hurry. Maybe all at once."

"Well, I'll give that some thought and get back to you. The sun is making me sleepy," said Tish as she yawned and closed her eyes.

Lily propped herself up on one elbow. Soon, she was able to blank her cousins out. She fell into the view before her: the river, calm at the edge, grave and daring in the center, a net of blue sky over and sunlight scorched into it. All the stuff that made River Oaks nearly perfect. A primordial screech from a pileated woodpecker and its long echo filled her. Tish smiled at the sound and put her thumb up.

Lily blinked as a kingfisher swooped from a tree and snapped at the brown water just behind where the boys had resumed tussling. Her peace was deflated as Marcel pulled down Jessie's bathing suit. Jessie shrieked. Lily looked away. Tish, woken by the sound, rose and charged toward them in the chest-high water. "Have some decency, you little shitheads," she yelled, stopping just feet away. When Lily turned back to watch, Jessie had pulled up his suit and was bragging and puffing up his skinny chest.

"Daddy said, and you heard him, Marcel, that I am the strong one now," Jessie said, then grabbed Marcel by the shoulders, hooked his legs under him, and pushed him down. Struggling, yet managing to hold

Marcel underwater, he counted aloud. At ten, Jessie's face had a wild look, a look interchangeable with Marcel's at his worst. Jessie's gritted scowl had a cloud over it, where rowdiness turned vulgar. The words, "I hate you both," rose from far down in Lily's gut.

Lily then stood up. Tish sensed the same danger. Perplexed, then panicked, Tish threw herself into Jessie, screaming. She pulled up Marcel, who, surfacing, gasped for air. Jessie looked stunned, maybe a little mystified by how far this had gone.

"Boy, are you gonna pay," Marcel snapped, panting. He then pushed up his own chest and began to laugh. An abnormal sound that hacked at the river. The whole scene seemed surreal and then took a stranger turn. Marcel looked at Jessie, and both turned their attention to Tish. Their looks oozed ugliness, and Lily took a step closer. Awful memories came flooding back. The boys went on either side of Tish. Marcel moved his arms to challenge her to wrestle.

"Come on sis, let's see what you got," Marcel said, as Jessie tugged at the back strap of her bathing suit, untied it, and pulled. Tish leapt backward, screeching, and pulling up her fallen top out of the river. Fuming ashore, she plopped beside Lily, who stood with her fingers dug into her thighs.

"On second thought, I do not have any pearls to share with you on tolerating them," Tish said. "I'm sorry that you, out of anyone, had to witness that scene. No more one leg at a time."

Neither Tish nor Lily warned the boys, when ten minutes later, a log slumped down the river toward them. They smiled to each other when they saw a snake coiled and basking in the sun on top. The log and snake bumped right into Jessie's back. Startled, he jumped backward in the water, falling over, his head inches away from the head of the wakened reptile. The snake slid like grease off the log and under the boys. They came out of the water, screaming.

"Like pigs squealing when they smell their own slaughter," Tish shouted. "Remember you're still on parole, arsonists," Lily added. "You can also go back for being perverts."

The boys left. It was just the river, the grasses, the sky, and them. Dar joined and commiserated with them over their account of events. She played diplomat at first, capping that with the caveat that girls must defend themselves by whatever means necessary. She said Marcel and Jessie's genetic makeup had fallen inferior to Tish's. Also, that there was no cure for being a dime a dozen and that snakes can be an asset. Dar then swam out to that grave center of the rolling water. She sank, surfaced in a full minute, smiling. Re-blessed and charged. "God, I love this place," Dar pronounced on shore, letting herself dry in the sun.

It was getting dark when Lily entered the house alone. "I am dog wet, drum tired, and thirsty as a leech," she announced to the empty kitchen. She looked about, at the contrast here to the wonder of the outdoors. The fluorescent glow on the hospital-green walls. The black-and-white linoleum, leafless, unearthly, a glaring tic-tac-toe board, shined from a recent scrubbing. Such a waste, she thought, as in minutes a million feet and a thousand pounds of food would cast that neat track into scuff, tromped greens, and spilled alcohol. She turned, staring back out the screen. The glass aglow in red and shades in purple, she almost reached back for the handle.

27

Second Half

Lily crossed the kitchen. She paused, noting a pot simmering wildly, the frothy overflow of what she thought to be potatoes sputtering and popping into the hot gas flame. A serious dinner was on its own. Shuffling to the stove, Lily turned off the heat under the pot. The aroma of meat and rosemary filled her nostrils.

Lily looked over the huge old stove, six eyes covered with varied pots and all working hard. It was a baffling crisscross of spills, a primitive system of cocked lids and pots half on and off their burners. It might have been professionalism, and for a second Lily tried to calculate the system. And then she was not quite sure which, if any, dishes would survive. Peering into the blackened inside of a pot that might contain collards, she clucked. Flames licked up the pot's sides. The smell of burning bacon and greenery filled her nose. Lily turned off all the eyes.

On the counter was a glass someone had left behind. It was full, the ice melted, the sides beaded with moisture. Lily took the glass and turned it up, swallowing as fast as she could. Except for the dilution from the ice it was pretty much straight bourbon. Belching and setting the glass in the sink, Lily ran a hand over her face and prepared for the crowds beyond. She smiled to this mostly unfamiliar world and its instant effect on her and swayed out.

Entering the great room, her head seemed to float, dragging the string of her legs along. She identified the sensation as euphoric. The room before her was as the kitchen, in disarray and struggling. Drinks had been traveling about, lost and restarted. Glasses were on every surface, leaving wet rings. Every hand was full and moving in tandem with their words. Lily discerned the tangles of disagreement, compliments, or things undetermined on every face. Tish was skirting away, blushing over a comment from Bev. She rolled her eyes to Lily and went up to change. The table places were set and shining and awaiting the charge. Lily's bare feet slapped across the floor. She threw herself in her chair and braced for flight if necessary.

"The potatoes are trying to tell us something. Perhaps that the collards next to them have died," she announced, not looking at anyone, but enjoying the little gasp and the plumbing of two sets of legs scurrying toward the kitchen. "I turned them off," she called over her shoulder.

Dar came downstairs and looked at Lily in mini shorts, a paper-thin white tank top with nothing under, spread-eagle with one bare leg slung over an arm of her chair. Dar rolled her eyes. Lily did not look dinner-proof....well, Bev-proof. "Lily dear, maybe you could put on that bright blue dress I bought for you last week. The belted one with the beautiful Mexican stitching," Dar said. "I'm sure you're just resting before heading up to change." Lily regarded her body once more, nodded, and without a dissenting word, sprang out of her chair. Her head vaporous, she ran across the room, and shot up the steps, managing two at a time. She passed Jessie, reeking of his father's British cologne, chewing, mumbling, his lips and cheeks covered in Cheeto dust. Although very tipsy, Lily felt refined in comparison. She returned within minutes wearing the blue dress and holding a small pearl snap purse Virginia had bequest to her from a box of such things she would disperse over the course of the reunion. In the purse, Lily had placed the bones from the plantation. She smiled and strode forward.

Dar looked on with wonder, thinking her daughter beautiful. A question mark grew on her face when she saw the purse, just not a Lily thing. She smirked at Lily's tangled hair. "Well, I guess I like it when your hair is a little wild," Dar said interrupting her conversation with Sarah.

The two male cousins were looking respectable in a corner playing checkers. Lily could hear bickering in the kitchen; Virginia and Bev were wrangling back and forth. She wondered, if it took so little booze, how everyone else was still standing. Lily shook her head, as if doing so would shift things into better focus. She hurried back to her chair, threw the purse on the table, slumped, but then sat up straight against the ladder-back. She was not sure how to act. Her mother five feet away, squinted at her, nodding with half interest to something Sarah said. Dar lowered her eyes to Lily's crossed feet beneath the table. With one raised brow, she hinted that it was forbidden to bring bare feet to the table. She then heard the harsh tones from the kitchen and shrugged saying it was forgiven.

The words around Lily soon became like drifting clouds, pushed by a strong breeze of the boisterous voices her male cousins. Virginia and Bev came in, both their faces terse, until Bev's grew in complexity and transformed to false joy. "What a glorious day we had."

"You look so nice, Lily," Virginia called across the room. "You should remember that," she added. Whatever had happened in the kitchen, Lily thought, was overtaken by sincerity now.

"Let's patch these up," Bev said to Virginia, shaking the watery ice in her glass.

Lily had the image of two warring sides coming out of their trenches to celebrate some holiday. Together, like twin mice, they ticked across the room, where, with her eyes averted, Lily could hear the silver tongs grabbing ice, and then cubes one at a time clanked into the glass. A second passed in that slow special moment, bourbon then a splash of water added.

"Oh, sweet Jesus," Bev expelled after taking a sip. "That's good."

Just then, Tish came down in a yellow dress, similar in cut and style to Lily's. For a second, they admired each other. From the bar, Bev looked at Tish, as effervescent and proud of her granddaughter as always. "Tish, you could make a blind man see again," she said. Lily had deciphered this as crudely poetic but true.

"Boy, did you brown up this week," Tish said, ignoring Bev and admiring Lily's tan.

Lily perked up in her chair, seeing soulful kinship. She and Tish had a good amount of gal-to-gal today. Lily thought to grab Tish and haul her into the kitchen. Get them both on the same fuzzy path. Tish looked around at each face, waved to her father, Mickey, in a blue shirt, pink tie, and white linen pants, nursing a beer. Looking bored, he tipped the bottle her way. Tish crossed over, straightened his tie and took a sip of his beer. Looking Lily's way, she grinned and took a second and bigger swallow, Mickey guiding it back down.

Dizzy, Lily swiped a hand over her brow. She watched Tish, who, swaying beautifully, made her way in small talk toward the kitchen. Lily thought to follow but felt sluggish. Dar sat down and eyed Lily. She followed Lily's eyes to where Tish stopped to chat up Sarah. Lily was watching Tish with fierce admiration, but her mouth looked downcast.

"Am I seeing a patch of littleness?" Dar asked. "That's not you."

"Still, I'd love to not help having that body," Lily slurred with a peculiar lisp, tasting of alcohol. Lily looked away, as her mother leaned back and frowned.

"You are outstandingly pretty." Dar squinted at Lily. "You are." Lily sucked on her lower lip and did not respond. "Lily, Tish is out of the ordinary, I'll admit. We should be able to accept that. You are svelte...tan and exotic," Dar continued. "Yes, like your father. Good thing you did not get my Georgia red clay looks."

"The emphasis should be on who's going to the ball and who's staying home to scrub the floors," Lily said.

Dar took Lily's hand; it was cold and damp. "I don't want to hear any more of this from you," Dar said. "It sounds ungrateful. You can't catch what you already have. You are stunning, Lily Hooper Smith."

"White lies are for acquaintances you may never see again," Lily said. "Stunning?"

"Okay. You're catching up. Adolescence is a long runway, honey." Dar sniffed the air between them. "Whew. You really have been drinking."

"That is a surprising statement coming out of any mouth in this room."

"Well, that is true, but I think you may have had enough." Dar stood and straightened her dress. "Wish me luck, I'm headed back in."

From across the room Marcel whooped, and Jessie swept the checker pieces onto the floor. "Sore loser," Marcel quipped. Mickey yelled at the boys. The boys yelled at each other, and Bev pitched a fit, saying that this was her time of peace.

Woozy, Lily reached for Dar's water and drank it. Crisscrossing her wrists on the table, she blustered through her lips. It was loud. Her mother rounded back and touched Lily's shoulder, just so. "Lily?"

"No one can cause a scene in a hurricane," Lily said, looking backward and up. "Why do you say we do this extended family thing?"

"Because we can't get out. If you tried, one day you would not like yourself," Dar said.

Lily looked back. "You pulled that out of your arse." She then leaned over and put her head on the table. Dar rested her hand on Lily's back. Lily wriggled to get her to massage her neck. Instead, Dar reached into her dress pocket, and with predictable, functionary movement, took out a cigarette. Just raising her head, Lily waved her hands in disbelief.

"Rescue me," Lily sputtered, as Dar took out her lighter, flicked it once knowing it would not light on the first try, and sniffed the fumes, listening to Lily moan at that admittedly terrible habit. With two more strikes, she lit up.

Rubbing Lily's neck with one hand, Dar held out her cigarette at arm's length. "They're not very good, anyway," she said. "And as things begin to look up, the cigarettes will be the first to go." Leaning over Lily, she snuffed out her unlit cigarette on her pie plate. "See...easy," she said.

With two hands, Dar continued to rub Lily's shoulders. "Partners?" she asked.

"Yes," Lily mumbled, straightening. With both hands, she played a musical ditty on the table and then clinked her water glass with a finger.

Dar watched her daughter, knowing that her sharp and witty child was also vulnerable. She became so frenetic at times. Like a fuse burning to an end none could see. Under her fingers, Lily purred, powering up her transistors, her queer and formidable brain planning assaults and defenses, or so Dar thought. Dar squeezed, then reached and placed a glass of water before Lily. From the cushion of her arms. Lily howled like a wolf. "Wine. Must have wine."

From three steps away, Mickey had been watching. He came forward and pulled Dar off to the side. Dar followed but shot a warning look at him. "Liking your daughter more and more, but maybe there's something she could take to calm her down," Mickey said.

Dar's chest constricted, but there was the fact that others had suggested similar things. She had been advised by Lily's school principal that maybe Lily should to seek counseling after she botched a frog dissection. Lily had turned the creatures into puppets and stitched their mouths into big smiles. The next week, there was a shoving match with some twelfth-grade football jock claiming that dodgeball was for sissies. Lily had kicked him in the shin so hard that the boy needed stitches. "Standard Lily stuff," the principal said to Dar. The fact was Dar did not want to change a thing about Lily. She raised her brow to challenge Mickey.

"Not that it is hers, or anyone's fault. Just trying to chip in to help," Mickey said.

"Mickey dear, your children at any moment might torch the neighbor's dog," Dar said. "And speaking of that, what about the little history we do know?" Dar nodded toward Lily.

Mickey looked to the floor and frowned. He then gazed at Dar apologetically and pointed at his sons. "You're right. ROTC for them," he said, pointing at his sons.

Marcel and Jessie shook their heads in unison. "What? What?"

"What, what," Dar called back mimicking a crow. Mickey turned on his heel and left. After a moment to calm, Dar assessed Mickey as a good man in a loveless marriage. Dar knew it took a lot for Mickey to act brave. He was a habitual man, playing it safe, and thus he made himself incapable of finding his inner self. Mickey would be fine walking down a flat and straight surface all his life. Dar tried to recall if she had ever seen a good belly laugh from him.

She went back to stand over Lily. "Poor Mickey," Lily muttered, then belched.

Mickey had joined Sarah and Bev by the front door watching the afterglow of dusk. Mickey, two heads taller, spread his arms over the sisters' shoulders. They leaned into him, and all three made a cooing sound at the glory of that view. Marcel and Jessie ran over. "What? What?" they pleaded.

Tish joined in. "Now, that's something," she said, taking Mickey's hand.

Dar took a breath and looked over at Virginia standing under twin-lit wall sconces. She was staring at an oil painting of the marshes near the old tea plantation. The light of the painting was similar to what the others viewed from the front door. Dar felt what her mother was feeling. That old place and its pristine and magical landscape was idle beauty waiting for a jump-start. The old homestead was in dire need of rescue. There were tenants, but they had no love. It had been reported that the barns, the house, and grounds had been taken over by weed and mold. Dar prayed Virginia did not compare herself to such loss. Dar knew inside that Virginia would not allow the place to go, and her mind settled.

Dar lay her cool hand on Lily's neck. Lily's voice called up. "Her brothers might be fucked," Lily moaned, "but Tish and I had a blast today."

"Honey, try not to express yourself with the F word," Dar said. "What did you drink?"

"Bourbon. Some of your wine when you and Mickey were discussing how best to deal with me. Gotta pee. I'm feeling better—in fact, in perfect order. Like radar in a fog," Lily added, slapping a knee. "Sorry for the tramp talk. But I am considering a tattoo on my ass."

"Wow, all that—you're gonna pay tomorrow." Watching Lily merge into a careful stroll, Dar recalled the potions that Virginia, on occasion, had used on her. The old standby for all the Hooper clan when wishing a little peace from a child. The fairy in the medicine cabinet. Paregoric. That drug, opium, mixed with anise and other things, was meant to treat coughing or diarrhea. The Hooper clan, including Dar, had discovered many uses for it. Virginia used it to set her straight, to calm her, and to babysit her when things got going in the adult world and kids were in the way.

All the sisters had kept "that little lady" on hand. Dar remembered drinking the milky substance, never wanting to leave her cozy bed, or the dreams, awake or not, constructed under the dictum of that sweet potion. Addictive, without proper supervision or self-control, one could be led off to be forever lost. That drug was now illegal, and Dar imagined the dire faces of mothers hearing news of that drug's demise. The Hooper girls for sure had hoarded it. Dar glanced over at Sarah, who she was sure was still addicted, buried so far under it and other substances that she could not hear a train coming.

Lily came back. Her face sparkled with the fresh water she had splashed onto it. Lily grabbed the pearl snap purse. Knew it might be time to get the house rocking. She walked the room, keeping to the periphery. She watched her mother's attempt to move into the pack. Trying to stand on ice, her sharp heels digging in. Sauntering up beside Virginia, Lily examined the painting. "Hope we can save it," Lily said.

Virginia winked back, her gaze saying of course. "Lily honey, I have something for you. The damage to the shed by those little fools is nothing. But your birds and the fact you notice and savor such are everything." She reached in the pocket of her powder blue dress and withdrew a folded card. "I made this two nights ago. My fingers and pencil do not play well together any longer. I'm sorry if it's not beautiful and that I could not find any colored ink." With that, Virginia held out the card for Lily to take.

Lily saw her name scrawled on the outside. A swirl was added below, a clip of tea leaves drawn. Lily looked up and smiled. Virginia looked on with her arms crossed below her belly. Two fingers wriggled in anticipation.

Opening the card, Lily took in the drawing; It was a lily, perfect in every way despite that her granny's fingers struggled in getting it right. "I'm not sure you know that," Virginia said, as Lily read the inscription below: "Lily, the flower of resurrection and rebirth."

"You are, you know," Virginia said, adding, "And you will see that soon enough in your life. We will rescue the plantation, and this home will remain intact. Mark my words. I hope you have a slew of children. This family needs a change of thinking. I pray I am here for that," Virginia added.

Lily knew the time was not right to bring out the bones.

28

The Ghost of Them All

The next afternoon, in the empty kitchen, Lily considered the dirty pots she would have to clean if she and Tish were to make dinner. Enough meat and potatoes. Turning on the hot water, she began to consider what pasta sauce to make and wondered where Tish was.

Scrubbing the big pot, Lily mused over her granny Virginia's hopeful words about the plantation and this house the night before. Her drawing of a lily, with the words, "resurrection and rebirth," spoke of transition. Lily felt an obligation to take the torch being handed to her. In that, Lily felt honor, but also sadness, as her granny was getting older. Her words in fact spoke of that, but Lily refused to see that dark line as anything close at hand.

With sudsy fingers, Lily tapped her shirt pocket. She had placed Virginia's card there that morning. "Resurrection for now," Lily said, and smiled. She lifted the clean pot above her head and thumped its side, just as Tish came crashing through the door.

"Sorry I'm late," Tish said. Dancing over, she reached and tapped the pot with nails.

"Let's do this," Lily said. "I have been craving pasta."

"Me too. I'm so hungry I could eat my fingers," Tish said and laughed.

"What would you think if we did Alfredo sauce? There's about six pounds of butter and enough stinky cheese for a quarter of Italy," Lily said.

"We could throw in some vegetables." Tish said, then both looked doubtful.

Two hours later, Lily and Tish sat as co-chefs, side-by-side at the dinner table. They leaned back. Each in unison ran a hand around their taut bellies.

"Oh my God, I think I ate a fat Italian man," Tish said.

"His fatter mother made me eat more," Lily said, wearing the makeshift chef's hat that she and Tish had made from newspaper.

The boys muttered some form of ridicule and then excused themselves to find their lost croquet ball and to finish the game they had started before dinner. "Better to find it in daylight," Mickey warned. "Bet that sucker is probably down river," he added, as they fled the room.

Clearing her throat, Virginia, sprucing up a vase of fresh flowers before the fireplace, began humming. As it grew louder, she turned upon the room, a brave woman knowing she would face doubters. Her voice trickled forward, fighting for volume. She paused and swallowed. Relaxing her jaw muscles into a brave smile, she then began to sing.

Dar had not heard her mother sing solo for years, and the room beyond went silent. Bev, Sarah, and Mickey turned as if seeing an apparition. Bev's mouth was cocked to throw out scorn, but she held it to see where this was going. The song flowing from Virginia's mouth was simple and sweet, her voice fragile and yet, determined. Dar, relieved yet perplexed, took Lily's hand. Virginia closed her eyes and upped the ante of her melody.

She followed the song to its source, hitting a point of spiritual hope and inseparable despair. It was haunting and beautiful. Gospel from the coast of Georgia filled the room. Words and melody sung under the breath and then reaching the same freeing crescendo as some of the kitchen help from the plantation long before. Virginia repeated several lines. Her face hung in the balance of wonder and of all the possible failings and suffering in that song. When Virginia ended, she opened her eyes wide and looked at her sisters. "Bigbee could have sung that better." Virginia said then blinked, waking up to the name she had spoken.

Sarah squared her torso with the mention of Bigbee. Bev pivoted away. Lily sat up. Her eyes danced between the sisters. Virginia's frightened face looked to pull back the name. Sarah shuffled about, unable to decide upon anything. She stopped, placed down her glass and started to mutter. Bev pretended nonchalance, even as her eyes stood rigid on Sarah. Lily prayed for escalation. Sarah looked ready to cave, Lily thought, and imagined her going down on her knees and spilling her guts until sunrise.

"What shall we do?" Sarah blurted out. Bev looked Sarah right in the eye. "I warned you to keep to drinks only," she hissed. "You are sloppy. Watch yourself, dream girl."

Hands out, Lily sputtered, "What the heck. BIGBEE! AGAIN!"

Having gone to Virginia's side, Dar took her hand. It was cold. She looked at Lily and drew a finger over her throat for Lily to back off. Whatever was going on here, Dar knew her job was to bring things to order.

"All this hush-hush for just Tish and me?" Lily asked. "Maybe Mickey, maybe my own mother." She rose. "I have a big ole question. Then some show and tell. Some tell from you. It seems Bigbee was more than the favorite family maid of yesteryear. Did she know more than she should, as most maids do? Do you suppose if history had been in your favor, Bigbee would have been your slave? Rather than the rosy kitchen help you call her."

Skirting the long table, Lily pressed her gaze into one and then another. Prowling to keep the intensity burning, she took off her chef hat, the fun of it gone. She watched her mother, who might have swallowed something too hard to get down. Dar's big dry eyes strained to see what most here could not. "Go, Lily," Tish called, crumpling her hat beside her plate.

"I'm sorry," Virginia whispered and hung her head. "How many years will it take for this bleeding to stop?" she cried out. "It's all my fault."

"You know that's the truth," Bev's cold voice interjected.

Dar's voice struck out. "What the hell's going on?"

"Boy, if y'all don't look like a den of thieves," Lily called out.

Sarah had not flinched throughout Lily's tirade. Her drug purse was on the table. The green circles under her eyes widened. Her shiny dead pupils, her pallor, and big splayed eyelashes made her seem doll-like. She blinked, sighting each, pausing on Dar with fear, mistrust, and hopelessness. Sarah then glared at Bev. Sarah picked up her empty bourbon glass, filled it with red wine and looked like she wanted to cry. Which, she did five seconds later, slumping into her chair without an apparent backbone to hold her up.

Eyeing Bev, Lily picked up her small purse. Opening it, she dumped out the bones over the table. She heard her mother moan. "Lily, please. Enough."

Bev muttered. "Don't even think of it. You've tried that nonsense before."

"Yep, those tinkling old bones again," Lily said. "Like I said before, slave's bones. I got some severed fingers here and part of a skull—a child by the thinness of it. A young girl, I'm supposing. Skull bashed in for misbehaving or to cover the evidence of pregnancy—you know there was no such thing as just a good spanking back then. They went for shredded meat. Only way to keep rebellion down. Boy, slavery was a cruel thing."

Bev growled, "This is disgusting. I will never hear of this again, Lily Smith."

Lily grinned, satisfied of her power over Bev right then. She considered that what she was about to say might be dangerous, as she peered straight into Bev's blue eyes. "What does it feel like to have had slaves killed on the grounds of the plantation?"

"Shush, you stupid child," Bev snapped, then tried to garner composure. Her left hand settled between her breasts, and she sighed, pretending fatigue with the situation. "Lily, you have quite an imagination, I'll give you that. A bit vile, at times. Crushed skulls and fingers? How would you think that to be true? We have gone over this before. I say they belong to raccoons."

Lily took the small handful of bones and dropped them into an empty wine goblet. One digit stuck up like a drink stirrer. Every eye in the room fell on that eerie display.

"History books," Lily answered. "Then logic. You know, the normal way for going about these things. Anthropologist stuff," she added. "I am not pointing fingers—no pun intended—at any of you. Heck, you were not even born when slavery was around. I just think as a family we should own up and make amends. Step one would be to educate ourselves against the stain of bigotry." Lily watched as indignation grew across Bev's face, into fear over every pale inch of Sarah's. "No telling where that will lead. I have always had the sense that you gals have so many funny things to share. God, I wish Bigbee was here. What a fun little reunion that would be."

Lily had not looked at Virginia, but if she had, she would have stopped right there. Virginia was plain ill, knowing Lily's tact was to get to more current issues. This had little to do with slavery.

Bev stomped forward. "You are a snide and arrogant little...well, I think we all know. You are just chasing your own tail, Lily. The only mystery here is how you got so full of yourself. Listen to your mother and grandmother. They know this is nonsense."

"Yes, enough," Sarah added, her voice sounding desperate.

Tish sat slack-jawed at the table, staring at the wine glass of old bones. Wild-eyed, she nodded for Lily to keep going and then spoke herself. "Gosh, Aunt Bev, don't know many plantations as old as ours that did not harbor slaves at some time," she said.

"Not on my watch," Bev called out, her tone seeking help from anywhere.

"Course YOU didn't, silly," Lily said. "It was abolished. But you had servants living on campus, paid so little they could not afford to leave. The difference is just semantics. I'm betting they were not always thrilled to be there."

Bev shook her finger at Lily. "Our help was happy to have a good roof over their heads and three squares a day. I'd like to tan your hide," she added. "Since your mother won't."

"Now, if that does not sound like a slave owner, I don't know what does." Lily said.

"Stop this," Dar called out, and walked forward. Virginia sat in her chair frozen.

"Tramp," Bev released through clinched teeth. Hunched up, she moved forward and stood a foot from Lily. "You are the most disrespectful creature I have ever known."

Dar, sensing danger, hurried her pace.

"Well, maybe then I should introduce you to Marcel and Jessie," Lily said back. "Course, their case is not just disrespect, but more so pure ignorance." Lily saw Bev's raised hand and stepped back as her palm swung by and missed her cheek.

Dar stuck an arm between them. "Whoa, dammit. This has gone too far."

Virginia began to cry. Lily turned to hear her sobs and flashed her anger back at Bev, "You want to whip me, don't you, Bev?" Lily shrieked.

Bev stared back. "What a little demon you've been raising, Dar," she said.

Sarah had risen. She licked her lips between hurried breaths, gripped her dress with tiny curled hands, and prepared to speak. She was perspiring. Her gummy mouth moved. Her eyeliner spread, and a maudlin tear of black ran down her left cheek. Sarah raised what little of her voice she could find, plunging her right index finger into the air before her. Her crazy aim was on Dar.

"God has stood by and watched all of us. And I am sorry for slavery. We, Lily, have done the best we can." Sarah raised her arms in exasperation. "So much work to do just to keep this family from smearing the Hooper name—oh God, I am so tired," she moaned. "We've done nothing wrong but set things straight and stick together...as sisters should." Sarah collapsed into a heap onto the floor. Mickey rushed to pull her up and then helped her to her chair.

"Wow," Tish exclaimed. Lily sat and took Tish's hand under the table.

"I hate this family," Lily said, looking down. She looked at Tish. "How do you keep smiling?"

Tish leaned her head on Lily's shoulder and whispered, "Because I know someday their nonsense won't matter and we'll be sad they are all gone," Tish said. To that, Lily moaned.

Dar moved to where Sarah sat as an abstract mess in her chair. Her mouth was the worst kind of sad, wet and twisted into deformity. "Sarah, nothing has ever been your doing. You are a fine person." Dar turned in a circle and continued. "We must somehow forgive and be done with this night. And the rest we will never know, God willing."

Real tears began falling down Sarah's cheeks. "I am so sorry," she sputtered.

"What's to forgive?" Bev snapped. Her gaze was oblivious to all that had passed, to the injured, or upon anything, except a pearl in her necklace. Which she took in her fingers, blew on, and polished between two folds of fabric in her blouse.

As easy as that, Dar thought watching. Dar took her sentinel position over Lily's chair. With shaking hands, she lit another cigarette and sucked on it until a quarter inch of gray ash hung. They both watched as Sarah, helped by Mickey, stood and shuffled to the bar. She looked upon her own horrified face in the mirror there. Dar had an awful feeling that things would get no better for her. The once spunky, coquettish girl with a plantation peacock on a leash was dead.

Lily, her head now spinning, felt like she was going to vomit and hurried to the bathroom. The urge subsided as she stood staring at the closed door. Then plugging the drain, she let the water run. She had tried tonight to hang tough and still she had no avenue to the truth. She had attained only a sense of sadness and maybe culpability to match the secrets she sought to unveil. Just as Bev intoned, she felt like a brat. No, Lily mused, I am just frustrated by this family. She thought of the hopeful picture Virginia had given her, praying for resurrection, and now knew that concept begged for forgiveness on a grand scale. Still, Lily was lost to the bigger picture of why.

Resurrection would never take to a family so in their cups, so bitter, and so hateful. Lily wondered if it were possible to feel sad when some were gone, as Tish had expressed. She turned off the spigot and dunked her face in the water, wanted to cry, willed it, and cursed whatever in her brain hardly let that happen. Pulling her head up, she let the water run down her clothes. Lily did not hate this family. She loathed how they tried to hide behind their big name. Maybe she hated Bev, Lily thought, and told herself to not feel guilty in that regard. Lily's mind spun, wondering if other families were so deluded and crazy. Her mother had said they all were. No matter where you stand, no matter the family.

Lily leaned and placed her forehead on the mirror. She looked up and said to the green eyes looking back, "Bigbee, who were you? I don't care anymore. You cannot have me. Keep your secret, and then I will not be like them." Then she slid to the floor.

29

Pulling Off the Cloth

Dar leaned over her mother's bed. She had tucked her in, kissed her on the cheek. She apologized for Lily's antagonizing move with the bones and how the evening had ended. Virginia reached and touched Dar's face. "It was a night, wasn't it?"

"What makes Bev so hateful, so contrary? When not being so would give her and those around her peace? Her bigotry, I know, is a culture thing. Selfishness, fear, and ignorance became a clubby, cult thing, I guess. But that's a lousy excuse. Hating gay people, where's that start?"

Virginia drew a slow finger across her covers. "For Bev, with Alden Carter."

"That name from the other day. How does one man change a woman's perspective on such a big subject?" Dar asked.

"Not a man, honey. A woman—well, a teen when it happened," Virginia said. "Bev had an incident. When she was eighteen. No worse for the wear, if we had not stumbled on them, I suppose. Who knows if she was really interested, or if it was just on one of her no-holds-barred exploits? I should stay away from this, Dar."

"Wait, wait, wait," Dar said, her heart racing. "Oh, sweet Jesus, please. What a glorious image I am seeing right now. You cannot wave this morsel under my nose and take it away."

Virginia sighed. "Well, Alden was sixteen years old. Bev was tutoring her in math for the summer. Alden was slow and a bit of a misfit. Even mildly arrested in development, though she was an exotic beauty. Jet-black hair and blue eyes. Tan at birth and a body that made all of us jealous. Bev and she got along well. Bev said Alden and she shared boy secrets." Dar slid to the floor, leaned against the bed, and rolled her hands for Virginia to continue.

"Well, Sarah and I were looking for the barn cat to move him into the tea cutting room, as we had seen mice there. We came up the ladder into the drying loft. Bev was lost to another world when we came upon them. Well, I suppose both were. Alden, was on top, talking sweetly to Bev, telling her to slow down and bide her time. They were both pure naked, kissing like they knew the greatest secret in the world. I can't believe I'm telling my own daughter. But I suppose you need to know, as it might give you some relief. You must never tell Bev that you know. There is enough trouble in this family. Lily, of course, can never know."

Dar lay back on the carpet. She was in ecstasy, yet her mind reeled in abhorrence for all the crap Bev had doled out.

"Bev first, then Alden, saw us standing there. Afterward, as we left them be—to get our wits back over what we had seen, they came down the ladder. Alden was smiling and nonplussed by the whole thing. She even leaned and tried to kiss Bev on the lip's goodbye, but Bev acted disgusted and fended her off. Alden never came back. Bev was reeling drunk and claimed to have been possessed by the devil. Said Alden had brought them some pills from home."

"Bev blamed the farm cat for us discovering her. Sarah and I drove the cat twenty miles away and let it go on another farm. Even back then, Bev's temper had no brakes. Bev said she would ruin us if we ever spoke of this again. We all had our secrets, you know. Well, Bev went into a state of frenzy afterward, railing in public against anyone who she thought was queer. She also began sleeping around more...with guys. Not being her picky self. It was in that same dark spell that there was the accident. Where a man was killed. You know the story."

With her arms folded over her knees, Dar shook her head. "I feel like I have gone to sleep dirty and woken up clean. Bev will, at least, feel my freedom."

30

Room Temp Jell-O Molds

A daddy long-legs crawled up the canvas of the wingback chair. Lily lowered the compact case mirror she had found on the ground and let the spider see itself for the first time. She hoped it wasn't disappointed. "See? You are about as cute as they come," she said. Flicking off the spider and dropping the mirror, Lily glanced down at her T-shirt with "Save The Virgins" stamped across the front. There was a drawing of trees around the words to advertise an imperiled forest on a piece of land proposed for a shopping center.

From the lawn, Lily picked up and sipped her glass of sugary milk coffee and began to review the night before. She had gained nothing but more sorrow and frustration. The drama was also wearing on her granny. The bones had been inspiring but had caused way too much anxiety. Maybe it did not matter about slaves or Bigbee. If history was to make itself known that would have to come by chance, Lily supposed. This family did not take well to excavation. They were just too set in their ways and lies. She did not want to be responsible for adding to Virginia's woes. Her granny had a hard job keeping peace and saving the things she loved.

The truth that Lily had learned was that her family was flawed, eccentric, and pretending poorly to be certain of anything unless it was in their favor to do so. The sisters held tight that there was a thriving plantation, that they were once beautiful and desired, and for some that there is nothing wrong with pandering and vanity. And then there was the truth. Racism and homophobia were living and breathing under this roof. More personal was the issue of her cousins, Marcel and Jessie. Lily had never really settled her score with them. It was not fair that she had to hide inside herself while they played scot-free. And soon their depraved side would mature into an adult form. Lily needed to do what she could to stomp them down but mused it might be too late.

Lily's thoughts went to their father, Mickey. While gruff and unsettled, something decent was trying to hatch out of him. Lily knew she should make more of an effort. Deep in her chair, she watched the sisters on the porch, where they had eaten breakfast. Virginia was placing a plate on a stack of napkins. Sarah stumbled across the deck to grab one before it flew off into the shrubs and polluted the world. Bev, finishing the last of her toast, nodded to them and went into the house. Sarah followed, looking back at Virginia, who wadded up her napkin and threw it down before joining her. Within minutes, Lily could hear their voices getting louder and was glad she could not discern what heated insults were being hurled back and forth.

Lily got up and went across the yard to her favorite patch of clover. She heard the door slam and turned back to see Dar storm down the porch steps. She went around the side of the house, her legs pumping to get lost. Half an hour later, Dar walked to where Lily was looking for four-leaf clovers. In her top pocket were three green bits of luck. Her mother took big unnatural strides toward her. Her eyes were red rimmed and feral looking. "Looks like you've been batted around a bit," Lily said.

"Always trying to fix the same old dent." Dar flicked her wrist across her hair. "Might as well give up trying to make peace. Too many angles, too much alcohol. I think they like arguing. Gives them a sense of purpose."

The screen door banged, and Dar and Lily looked back. Bev had come out onto the porch. She carried a tray. A bottle of vodka, a pitcher of tomato juice, and a bucket of ice. Sarah and Virginia tottered behind. They looked old up against the house's bright siding.

"Running out the clock," Lily said, and began digging for worms with a stick.

"Yes, the minute hand is flying up there," Dar said. "It will almost be a wonder if someone is not carried out of here on a gurney." Lily looked up, hurt and startled.

"It won't be Virginia, mark my words," Dar said and smiled.

"I wonder how long it takes for a broken worm to grow itself whole again?" Lily asked. She held up a worm she had accidentally severed while angrily picking at the ground. "Just sometimes seems so...hopeless." Lily nodded to the porch.

"You know, Lily, they were rich, spoiled girls. That made them blind to what they were getting themselves into. And they always got themselves into something big. Thinking small was never an option. Even Virginia. Nature gave that worm what it did not give to humans."

"I will say one last thing you need to think about, Lily. Maybe it holds true. Before we assume those three were aggressors all their lives, consider that they might have become victims somewhere along the line also. I think that is something we might ponder. Even as we may never know, it might help us deal here."

"Let's hear more about Bigbee." Lily said, changing course. "Only what she was like. I'm done wanting anything else on the matter. Just think I should know her from a distance."

Dar sighed and smiled. "Bigbee was a woman of high winds and sometimes just like our river here. Both mad and sane...both tempest and calm. She could wield a cleaver over a live chicken and sing a lullaby at the same time. She had a haze in her eyes that in my youth scared me. When my brother died, my mother got the same fog there, and so I guessed then that Bigbee must have lost a child. I had no reason to think different."

Dar stood and pulled Lily up. She sniffed the air and smiled to where the sun was calling off the river. Hand in hand they headed away from the noise on the porch. "We will never understand the all of her. She arrived out of nowhere, no answers ever given as to her background. Sage, as you might know, in her final years, took her in. When Sage died, Bigbee stayed on to help Virginia. They raised my brother together. It was truly like he was part Bigbee's son. Her grieving was so powerful, Lily. But I have told you that. Though they left the plantation, she never left Virginia's side, until years later, when Bobby became ill and died in that tub. I suppose she did not want to see any more death come out of this family. She left. Don't know what else to say. Though, as you, I suspect there's more. There always is in this family. That's all I got, Lily."

Dar turned and stroked Lily's head, releasing her name in a long tally. "Remember, you need to look at this as a cumulative thing. All families are that. By God, there is nowhere you can stand atop this family where it is not steep. Like being atop a marble. Round, slick, and a long way to fall. Easier just to stay put and live with what it serves you, I guess. Those swirling colors inside are like an answer we cannot have. It's like having faith without proof. So, we keep our feet tight to the surface. It also becomes a damn habit. So that we do not want to leave. Well, maybe until we are too afraid to stay," Dar added and laughed.

"Wow, that's some heavy stuff, Mother. You can be such a redneck and then not."

Dar shrugged and pulled a napkin from her pocket. Opening it, she yanked a piece of fat off a slice of ham she had snatched from the kitchen and tossed it out into the water. That action made for a chaotic moment on the river's surface as fish hurled themselves at the meat.

"Whoa," Lily said. "Are there that many fish in the river? Why haven't I caught any?"

"Everything likes fat, honey," Dar said.

"I have had an epiphany, Mother." Dar screwed up her eyes at the word. Lily rolled her eyes. "Something has revealed itself to me." Sighing, she continued. "At birth, each person is given an allotment of people they are not required to like. Relatives or not. I am determined to accept this without guilt."

Dar patted Lily on the leg. "Can we really manage that?"

It was just after dusk. They were on the porch having just finished dinner. Mickey had grilled burgers. They were digging into watermelon having pushed aside a green Jell-O mold Bev had placed on the table. When mosquitoes poured over them, all rushed to gather whatever they could carry indoors. Dar grabbed the Jell-O mold and hurried around Lily, who had just bumped into Mickey flying out the door to gather the grilling platter. Swatting wildly, mosquitoes covering his face, Mickey apologized.

"My fault," Lily said. Mickey's eyes widened and he smiled. Lily grinned back and for a second each pondered the other. Lily swore that something lifted in this moment, a crossing in solving the dilemma that had faced them for too long. Lily reached into her top pocket and from it withdrew a four-leaf clover. She showed it to Mickey, slid it into his shirt pocket.

"Well, Lily, that is very sweet of you," he said.

"My pleasure," she said, as Mickey, swatting madly, hurried to the grill and then fled back into the house. She watched him and was grinning when Dar came back out. "Hot diggity," Lily said. Dar approached her. Lily was swarmed with insects yet seemed oblivious.

"Have you been drinking again?" Dar asked, turning her by the shoulders toward the door.

Lily feigned weakness and leaned into her. "It is not always that," Lily drawled. "Hardly."

Later, in the bathtub, Lily sifted through, what was, overall, a great day. There had been villains, but the good side of the family had won at every stroke. The day had been maximum hot, and the honeysuckle in the ditch out along the road sweeter than in past years. Sitting up, tucking her knees to her chest, Lily decided she should share her happy vibes with her mother. She got up, dried off, and put on her pajamas. Her mother lay fully clothed on top of her covers, half lidded, her mouth part ugly by weak sleep.

"Today, Mother, was the buffet that excites me, eggs me on, sunny-side up," Lily announced, standing over her. "This is an amazing place;

the house, everything. Every year, the whole place explodes before my eyes, and I discover something I never knew existed. It is like Krakatoa was to all those salivating scientists. Let's make this ours. Take over River Oaks and then the plantation. We have a whole life ahead."

"Flushed the Jell-O mold down the john. Went down like nothing, like a song," Dar slurred and giggled. "What's exploding?" she asked shuddering then puffing down to sleep.

Lily looked down at her mother and smiled. She backed out of the room. Feeling rambunctious, she snuck down into the darkened house. From the kitchen cupboard, she brought out a bottle of red wine and, with opener in hand, tiptoed back upstairs. Seeing the strip of light under Tish's door, she knocked and went in. A half-hour later the bottle was empty, their lips and teeth purple from swigging out of the bottle. They began to share their most intimate secrets. Lily described her only kiss with a boy whose name she could not recall no matter how many times she smacked her forehead. Tish railed on about one kiss after another.

She then went on to tell Lily that yes, she was still a virgin. "But I hope for not much longer," she slurred. She did not blush. It was just a decided thing.

"I don't have enough specifics in that area of my life yet, either," Lily said, pointing to the Save The Virgin shirt she had thrown back on after her bath.

Tish and Lily were passed out, spooned back to back, when Dar came in the next morning looking for Lily. The empty bottle lay between them. Dar had left the door ajar and went forward, giggling. When she heard the cousins' voices in the hallway, she hurried backward to shut the door. Too late, as Marcel and Jessie stood grinning in the narrow rectangle of space.

"Lookeee there, Jessie, our sister has a lover," Marcel said. Dar came out the door, grabbed him by the ear, and twisted until he screeched. She eyed Jessie who had backed off. He hurtled away. Marcel followed, holding his ear and mouthing off that there was no way he would let this news pass. "Tish and Lily are homos," he screeched down the stairs. "Ever seen a stuck pig, Marcel?" Dar called after him and then turned to get the girls up.

The ruckus had wakened them. Dar faced the two heads as they lifted. They were beautiful, sleepy, and seemingly unscathed until Tish's sudden realization of what had occurred and what she would face downstairs with her brothers. She moaned as Lily picked up the empty bottle. Tish half smiled and fell back into the covers.

"It's not exactly the prize in the box of Cracker Jacks, girls," Dar said, smiling back.

31

Morning Glory

Lily slushed through the kitchen door in her bare feet. She had re-colored the shamrock on one big toe and added a row of flowers on the other nine. She and Tish had remained in bed playing Go Fish until they felt back on level ground.

"Well, sunshine, how we doing?" Dar asked, scouring Lily's face and body for any signs of a hangover. "Youthful resilience, what a blessing."

Sarah, holding a box of baking soda, came out of the pantry. She looked hollowed out. Lily snaked around Dar, sniffed the air, and exclaimed with glee, "Cinnamon rolls." She shoved her fingers under the front waistband of her pajamas. Dar glared at Lily and nodded at her hands.

"Well, don't have kittens, y'all, I'm just a girl looking for sweets," Lily blurted.

Sarah shook the box of soda. "Fridge stinks. Needs cleaning before we leave."

Bev frowned at Sarah and then lifted her head to Lily. "Hey, don't you fret about those young cousins of yours. I already set them straight. Nothing wrong with a little girl time and a bottle. And no way Tish the Dish is ever going to switch tracks."

Dar eyed Bev over the remark, thought of Alden Carter, and leering at her, wondered if Bev had managed to wash away that incident.

Lily deplored the ignorance of Bev's remark and was tempted to tell her what an amazing kisser Tish was. She withdrew her hands from her waistband and placed them on her hips as Mickey walked in from the porch looking perturbed.

"Am I on the most-concerned-about list again?" Lily asked him, a bit bewildered. Their progress the prior night seemed now imprecise. "Gosh, I feel like I am always the cow that crossed and crushed the field of okra." She figured Mickey had heard about her and Tish's spend-the-night party. "Oh hell, Uncle Mickey, were just kissing cousins," Lily cackled.

Mickey took a deep breath and managed a weak smile. "It's just Marcel and Jessie. They just don't need any more juice in their engines," he admitted.

"Maybe you should go change before breakfast," Dar announced. She reached to redirect Lily who looked at her pawing hand, smiled, and pulled away.

"Bev, thanks for the support," Lily said. "It is such a nice morning, don't you think? A bacon and cinnamon morning?"

Beside Bev, Virginia's eyes brightened, relieved. Bev shrugged and smiled also.

Lily moved close to Mickey and spoke in a hushed, just-between-us voice. "Mickey," Lily began, and paused. "Let's have a beer soon," she whispered.

Mickey pursed his mouth. "Good morning, Lily," he replied and squinted at her.

"We can just have tea. Today, maybe tomorrow," she said. Mickey scrunched up his mouth and shrugged, an affirmative yes to Lily. She was determined get to know the real Mickey. Not the one made by his defenses, or hers for that matter.

In slow crow steps, the sisters approached the stove to check the rolls they had all chipped in to make. "Let them sit a few minutes more," Bev said to Virginia.

Lily raced over, reached between them and grabbed a piece of bacon. She twirled on her heels with her prize held high and then sauntered away. "Yum, I'll be back for those rolls," she called back pushing through the swinging door. Virginia followed Lily into the great room, mouthing a thank-you to Lily as the door closed behind. Triumphant, Lily grinned and headed upstairs to change.

She paused, peeking down from the triangle where upper floor and stair converged. She watched Virginia stride across the room below. She appeared motivated and safe from provocation, her posture straight, Lily thought, squatting to watch through the balusters.

Just then, sunlight filled the stained glass behind Lily. Colored light fell onto the floor below. Virginia stretched her foot and tapped her toe into that pool of green and red. Lily saw her granny's contentment, her vulnerabilities deserting her one by one. Each summer, the old house, the river, the old memories here, added rigor to her steps, stripping years away. All this, Lily mused with hope.

From the kitchen came the sound of an ice tray cracking. The great hall was safe from her sister's for a while. Virginia bowed and twirled with awkward rigidity then she straightened, brushed her sides, and smiling, filled her lungs with air. Lily envisioned some bygone era; Virginia's head held high and her posture straight. Lily imagined her pulling on one elegant glove then another. She was young, maybe in love, with no signs of life's present or future woes. And then Lily recalled a similar view from a decade before, when she had seen this woman in the arms of a man who was not her husband. Hardness grew in Lily's chest, as that night remained strict and unresolved.

Her granny's affair had ventured in and out of her mind over the years. The last even more so with her father's dalliance. The clandestine forces upon adulthood, foul and life wrenching. Lily sat down hard on the step. Staring down, she felt weighted. Why, she asked, did this matter any longer? Why were minutes of one night, so long ago, still like slippery air between she and her granny? It seemed silly, Lily mused, thinking back to that night.

Lily was staying over at Virginia's and had awakened to a clamor in the house. Virginia's second husband, Bobby, was driving with Dar to the plantation to pick up an old armoire for Virginia's living room. In a fog from the milky tincture Virginia had given her to drink when she tucked her into bed, she had snuck onto the stairs. Lily, about five, had looked down upon Virginia talking with a stranger. They were inches apart and whispering. Then touched and hugged. At first, Lily smiled. Then they moved, almost falling against the wall where a bookshelf had been taken away to make space for the furniture Dar and Bobby would bring. Their bold shadows from the moonlit window groped and pushed. Malleable ropes twisting, knotting, and then releasing to be retied. Lily's head was awash between reality and trance, the paregoric she had been given making her dreamy. There was little she could validate.

The deeply shadowed bodies, hand in hand, at last sprawled on the couch. Their hard breathing and occasional cries made Lily want to flee back to her room but at the same time, immobilized her. At last they lay there, immobile, tangled like landlocked fish taking small quick breaths. Or so, in her delirium, Lily thought. Before she rose, she swore Virginia saw her watching, as her eyes flashed toward the stairway where she was sitting.

Lily had awakened the next day with a head full of cotton and a bad dream feeding her. When she came downstairs, the armoire was set in place over her mental imprint of two twisted bodies. She pushed down to subdue what felt vulgar. Then found it easier to lift the night behind into the spaces reserved for misunderstood dreams, flying, and peculiarities, like why a chameleon can change from blue to green upon a leaf. All laws of nature meant to be elusive.

Still the tacit parts of Lily's young mind dug in and remained muddled in the perils of there being two men in Virginia's life. Any wrong felt secretive. The right was in the exactness of those two in that shadowy room, like a practiced dance between trusted partners. Lily never confessed what she had seen to anyone. The danger went away as Lily never saw the man again, and she learned to sway her misgivings when the need arose. The magic of carefree years took Lily's small hand. Yet, that night remained as something unproven and surreal.

Staring now at her granny, poised in such elegant peace, Lily thought of Virginia's second husband, Bobby. He had died maybe a year after that odd evening. To Lily, Bobby was just a vague outline of bright shorts and shirts and a mouth that was loud. His passing was a memory of flowers and her first funeral. It was only in later years she heard grumblings of what a scoundrel Bobby had been.

Her parents' slow year of dissolving diverted Lily's attention away from that druggy night. Her father's indiscretion was somehow different than her granny's. Her parents' tears and raised voices made their situation hard as stone. Then it was like a knife had cut each away from the other. Her granny's night was soft and quiet and had pushed around in Lily, but never violently came through her skin, like it had done with her parents. Still, living and scratching inside was the fact that Lily and Virginia seemed to touch without full commitment. There was an undertow as they approached, crosswinds when they stood side by side and in things unspoken, and by the way they hugged with air between them.

Standing, Lily recalled the drawing of a lily given to her by Virginia. She was to take the baton. The image of them never hugging as she did her mother and father seemed now impossible and wrong. She wanted to tell Virginia that any sins in her life would not find her here. That, in this house, was absolution. Lily then and there understood the power of secrets. In them is harmony, pain, as well as the disjointed things freed from keeping them, and the longing to share them to keep one's sanity. Lily raced down the stairs. At the bottom, she strode to Virginia, startling her. Wrapping her arms about her granny, Lily pressed through the layers of doubt, pushing her heart in through the pockets of air into Virginia's insides. "I love you, no matter what."

32

Bliss in Old Ruins

Virginia's door was open. A gale of air was being sucked through her open window by the attic fan two stories up. Virginia was sitting at the vanity when Lily entered to say goodnight. Looking over her shoulder and greeting her, Virginia laid down the alcohol pad she was using to scrub rouge from her cheeks. Lily hovered behind in her pajamas, as Virginia, with her right then left index finger, punched up the skin under her cheekbones. Lily took in her fragile neck, her head as it turned back and forth, checking her face in the mirror. Virginia squinted in the glass at Lily's curious face. She reached back and took Lily's hand, clasping it to her bony shoulder.

"The mirror is the window looking at your maker's craft and at man's failing in execution of his exact plan," Virginia said with an aggrieved drawl. "That is what my mother said once, each of us lined up behind this very vanity. She wasn't just talking about physical beauty. But of course, that went right over our heads. She was talking about conscience. My mother's intent was for each of us to have our turn in this chair. She warned us that you grow beautiful from the inside out. Also, that beauty on the outside can grow to ugliness on the inside. Rather than see the sense of that statement, we shoved about to argue who was the prettiest." Virginia cackled and took a sip of her watery drink.

"Sage was always patient. 'Litmus,' she said, leading me to sit first. 'Now, let's see how you handle judgment,' she said. 'If vanity steers you then the mirror will tell you; plaster it in your own eyes for the rest of your life.' She told me that I passed. Bev was to sit next. She looked frightened and made an excuse about being late for something. You see, Sage already knew what would become of Bev. She was just hoping Bev would focus and see it herself before it was too late. She was already the wildest of wild."

"There is so much more we need to know about the other," Lily said, and her granny swung about in the chair to face her. "You know, when we get back home, I will make more of an effort."

"Of course, we will," Virginia said, and leaned to pick up her brush, which had fallen to the floor. Behind, she heard Lily gasp. Virginia pulled herself up with the help of the desk. She followed Lily's gaze to an object tucked beside the mirror. Virginia's pulse quickened as she cursed herself for cradling the bottle Bigbee had given to her all the way from home. She had meant to place it away forever. Beyond what Virginia did know about the bottle, there was something much darker within its core. That much Bigbee had hinted of.

"Where did you get that?" Lily gasped, and then blushed, as she had purloined the thing from Virginia's trash long before. She had ridden her bike to Virginia's for a visit and having found her sound asleep went back to where her bike was propped up against a tree in the alley. On the curbside was Virginia's trash bin, the lid off, as some animal had been rummaging. Trash and food scraps lay about. On the top of the container, half exposed in a pearl-colored handkerchief, something glistened. Lily unwrapped what appeared to be an old perfume bottle, guessing that her granny had been cleaning out her attic, as she did once in a while.

The jar was filled with what looked like gray sand. Lily had tossed the bottle in her bike basket, where it became lost among myriad piles of other favored items. A month later, she thought of it and took it from her basket. Twirling it in the sunlight, she saw something buried in its center. Dumping out the contents onto newspaper, she withdrew an old key, made possibly of bone, which excited Lily to no end. She had meant to ask Virginia about it.

Lily reached for the bottle, wondering how it could have gotten here. Virginia's tiny pink fingers folded over Lily's thin wrist. Lily let go of the bottle as her granny's eyes pleaded to her. "I found it in your trash out by the curb," Lily said. "It disappeared, and I figured some creep had stolen it. It is kind of cool, you know."

Virginia frowned hard, her gaze curious, then sharp on suspicion and then anger. "Ah," she said. "I now understand what happened. I saw it in your bike basket when I came to see your new home, and took it back, because it belongs with me. It came from Bigbee."

Virginia's mind flashed back. Bev. She had not thrown it in the trash. The bottle had vanished from her bedroom at home. Bev, Sarah, and she had been arguing over the necessity for keeping such a thing. Bev had slapped a stern hand down, saying that since it came from Bigbee, the whole package was likely of the occult. "You know how those people use magic," she had said to Virginia. "Why do you suppose Bigbee gave it to you? God knows what that key's to," she added, shuddering. "You have to wonder if it's not a curse."

Virginia had reminded her that Bigbee was family. "In no uncertain terms, if you recall." Virginia had told her to shut her down. Sarah had refused to touch the bottle and began to weep. All this was the worst kind of curse, leaving them holding the whole shenanigans of every bad deed in their lives. After shooing her sisters away, Virginia put the bottle back into her bureau for safekeeping. The next week she had gone to move it to a better hiding place. The bottle had vanished. She had joked to herself that if she could not find it, neither could her sisters. She now felt guilty about taking it from Lily's basket and wondered if that had not been a better place for it. "Should have put it in the attic here with all else," Virginia said, palming the bottle.

"What is that bottle? And the key? What does it fit?" Lily asked.

"No one will ever know what it means in whole," Virginia answered in part truth. Reaching with her free hand, she picked up her bourbon glass and drank the watery remnants.

"You know, I took that key out once. It's made of bone. How weird is that? Do you think it's human, you know, like the ones I've got?" Lily asked.

Virginia rolled the bottle over in her palm, tumbling the soil. The key was just visible. "Patch me up, will you?" Virginia said to Lily, holding the glass over her shoulder for Lily to take. She watched in the mirror as Lily hesitated. Lily leaned, eyed her dead-on and snatched the glass. "In the blue crystal decanter inside that cupboard," Virginia added.

Virginia's thoughts flashed back to the day the bottle came into her possession. Marshall, her son, had died months prior; it was a stew of time that owned nothing but suffering and loss. Her husband had vanished in his own exile, never to return.

Sporadic showers were sweeping up the coast, but that had not kept Bigbee from her Sunday walk, nor Virginia from picking blue flag irises for the house. Virginia passed by Bigbee's room behind the kitchen. The door was open, as was the single window on the east wall. Rain misted over the sill. Dead flowers sat in a pot on the bedside table. Wary of this trespass, Virginia entered with a handful of flowers. Placing the wilted flowers aside, she arranged the fresh stems, closed the window, and then turned to view the room.

Virginia crossed to the old white bureau, which within that frugal room was a shrine of personal effects. A rusting pocketknife was set atop a huge black feather. Two carved pieces of driftwood, one resembling a man praying and the other a mother under the burden of two stick-thin children, stood side by side. There was a simple tin cross. A locket of long gray hair was wound around it like a vine. Seashells lay about the table's entire surface, strewn about as they might have been found on the shore. Virginia picked up and turned a bottle of sand in her hand. Inside, up against the glass, was a key. As Lily said, it appeared to be made of bone.

The room was humid, and as Virginia swiped her forehead with her palm, Bigbee came in behind her. Virginia turned and gasped, searching for an apology for being there. Bigbee looked at the fresh flowers and smiled, as in her right hand was a rain lily. "Resurrection and re-birth," Bigbee said, and held out the flower for Virginia to take. She then frowned, noting the bottle in Virginia's hand. Virginia placed the bottle back on the table and felt her face grow hot.

"My home," Bigbee said in a weak voice, staring at bottle. "It is gone, painted over with tar, and everyone might as well be dead, living beside that mark of cruelty." With that statement, Bigbee grabbed her bosom over her heart and might have torn it from her chest. Her voice filled the room or maybe it was just the tenor, a growl covering so many emo-tions. Bigbee lowered her hand and looked past the bureau; maybe even through the wall. Her face appeared full of tears without a single drop present. Her lips blown full like she might any second bluster and fall. But there was something else Virginia would never forget, and it was the thing that kept Bigbee standing, Virginia was sure. Never had she seen such venom in a person's eyes. That poison then flipped to agony. Vir-ginia placed a hand on Bigbee's arm. Her flesh was cold. Bigbee shook her head. "It is forever, and at the world's start was an unkind force, Vir-ginia. There is nowhere else to go now but to pray it will be different after God swipes his hand to clean the earth of man."

Virginia had tried to hold her, but Bigbee remained as stone.

"Black folks are here to suffer and survive only when we are buried. But then, all will suffer in the end. We were your hope, Virginia, your test, and your world failed the first time you laid eyes on us." Bigbee's voice was as cold as her skin.

The "litmus," Virginia mused now, recalling what Sage had said and that she had just shared with Lily.

Standing before Bigbee, Virginia was stymied for words. The flower of resurrection and rebirth in her hand felt like a cruel joke. Bigbee touched Virginia's arm. "You are one of the blameless ones, Virginia. We cannot help where we are born."

In a way, that bottle is God's guilt over letting his soldiers become so cruel. I walked away from my island thinking God was full of malice. Every grain of sand in there is a man who has suffered. The key is so I can revisit my humiliation. It is a key to our now padlocked church." She paused to look at Virginia. "When I get home, I am going to resurrect the children who then will bring the soul back to God and our house of worship."

Virginia recalled the day Bigbee left for good. "You carry my guilt. I will carry yours," Bigbee had said. When she walked away forever, what Virginia wished to see in her eyes was not there. Maybe shared sorrow and guilt. Instead her brown eyes were filled with redemption, a look to haunt Virginia forever. Virginia remembered how she had implored Dar to name her child Lily. She never told her why, but that name in their family might offer them all hope.

Lily came back and set the straight bourbon down. "You were mumbling, Granny. Kind of spooky stuff about God and guilt."

Virginia reached, swallowed, and coughed. "Just something someone said once." Virginia heard Lily's frustrated sigh and caught her beseeching gaze in the mirror. Staring into her beloved Lily's eyes, she said, "I don't know half of it myself."

Lily dropped her hands to the back of the chair, hearing her name. "Please, Granny, tell me what you know at least," she said.

Virginia nodded into the mirror. "Oh, what the hell," she said, sighing. "I know Bigbee was haunted by her past. I thought maybe she had lost a man. I asked that once, and by the bitterness on her face, I knew to never ask again. When she left my employment, she asked me to pray with her. She made me retrieve this bottle," Virginia said, nodding to the table. "She wrapped her two big hands around mine, holding it, recited a prayer I had never heard, then opened her eyes and told me that when I hold this glass, to feel its weight. 'Of a hundred human hearts blanked out,'" Virginia quoted. "'This bottle,' Bigbee said that day, 'is the scale between the weak and the strong. The key inside holds the power to make it right again,' she told me." Virginia did not relay the last thing she said. *I have done my part here. The rest is up to you.*

"Granny, this is amazing stuff. Is all this superstition what's gotten everyone's tails bunched up? Oh God, did Bigbee ever scare the bejesus out of all you gals." Lily paused. "Still, that bottle kind of scares me, too."

Virginia turned from the mirror and smiled. "There's nothing more, Lily. What you've ended up with is to witness what women look like when they have not deserved half of what they have gotten. We chose relationships and husbands poorly. Built a castle with halls of white lies we can no longer follow. So, don't try to understand, Lily, because I don't half the time." Virginia drank again, and then looked back. You're not a child anymore, that's for sure. You are sprouting into a real lady. A keeper for some lucky man. You will have children of your own. They will have your veracity. The next links in the chain of Hooper pearls. Nothing for them but the sultry plain of summer porches and hard rains."

Lily remained silent. She looked down at her body, in disbelief that a child might someday cling to her insides. Lily blushed and hunched her shoulders. "I just love when as a family we peel onions," Lily proclaimed. Her impish smile swarmed over Virginia. She gripped her hand and released it. "We can finish peeling this one whenever you want." She paused. "Though it will be just sad when all the layers are gone."

Virginia nodded. "Of anything that has been said in this reunion, that is the most profound. Also frightening. Let's just see to it there are always layers left. Just for dignity," she said, and clasped their hands together. "One layer, Lily, I pray we have thrown away or at least bruised on the outside is the argument of selling River Oaks and the tea plantation."

Lily leaned over her shoulder. "Never going to happen," she said. "Goodnight."

Up in her turreted room, Lily shot up in bed. She rubbed her eyes and looked to the ceiling. "The attic," she mouthed. Her granny had said she should have put the bottle in the attic. With all else. At dawn, with only the smell of coffee wafting from below, Lily dressed, crept up the narrow spider-webbed stairs, pushed open the creaking door, pulled on the light cord, and shut herself in.

33

Salt in Our Wounds

By the look on Dar's face and the way she ruminated on the entire sky and all unseen beyond, Lily suspected her mother's morning had not started well. She seemed small down in the canvas of her chair, maybe like she regretted that she could not go deeper.

Dar acknowledged Lily by wriggling one dangling foot. She brushed her with a look that said she was fine and then not. Standing over her, waiting to be invited to stay, Lily shuffled this way and that. At last, Lily sat down in the chair facing her. She brought her knees up into sharp points and busied herself by scratching at the old wood on the deck below.

"Someone did it again," Dar at last said. "Left a pair of golden baby shoes at the bottom of the stairs. Who does that?" Dar asked, and looked at Lily like she might somehow find the answer. "The thing about baby shoes is that they can be mysterious, as everyone argues who they belong to. Some pair always missing, leaving someone out. They can bring either great happiness or sorrow. They are also as odd as they are cute. The same person who invented Hallmark cards invented Mother's Day and baby shoes. All to make money at the cost of someone's heartbreak. The thing about these shoes is in the day they show up. It is cruel even if the person meant well."

Though Lily was armed with questions from her attic discoveries, the woeful mood of her mother superseded that. She could not recall ever knowing about this bizarre tradition and wondered how she could have missed it.

"It is like that science ride at the fair in Atlanta," Dar said, after sipping her black tea. "As you know, the fair comes the same day each year." She then looked straight at Lily. "Those shoes were not mine." Her tone was solemn, riddled with possibilities. Lily decided to just listen. "Someone placed the same shoes there last year. They'll disappear after lunch. You know the ride at the fair, the one in that big metal cylinder, where you finally understand the power on your body by moving so fast in a circle? You are spinning really fast, and then the floor drops out from under you, and you stick to the wall like a chigger. That was the force of seeing those shoes, reeling me back into seeing the uncertainty of everything I thought I knew. And, honey, we are the chiggers. This small Hooper dynasty is that unwieldy machine. We are waiting for the floor to drop out from under us." Dar let out a groan and looked into Lily's eyes.

The look her mother carried was an offering, Lily understood. Forged by mother to daughter, saying if she were to look deep enough, the comparison might make sense. Dar put her face to the mug and drew in the fumes. Like she might not return, Lily thought.

"Just as that force of nature, real tragedy is a sting you feel forever," Dar said. She leaned and squeezed Lily's knee. "And, my sweet girl, someone—sometimes an idiot, sometimes a friend—will always be there to remind you of anniversaries. Even the ones that are painful. So the floor can drop out. And that's just wrong. The shoes belonged to my brother. The one I told you about who died when we were little and living at the plantation. I mean it when I say I can only guess who put them there. They all have their reasons. Some pure. Some sinister with an eyedropper of innocence. Some might feel the pain alongside me, as today is the anniversary of his death. Others may think they are helping, thinking that their deed is charity."

"Either way, it is just weird," Lily said.

"I have asked every single one of them who is responsible. They all claim they do not know. Maybe they do it all as one, three toddling emissaries thinking they are doing the right thing. Doing it for me? Or in memory of Marshall without a shit care about my heartstrings. Like they are just suddenly so full of the right thing in the middle of this storm they call a reunion. I wonder if seeing those shoes bothers Virginia, or if she finds some relief that is alien to the likes of me? Yet, even as seeing them hurts me to the core, I let them sneak in and take back the shoes to whatever sanctuary they keep them in."

She again bent her fingers over Lily's knee. With that touch, too hard to be loving, she might have been reflecting on the graveness of such a true and hard story. A clatter of footsteps behind them caused both to start. Dar braced. "As I said, I expect the shoes will be gone by one. That is when the coroner said my brother most likely perished."

"Wow," Lily said, leaning back with the cold force of that comment. The screen door flew open. Marcel and Jessie raced into the yard, oblivious to Dar and Lily. "They seem to be able to skip past the beauty here," Lily said.

"We learned long ago that they're not just boys," Dar said, looking at Lily, then away.

Lily's face registered disgust.

"I have settled my hatred of them because of the blood relation thing. Relatives must attempt to make amends, even if the sense of it cannot be put into words. I am really trying to believe that. Though I have just about given up on God." Dar paused, as Lily put her hands up.

"Those shoes represent more than just little feet. They are, in a way, anchors to my past. And yours by heredity. Let's let Marshall's shoes be a bridge for us. Instead of something weird and cruel, let's celebrate those shoes. I say we take them as an invitation to cross over and bring the plantation back to life. I don't know how we can afford to do it, but I am going to dream we can. I am sure you are right that our forebears owned slaves. Do you bury things like that, or do you bring the place back and somehow make amends? And how do you make amends with things so heinous as that?"

"By changing the blood," Lily said, and shrugged. "Put a new engine into life and promise to never go back to the old one. Give a ride to someone in need, no matter how far they want to go."

Dar stared at her. "You are something else, Lily Hooper. Now, I'm going to go get those baby shoes before they vanish. See you later, crocodile. I mean alligator," she added, when Lily buried her head in her hands.

Lily watched her mother walk inside and then heard her greeting Mickey. He walked out and looked down at Lily. He seemed distracted and walked down the steps toward the river with his hands in his pockets. Tish, with a towel and book in hand came up over the riverbank. As she passed her father on the lawn, she stopped, rose up on her toes, and kissed him on the cheek.

34

Crossing

While the others were arguing over a Scrabble word at the dining room table, Lily snuck away. "'Don Juan' is not a single word. And a fictitious man, not even legal," Dar said to Bev.

"It can be substituted for womanizer. Like Falstaff is for beer," Bev, tipsy, retorted.

Lily came onto the porch and found Mickey. He was asleep in a chaise lounge with a soiled napkin in his lap. A can of beer, manacled and tilted between his thumb and palm, rested on the deck below. An oblong puddle of foam had collected on the wood. Two yellow jackets circled it. Lily tapped her foot and smiled, watching them dart up and about at breakneck speed.

Mickey opened his eyes, startled to see Lily standing over him. He swatted as a yellow jacket brushed over his lips. "This is how days should pass," he muttered. He had eaten a late lunch of fried chicken, fresh beans cooked with ham, and other casseroles and fixings. His plate sat on the deck beside him. He stretched, then wiped drool from the side of his mouth.

With hands in her pockets, Lily nodded.

"You know it's good when you're so full you can hardly get an after-lunch beer down," Mickey said.

Lily frowned, as he sounded uncomfortable with his assessment of this grand life. She tried to figure out how to steer Mickey into gainful conversation. Mickey patted his belly. He looked like he might close his eyes and go back to sleep. She felt frustrated. She was sincere about making progress, then reminded herself she was the only one aware of this goal. The two of them needed to get down to just being frogs in a single pond.

Mickey flopped his legs on either side of the recliner, his feet thumping on the deck. Big frog feet. Already back at the foam, the yellow jackets threw another fit. Mickey looked appalling, sweat rolling down his temples, and Lily supposed that to any fifteen-year-old girl this posture in men would appear gross. He brought his beer up, took a sip, and then frowned. "Hot," he said, and put the beer down. Then he undid his belt and sighed with relief, as Lily looked away toward the siding on the house. "Sorry," he said.

Lily scrunched her mouth and almost gave up. With his pants undone he seemed to be about to unravel, and she would abandon her mission and walk away when it happened. Mickey rescued the moment. He turned his face into the warmth reflected off the house and nodded like he knew something the small world around him did not. He looked genuine and content, maybe humbled by the great house above him, as he looked up and took it in. He sighed, reached and patted the siding. "Yep," he said, "You're something, old man." Mickey eyed Lily, and raising his right hand, blocked the sunlight. She shifted to the side to shield the sun from his face. He nodded to the empty chair. She declined and moved over to where a bit of shade from the charred oak fell.

Inside, the sounds of the kitchen echoed. Marcel, Jessie, and Tish yelped happily across the distant lawn. Lily felt Mickey staring at her and turned to face him. He looked perplexed. Maybe because she lingered, when she normally did not. Maybe, she mused, he felt as she, that there were unwritten laws on the matters of forming adult-teen friendships. They were just both ignorant of how to get there. She decided to start with familiar territory. Risky, but she considered it as a path they were at least familiar with.

Lily pointed toward Mickey's kids. "Paint what you see," she said, holding up her thumb toward the yard and squinting. "It's for the eye of the beholder, I guess."

Mickey shook his head, showing part displeasure. He then folded his hands and smiled. "Why can't you just talk straight?" he said.

"Guess you know how I would paint them," she responded, ignoring his plea.

"It's not always pretty," he agreed, with a weak laugh. He poured out his hot beer and watched the bees scatter then resettle. He belched and apologized.

"I like to imagine great things in all our futures, Uncle Mickey," she continued, though unsure how much she thought about that.

"You're not old enough to be so smug," he said.

"I'm not saying you're not already successful with your appliance stores. I'm talking about families. Where do we find success to be one? This little reunion has been a bit of a chore all the way, don't you think? Almost a barnburner, in fact," she added, looking toward the charred shed. She looked up into the big oak and thought of Nessie and her brood.

Mickey looked back, wide-eyed. "That was an accident. As for the rest of it, you just look too hard at things. I think most families struggle." He stood. Shoving his hands into his pockets, he paced to one end of the porch and back, then stopped before her. He shook his head back and forth, his gaze on her yellow flip-flops. "Nice tan, Lily," he said, pointing at her feet. "You and Tish really brown up," he added, trying to get this moving in another direction.

"She is my bud. You have a real keeper there," Lily retorted, and then noted that he was appraising her comment with admiration. She wondered how to continue. She focused on the fact that this would be a win for them both. "Uncle Mickey, I like you. I think you are a saint of sorts...but you act like life doesn't get any better than this, and if that's true at your age, then that really scares me. You, me, all here need to know there is progress in our lives. And even in our moving forward as a family, though we might need to stick to individual achievements." Lily looked out to Marcel and Jessie. "Unfortunately, we do not all heal as worms," she said and looked back. "I know you are dealing with a big bucket of hardware. Bev, the bluntest tool in history, your wife pulling a no-show—again—the boys trying to stay just delinquent and nothing worse or better."

Across the way, Mickey stared like he would remain silent for the rest of his life.

"And where is my own progress?" she asked and looked down. "I feel stuck in orbit around things and people that really matter to me. At times, I feel like I will forever be jammed there. My mother divorced Dad, and she is now a lesbian. I'm supposed to think that is progress, but...like that did not affect me," she said and looked up. Mickey nodded back.

"I am kind of thrown in the hamster cage, and I hate the wheel," Lily stammered, shaking her arms. "If my mother is happy, that is all that matters. Right? Yet, if she is filling an empty place with more emptiness, that makes me worry. I like and love her, by the way, whether she is gay or not." Hearing herself, she paused. She wanted this to be about her hard deal with Mickey.

He sat and leaned back, looking out between his bent knees. "It's not easy, Lily. We all have our challenges." His sight trailed to the yard and then way beyond. She speculated that gaze went past the river, south, then east to the coast where his wife was with her friends. In that moment, she felt sad for him, split away from someone he loved. She knew how that felt.

"Do we all just get used to the cold routine of laying eggs, not ever seeing or caring whether they are nurtured or scrambled by uncaring monsters?" she asked and felt her body clench. She did not expect an answer and moved to sit on the deck below Mickey, who looked perplexed. His hands were clasped in patience. She was then filled with a sense of well-being. He smelled good. It was lived-in, a little woodsy. Her father's skin smelled like that of a green apple, but Mickey's smell was okay, too. Mickey rolled his neck, grinding it loose.

Lily then knew this had only a little to do with getting to know him better. It was about going to another place. It was about pain. About

Marcel and Jessie. Her eyes welled up. She swallowed hard. Her disdain for her male cousins was known. Yet the true visual of what had forged that disdain had been as looking through a cotton ball, because that is the way she made it. She had practiced pushing away the day that broke her back. She had kicked it, stomped it, spit when she thought about it, until all that was left was revulsion. But being with her cousins for this solid spate of days had reawakened everything. Lily looked out to the yard, her eyes screwed up in anguish and near hate for her own blood.

She did not like the idea of recalling that incident. It was awkward, even as Mickey knew all about it. He nodded for her to continue. She had a hard time opening her mouth. That day left hard, welted edges for them both, though hers were far more personal and hotter than the sun.

Mickey pulled himself up, his big feet again plopping like tombs on the deck. His look wavered from soft to firm, his eyes bouncing around her. How to square up his two monstrous children to a world that waited for an answer? More so, his expression appealed for truce, thinking maybe they would not have to get into specifics. His posture relaxed.

He contemplated how he could set things straight. Though only time, maybe not even that, could heal such a wide-open wound of the soul. He saw the peril of Lily's young heart. She held the palm of one hand on her stomach as if holding in her guts. He decided to change the tide of things definitively. He pointed a finger at her, paused, and then smiled. "I always liked your father," he said. "A bit of a bohemian like his daughter, but he is a really good man. Like his daughter...in a generic sense, you know what I mean."

With the mention of her father, Lily felt her heart rise and fall. She imagined her father standing beside Mickey to help him through this. He parted his lips, licked his mouth, and looked at her with a twinkle in his eye. "And your mother is a force. I'll always want her on my side and never against me," he said, shaking his head and smiling.

Bitter and sweet converged in Lily. She stared at the yard, blurred the shapes and sounds of her cousins. She realized he must have a purpose in bringing the goodness of her parents to stand beside him. That maybe she needed all of them to survive the next moments.

"Truth becomes muddled in wars," she blurted. "In bad marriages it's all about barbs, winning small-pitched battles, and everyone walks away gaining nothing. Divorce is like its own God." Mickey watched her, letting her unroll this long, ugly carpet.

"During that divorce, Granny told me that just like in war, the goodness of a person is the first to go on the battlefield. His affair was awful, still hurts me, but I think they both drove the other toward their weaknesses. I lost my goodness, I think, in their war. I should have expressed my righteous feelings for my father to my mother. But, of course, her hurt was too deep. I should have told him he would be remiss without her radiating walk and personality. Would they have seen what they were blind to?"

"Would it have made a difference?" he asked and looked down.

She ignored him. Her ears went back to the crow sounds of her cousins.

"Yes," he said. "Your dad was a dreamer. Maybe too much so, in terms of compromising. Your mother needed all four of their feet planted. Tried hard to make that happen, thus kept him down, I think. All that is because, in my humble opinion, your mother works very hard to not be a Hooper. But at the same time, she would not give up this place or the plantation to save her soul. Would go back as a tea maven tomorrow. As would you, I suppose."

Lily looked back at him, astounded that he put such a complex package into words. She giggled, adding, "I think there's another reason my mother fidgets to keep her feet planted. It's the fear of that wild Hooper gene. She needed someone carrying tent stakes to hold her inclinations down. My father had no stakes; had wings instead. She could have dreamed with him. And he could have been less stubborn and accepting of her. That is the anger I hold. That could have held us together. To me, he was the only man to walk on the moon, to have seen the earth in its beauty, and thus its fragility and peril. He loved just breathing. And he loved my mother as much as she loved him, though neither expressed it well enough to save their marriage. But then my father stumbled. I love my mother. She is the best friend I see every day."

Lily took in Mickey, who was looking like he might hug her. She looked away.

"Well," she heard in a wash of air from his mouth. "You are wise for your age. I know this has been so hard on you."

His words struck her. She knew she could not walk away from what held them apart. "Look at your kids out there, Uncle Mickey. You wanna know hard? She shook her hands toward the yards. "Tell me, am I better than Marcel—than Jessie?"

"No, you're not better than my boys. As a father, that is what I am supposed to say. But, in truth, they certainly are not better than you. I can only pray they will have your merit. There is just no excuse to some things, and only a lousy, self-serving parent living in a paper bag would try to argue their case." He looked at Lily and flushed red.

"Wow," she said, and gulped. "Yeah, I know, girls mature faster than boys. Girls are quicker on their feet. More agile in their brains. Can read well beyond their years, as guys are still stuck on *The Hardy Boys* and waiting for their armpit hair and the rest to grow in. Girls are already bleeding to death. Well, except me." She then blushed, realizing she had divulged more than she ever wished to.

Mickey's brows went up. She took in his broad, sunburned, and peeling face. She considered if she were satisfied with his statement about his sons. "They are my cousins, so I would like to see them ride off to see that the world is not flat and that they are not part of a secluded and protected tribe named Hooper," Lily said.

"I never apologized like I should have for what my boys did long ago. And I know their forced apology did not mean enough at the time and never will. You were far too young to experience something like that." He ran both his hands over his damp scalp and held them there. "If they had been older, I would have sent them off to some remedial school or maybe the army, if that's any consolation."

"If they were much older when they did that, they would have gone to jail," she said.

"You are something. You manage to find light in all this. I am just so sorry—about a decade too late," he said and looked to the sky. "There are no right words. All I pray is that they did not lose their goodness in the battlefield they themselves have created. Despite them, you have kept yours."

"Uncle Mickey, I have found humor in many things, but for them I have accustomed myself to just loathing." She looked out where Jessie was crying on the grass. Tish stood over him ready to finish whatever he started. Mickey and Lily looked at each other and smiled.

Mickey walked forward and gave Lily her a hug. It was, she thought, the only embrace he could manage in his own state of flux, his arms encircling, but just touching. Releasing her, he said, "You can loathe them as long as it takes. If it takes forever, that's okay, too. I am afraid that we might have seen what we are going to get out of those two. But, as a father, I have hope." He then turned and walked back into the house.

Alone and sitting with her back slumped against the warm siding, Lily stared to the far side of the river. She tried to imagine herself running through the bramble there, cutting her skin. Instead, every fiber of her spun on this time with Mickey. And then upon what Jessie and Marcel had done to her long ago. "Horrible, unforgivable curiosity on their part." That is what Mickey, with his big red face, had called their behavior well after the incident had occurred. The word "curiosity" had struck Lily as wrong and had made her despise part of Mickey for so long. Like his two boys were just being nosey. Like it was okay if they were just curious.

They had been playing together in their basement. Hide and seek, tag and such. Tish had run off crying, for what reason Lily did not understand, as Lily had been hiding in a cupboard. With Tish gone, the boys found Lily and pulled her out. Marcel plunged a thumb into his skinny chest, boasting about being the Master of the Universe. A wrestling name he had bestowed upon himself. Lily was taking no guff and asked what had happened with Tish. Jessie said she had pinched her finger and would be back after she got over being a baby.

The boys began teasing Lily, saying her father was a dirty hippy. They coerced her into wrestling, had her pinned to the floor. Marcel touched her chest with Jessie going along, which she could not understand, as their bodies up there were no different than hers. They began to explore, plunging their hands all over her. She had thought it strange, then frightening and began to fight. Jessie held her buy her ankles and Marcel lowered her shorts. She was out of breath as Jessie tickled her on her belly and then upper thighs. They began sticking their hands down her underwear and laughing. Marcel stuck his fingers into her vagina. He squealed. Scared, Lily had urinated down her thighs. "Gross," Marcel laughed. Tish came back, pushed them away, grabbed Lily's hand, and ran away with her.

Lily had nightmares after that. But unlike the ones she was used to. These were of smothering under humans that expanded in form, their bodies ballooning to ten times their size, then shrinking. Another of being caught under falling mattresses, heavy damp mattresses thumping down on her, one after the other until she woke atop her real one drenched in sweat. This had gone on for six months or so, until Mickey found out from Tish and told Dar.

Her mother let Lily sleep in her bed, as her father was out of town. Dar let her steer the car whilst sitting in her lap. They had stopped reading *Grimm's Fairy Tales*, skipped doctor appointments, and gone out for lime freezes instead. They made plans for a dog when Lily was a little older. Dar made her play after school with both girls and boys, though Lily tried to reject the latter. This, in later years, had culminated into Lily's love of dodgeball. She loved winning, being the last one standing, loved slaughtering the guys, seeing them all lined up and seething on the sidelines as she swayed and yelped for joy. Her father had not been told. When asked about Lily never wanting to go near Marcel and Jessie, Dar made excuses to correlate with the moods of her aging. "I can just get through Thanksgiving myself with those two," she said.

Eyeing the cousins now, Lily stood. She would never forgive them. Nothing had changed. She strode down the steps, crossing the yard to where Tish was arguing with her brothers. She saw lewdness in Marcel's eyes, whether there or not. Seething, Tish turned to Lily. Stepping in front of Tish, Lily planted her feet before the boys. Marcel turned to Jessie, smirked, and crossed his arms in challenge to Lily. She slapped him as hard as she could, following up with one to his brother. Their tears were as glorious as sunshine and the sting on her palm sweet.

35

The Writer's Bloody Sword

Virginia was at the water's edge taking in the view. She sat in a low-slung chair Lily could not imagine her getting in and out of. Virginia greeted her. "Hey sweet thing." Lily had waited to find her granny alone and away from the house. Plopping down cross-legged on the grass, Lily set the satchel down. Virginia glanced over it with a glow of recognition, then a look of challenge. Her mouth then hitched up into a tiny smile.

"Seems you have been in the attic, young lady. Well, I suppose some of the stories I promised to share with you are buried in those pages."

"Sam Green first and then Malcolm Squibb's death. I peeked but left the juicy stuff for you."

Virginia sighed. "Yes, I was a good little author once. Stirred up a lot of town juice with those stories. I believe you have a sense of how we got there. What we were born to, we were meant to seize. You know, we had to practice being spoiled until it became second nature," she added almost apologetically. Lily laughed and Virginia continued. She wrapped up the history of the tea plantation, spiced it up with descriptions of its magic, beauty, and a smattering of their antics, as if the land and three girls were inseparable from the other in cause and nature.

"Sounds like a fairy tale," Lily said. "Next time we are there, I want to see the beach and dunes. For sure some alligators. And I wonder how hard it would be to lasso a wild horse."

"What I learned growing up is that dreams can come true. Getting tea to prosper on land and air that tried to clash with it was something of a feat. And getting three wild girls to slow down proved to be a constant task for my parents. But as for tea, the southern market was ripe, and my father would not take a no from that soil. He gave up saying no to us. He was so much better at saying yes," she said with a wily grin. "My mother dealt with us by saying our roads had already been paved, our futures known to her at our births. I explained some of that to you in my room. Sage said that just as religion spoils its prodigy with free tickets to both sin and forgiveness, so does wealth. We would find our licks in due time," she forewarned.

Virginia paused and took hold of the wooden chair arms to adjust her body.

"Now, tell me about these articles," Lily said, patting the old brown satchel.

"Patience my beautiful child." Virginia leaned to pick up her glass. She took a long swig, moaned with pleasure, and continued. "We had our youthful larks. Those blossomed into a big dose of sexuality. That is probably what you are here to know," she added and winked. Virginia took in Lily; whose face extolled her awe at the possibilities going forward.

"Story one. We were all lined up as teens. It was at an all-girl party to celebrate my fourteenth birthday. I remember I was in a crisp white party dress. Oh, Lily, that was a day. I think the big gates really opened then. I had cut the cake. Minutes later, on an urge that is not meant to be explained, I ran through the sprinkler and disrobed down to just my panties, urging my sisters and friends to join me. Sarah, yes, the prude of today, and two other girls rushed out under the arch of water and stripped down. Bev grabbed a boy of twelve and dragged him over, prying his fingers off his covered eyes. Bev teased him that he peed himself, but I think it was the sprinkler. The scene made for awkward minutes for the parents hanging around for festivities that never included them. My father just then was leading a pony from the barn—my birthday gift. I danced so hard, Lily, I fell, pulling down my best friend into the slick grass beside me."

"Too bad there were no cameras back then," Lily expressed, wriggling on her butt.

"There were, silly, but no need, as that day is etched in all minds," she said and slapped her knee. "One minute, I was as precise and poised as a ballerina, the next, a stormy bohemian in a maypole dance. My father was one of only two men there and was quite embarrassed with his teen daughters and their friends naked in his yard. My mother, while drying us off, consoled him as he stood holding a horse blanket to shield the guests from our huddled bodies. She had such a way with him. I will paraphrase her calm words to him that day to the best of my ability." Virginia pulled herself up.

"Our daughters are thoroughbreds, Winfield. That kind wins not so strictly by muscle and training, but by a blind perception that there is nothing else on the track in the way. That there are no judges. There is just no other way to win but to have the rest of the world behind you. Your daughters have that kind of confidence. That said, Sage let us finish drying off ourselves, went around the blanket, and kissed my father so long and firmly that all others about dispersed. 'Today, we have witnessed what we knew was coming,' Sage said, releasing him."

"Boy, I didn't get that kind of confidence," Lily said, and yelped.

Virginia cleared her throat. "Well, we had a lesson coming. Sage, gripping Sarah and I by our bony shoulders said, 'Sound judgment must live hand in hand with erring. They are never in contradiction when in balance.'"

"Wow," Lily responded, then asked, "Where was Bev?"

"She had corralled herself within her girlfriends. She got hers later, but from my father, which was not so full of wisdom as it was a sting she talked about for days. So, let's get down to these articles. Oh, those were wonderful times. We were pretty, charismatic, devilish, and insatiable in experimenting with the platter set before us—off to the races, to use Sage's analogy. All our individual talents were used for the benefit of the unit. What began as mischievousness aged into sophistication. The playground got bigger. Boys became men. Sage filled us with her positive spirit, confidence, and the clothing to make us sharp. I found I had imagination. Start at the wild edges, because the middle is mediocre, was what I always said," Virginia added.

Lily snickered and Virginia reached sideways and tussled up her hair.

"It was a consequence of having power over men that I began to call myself an author. I was no good at turning back those men. But I always called the shots," she said.

"Virginia Hooper, you make me blush."

"Hummpphh," Virginia responded. "My mother was my coauthor in spirit in my decision to write. She furrowed the path, planted the seed, and watched it grow after I sent in my first piece of writing to the local paper. With a nudge from my mother to the editor, it was printed. They had struck a deal. The paper needed some pizzazz. The deal was that my words, even as they were not, must appear as fiction. And so, while most others in high school were in doubt or in peril, I forged ahead with glee and contentment. I had an eye and smell for the irregular, for the scandals, and for the chemical that jettisoned the blood of a small, rural community. Once a month, my voice was to be heard in the thin local paper."

Lily, with keen eyes, nudged closer.

"What I exposed I did for the betterment of society. It can't be all fun. We must have social missions," she said, then watched Lily furrow her brows in doubt. "In the early stages, I was careful, only exposing low-end culprits, nameless drifters, or town riff-raff. I made these characters generic and unverifiable, as promised. My mother and I understood the real ticket was coming. I was practicing for a big fish. I had told no one that I had one such on the hook. Yes, my dear, I was closing in on flesh of a bigger sort. Under my pen, my fame and another's suffering were interchangeable parts. Still, I remained pure to the cause to better our environs by clearing the scraps off the table, if you know what I mean," she said.

"You should be ashamed," Lily joked.

"As the townspeople clung to my stories, I was spurred on. Every paper in town vanished from the two stores that sold them. This warfare of sorts stirred my primitive desires and opened my literary eye. My writing became confident and playful. You know, Lily, those vermin could fall off the blade of my articles anytime by being better men."

"Were there that many in such a small town to keep you busy?" Lily asked.

"As many as sweet onions, only these were spoiled," Virginia answered, and Lily spidered her body around to face her granny straight on.

"By my fourth article, I began to describe the profile of the swarthy man I had in mind from the start. In weekly installments, I wrote of a man who had his way with a whole town. He had all believing that his charisma had only one side, as a gift to lift their spirits. 'On first impression, like butter on a pancake,' I wrote. That surely spurred my readers to look around them. I suggested that our man had always marked the ones he intended to take. He was like a predator. His prey was the beautiful, or anyone with something shiny to offer, or none of that at all, because he got pleasure out of the hunt and the kill. Things as small as a good deal on a car, an extra helping of pie at the Lickity Skillet, or a stiffer drink at the bar." Virginia paused. Her mouth grew hard. "Or a girl to conquer and leave stripped and scared," she murmured, looking out across the river.

Virginia drew a breath and continued. "Yes, as if he were a caricature of many, I drew a picture of a man whose charm had gone too far. Whose ego made him think himself invincible. My readers were fascinated. I was narrowing down on the one. Being abstract is good, my mother said, but let's hint a little more with Sam Green in the next one," she told me.

"Whoeee," Lily squealed, sticking her hands under thighs and rocking back and forth.

"A doll without eyes. That is how my next barnburner story began. That was some spooky imagery. Down the way, every woman ever snookered by Sam Green would repeat that. He had that look, his eyes so still, so blue, and deep—by practice, pretending to be so misunderstood. One just wanted to soothe him, to find what smoldered in such a handsome desperado. 'Smoked away by the devil,' I said of those two eyes."

"Get 'em, Granny," Lily said, punching the air with her fist.

"I knew this might be my last article. I was breaking the rules. Sage reminded me that justice held the oars. 'The roach is underfoot,' she said. Soon, I would put this man on the scales of judgment, even as I would never mention him by name. My readers were hot to measure and casket our villain. I considered that some, his victims mainly, must have figured out his identity. They remained silent, but surely hope stirred them. Sam held them paralyzed through blackmail, gifts, fear, and his infectious charm. Bastard." Virginia sat up, her blue eyes firing.

"'Like a bad dog under a porch, sometimes it needs love, at other times, a good scolding.' That's how I began the next one. 'A beast of God has bitten some and fooled others.' Lily, in the end, I honestly don't think Sam Green felt the pressure mounting against him. Around that time, I had run into him and saw nothing in his eyes but the surface of a muddy pond."

"I remember this part," Lily blurted. She blushed for having skimmed the articles. "'The rest of our man is by now under ten feet of dirty water,' I think you said. I liked that. I only read a little bit, wanted to hear the rest from the author, my very own grandmother—wow." She grabbed the satchel and dug through it until she came across the old sheets of paper. Pulling the article out, she handed it to Virginia, who pinched it between her excited fingers.

"'Clark Gable eyes, the wild hairstyle of a rakish man,'" Virginia read.

"Granny, that's cool stuff. 'With a greased curl hanging over his right eye, he tried to hide his measure.' Boy, they had to know who he was then."

"Yes," Virginia said, and held the article closer. "'The shadow of porches cannot hide him any longer. Those vines of glorious hair, like the lids over septic fields are there to cover filth. When he slithers rather than walks away from town, knowing he is out of language, do not offer him comfort.' That was fun stuff. He had messed with a Hooper, Lily," she added.

"My, oh my," Lily said, and shook her head. "You had that scoundrel pinned down."

"Yes, I stuck those words into his mouth like a lollipop. Into that of a child after his first buzz cut, for the world to see," she said with pride.

"We have that snake tied in a knot," Lily called out. "Okay, what the hell did Sam Green do to you?"

Virginia perked up. "My attraction for him began as a lark. I had my eyes set upon a purebred horse I knew my daddy would never buy for me at the price. But a conquest, at that age, is a battle to enjoy. Sam Green, four years prior, was my seventh-grade math teacher, and he was the owner of many fine horses. Sam was twelve years my senior. My error was remembering him as a pushover as a teacher. I did not comprehend that his guidance to the right test answers, his fatherly hand on the small of my back, was a sort of mentoring for a perfect opportunity down the road when I became legal. Well, you know what I mean."

"Whoa, Granny," Lily said, and shook her head.

"As for the horse, I needed to move him along into a better deal," Virginia said, and blushed. "I went to his farm. I had dressed to eliminate any guessing and to incite the man's bargaining in my favor. That's just what we did back then. A bit of swaying outside the training ring, as the foreman ran the horse through several routines, got Sam's attention. As I leaned into the rails, stretching out to view the graceful dance of 'my horse,' Mr. Green stood in dream behind. Lily Hooper, if you are, by that look on your face, thinking I was leading him on, you are correct. The unwritten rule at that age was that girls could practice, where grown men must restrain themselves from anything outside of admiration and polite comment."

"Yes, we should be able to flirt without worry, but you girls..."

"Well, I had not heard but a few rumors about him. Stuff that in a small town could be just boredom or viciousness. He had, after all, been my teacher. I did not listen to my brain hissing. My desire for that horse got the best of me."

"I will try to not let that sway my opinion of you," Lily said, and smiled.

"So, by whose insistence, his or mine, I cannot recall, I snuck out and met Sam Green early the next evening in the forest near my home. We smoked, drank bourbon, and kissed a little on a blanket thrown out on pine needles. Things were getting hot. I thought that because of my age, he would respect limits. I wriggled away and straightened my dress. You know, to show him that we had played and that I was flattered, but not committed."

With a hand, Lily lifted the hem of her shirt and fanned it over her belly. "My lord keep it coming, Granny," she said, and Virginia covered her grinning mouth.

"As he fumbled to regain his wits, I began talking about the horse. He started to paw at me again. Inexperienced when things were not in my control and feeling a flash of panic, I let slip a couple of innuendos about what I had heard about him. You know, asking sweetly if he was a cad and should I be careful. My knowledge was not well-suited for this man. He smiled devilishly, pinched the sharp curl of hair shrouding his eye and swept it back. I was afraid, though I let him kiss me again. His mouth dropped to below my neck and his hand went to my thigh. I tried to twist away."

Lily looked at the faces of Marcel and Jessie standing out like hot reflections. "I put him on his side in the grass, Lily. But he looked back more bedeviled than before. Like I was about to fail the test, and there would be no more free answers. That he was going to spank me. I had not considered that Sam Green might not succumb to my plot that evening. Angry, I spit out more of what I had heard. Yet here was a man who knew no caution, saw no future but the one a second away. I knew I was in danger. He rolled up his sleeves, exposing his strong arms."

Lily chewed her lip as Virginia continued. "I was young and stupid. Don't ever be that stupid, Lily. Sam Green locked on me, chin up, eyes down. His sweaty head was like the slick cone of a missile. His wantonness, and confidence in that, was all I saw. I had assumed that the allure of my sun-tanned body was a way to get a horse. Here was a man who would just keep moving. He was used to the fact that any incident here would be bogged down, redefining itself as a rumor. He had, after all, not dragged me there. Suddenly, it was a larger world than I had ever imagined. Knew this, as he rose to his knees and looked down at me. His hand was on his buckle, his eyes perched on the frozen vulnerable glow of my body. The glean in his unhidden eye telling me that he never lost."

Lily waved a hand for her to continue. "Sam Green seemed to relish his effect on me. Then his arms moved in like tentacles. His hands pulled at me, ripping off my dress. Rising, he carried off my clothing. With his lighter, and gas from a can in his car, he burned my dress as I watched, frantic and hiding behind my thin arms. My mind bounced about in stories I had read: 'She was a fine girl, but no one knows where she is.' Sam Green laughed, telling me that I was but a child, and he was not that kind of criminal. He made me walk home, following the settling dust of his horse and buggy in the dark."

"Oh Granny, I am sorry."

"My sisters rescued me, bringing a dress to the barn after I pelted their windows with stones. My mother saw Bev leaving with the clothing and followed. I sat on a stool in panties and bra, sobbing to Sarah. The sharp and herbaceous smell of freshly cut tea leaves filled the structure. But all my mother smelled upon coming in was my fear. Like I might have been dishonored. Her gaze searched mine for how far things had gone. While continuing to sob, I summarized my predicament. Sage knew the allure of the dress I had worn in my bid for a horse. She knew the infamous area of forest where I had walked without coercion to meet Sam Green. For decades, that wood and meadow had been a lair to both sexes for meeting in secret. I shook my head to tell her that I had not been raped. My mother knew she must keep the news from my father, as he might quite literally kill Sam Green."

Lily scoured her granny's face, as she was quivering and digging her toes into the grass.

"As I dressed," she continued, "Sage paced the hot barn, spoke to the long row of stalled horses as if they would tell her what to do. It was a dilemma. Her daughter's dignity had been spoiled. Sam Green must suffer in a bigger way than he could being dead. And so, with that in mind, a career in journalism spun off the wheel. If only we had a crystal ball to see the gravity of our future."

Just then, Dar called out from the house. Dinner was ready. "We can finish all this nonsense later," Virginia said, allowing Lily to help her up. "Let's just say that Sam Green left town by whatever energy he could muster. Truth had gotten the best of another man."

36

Beauty and Dead Eyes

Lily came into Virginia's room at bedtime. She lay propped up and reading a magazine. "Now Malcolm Squibb," Lily said, dragging the vanity chair to Virginia's bedside. In her hand, she held a picture of Malcolm torn out of a yellowing newspaper. His name was below, yet no article was attached. He was smiling, but his eyes had been penned and torn out with X's.

"Where's your news story about this guy? And what's with the dead eyes?"

"There is no story. The paper dumped me because of the Sam Green piece. Can you believe it? Even though the editor sold a ton of papers from that. He said that tying someone to the tracks just because he was a cad was not journalism. I had broken our deal. He would not accept my argument for continuing. Everything in town here is real, I said. There is no fiction. There are no misconceptions in what you see or hear, no accidents, and even faith is about believing in all possibilities. Spells exist. People dead or alive can walk through walls. Alligators can talk at night. That editor looked at me like I'd gone mad. Sam, I argued, believed in only his lust and con jobs. I reasoned that a man as that, banging his own selfish pattern into everything, must be entombed in ink. The editor did not buy any of that, poor soul. He was from Philadelphia. Anyway, that picture was taken after Malcolm was awarded a grocer's association award. Bev tore it out a week after they met. Pinned it to her bulletin board. Later, when things went awry, she took his eyes out, but left it up. I took it down as bad juju."

The idea of man's eyes being dug out in the safety of a picture sent Lily's mind racing.

"Bev, as you know, spent an inordinate amount of energy getting the attention of men. And it was not just praise Bev wanted. She had an affinity for tantalizing...to watch men and boys squirm. She said once that provocation was like holding a worm over a fish in a starving pond, never letting it in and pulling away as they jumped. Bev thought it a simple courtesy for men to notice her. And so, she played. Bev was a performer. Once she had them squirming, Bev would lift away with a sway that shaded even the Negroes working in the rows of tea bush."

"This is getting better than anything I could imagine," Lily said. "Criminy."

"It gets better and, in the end, much worse. Bev's sexuality evolved, becoming extreme and hyper. Her body evolved like magic. And she developed the cunning of a spider. I think the Malcolm Squib fiasco never fazed her. It began when she was given more responsibility in the family tea business. She was seventeen. Bev hated bush-trimming time and was useless. Sarah and I did not mind." Virginia laughed. "Our father said we were slower than two creeks of dry mud. Sarah and I took trimming time to plan for the coming months. On the back rows, we gossiped over the past and of days that had not even begun. In snake boots, bathing suit bottoms, and lathered in oil, we formed imaginary alliances and pondered the wills of boys."

"Wow, that sounds like the stuff of dreams," Lily said, frowning and slapping the bed. "I want to live on the plantation and do all this stuff."

Virginia shook her head and sighed. "No. You go there and live your way." She then continued. "Well, Bev turned herself into an apprentice at negotiating and expediting new avenues for marketing tea. She had shown some aptitude for creating product image. She changed their label and proposed planting the up and coming foreign teas, and even perhaps mixing in dried fruits in some. Orange, lemon peels, or ginger. Our father knew the transition would take time for new varieties to be planted and for the southern public to take on something with fruit they could not chew, but he was proud of Bev."

Virginia yawned. "Our father trusted only himself with the existing accounts. He feared the possibility that Bev's high style flirtations might hijack his business. Bev had just begun to 'roll,' as she liked to say, when Malcolm Squibb, one of our best tea brokers, showed up unexpectedly to the converted tobacco barn, turned into Bev's office."

"Father had gone across to Macon to preview a piece of equipment. Malcolm was one of those in the existing account category, our father's explicit territory. Bev and Malcolm had met before. She thought him, though attractive and youthful for an age of twenty-six, as always surly and inattentive to her. All business. Which to her was inexplicable. A dire future looked at him that day. Malcolm, in Bev's hands, might as well have come in, reached in his pocket, and just rolled dice across the pine floor. He might have read them and kept on moving to the other side of the room and out the side door. That might have saved him."

"Man, oh man, is this guy in trouble," Lily said, and leaned closer. Virginia tried to smile.

"Malcolm had been surprised to see Bev behind the oak desk. She was filing her nails and had her legs draped lazily over a drawer she had pulled out. She wore green, she told us, bragging of how well that color works on her. Malcolm, she said, bit that worm and hook and didn't care where it took him. In fact, Bev told us things I should not repeat to my sweet Lily."

"Virginia Hooper, don't you dare leave me at the bottom of that well."

Virginia grinned, and wriggled her toes under the covers. "Well, Bev drank him in, as he did her. He stood there imagining Bev, in almost certain impropriety, I am sure. I get the sense that minutes passed in playful banter and flirtation. Aroused, Malcom guided himself down into the chair across the desk." Virginia paused, as Lily was blushing and looking down. "Do not tell your mother I shared that raunchy detail."

"You know I will," Lily confirmed, but still would not look at her granny.

Virginia continued. "Bev knew she had the upper hand, but at that point it was just for pleasure. He was, she later told us with tremendous joy, 'a butterfly, alive and pinned by the wings.' Bev then began to play coquettish, scribbling a note on a pad of his visit for her father, even saying she could not help him, as she was with new accounts only."

Virginia shook her head. "At that point, Malcolm mentioned an expansion of an existing account. Thus, in a manner, making it new to Bev. One of the smaller South Georgia grocery chains he dealt with, he informed her, was attempting to merge with a larger Alabama concern. Bev calculated that to mean a financial boon was in the making for the man standing before her. He placed a finger to his lips, pantomiming the secrecy of what he was telling her."

"'My business will explode,' he said, 'If my client, Peter Lund, has his way with this merger.' The mention of that name caused Bev to drop her pen. Peter Lund's son, Luther, was Malcolm's friend and inside track to making him the preferred broker for this new mega chain. The fact was that Luther, a dashing twenty-three-year-old, had devoured Bev in passion and deceit one year before. She had sought revenge since. Luther had toyed with Bev over a period of two weekends to the point that she almost believed the years between their ages had no bearing. She imagined herself in the Lund plantation near Mobile. As it turned out, Luther seduced Bev just to get hold of—to steal, by the amount he paid—a valuable stud horse left to her by a business relation of our father. Luther described the transaction as a rental and said he would return the stud once the animal had performed his requirements."

Awed, Lily slumped forward then back up. "Good golly, Miss Molly. What is it with you all and horses?"

"Well, Luther by then had plied Bev with images of their weeks of dalliances spanning years. Bev should have known she was on a slippery cliff. Whatever paper Bev signed," Virginia said, propping herself up, "she had done so without our father's consideration. Bev was left with a very thin envelope of cash. Well, by means of rumor, the incident reached Winfield's ears. Bev had portended of course that it had been a sharp transaction on her part. Lied that the fee was to quadruple if the stud did his work. Of course, none of that ever came to pass, as you will hear. Luther, as you can imagine, kept the horse. The paper she had, in love's delirium, signed, was a sales transaction."

"Is this for real? My life is plain Cheerios," Lily moaned.

"Now, back to that room with Malcolm Squibb. Remember, the name Lund was right before her. The opportunity for retribution seized her. Malcolm, she said, had been delivered to her by her guardian angel." Virginia paused, and grinned. Lily nodded for her to keep going.

"Well, Bev went to the other side of the desk and wordlessly smoldered over Malcolm. He sprang up like a child and Bev allowed him to have a smidge of his way with her. You know, letting him kiss her and then her enticing him that of course there was more."

"No, I really don't know," Lily answered. "But, whew, is this juicy!"

"Bev," Virginia said, "was determined to sabotage the Lund merger. She knew she would need Malcolm to reach this goal. Bev ended the meeting and said she would pass the news on to her father, which of course she did not. This was tricky business, Lily. We told Bev she was out of her league and that someone might get hurt. She looked at us as if we had four heads. Said she had trouble feeling sympathy for a man so directed by his weaker emotions as Malcolm had been in her office. 'And besides, it's Luther that's going to lose.' Well, I wish we could have changed things then and there. Maybe told our father, but we were in a contract to always believe and protect. What a foolish deal."

"I'll say," Lily agreed, thinking to know how this ended.

"Bev had a plan," Virginia continued. "The next week, she made sure to bump into one of our father's good friends outside the liquor store he frequented every Friday after work. A judge with far-reaching influence. When he saw her eyes rimmed in red, his sympathy was immediate. Bev had spent five minutes pressing her knuckles into her eye sockets."

Lily stood up and paced. She said nothing. Just listened.

"I will try to tell you just like Bev told us what occurred in that meeting," Virginia said. "'Bev Hooper,' he said, 'You are looking every day more like your mother,' Judge Winthrop hugged her. Releasing her, Bev made no attempt to hide her sullen face."

"'The fact is, Judge Winthrop, I came here to see you,' Bev began. She told him our father did not know she was there because of the very personal nature of the subject. Bev said all needed to be under the strictest confidence. Not in the middle of the sidewalk. 'I know you law men know all about that,' Bev told us she said to him. You all right with all this, Lily?"

"It's fine, Granny," Lily urged, her adrenaline racing.

"'We could go sit in my car, but I am not sure how that would look,' the judge said. Bev, at first, pretended to agree, but then said she would just duck down if need be. With a brown bag of liquor tucked under one arm, Judge Winthrop led Bev to the passenger side of his Lincoln. She slid in. Her desire to take down an unscrupulous man overrode any need for integrity."

"Bev worked her tale. Tears left her, calmed by the judge's soothing words and handkerchief. She told him she was seduced a year prior by a man from Alabama. The judge hated Alabama. Bev had overheard him at a party at the plantation, saying there were more crooks in Alabama than the rest of the country combined. Alabama, he said, relied on deceit to make an already slender economy work. She overheard that same night the judge's hatred was because a court in Alabama had found his son guilty of money laundering through a few churches he had formed. I must admit, Lily, she is shrewd. When the judge asked Bev who started what, she acted confused. 'I'm just a teen, Judge Winthrop,' she said."

"I need my water. I'm parched," Virginia said, reached for her glass on the bedside table and drank. Still holding the glass, she continued. "Bev told the judge the man's name was Luther Lund and added that he had seduced her to sign away her stud horse forever. She thought he was just borrowing it for a little money in exchange. The judge said he knew Luther's father, Peter. Said he was an unscrupulous businessman.

Judge Winthrop then asked why Bev had waited so long to come forward with this, or at least why she had not told her father about the seduction. 'He was just so mad about the horse, and I wasn't pregnant or anything. What if Daddy had killed him? That would have been the end of everything.' Bev loved telling us that part."

"The judge said he supposed she was right, but again asked her why now bring this up. Bev told him she was tired of living with the memory of that night. 'My friends go out, and I stay home, because boys just scare me. Things just need ironing out so I can be free again. Do you just think you could give him a good talking to? Scare him into thinking he can't treat girls that way. I will admit that I did consent a little to what he did, but that does not make it right. I do not want to press charges,' she told him. The judge smoothed back Bev's damp hair until she stopped weeping. This all makes me sick, Lily. Bev leaned against the door and in an offhand manner mentioned the proposed merger of stores."

"What a sinister bitch," Lily said, and apologized. Virginia waved it away.

"When the judge smacked the dashboard over this news, Bev repeated she did not want anyone to go to jail, prayed he saw the opportunity to handle this in a different manner. Bev could see he was ruminating on an idea. The horse, he told her, was also a big matter. They used to hang horse thieves. Music to Bev's ears, as the horse was what she wanted. He told Bev he would have a hard time going after Lund for their tryst. Though it was improper, it would appear consensual. Bev agreed that was understandable. When Bev added the Squibb name to the mix, the judge turned a happy eye to her. Malcolm's family had been a public embarrassment for many years, he said. The judge said he would deal with the matter. 'An Alabama company owning part of Georgia, well that is why God made me a judge, and that Lund and Malcolm boy are weak sons of a bitches,'" Virginia quoted, using the deepest voice she could muster.

Lily rolled back laughing.

"Two weeks later, Bev heard the merger might be off. Judge Winthrop, it seems, had used his influence to convince the lawyers overseeing the merger of the poor business practices of that Alabama company. This was bolstered by a crisscross of other paperwork mentioning questionable money transfers to overseas accounts and other shady business."

"Wow, this is the kind of stuff I always knew was out there, but hiding," Lily said.

"Judge Winthrop reinforced to Luther and Malcolm that any criminal findings past or present would amount to jail. He even mentioned knowing about illegal migrants working in the Alabama stores, and hinted at either Malcolm or Luther being involved in the seduction of a teenager. He advised that if Bev's family received the horse and three times its value in money, a year's grain and hay, plus a substantial legal fee to be delivered to him, then he might reconsider his influence on the matter and let the merger go through. The same week, Bev's horse was returned by a tiny underage girl driving a Chevrolet truck and trailer. The girl handed Bev a thick yellow envelope. The judge backed out of condoning the merger."

"Holy moly, does this kind of thing still go on?" Lily asked.

"Right under your nose," Virginia said, and then turned her head down to continue. "The judge was not finished. Peter Lund was apprised that the failure had something to do with his son, Luther. That Luther and Malcolm were stacking the odds in their favor to usurp their own families and had planned to control the merged companies themselves. Luther was pushed down the corporate ladder by the huge angry paws of his father and told to stay there until he was smarter. Malcolm went down with him and had to start from dirt up. Three weeks after Bev got her horse back, Malcolm was drinking in a new bar called The Bacchanalia. He drove off and hit a tree at one hundred miles an hour." Virginia crossed her hands over her stomach under the pink sheets.

Awed, Lily spoke. "A kind of innocent man died."

"A sad state of affairs," Virginia answered.

"So, in a way, Bev killed him? That's the big secret around here?" Lily asked.

"No—well, yes, in a manner. Sarah and I shared the truth with Sage," Virginia said, changing the subject. "'There will be a good man to take that bad man's place,' Sage affirmed. That cold statement haunted us, and as life goes on, I wonder if she had not been wrong for the first time in her life."

"What about Bev?" Lily asked. "Will she be sorted out?"

"What about any of us?" Virginia asked. "Now, goodnight, my sweet girl. You will save and replace us all."

Lily turned off the lamp and left, her mind spinning.

37

Threads to Darkness

When Lily could not find her mother in her room nor in the darkened house, she took a stab at the great outdoors. The night was hot and sticky, a tepid breeze rustling the oaks. Dar lay half-dozing on the porch in the dark. She had changed into her white nightdress. Her hands were placed over her slim belly, her red hair balled up under her head. The moon illuminated her, turning her skin a milky blue. She might have been dead but was just sleepy drunk.

Lily stood over her and began sputtering about articles, men dying, and naked teens under fountains. When Dar mumbled and fell back asleep, Lily announced she was ready to spice her life up with a man. Dar flinched and looking up tried to gather in the disjointed mouth moving above her. She breathed back wakefulness and Lily's provoking comment. Dar leaned up on an elbow, wiped her mouth, and began calculating how to attend to her daughter's loquacious state of mind. Nocturnal and hunting, Lily would be a handful.

"Did you know a man died? And not the guy Bev wanted?" Lily asked.

"It's not like anything should surprise you by now," Dar answered, and patted the deck beside her. Lily sat in one fluid motion.

"Yes, I knew a little about Malcolm and company. Lily, honey, as for that death, you are just worked up over images. No one wanted anyone to die. Not even Bev. Malcolm drove himself into that tree. Either of those two involved would have done Bev harm, did in fact. Horse stealing, playing house with a teenager. They were taking their chances with Bev."

Exasperated, Lily sighed. "There are just way too many secrets around here. Traitor."

Dar sat up and picked up her glass off the deck. She was about to drink when Lily pointed at the bug swimming circles in the wine. Dar frowned, stuck a finger in the glass and slid the bug up to the rim, where she flicked it off. "Good as gold," she said, and drank. "Forgiven?"

"Maybe," Lily mouthed.

"All I know is we're lucky Bev is a weaker version of herself now," Dar said.

"I don't believe that for a second." Lily responded.

Dar nodded. "It's a blessing Virginia turned out so well. Sarah speaks for herself. You know, she brought wounded birds home from the marsh and beach back then. Guess that's where her good side got its start." Dar paused. "But there was a weird side to her, when you gotta ask where compassion meets darkness. We are talking about drowning kittens, because that really did happen. Sarah found six of them in the barn. Took them to the ocean in a burlap bag and tossed them in. Seems kind of strange bringing dying birds back from the ocean to save and returning with cats to kill." Dar looked sallow. "Yes, dammit. To rid them from an overpopulated world. She was only sixteen."

Lily's mouth went slack. "And I thought clowns were an image to haunt me for the rest of my life. No one sane does that," Lily said, shaking her head. "Those poor kitties."

Dar reached and patted Lily's shoulder. "On a happy note, never told you Sarah owned a peacock. Paraded it on a leash when her friends were there, or when Sage and Winfield had a party. Standing in her elegant dress and holding that crying bird, Virginia told me she would sidle up to just about anybody and talk for an hour. Virginia claims she was long-winded and engaging to the point of being hypnotic. She was a library of facts. Evocative and charming." Dar squinted. "Really hard as the dickens to imagine her being the brightest thing in the room. Where'd that go?"

"What about men?" Lily asked.

"I heard boys really liked her. But Sarah stifled them, because all she talked about was a world beyond their minds' capabilities. She was just so lovely, they hung about and listened. I believe you have some of her in your genes."

Lily frowned back and Dar chuckled. "Example. Sarah, on a lark, began to give advice to her friends whether it was wanted or not, and charge for it. You'd have done that. A nickel for simple guidance, a quarter when it involved her girlfriend's crushes. She claimed to have read all about the history of love in Greek lore, so was an expert. Sound like you? When Sarah's jar was full, she stopped. Donated the coins to an old man who came around selling brooms."

"Amateur," Lily said. "So, what made Sarah change? When did she start drugging herself?"

"Well, there are many levels to that answer, but Sarah started using substances beyond booze...as I am not letting that count...when a man left her two weeks before their wedding. That beau had been figuring on getting his feet set onto the plantation, but then realized he would have to go through her sisters to get anything. Tortured to find her identity, Sarah next attempted to marry someone whom she deemed to be a universal man. A minister. He was universal until it came to accepting Sarah's firm views of an evolutionary world. His sights were narrower. He left Sarah on the altar of his own church. Isn't that ironic? In her purse, she found more pills."

"No wonder she seems so frigid. That woman has been jilted."

"Frigid, she is. It's a good thing Sarah had warmed her hands by so many fires when she was young. She had a bit of sugar in her for men who could speak her language. Virginia said she was conspicuously loose for a few short years." Lily's gaze went wild.

"Sarah gave up drugs when she began her charity work. Then, she suddenly jumped back into paregoric about a decade ago. Virginia said it was to get her thorough the memory of seeing Bobby's body drowned in the bathtub. Sarah had come over to check on him, as he had been ill for several months, and found him dead. A heart attack, as you are aware. Virginia had gone to the plantation for a couple days. I believe you might recall...or not...that drug. I gave it to you a couple of times for a cold when you couldn't sleep. Uncle Sam took it off the market."

Lily nodded, recalling the milky substance Virginia had her drink the night of her rendezvous with a lover. "My God, Mother, how much did y'all stockpile?"

"Enough to stop every war between every friend."

"That's messy stuff," Lily said.

"You know, I think that Bobby's gruesome end was just a piece of it for Sarah. Fighting her demons over never having been loved was the real crux. Let's just get out of this reunion with bruises, Lily. Don't want to end up like Malcolm."

38

Sleight of Hand

The rain fell in tangents, grayish lines on the windowpanes, as Lily set down her book. "Everlasting" was the word that came to her mind, as she *felt* the fragrance of that romantic story's end. She looked down at *Wuthering Heights* feeling both tense and dreamy.

Out the window, she could see the sun peeking out through the clouds. She heard Mickey's muffled voice down in the yard, punctuated by a tapping noise, and knew he was setting up the yard for croquet. She smiled, proud that she and Mickey had discovered at least a corner of one another. An adversary had been traded for a friend. And slapping his sons had been like winning a trip around the world.

Lily's thoughts moved to her freshened bond with her granny. Any discomfort between them had been replaced with downright love. Lily looked down at her bedside table. There sat three little bottles with foggy magic inside. After last night's chat with her mother, Lily had crept to the door of Sarah's room. Thinking she could rescue Sarah and have her once again leading peacocks on a leash, she had creaked open the door. Sarah lay unconscious under a dome of drug euphoria. Night light painted the sheets. A limp arm fell over her eyes. Her mouth lay open and was skewed, her brow furrowed as if in consternation. That look told Lily she was doing the right thing. She shot about the room, finding one bottle in her purse and two more in her underwear drawer.

Feeling the squeeze of time left at River Oaks, she stashed Sarah's bottles in her drawer, and a minute later was pulling on the pink dress her mother had wanted her to wear. "The reunion is winding down, sweet pea," Dar had said, holding the clothing out the afternoon before. "It's for them, not you." Now pulling the dress half over her body, then off, Lily flung it on the floor. Spotting the long, sheer silk window curtains, she yelped. She managed to pull a set off the rod. The rest of her search involved sneaking into other rooms on different levels of the house. A half-hour later, she had become something between a gypsy and a lady of the moors.

Hocking up her attire, she took a dive down the stairs, grinning. Hearing the voices below, she had a sense of entering a long boulevard. The final parade gathering. In head wrap, layers of silk, earrings, necklaces, silver bracelets, and a make-do ink tattoo of a lily on the side of her neck, the hardest to achieve by all measure, she hit the pine floors flat-footed. Swaying and enjoying the swish of fabric, she just avoided slipping on marbles spilled on the living room carpet. She thought of the danger for her grandmother and aunts crossing and of the pitiable aptitude of her male cousins. Lily was lamenting Marcel's name aloud as she stepped onto the black-and-white checkered floor of the kitchen.

Dar greeted Lily with a burst of laughter. She came over and hugged her with a gentle tug on the hair coming from out under the headscarf. Lily smelled the natural perfume of her mother's vacationing, her head damp from the river. It was Saturday, and that made the fragrance special. The final second to a tale they had so far survived.

Behind Dar, there was a hum, murmuring, and a single gasp. Lily whispered to Dar about the marbles. Dar grimaced and swung through the door to clean up.

The others spoke in soft voices, introducing awkward, yet cheerful "good mornings" to Lily. Whatever, this was a good start. Or end, she thought, then smiled with a little melancholy nestled in her chest. Yes, this week's ballyhoo was coming to an end. Lily looked past them all. The back door was open. There, a sheen of blinding white sunlight struck the deck and wet lawn. There were thick towers of clouds to the east and something darker brooding behind.

"You know a place is special when you're happy with any kind of weather," Lily said.

"You look fun," Bev announced, her tone sounding bewildered. Virginia said she looked rested and lovely.

Mickey smiled, his eyes bright and sure. "You look fabulous," he announced. Bev swung about, eyeing her son. Lily and Mickey, thick with one another, was too much for her.

"I'm celebrating," Lily said, spinning for Mickey. "It's been such a great reunion." After a second turn, her gaze fell on Sarah. Lily wondered what her state would be when discovering that her drug was missing. Sarah's stance was akin to one on a tightrope. Spread your arms for balance, she wanted to say. Sarah took a steady breath, her unmade face showing she could do this. She looked Lily straight on, her puffy gaze garnering pink light from the window.

"I like the outfit, Lily. Isn't that red sash from a curtain in my room? And my silver bracelets from Italy?" Sarah asked. She had spoken as if each word required thought. She then reached for her hot tea, her hand trembling.

"Yes ma'am, they are," Lily answered, jangling both wrists. "I hope you don't mind. I just got carried away, and they are so lovely. I have admired them."

"I think you are just so great, Lily," Sarah said, her tone certain.

"And my silver and turquoise necklace," Bev stammered. "What the..."

"*My* necklace," Virginia countered, "that you borrowed last year. What is that mark on your neck, Lily?" she then asked, shuffling forward in her fluffy white slippers.

"It is a lily. You, of course, know what it means." She winked and leaned to kiss Virginia's cheek. "The rest of me is gypsy. They are free...well, by their way of seeing. They are actually subjugated to encampments, eating squirrel and dumpster fishing...but what do you do?"

Dar returned, holding a silver bowl of marbles. Dar shook the bowl toward Mickey, then nodded for Lily to follow her out. In the living room, Dar swung about and opened her other hand. In it was a single vile of Sarah's paregoric.

"Went to your room to get a brooch to hold your head scarf better. It's too late, Lily. She needs her escape. Maybe she deserves it. She is lonely. You have me, Bo, and a new house. Besides," Dar said, "going cold turkey doesn't work with Hoopers, though I can't say I know that for sure, because I don't think anyone has tried. That vial is as addictive as sleep, Lily. I'll put them back. She wouldn't be able to just walk away."

Coming back to the kitchen, Lily adjusted her head covering. Reaching behind, she clipped her hair brooch to the scarf and pinched the fabric down to a point. Dar came back in. "Boy, I could sure use something to eat. Pancakes, eggs, bacon," Lily said. "Would that be all right, Mom, if it's not too late?"

"Never too late, hon," Dar said.

As Dar made pancake batter, Lily hung near her and took it all in. Except for the tap of Dar's right shoe, the kitchen was quiet. Bev was smiling and held her hands over a warm skillet of cooking bacon. Mickey rubbed his hands together, excited to get the day started. He smiled, reached in the refrigerator, and took out the orange juice. Even Sarah was beaming, motioning with jubilation as a hummingbird sipped upon the red nectar in the feeder outside the window. Virginia, the queen, was looking about as pleased as she could be, like she might exhale all worry. Just then, Bev turned to her and said she had a wonderful dream about them as kids. She took Virginia by the arm and retraced the dream, and within moments, they were tittering.

Lily knew her mother would tell her that this rare snapshot of contentment was "baked into the blood that binds us." She had said that last summer when the family had, by some unseen force, sat around the dining table and began playing rotating rounds of gin rummy. "In a sense, it's the same power that brings us all to these reunions. Even though it feels like obligation, Lily, it's so much more. I lost a dog once," she said. "A hundred miles away from the plantation. We looked but never found him. Somewhere beyond fifty creeks, rivers, swamps, and highways, that dog was lost. Beyond a million god-awful reasons to get hurt, shot, or find another home, Blue showed back up two weeks later. I don't call that a miracle. I call it the power of bound spirits." Lily liked the dog story but not her mother's addendum, saying that all families were the same. That to Lily seemed frightening if true. And incurable. Dar looked about and whispered sideways to Lily. "Like to put this in a box and lock it."

Beyond the door, the yard darkened and it began to pour. In seconds, a solid sheet of gray water spilled from the eaves and valleys of stories above. Mickey reached in his back pocket, took out a pack of cards, and smiling, shook the cards to Bev and then Sarah. All of them peeled off into the main body of the house. Lily ran out the back door into the rain.

Virginia looked out the window. "This is going to put a real shine on this morning once it clears," she said above the roar of earth-pounding water. She held out a carton of eggs for Dar who placed them on the counter and wrapped her arms around her mother.

"I wonder if whoever resides up there might acquit everyone in the rooms below him. And just start from scratch," Virginia said.

39

Back on the Front Lines

Dar had driven eight miles to the store for Lily's "beginner's kit," as she called the things they would need for Lily's period, which had begun while Lily danced in the rain. Lily had remained behind and secured herself next to Tish. One by one, the sisters drifted by to assess Lily's demure form. Their voices were low and funereal. It was an awkward parade of accolades, coddling, advice, and warnings of how much worse it was going to get.

Bev had told the boys of Lily's new development. Dar, in returning from the store was forewarned by Virginia to this. Hustling Lily to the bathroom, she left her leaning on the wall inside holding a paper bag filled with "goodies," as she called the contents. "Hold it there," Dar said and bolted out in search of Bev, who was standing on the deck admiring a ring on her finger. "Well, Bev, you have given napalm to the Viet Cong out there." Dar pointed to the yard, where Marcel and Jessie were sneaking along the hedge looking for God knows what. "If I must play their bad mother here today, I will. It will not be pretty. Never wanted boys, anyway."

During dinner, Marcel and Jessie, seeking compensation for Lily having slapped the bejesus out of them days before, began with their slurs. Mickey rushed over when he heard Marcel call Lily, "'Miss Cram a Tam." He twisted both their ears until their shrills filled the room. When Mickey let go, Jessie covered his hot ear and Dar was sure he shed some tears. "I did nothing," he whimpered. Marcel stiffened his lip and looked with hostility toward his father. "The army will take care of that attitude young man," Mickey said.

"Bless you, Mickey, for saving them from me," Dar called out.

The novelty of Lily's first period vanished quicker than she could have imagined. Late to the game compared to her peers, Lily had witnessed, as one by one those girls matured into this crossing. One classmate had described this marvel to Lily. "It is like your fun, bouncy self, hitting a waiting fan at high speed." Lily had the wisdom to think that an exaggeration. Most acted with repugnance toward this change, although some flashed it about as a cool club thing. Lily never liked those latter girls anyway. Tonight, Lily accepted her fate and that there was nothing cool about it. There was nothing but the fact that every month for days she would feel dirty, and according to Dar, irritable as a poked snake. The bathroom talk at school was now firmly proven in the court of her body on many levels. And all the eerie warnings she had heard over the years played in her head: That having a finger slammed in a car door was nothing in comparison to the misery she would feel, that dogs would follow her, that she would imagine every boy at school sneering, that she would become a solid bitch, and that her mother would ask her every day, "Are you hanging in there, honey?"

It was after dessert. The night became a little giddy for some, a little wistful for others, as the reunion was about over, and the horizon of their homes came into view. Mickey was thrilled with the thought of being with his wife soon, as he had mentioned her several times. The elderly sisters were playing by the bar. Dar, with her wrist cocked around a gin martini, leaned into Lily and said of that scene, "They act like fresh kittens who do not yet know they are related. If I were a kitten, I would be careful around the one called Bev." Lily and Dar howled over that. Being the final night, Dar was going all out and went to make another martini. "If we don't drink it here, it'll all end up in Bev's trunk," she said, coming back to the table.

"Gotta go to the bathroom," Lily said, frowning and rubbing her belly.

"Hang in there, honey," Dar said and watched Lily scowl.

As Lily walked by his chair, Marcel's two sly eyes looked up. He eyed his father, who was laughing with Virginia. He moved to speak out of the side of his mouth. Lily stuck a warning finger up before his face. "It's just blood. Some people drink it. Some die losing it."

As Lily returned from the bathroom, Bev was coming out of the kitchen with another bottle of bourbon and a hot kettle. "At least we are not out of booze. Now *that's* careful planning."

Lily got up and went to stand beside Virginia. "Granny, I've been thinking about Bigbee. Do you think she'll come back to visit you? You were, after all, a big part of her life."

Virginia's smile went cold, and she took a labored breath to answer. "Bigbee has gone on with her life, and that is what she deserves. So, let's move forward not backward. I have had to try do that." Softening her tone, she added, "Let's just leave Bigbee heroic."

Frustrated, Lily frowned.

"Things have changed, dearie," Virginia continued, stroking Lily's hand. "Soon to change even more," she added, taking in Bev across the room. "The Hooper resurrection needs a little push." Virginia rose and left. Lily stared, wondering what she meant.

Lily found Dar standing on the landing, toiling with a word in a crossword puzzle. Her mouth was twisted. Glancing over her shoulder, Lily noted the puzzle was, to say the least, dated. The newsprint around it was yellowed with age. "Pinstripe," Lily said, as Dar tapped the clue with a pencil. "Suit worn by contemporary men."

Dar looked back. "That's it, smarty pants. How did you know that?"

Lily smiled. "You know, since hearing all these great stories from Virginia, I have decided to write a book about this family. I'm gonna need a lot of help with that."

Dar tossed her pencil and puzzle back into the bureau drawer and shut it. "You know, Lily, persistence is not always a virtue. And, besides a lot of people read fiction."

"I can't fill a book with white lies." Lily's look was full of insinuation.

Dar laughed and patted Lily's arm. "Even God has had to lie." Lily stared back in awe at that. "Let's get back to fun. Your granny and what you have witnessed here through the years has given you enough to fill any book."

"I am going to have a farewell drink with Bev," Lily announced. "She's snookered enough to sing like a canary."

"Good luck there."

"Don't you hate a prude?" Bev slurred to Mickey, as Lily approached. Bev was disgruntled that Sarah had just been sipping tonight. "The last night, and my sister has a been a bore—kinda like a rented priest. The kind she wished she'd married."

Sarah heard, but smiled. Lily veered off to avoid the scene. Bev was drinking a hot toddy, a drink she liked to call a "shot to the brain." Seeing Sarah was ignoring her, Bev waggled her drink toward her. Venom spread through her eyes, and her mouth went rigid. Mickey put a hand on Bev's shoulder and said she'd had enough.

Bev held her head high, flashed her eyes at her son and laughed in his face. No more kittens by the bar, Dar mused, approaching and noting Bev's condition. Bev continued to laugh. The sheer noise of it brought Sarah to attention. She threw Bev a look of irritation.

"What a little Girl Scout you are today, dear sister," Bev said, and rolled back her shoulders.

Mickey snapped, "No more." Bev sputtered something back.

Lily cringed. Thinking of the rare goodness in the kitchen that morning, she looked to the floor. "Norman Rockwell has turned down our family portrait." Lily said to Dar, but she did not hear, as Bev was bellowing.

"Sarah is always confused. Waiting for her reasons for being born to come to light." Bev choked on a deep swallow of hot bourbon. Mickey reached and took the drink out of her hand. Bev eyed him with the most poisonous look Lily had ever seen.

From across the room, Virginia called out. "Sarah is the shadow that swims beneath us. That binds us. All muscle of kindness. Her patience with you is the only fault she has."

"That little drugged up carp is scared of her own shadow," Bev responded.

Mickey snapped his fingers at Marcel and Jessie, who were playing checkers. He nodded for them to head upstairs. They stood and looked to Tish, who he had not summoned to leave. "Just do what I say," Mickey mouthed. The boys dumped the checker pieces into shirts held out from their skinny bellies, grabbed the board, and went off mad. "Mother, we were having a decent day. Let's not ruin it." Mickey's voice was stern.

"Oh, just have another beer. Don't try to sound like you know what you're saying. No one's going to believe that," Bev said with a dismissive sneer.

Sarah threw up her arms and stormed off toward the stairs.

"Going to find your dreams?" Bev asked to her back. "They're in your purse."

"Mother, this is when I can honestly say I don't like you," Mickey said.

Bev glared. "Just trying to have a little fun with my sister. Y'all need to loosen up and see who brings life to this house."

On the other side of the table from Lily, Dar stepped forward. She could take no more. "Bev, you have been the bane of this reunion, always looking to place others in your tiny little dark courtroom—where the rules and laws are about as couth as flinging horse shit."

"This from a woman who would rather lie with a woman than her poor husband," Bev said, and smiled. "Guess that.... lack of.... was why he found sweeter flesh?"

Dar saw white. She was unable to grab back the words as they left her mouth. "This from a woman who closets herself. A woman, who took a tumble in a hayloft with a girl. I heard tell of how you moaned when she kissed you all over."

THE STEEP SIDE OF THE MARBLE

Virginia's cry filled the room. "No, Dar. Please, Bev, stop."

"Holy cow," Lily and Tish said at the same time.

Mickey grabbed the table and slumped. Bev's face went into freefall, her cheek rouge purpling, as she went back to an incident she had pushed away as belonging to someone else. Through the sludge of that, her two hot eyes latched onto Virginia. Bev could find no words.

"At last, you have nothing to say," Dar said.

"You whoring lesbian," Bev screeched. "Your husband found a better woman than you will ever be."

"After that girl tumble, you put a man into a tree at a hundred miles an hour," Dar said. "I am a lesbian. Not wicked like you. You have no conscience."

The sharp ring of steel pierced the room. Bev had reached onto the table and grabbed the butcher knife from the carving board. She shook the blade, threatening Dar. Mickey lunged out to grab her arm, but Lily was already there. As Lily reached from behind to take the knife, Bev started to cry, or scream, or maybe just catapult into insanity. She flung her arm down to her side and looked to the ceiling. "I have done the best I can to hold this family together," she screamed.

Coming down, the blade had slashed Lily's hand. As Bev saw the blood pouring off Lily's fingers, she dropped the knife, grabbed her chest and sat down hard on the chair next to her. "My heart—you bitch, look what you've made me do," Bev screamed to Dar.

"Dear God, what have you done?" Dar yelled, as Tish went to get a towel and Mickey grabbed the knife from the floor and stood over his mother like he might stab her.

Virginia came forward in slow motion, shaking. "That seals it, Bev Hooper," she said.

"How much does a girl have to bleed in one day?" Lily asked, dazed and falling back into a chair.

40

Home

With one last visit to the river, Dar tried to think of Chantelle. Nothing. Even as they were minutes from heading home, the image of her did not leave Dar in wonder or move her heart. That frightened her. Maybe the reunion had whittled her down to numbness, down to where not a single nerve ending stirred the juices of affection. Not even fondness from a distance, as they say. Dar left to finish packing the car.

The day was a scorcher. Dar, then Lily, stripped down to as little as possible for the hot drive. Upon leaving, Dar opened every window in the car. Backing out, her foot hit the pedal hard, spitting driveway sand. Soon they were eating up the straightaways of the steaming back roads. Her mother's face was about as chagrined as Lily had seen. The problem was that there were too many reasons to be miffed. After last night's grand finale, the good of the week would take time to struggle forward.

Heavy black clouds gathering in the west held off, but the front's wind ransacked every loose component of the car. The open ashtray was emptied, butts to the floor, ashes filling the air. The pages of Lily's diary chattered like they would tear. Ditch leaves swarmed over the car. A paper bag blew in, settled, and blew back out. In the rear seat, Lily was taking the brunt and wore a red and black bandana over her nose and mouth. At last the wind settled. Dar sighed. "What the hell. That's some kind of last word." Lily shrugged, having not heard a thing.

Dar looked at Lily's hair and then at her own in the mirror. "It'll take a week to comb this nest out," she yelled back. "If only for AC," she added, and concentrated on enjoying the lowland swamps to the right and left. She then hung her arm out the window, rapped the side of the car, and sneered at the world flashing by. Quarter-sized globules of rain began to splatter against the hood and windshield. In an instant, tepid water was blowing sideways into the car. Dar and Lily raced to crank the windows back up. The car was like a sauna, the roof over, a drum. Soon the rain passed, and the windows were back down. They drove on in relative silence. Lily was in her own world and singing just above a whisper.

Dar considered breaking into Lily's space but thought better. She might be dealing with her own measure of things, ragged cut hand, period, and all. Sighing, she thought back to the last minutes of the reunion. Bev had arranged her driver to leave at sunup and had not said goodbye. Sarah, after a hundred methods of apology, had promised for a better reunion next summer. Virginia had peddled herself to Dar as happy and forgave her for divulging Bev's secret to the family. Virginia had hugged the life out of Lily, or so Lily had joked. Mickey's clan left after Tish and Lily made sleepover plans. Mickey hugged Lily, saying, "Thank you for everything. Sorry about the hand." The other cousins wrestled each other into the car without declaring to anyone they had been anywhere for the past week they were thankful about.

Dar turned her confounded look back to Lily. She wished she would come up front with her. With whipping hair hung up on her lips, Lily called out. "We came. We conquered," she said, and pounded her chest.

There was purity in Lily's look that settled Dar's nerves. Her bright eyes like promises to a world of good. Dar sat up straight. She rolled up her window a bit. "You certainly scored some wins this week," she said. "With Mickey, and you and Tish like dogs in a park. And, my gosh, Virginia and you were like Indians sitting around a fire."

Lily had turned her head and cupped her hand to hear ear. "Tish, dogs, Indians, all good things," Lily said, piecing together the positivity of Dar's comment.

Dar shook her head, thankful. "We are free and in one piece," she said to herself, then raised her voice. "I will bet a week's worth of wine that we will come to grips with the silver lining of the whole mess." Lily looked up, nodded, then wriggling forward, hung over the seat.

"I would say the worst casualty of this week was Sarah," Dar said a second later. Lily wriggled her bandaged hand over the seat. "Well, there's that. But that'll heal quickly. Sarah's math for saving herself has taken her somewhere that might not give her back. She might need a vacation in one of those places," Dar added, looking sideways and then back for Lily. Lily had stretched out on the seat with her knees up. There was a wind-bruised gardenia blossom she had picked from River Oaks behind her ear. "That's pretty, honey," she yelled, adding, "As I said, alcohol and opium are addictive and may require some hard time locked up."

After a good five minutes of silence, Lily spoke. "Sarah needs a dog, that's all. And I'm going to need a tampon."

"Got it," Dar barked. "7-Eleven at the next intersection."

After stopping at the convenience store and using the filthy bathroom, they continued on. A gentle breeze brought down the humidity. Lily hummed in the backseat. Dar was worrying over her adjustments going forward, just as Lily spoke. "Feeling pretty chipper—being suddenly grown up and all. Ready to meet boys on their own terms," she said, and waited for response. Dar brought her neck around with a jolt that hurt, and Lily laughed. "Forewarning: Tish and I have some mighty plans for lining up boys. Like bowling pins. Though, one at a time, Mother."

Dar sighed. "There is no sexy and grandiose chapter ahead, dearie. Periods will become a holy nuisance making nine stitches without Novocain a fine day." Lily shot back scorn. She had been brave, white-knuckled, gripping Dar's arm while the only doctor near River Oaks sewed her up, apologizing over and over for having run out of that numbing drug.

"By the way I am done with my male cousins. I will no longer be using their names. They have been narrowed down to fit on a neat shelf. Artifacts given to me by relatives, they will remain on display far away from me. I will not be bringing them down to play with any longer," Lily said. "And have accepted that it is okay to just loathe them." Lily unwrapped a grape sucker and shoved it in her mouth.

"Well, I guess that's dandy Lily," Dar responded, confused. "Grudges are never healthy, but with those two, I think it might be acceptable."

Arriving home, Lily and Dar found a path to the kitchen table. They left their bags piled at the entry. The kennel was closed, and Lily was mad about that. "We could have skipped that ceremonial lunch of weird potato casserole and been here in time to get him," she moaned.

"You know it's tradition, Lily. Except Bev wasn't there. She certainly skedaddled, but then her absence was kind of luxurious, don't you think? By God, we needed a little comfort food. All that cheese, sausage, and red-eyed gravy mixed in," Dar said, trying to console her.

"No one talked the entire meal. Should have buried lunch and had a funeral," Lily said.

Dar looked toward the kitchen window. The setting sun was lighting up the treetops. "Home," she purred. Dar rose and pulled out a bottle of white wine from the refrigerator. She poured two small jam jars full and slumped back in her chair. Dar raised her glass and clinked it against Lily's, sitting untouched before her. Lily looked at the glass and then at Dar.

"It's not some spider, Lily," Dar said, nodding at the glass. "We are surrendering to our better selves, that's all. Besides, you have suddenly grown up. Time to celebrate."

"This family makes more reason to celebrate than someone rescued from certain death," Lily said, lifted her glass and drank. "Mother of God, that's good," she crooned, hoping Dar got the quote reference from Bev. "I write those things down...for the book."

Dar looked confused, then pointed at Lily and smiled as she recalled the moment.

Lily felt a wonderful pull in her chest. "River Oaks doesn't end just because we walk out the door. Right? The river didn't dry up. The house will be there next time, unless Bev tears it down while we sleep." Lily looked across at her mother for an answer.

"Over my dead body. We will be back next year."

Lily reached and clinked her mother's jar. She swallowed and wiped her mouth with the back of her hand. "Mother, I will probably leave this family high and dry...if you and I don't get the plantation up and running. You promised. Now that we have stolen those baby shoes."

"Once again, that was a symbolic thing. Like carrying around your lucky buckeye. We have no say in that, and we cannot afford to buy it. Who knows how much money Virginia's got left? Bobby spent an awful lot and supporting her sisters is a big drain." Dar ignored Lily's scornful expression and looked about the kitchen, realizing with the talk of finances that she was thrown back into her real obligations. Her job prospects were going to be temp jobs until her luck improved.

"You gonna call Chantelle?" Lily asked. When her mother twisted her mouth into a knot and did not respond, Lily rose to use the bathroom, grabbing her little kit.

With Lily gone, and her question sitting on the table, Dar's gut wrenched. The long drive home had not improved her longings. Chantelle had settled to the back of her head, in the same category as jobs. Here she had announced this massive change, as prideful as if she had selected God as her eternal sidekick. No turning back, she would have sworn on a Bible. Now, she had to wonder. Had Chantelle been a tryst to free her mind of loneliness, a fix for a flat tire, a ding pushed out in the uncertainty of her divorce? No way, Dar thought. She had been passionate with a woman, the first in her life.

Dar squinted, thinking back hard to that beginning. In that new world, Chantelle had led her through the darkness of that scary house. She recalled feeling nervous and, for a long humid moment, dirty. Their first intimate touch and then kiss, in reflection tasted personal, raw, and powerful. Then she had gotten jittery, as if she were another person, watching and unsure. After several drinks and some frisky and then tender moves by Chantelle, Dar had found her appetite.

Dar confessed now that she felt neither crowned with new purpose nor let loose in a fenceless pasture. As with her husband in the first feverish weeks of their relationship. Finding herself drawn to the image of him, Dar began to chew her nails. She sought Chantelle's face and body. Was the butterfly-shaped birthmark on her left shoulder or her right? Dar searched for a thread to connect them in a positive light. She recalled that she expressed to Lily that being with Chantelle was like traveling to somewhere exotic. Or had she? Dar wondered, feeling lost.

She shook the last drops of wine onto her tongue. She felt contrite and bitter and wondered where Lily was, missed her right now like a best friend. She then cursed herself for giving nothing up for Chantelle, who had been trying so hard to make things easy for her. She was not being fair. Dar recalled the things she had shared with Lily on the shore of River Oaks, describing "all things Chantelle." That had not felt like a lie. Like she said, she could just walk and talk with her for endless hours and not want to turn around. Confusion welled up in her heart. She wanted to scream.

Rubbing her right hand up and down her left wrist, Dar consigned herself to see how things went when she saw Chantelle for the first time. It would not be fair otherwise. If it turned out she felt fickle, her sexuality confused, or that Chantelle seemed like a different animal, she would deal with that. If though, Dar calculated, she had taken the wrong fork in thinking she was gay, she would never eat crow with the extended family. She would pretend to be gay or hide until Bev died.

"Mother, Mother," Lily was saying, and Dar shook free.

Dar reached and gulped Lily's wine. "I can't, Lily," she said, looking Lily straight in the face. She rose and left the room, bewildered by all concepts except a bath and bed.

41

A Glass Half Empty

The following night after dinner was done and the dishes were dry, the phone rang. Dar raced to answer it. "Hey there," she said. A muffled accord of consensus filled the space from the other end. Dar whispered back. "Me too."

At the table, Lily cringed. She pushed back her chair to escape. Dar waved her hand for Lily to sit back down.

"I can't wait to see you either," Dar said, and then shot a glance to Lily. "Yes, she is sitting right here. I don't know... well.... hmm." Placing a hand over the receiver, Dar looked Lily's way. "Chantelle wants to talk to you, says it is time you two meet."

"Meet? Are you kidding me? Never met anyone for the first time on the phone. Well, the operator once. Her name was Mildred, a lively woman who had a daughter my age."

Dar walked the receiver to Lily. "Just love this long cord," Dar said, blushing.

"My God give it here," Lily snapped, took the phone and placed it to her ear. "Yes?"

"Lily, we haven't met, but this is Chantelle."

Lily rolled her eyes. Duh formed on her mouth. She eyed her mother and pointed to the instrument in her hand. "No, we have not," Lily answered, chirping politeness.

"I will make this quick. We can have a long little talk in person soon," Chantelle said.

Lily hated when grownups used the word "little" with anything. And also, long and little didn't mesh. It all sounded patronizing. Lily wanted to tell Chantelle that every aspect of her life was big. That there was nothing she did not know.

"Yes, I will look forward to that," Lily said. She knew her tone was plain Jane, but that was all she could muster.

"For now, I want to impart a bit of advice," Chantelle began again. "You should not have to, or need to for that matter, understand. Just let Dar be happy. I will take care of the rest."

Lily was stupefied. And angry. She held the phone away and stared at it. Chantelle's statement was trying to rob her of something. Of the bond between her and her mother. Like she could slip in between them like cold oil. Without looking at her mother, Lily stretched her arm for her to take back the phone.

Putting on her happy face, Dar raised the phone. "Thanks, Chan, I guess I will have to call you later." Pause. "That's all right. Gotta start somewhere." Dar crossed the kitchen, hung up the phone, and turned to face Lily. Her daughter's gaze was a mix of blind amusement and fury.

"Guess Chan wants to get this whole thing wrapped up pretty quick. Where do I sign? Guess the same place you did," Lily said with bitter intent. She held out her wrist as if waiting for shackles and sharpened her focus on her mother's tightening expression. "You don't meet people on the phone," Lily repeated, rising from her chair.

With Bo wagging behind, Lily escaped to her room. She shut the door and then took her small desk chair and shoved it under the doorknob. Sitting down on the edge of the bed, Lily felt anger welling up. Then tears. Dar tapped on the door, turned the knob, and pushed.

"Lily, honey, it's dangerous to do that. You know, fires and stuff," Dar said.

"It's for our own good, Mother," Lily said. "I will try to not let that pissant call ruin a good mood. I will be thankful for the 'little' things, as Chantelle likes to say."

"I am sorry about whatever Chantelle said. You probably took it wrong. She's a good person. Just a bit direct at times. Get some sleep, honey, and take the chair away from the door." With her knuckle she gave two sharp taps goodnight.

42

A Hard Change of Venue

Virginia was back in her quiet Victorian home. For four weeks, she had savored the peace, the sense of disbelieving that no one was arguing, that meals could be staggered or skipped all together, and that she could remain in her robe for most the day. In this very moment, those were musings on hold, as Virginia was dealing with indescribable confusion.

First it was the double vision, then the narrowing of her gaze into the browning flowers on the azaleas beyond the white porch rail. She did not know she passed out, only that she woke with a splitting headache and that her tea glass was shattered on the green boards at her feet. She picked the lemon out of her lap, watched it go from mauve to bright yellow. She felt moisture running down her chin and wiped at the spittle.

Virginia looked out to the street and there she recognized her daughter. Getting out of her old blue-and-white car, Dar waved. Virginia raised her left arm to wave, but it was stuck. She lifted her right arm and watched as the fingers and hand moved back and forth greeting Dar.

"Mother, you dropped your glass—Virginia, are you all right?" Dar asked as she came slowly up the steps. She rushed and knelt at Virginia's side.

"I'm fine, silly. Just had a little nap," Virginia said in garbled words.

The right side of Virginia's mouth was not moving. Dar rose, went into the house, and called an ambulance.

Many hours later, they were back at Virginia's. Dar had tucked her in on her sofa and now looked down at her. Virginia looked and acted normal. The hospital said she had a small stroke. The curt nurse talked about her own mother, who had become pretty much an invalid after such a thing. The doctor came in and said there did not appear to be damage. Scans and monitors all fine. His terms after that were technical and confusing until he ended with, "Just watch her."

Back at Virginia's, Dar went over the doctor's words that were stuck in her head: "She may never have another one. She may have more. They may be worse. Temporary paralysis is not uncommon. Face, mouth, an arm, maybe. Permanent paralysis is possible." He did not use the word death, though that was laced in his expression when Dar opened her mouth to ask but did not. "Not much else you can do but just watch her," the doc reiterated, looked at his watch, and rushed off.

Dar decided not to tell Lily. She did not need that stress. Lily was having her second period, and it had turned her into an emotional and physical mess. Dar was handling it with hard love and a soothing voice that Lily said reminded her of Chantelle.

When Dar arrived home, Lily was on the phone and shot snake eyes into Dar. "I have a mother," Lily said into the mouthpiece. "I think." Lily could not fathom Dar having brought her girlfriend into the fold of something so personal as her period. "Gotta go do lady things." Lily slapped the receiver on the counter. "Dear Abby wants to speak to you, blabbermouth," Lily said to her mother. "Maybe she's got advice on that condition, too."

Until that moment, Dar had promised herself to let the relationship follow its course. Upon reuniting, Chantelle called their bonding seamless. "Two sweet peas sharing a pod," Chantelle had said. A bit irate and reviewing that, the statement sounded borrowed and possibly used in relationships of old. Picking up the phone, Dar asked Chantelle to come by later to discuss things and share a bottle of wine.

Chantelle arrived at ten. Lily had been in the living room five minutes prior and had vanished. Dar was sure she must have seen Chantelle's headlights at the curb. Chantelle walked in, all aglitter in greeting Dar. "Sixth time in a month. Must be we are happy," Chantelle chirped.

Dar smiled, then got down to protecting her daughter. "Chantelle," she said, while pouring her a glass of wine, "It's not your place to raise Lily. And you could do better to not be patronizing. Lily sees through metal."

"I apologize, Dar dear," said Chantelle, flicking a hand through her hair.

"Don't," Dar said, her ire risen by Chantelle's inexcusable addendum of Dar dear. "You know, patronizing kind of pricks me, too. Everyone for that matter."

Chantelle cleared her throat and took a tiny sip of red wine. "We all have our insecurities."

Dar leaned back and crossed her legs. "Let's review. You're not helping my situation here by getting yourself involved with Lily. Simple as that. Now, let's move on and enjoy ourselves."

Chantelle's voice cracked, and she chuckled. "Oh, Dar honey," she said, leaving a trail of wonder to die in the two feet between them.

"Again, patronizing," Dar responded. "You do not even have children. You have cats that kill every bird in your yard and a parrot that tells you to, 'Shut up, Stupid.' Your last girlfriend taught him that right before she left. So, leave your lessons at my front door."

Chantelle counted aloud so Dar could hear. "Wow, a real argument." In a sugary voice, she added, "Dar, sweetie, let's always preserve the good. We will always disagree about some things," she added. "You should not dote on Lily. She needs to grow up."

Dar's ears became hot. She said nothing. Instead, she made a hand motion of hanging up a phone. "Click." Chantelle chugged her wine and left.

The next day, Dar found a card in the mailbox. On the outside of the card was an abstract painting. Colorful swirls cut through with angry black slashes. The saying inside was what Dar called intellectual sap. A script, as intangible as the painting, phlegm about order and chaos, about inertia being the death of love, and of time being the healing force. Chantelle had left a secondary message below the printed one. *We are kindred souls in this universe. I am sorry for getting involved. It's the Italian in me to wear truth on my sleeve.* The word "truth" stung Dar. The woman could not turn a phrase without her righteousness ruining the rest of the meal. Dar's first instinct was to wad up the card, which she did and felt decent about. Staring down at the wrinkled paper, her better side gave in to Chantelle's effort, and she decided to give them a day or so.

43

Our Unfaithful Minds

For most of that night, Lily did not sleep. Cramps ran through her in unpredictable waves without warning. Hope of sleep left. The hot water bottle had grown cold and felt creepy, nursing against her side where it had fallen. Lily pushed the rubber bottle to the floor, where it took an eternity of seconds to stop sloshing.

"Blessed God, I am bleeding out," Lily cried out, at the bewitching hour of three. Just as she found the sweet spot in the nest of covers and pillows, a giant moon threw a searchlight upon her. An hour later, illuminated in eerie blue light, the cheery-faced troll doll on the bookshelf across the room began to stare at her. Lily threw her shoe at the orange-haired monster at half past four. She could not have hit it in a million years but did, also knocking to the floor, and breaking in two a ceramic antebellum bank made to resemble Scarlett O'Hara. It had been a gift from Bev. Lily had never dropped a coin in it, for fear she was donating to ignorance and bigotry. Lily pulled a pillow over her head and failed to suffocate herself.

Twice, around five, Lily said, "Mother, I hate you." This was for Dar informing her of a famed Hooper curse, after shoving the scorching hot water bottle up against her belly. "Every one of us, Lily, has endured periods so regular, to the minute, round the clock for six exact days, so vicious and cruel that I think that at least one Hooper in the last century took her own life." Lily had stared in awe at that statement. "We just need to know what we are facing, honey," Dar added, fluffing up the pillow around Lily's enraged face.

Lily was relieved when dawn struck her curtain. She lumbered downstairs and found her mother at the kitchen table. Dar looked up and noting the rings under Lily's eyes and hummed her sorrow. "Day four. That's when things start looking up," Dar said.

"Kill me before I kill," Lily said.

"Get some coffee. Studies are showing that it helps," Dar said, her tone unsure of that.

Lily sat. "Why in summer?" Lily said, then placed her head down on the table.

Dar reminded her of her tough love, "Twelve months of the year, no give or take." Dar then got up to get dressed, saying that the temp agency had set up an interview for her.

Lily's mood continued to swing down. By noon, so did her judgment. The house and neighborhood were dead quiet. Even Bo, asleep on the floor, breathed in solitary wisps. She tried to call Tish, and no one answered. She tried to read again, hating a story she used to love. Looking out the window, she decided to get out. Her breath felt hot and feverish. She brushed her teeth for the third time.

Her mind tried to tell her to stay put, let the poison of her foul mood work itself through her system before she entrusted herself to the world. It was not just her body and emotions. Chantelle had gotten under her nails. Lily was worried her mother had made a terrible mistake. She looked in the mirror. She was unruly, her hair unbrushed, and she had goblin circles under her eyes. Contained by bedevilment, to maybe inflict a little pain on the day she could not enjoy, she left the house. Bo's cries from behind the front door did not sway her.

The air had a dangerous feel. Lily had stolen two cigarettes from her mother's room then swallowed a huge mouthful of gin out of the bottle. That felt like a good place to start. Walking about the neighborhood, she convinced herself that every person was out to make ruin of her and judge her. One woman, watering flowers, eyed her as a helpless child. Men stopped mowing to glare, a cat ran away, and when she waved to a child and her mother passing on the sidewalk, the mother whispered.

Telling her child to stay away from those types of girls, Lily was sure. This was a practiced, towering, and cruel world. And she was not invited.

Lily saw a group of boys her age. Her urge was to test her charms in that way to get out of these doldrums. She walked up with a cigarette dangling from her hand, thigh level, flicking the tip like she had seen people do when hanging out. They turned away disinterested, passing a cigarette between themselves and snickering. It's fool's gold to think you are on the competitive front, she told herself. A girl with the figure of a boy has no hope.

By midday, Lily found some playmates. They were just small players; vapid and far too young for her. She was hanging tough. Go home, a voice told her; these are children you are playing with. Yet her juvenile act was moments away.

Lily had met these kids once and didn't really like them. Their coolness had not yet set in. The brother and sister twins had unnatural-looking flaming red hair, too many freckles, and to top it off, their names were Brick and Doe. They seemed too happy, too fairy tale in their innocent speak and sweet, home-baked apple pie smiles. Their cheeks, fertile and pinched lovingly by a relative at every step. Lily was the newbie in the neighborhood and wanted to tell them how in charge she had been in her last.

In minutes, lines were being drawn as to who had the most right to be hanging out at a new home construction site on the cul-de-sac. Brick and Doe, with stolen lumber, had already built a little fort in the woods behind the house site. They bragged of how well camouflaged it was. They pointed in that direction, shaking their heads in the exact same moment and in the same manner. They smiled with sweet sincerity at Lily's sidekick, a square-bodied boy of ten living down the street, who, though she did not know it, had followed her. The boy glared back at Brick and Doe's pastoral glow, spit on the ground, and claimed this part of the neighborhood as his. "What are you going to do about it?" he said, even as they remained silent.

The words escalated, and predictable sides formed. Brick and Doe, though innocent in face, knew some real foul words and by the miracle of twins said them in unison. Lily would usually have never sided with her young companion, as he was cocky and spat continuously, drawing an angry hand across his mouth each time, but she needed him. Insults were passed about, denunciations about mothers and fathers none were familiar with. Lily was not herself. In her mind, the twins were defending their right to all corners of a better life than hers. How things escalated was a blur. Throbbing in her head was the message that someone was going to get hurt.

Too late. The cutoff ends of two by fours were readily available to Lily and her now two companions, that baleful-mouthed boy and his tiny innocent sister who had arrived out of thin air and for whom the boy was responsible. Chunks of wood filled the air. An unstoppable dogfight ensued, as Brick and Doe fled behind a barricade of shrubs. The young girl was baffled and so scared that she peed in her dress. Her screams, hands over her ears, as urine streamed down, stinging her legs, set the whole scene on edge. And might have stopped this poor-sighted melee if tempers and distress had not reached the stage they had.

Lily's accuracy that day was just meant to be. She could have been blind, and those missiles would have found their target. This was where a hypothetical toss met certainty. Where life's lessons were unfathomable but true. She turned mechanical soldier. The first pieces she threw were direct hits into the shrubs protecting Brick and Doe. The fourth piece of wood she hurled arched in what seemed slow motion. Simulation in its perfect scroll across the battlefield, as it seemed so impossible and yet probable in its lesson. She could not even see the two hidden twins. The wood hit Brick in the center of his forehead, splitting the skin wide open. He stood up, bug-eyed, as crimson sprouted and ran in a torrent down his face. By the bloody image and his screams, Lily assumed he would die. She deemed herself a total reprobate and fled.

When Lily got home, Dar was standing in the kitchen talking on the phone with Chantelle, or so Lily assumed by the childlike manner of her murmuring. "Chantelle," Lily whined aloud, stung deep by her misdeeds that day and by her pent-up anger against that woman. She stood her ground, as her mother's mouth froze halfway into a word. Dar had been attempting to file her nails, the phone wedged between her shoulder and chin. She mouthed, "What the hell?" In response, Lily mimed wrapping something around her finger, hoping Dar got the riff toward Chantelle's manipulative traits.

Dar whispered in the mouthpiece. "Crisis. Better call you back, hon," she said. Dar placed the nail file down and stared at Lily. Before Dar could speak, Lily crossed the room.

Seeing the phone cord blocking the refrigerator door as the perfect avenue to pick a fight, she spoke. "A girl can't get a little food around here," she said, and shook two angry hands toward the obstacle before her. Dar crossed over and hung up the phone.

"What, did you lose at dodgeball?" Dar asked. She knew Lily had skipped practice due to her period. Dar had not meant her words to be cruel, as Lily never lost at dodgeball. Lily was pricked by something more than Chantelle. Lily's eyes flickered and narrowed. Her posture was clenched for self-destruction. Dar had seen this a couple of times before. Lily looked fist vicious.

Lily saw Brick, saw her life spiral in shedding his blood. She was angry at herself, at her mother, at Chantelle without a doubt, at Bev for everything in the cart, at this new neighborhood, at the unyielding heartbreak of divorce and the broken dam leavened upon their lives. At her skinny-ass body. At everyone telling her she was beautiful when she felt so ugly. At the unequivocal cruelty of her male cousins, whom she would dig her teeth into if they strolled in right now. She ripped her hands through her hair, watched the mural of her mother frozen and wondering how to calm this tempest.

Lily felt a high-pitched squeal leave her chest. And then a soaking rain of water leave her eyes. The kitchen before her seemed to shift on an axis. And then something took hold of her. She followed what needed emptying. Her body and mind felt channeled out, and she began to breathe again. Chantelle's face reeled before her, a snide face. She wanted once and for all to dispel the notion of her. She had a right to challenge Chantelle.

"Chantelle, at this juncture, is not open for negotiation," Dar said, seeming to read Lily's mind. "I'm sorting that out."

"Seems that's all we do anymore. I wish we could pull this past year back onto the spool. We could use all we have sorted out and get back my father." Lily felt her face flush hot with anger. Then a spotlight shown on her senselessness. Who the hell am I? she mused, seeing how the day had unfolded. Lily took a deep breath. "Oh God, I'm like all the people I loathe."

Dar took two steps forward. "You are low on iron. Sit. I'll get you some tuna fish. Wow, where is this coming from? I thought you were trying to be okay with Chantelle. I know I am." Dar opened the cupboard. "As for your father, you know how much that killed me."

"I was never trying to be okay with Chantelle," Lily said. "You made that up in the wishful thinking department." Lily sat. A sharp pain ran from her gut to her back, and Lily cursed. "Shit." She ground her teeth. "You gotta be kidding me. For the rest of my life?"

Dar watched her daughter's wild gyrations of mind and body all tallied into a single look. Lily wanted to hurt her. "Almost," Dar answered. "But with lots of good days between." She then looked at Lily head on. "What kind of trouble did you get into today?"

"What will your father say when he gets home?" Lily whimpered. "That's what a girl in a solid family would hear. That's what I want to hear."

"It's gone," Dar said. "Lily, I know there are a lot of things needing straightening out. But I ask you again, what bad road did you take today?" Dar had opened the can that stood in her palm. She looked at it, shrugged and placed the tin and a fork before Lily.

"I am just bored with the possibilities that never arrive." Lily stared at the can of tuna fish and could not help but smile. "No use wasting time with mayo and bread. Or creativity."

After their laughter subsided, Lily told her mother the truth about Brick and Doe.

"That poor little girl peeing down her legs," Dar said, shaking her head, as Lily finished.

"I feel like an orphan that has knocked her own teeth out," Lily said.

"I have to take some blame, Lily. For kicking us into such hard times over the last year or so. For being too consumed, with this and that."

A smile lifted to the corners of Lily's mouth. "For your slack vision of house," she said, pointing about the kitchen. "For the whirl of your frantic beauty that has yet to find a decent mate."

"That's just not fair." Dar leaned back in her chair. "I am doing the best I can."

"Remember, we're not allowed to use that. Neither of us, by your rules, after I failed math and tried that same expression."

Securing a toe to the floor, Dar balanced the chair on its back legs and contemplated Lily. "On the subject of bloodying Brick," Dar said. "It's the chances you take in the neighborhood. For both of you." Dar was dead serious. She knew that Lily needed perspective and humility, and so she told her about Virginia's stroke. That news knocked Lily back into orbit. Within ten minutes she was dressed and riding her bike to Virginia's house with Bo racing at her heels under the streetlights.

44

The Pith of Summer

The next morning, Dar entered looking unruly. Her hair, a pile of straw about to be lit, Lily thought, perplexed by her mother's faint greeting. Lily pondered whether Chantelle had come over while she was at Virginia's. The thought made her stiffen. Her mother's unbridled assembly and lack of greeting spoke of many variables to the evening behind. Maybe, Lily thought, last night had taken a wrong turn. Maybe her mother was just worn out. Lily did not want to think of what might have led to the latter.

There had been a note on the kitchen table when Lily came back from her granny's. "Only bother me if Virginia was not herself. Fried chicken in the fridge. M."

Lily eyed her mother now, washed up like green flotsam. Her way-too-short, silk olive-colored kimono made her look rented, Lily thought. With legs bare almost to where they ended, her mother reached to the cabinet above for the can of Luzianne coffee. Lily covered her eyes.

"Romp or ruin?" Lily played with, until the words popped from her lips. Dar had not heard, as the cabinet door banged shut.

Lily spun her cereal bowl. She cringed at the thought that Chantelle might at any moment come falling into the room, besieged with a long night of puppy play. "Romp," Lily, mad, called out, though the water was running to fill the coffee pot.

Lily thumped the table with her palm. If Chantelle had stayed the night, that was a first. She then considered something she was nowhere near ready to accept. The possibility of Chantelle maneuvering to live under this roof. A protective wall went up in her. Her first instinct was to pack and move in with her father. That news alone would shut down the whole shebang. It was not hard to envision Chantelle as a charlatan, secretly thrilled with the fresh stock of Dar. Her gorgeous mother right out of the river, untainted, and hers to shape. Lily's fingers clenched the *TV Guide,* and she tossed it across the table. It had come in the mail as an enticement to subscribe. They had no TV.

From the sink came a peculiar sound. Could have been an impatient moan or a delightful tremor. Dar tapped the top of the coffee maker. "My, oh my." The sound was sensual, or maybe a melancholy, Lily thought, once more taking in her mother's body smeared up against the cabinets. This was hardly the mother she knew, the one with at least one finger on the steering wheel. Arms crossed, Dar shot Lily a weak smile, nothing to even make a girl feel homey.

Crossing her arms around her cereal bowl, Lily thought of how well her mother had handled the whole mess of her meltdown the day before. If she could handle that bag of snakes, then she could handle manipulative girlfriends and dump them like trash onto the floorboard of a car. In that vision, Lily looked up, sure that last night had not gone well.

With the coffee pot at last gurgling, Dar let out a relieved sigh. She turned to Lily. "Hey, sweet pea," she called, then cleared her rusty throat. "How are things in the neighborhood this fine Sunday morning?" Her sight was squared up with Lily's. "Guess your granny was doing well, or I would have heard from you."

"Doing a crossword puzzle when I got there," Lily said, studying her mother. "Worked on a Norman Rockwell jigsaw after that, until she wanted to go to bed."

"That is wonderful. Maybe it wasn't a stroke. That nurse was a quack, and the doctor was a tired old pessimist with more important matters to attend to."

Lily looked her mother up and down, then with purpose at her new watch. A gift from her dad, left in their mailbox, as a token to celebrate that they were now two miles closer. Dar looked at the watch. Lily thought her gaze was pensive. She shook the watch to wind it.

"Lunch soon. Is she staying over?" Lily asked, fishing.

Dar leaned back against the counter. Her kimono opened up at the chest a few inches. Lily stared in disgust. Dar's expression pleaded for Lily to understand she did not fathom things herself. From under the table, Bo got up and came to Lily's side.

"Oh Boyyy, Boyyy, you are such a gooood boy." Lily leaned to kiss the dog's nose. Excited, Bo's long claws scratched hard at the floor, drawing a futile glare from Dar.

"So, what did you do last night after Virginia's, besides read my old diaries, which I mistakenly left out, and eat fried chicken in your bed...both of which are forbidden?" Dar asked, changing the subject.

"Well, I managed to stay sober enough to spoon with my new man-friend on the kitchen floor," Lily announced, and then began to giggle.

Dar stood dumbfounded. "That's not funny, lady." She then turned and fumbled with her empty mug, which slipped from her fingers into the sink with a crack. Dar's hands went up, and her fingers interlaced above her. Counting patience and nerves, she took measured breaths.

Lily shrunk in her chair and stroked Bo's back.

"Ever since we got back from the reunion, this place has gone to hell in a hand basket," Dar exclaimed. She then aimed a weak apology toward Lily, which came in a proxy of mouth, air, and a wave of her hand.

Lily got up from the table and went to her mother's side. "I'm sorry for saying that. I just barely know what spooning is, though I now know what precedes it and might come after," Lily added, thinking a light joke would loosen things up. "You never told me you were in Scotland. Did you see a castle? Diaries are a great way to get to know someone."

Dar, clinching the robe about her breasts, turned to get another cup. She filled a fresh mug, threw in two lumps of sugar, and without stirring, faced Lily. She looked down at Bo, who stood with his head tilted at almost the same angle as Lily's. Dar began to laugh.

"Yes, two castles, and they were cold."

"Wow, a cold castle. Imagine," Lily responded. "So, mother, what do women do to entertain themselves when they are glad there are no daughters around? I guess we need to straddle these things to move forward." Her face showed more curiosity than malcontent. "I just really want to know, are you really happy?"

Dar sipped her coffee and gave a faint smile. "You, my little Columbus, are far too direct to keep up with. It's Sunday, and I'm going to read in bed."

Lily got up and followed her mother. At the room's threshold, Dar turned and wiggled a crooked finger at Lily. "Bring a book. I intend to read, not to answer questions. Chantelle left in the middle of the night. We had an argument. A real one."

Later, with her book face down on the covers, Lily stared over at the crumpled card on the bedside table. Beside her, Dar's head was squashed into a mound of pillows, her mystery novel a foot from her entranced eyes. She leaned and picked up the wadded paper and, flattening it out, shook it at Dar to get her attention.

"Yep, that little gem was the crux of our big row," Dar admitted and tossed her book down. "It's that darn red wine over white that got us started last night. I figured Chantelle, in as light a mood as I had ever seen her, would take my honesty well about that card. I should have left it in the trash."

"Doesn't sound like that darn red wine over white had much to do with it," Lily said holding the card up to Dar's face.

"Yep, she was ripping mad. You did this to my sweet lovely words," Dar whined, mimicking Chantelle's initial reaction.

"Wow, I guess I get how that lit up all that booze in your brains."

"It went both ways, Lily. When I said I didn't understand a lick of that card, she laughed at me and said I was a better bonbon person than art lover."

Hearing that, Lily's mind constricted. Chantelle's perfect Roman nose that Dar had described grew into a hook, her pert rosy mouth deconstructed into flat and pasty mush. Lily's already dim view of Chantelle darkened, and she crushed the paper back into a ball.

"Yep, that was a real insult," Dar said. Taking the card from Lily's hand, she tossed it across the room. "She was so pleased with herself. Yet I must say that in response to her rudeness, I held myself to higher standards. You know, like how you stand before a big wave, your feet dug into the sand. When she got that I was not swayed by her cockiness—possibly forever—I used every obscure word in my drunk brain to sum up that card."

As Lily began to laugh, Dar added, "Sense be damned. You can get into real trouble using words you don't understand yourself. And never compare that kind of art to frozen vegetables to a sincere guru of the arts. She was fuming. I thought she was going to scratch out my eyes. I think that was just her fear of maybe losing a hot ticket like me."

"Maybe?" Lily asked.

45

The Tricky Prism of Health and Nostalgia

Monday afternoon, Lily returned from a spin on her bike to check on Virginia. Dar was on the front stoop in shorts and a bathing suit top, looking glum. Lily noted a passable smile to cover that. She sat beside her mother.

"How's Virginia today?" Dar asked. She had visited her hours before, bringing over a small pot of vegetable soup, and had left concerned.

"Was eating soup she said you brought her this morning," Lily answered, frowning. "Maybe we should be checking in on you. Memory seems to be off," Lily said. "Granny was a bit flummoxed, she said, by all the visitors, but had the answers for most of what I asked."

Dar patted her knees. "Bev and Sarah called last night, one on one phone, at Bev's, one on another. They informed me that the tenants are throwing in the towel at the plantation," Dar began. "It was inevitable. They were wannabees with no experience and have not paid the lease in months. Seems they gave up on tea and told nobody. Then tried to get fancy with olives...didn't even tell Virginia...what a concept. Olives. Who the hell thinks this is Italy? Besides Chantelle."

Dar looked at Lily. The news had shaken her. Dar knew that Lily could surmise the direction of things from here. The plantation was now on the docket for serious decisions. The worst-case scenario was Virginia giving up on the dream. For sure, another tenant was off the table.

"Good thing Virginia sent someone to check up on them, as they had already burned one row of tea bush to make room for their loony venture. They are gone now, the place resting in the hands of what, I don't know. Nature will swallow the place up in one summer," Dar moaned. "Of course, Bev, when she called, tried to act all full of melancholy about Sage and Winfield's dream sliding away. You could hear the opposite in her breathing and the way she tossed a celebratory drink down between sentences," Dar said, and paused. "Then Bev used the 'we' word. 'We will let you know when we decide what we are going to do with our place.'"

Lily sat frozen. The plantation was, as the Hooper name, like concrete. She remembered a time when she had not known the splendor of that place. When she was ten and eleven, she was made to work to get the place to resemble its fairy tale past. It had by then been left idle for three years. She had left with dark impressions. A place of mildewed boards, ten-foot weeds, snakes, peeling paint, and dankness lurking where light could not hit. Mickey, the cousins, Dar, Lily, and her father were tired, scratched, mosquito bitten, and itching over their legs and arms.

On further visits, the magic of the plantation had set itself into Lily. Bitten her, like her mother had assured her it would in time. The plantation had come out of a cloud of mist, its frame of marsh, lowland, and wildlife, irreplaceable. The house itself was a sprawling jewel. The porches alone could support a human heart. That the plantation might be sold, its bounties never explored by her, was a thought that made Lily ill. Now, the Spanish moss in her bike basket seemed like a remnant of the past more than a reminder that she would someday return. She looked at her mother, praying she had come up with a plan of rescue.

"Something that grand turning back to forest now seems plausible," Dar said. "A once beautiful story, my grandparents' dream." Lily's face went to stone. Dar put an arm over her.

"Virginia's mind is not the same. It's been like a tidal thing. You never know what's getting brought in our taken out. And Bev is really bombarding her now. Trying to act like she has a say, dragging Sarah in, moving her mouth and arms like some puppet. By God, Virginia bought their share of everything. Now Bev sees a chance of selling the same horse twice. Sarah just sees the place within homesickness, of when she was beautiful and desired," Dar said. Beside her, Lily was pensive and spun the wheels of a skate that had been sitting and rusting on the steps.

"Well, you and I and Virginia are the ones with the most heart dug in," Dar said. "I thought the plantation would wait for me. God, I have been neglectful." Dar pulled Lily in closer. "Sitting on that massive porch every day and watching tea grow. You, running about with your kids. That's the dream I'm keeping."

"Porch and tea sound perfect. I have faith in Granny. She will not let Winfield down or let Sage's ghost go unattended." Lily felt a sense of urgency, thwarted by hearing over and over that she would be going to college. Her granny had started that mantra in the past year. No matter what, over hell and high water, she said.

Dar did not seem to have heard a bit of what Lily said. She reached out and ran her hand through the dappled shadows as if they would turn with her fingers. "My brother's passing put the brakes on it all. If there is a God, he has awful skills and not a lick of compassion."

Lily watched her mother stiffen. "Even we must come to terms that Virginia's stroke changed something in her. When I brought up the plantation this morning, she had no oomph to describe any will that might be lurking. Her mind was instead on crocheting scrub pads and asking me what color I wanted." Lily could not remember her mother seeming so sad.

"When I brought up those lousy tenants, she looked at me and said I was sweet to worry about such things, but she was not. Said it like she had a secret magic wand, smiling like a child. Damn this world. When you think it just can't be, it can," Dar said.

Even as the stoop, house, and their frail skin was lit up, scorching under the midday sun, Lily and Dar sat ill affected by that. Their eyes met.

There they lived in similar pain, both learning. Lily understood that this was the kind of hurt neither could part with nor push away, for there were things to be done with it. She watched her mother's expression, hoping for her gaze to explode with a plan. Her red face remained covered with fear.

Dar drew a hand across her face. "Damn our fallible minds." Her posture tightened. "Yep, God's a tricky one, harvesting what he's planted before it's ripe."

Now, Lily wondered if any of them were prepared for losing Granny. "Things like that don't happen so fast, do they—to the mind?"

"No. Yes. I don't know. I guess illness can do anything it wants. But I won't be mentioning my concern to Bev. She'd take any of this conversation as a sign of hope. Bev does not wish her ill. She just needs her infirm enough to be without a will. Damn her. Lily, maybe you're right, this is too fast for such things to come on."

In the stillness beside her mother, Lily felt a huge sense of need leavening in her gut. Panic to rush to her granny, grab her hand, and go back in days, in seasons, in years. To the summer home. To the plantation. Lily's heart wailed, like the phone ringing in the house behind them now that no one could budge to answer.

"It's the plantation calling to say it will stay intact until we get there." Lily said and patted her mother's hand. Dar pushed up to go answer the phone, which had begun to ring again. Lily ran to the backyard to get her bike, her mind on every shortcut to get back to her granny.

Lily found Virginia as she had left her, reading a Nancy Drew book. Lily was not sure the page had changed. Dried soup was stuck to her chin, which Lily wiped away with a napkin dipped in Virginia's cup of tea. Lily then took out a blanket from a guest room and took her hand. She towed her, smiling, out to the back lawn. Lily helped her down onto the blanket she had spread in the shade of a fig tree.

Lily stretched out on her belly. Beside her, Virginia wriggled to find comfort. With legs at last comfortable, Virginia leaned on one elbow and with her free hand searched the grass. Lily found two four-leaf clovers in one minute. Virginia had found none, which, of course, they both knew would be the case. Just as Dar, Virginia did not have an eye for zeroing in on the prize.

"Same spot as last summer," Virginia said. The fact of that recognition comforted Lily.

"Clear your mind of all but being frivolous and fun. Catch an exceptional tree, not the forest. You're only seeing one thing," Lily said, redirecting her on the technique of clover hunting. Ten minutes later, Virginia still had not found any, refusing the one Lily tried to press into her hand. "Your fingers were poised right over this," Lily said.

Virginia at last sat up straight. "I was never good at that. Sarah could find them like that's all there was in the lawn."

"What about Bev?" Lily asked, sitting up to face Virginia.

"She claimed she found them all the time. Though, of course, there was never a witness or evidence of that," Virginia said, and smiled. Lily found comfort with her granny's acuity in recalling those details, even as her mother said the long past would stay sharp.

Noting that she was struggling to get comfortable and was sweating, Lily went to the kitchen for iced tea. Returning, Lily pulled over a metal lawn chair and helped her granny into it. Virginia took a glass of iced tea and a cookie from Lily's outstretched hand. Plopping down on the blanket, Lily stared as Virginia held up her right index finger. She smiled down into her tea, plucking out the lemon and squeezing juice into her glass. "By God, I pricked myself with those old sewing scissors an hour or so ago. Put lemon juice on it. It's a good way to clean a wound," she said. Lily smiled, ever confidant of her lucidity.

Satisfied, Lily asked of the plantation. "That place has lodged itself into me. But like a book where chapters have been torn out," she said, urging her on. "The more I know, the more I need to know. And I want to live there and write a few chapters myself."

"It is magic and hard work. I think you know I was the last to live there. Dar's father wanted nothing to do with it. Tried to act the part of beating back the vine, trim the bushes, but gave in to his true self.

A party boy licking his wounds over his friends spreading their wings in the big towns. He'd come and go, heading back to the plantation to see if things had changed. He had a million schemes to make us rich, no matter that we already were in many ways. As I think I mentioned, we made a lot of money selling off some beach and marsh way off from the plantation. I never had an intention of ever leaving, Lily. Sarah and Bev piddled at the idea of the plantation's future until they realized that it would not bring back the past. In that foolish despair, they sold their shares to me. Dar's father left soon after our boy died," Virginia lamented. "You know most of that."

"Who leaves a family behind like that?" Lily asked.

"One who has no family sitting in his head," Virginia answered. "Let's not talk about him, instead the plantation," Virginia added, and took a deep pull of her iced tea. "One human alone cannot keep that place whole, Lily." Virginia rolled the glass over her forehead. "It is a lover that does not understand infatuation. That land needs real love all over again as it has been shunned for so long. It is now timid in its trust. Its mystical power and passion will be revealed by someone's loyalty, someone with staying power and the strength and will to caress that landscape. Then the plantation will come out dressed in its flowing veils and you will think you have never seen such beauty or feel such friendship."

"My goodness, Granny, you make me want to pack up now."

Virginia's sight glazed over and she smiled. A frown covered that in seconds.

"And then there was Bobby. He was a curse and I took hold of it. Marshall's death, I think, made me insane. If I had not had Bigbee with me to stand as my friend and protector, I would have remained that way." Virginia's expression looked to escape.

Lily moved over to her side and pried the glass from her hand, set it down, and ran her cold fingers through her palms to warm them up. Virginia looked up and around, stretched her white throat, and took a hard breath. "Bobby wanted nothing that did not have his name on it.

He also hated physical labor. I don't know what I was thinking. I should have stayed at the plantation. Now look where it is." Virginia looked at Lily. "Men are like rivers: they rush off when it begins to barely rain. It's in their chemicals." Lily moved closer, until their bodies were bound side to side. "We must sit on the bank and wait for the ones whose words sound smart and prosperous. You will have better luck than I."

Lily was about to speak, but nothing would suffice. She was thinking about her father. How lucky she was. She needed to tell him.

"Few are forever noble," Virginia said. "But there are enough good ones out there to wait it out. I met a few. One, that stood out." Eyeing her, Lily fidgeted with her watch. Their silence confirmed of whom she spoke. Virginia had no righteous words to convey the wonder of that night with the consternation it had caused her precious granddaughter. She reached and hugged Lily, their embrace once more confirming there were no more barriers.

Lily helped her granny back into the house. As Lily mounted her bike, Virginia, standing on the porch, waved with the white napkin she had carried from the yard.

"Don't you worry about the plantation," she called out.

46

Where Parallel Tracks Really End

Virginia leveled out, and Dar and Lily had begun to breathe easier. Weeks passed as Virginia was even driving and running errands on occasion. Her mood was upbeat, even suggesting that next summer they spend some long weekends at River Oaks and get back to putting life back into the tea plantation. "Tea will forever be popular," she said.

And then Dar was summoned by Bev. Bev's performance on the phone was brusque, her tone meant to have Dar on her doorstep in an instant. She was kind enough to add that no one had died.

When the call came, Lily was just returning from a long bike ride. Her gaze was aglow from the wash of those free and lazy hours. Dar took one second to admire Lily's red, green, and blue nail polish before turning her about, grabbing her car keys, and pushing her back out the door to the car.

They walked through the back door into Bev's kitchen. Bev was nursing a gin and tonic. Her face took on every inch of prophecy and a pinch of distress for what she had to divulge. That woman's like a chameleon, Dar thought, prepared to be angry if this was another charade. Sarah cleared her throat and shook her head back and forth over hunched shoulders. Bev eyed Lily and blinked a few times.

"Is this for children's ears?" Bev asked.

"Don't see any here," Dar said.

This was the first time Lily had seen Bev since River Oaks. Bev had still not apologized for slicing up her hand. To Bev, the whole thing had been an accident from dysfunction brought on by another. If cornered, she would have called it an expression of her passion. She did not care about Virginia. She was a predator, seeking out her favorite food: winning. Lily raised her hand to show Bev that the stitches were gone but an ugly bluish scar remained.

"Oh, that," Bev said to Lily, her brows still set high on Dar.

Bev frowned, as all were wasting precious time. Sarah shook a single piece of paper toward Dar. "In case you have doubts," Sarah said.

Dar shivered. "It's freezing in here," she complained.

"It's summer," Bev said, annoyed, as she did not enjoy her task being sidetracked. "AC's running. But of course, you would not understand a luxury you do not have."

"Just had an attic fan put in. Reminds us of Virginia's plantation house," Dar said, emphasizing her mother's ownership and her suspicion as to what this was about.

"You need to face facts," Bev snapped.

"What now?" Dar exhaled, and tensed for this drama to unfold.

"Well, Virginia called me two nights ago, claiming that someone was walking around her house while she slept. She had already called the police. When they arrived, all the windows and doors were locked from the inside. They called her back on her phone, and she told them she was mistaken and to go away."

Wincing, Bev rubbed her right arthritic shoulder, letting Dar and Lily absorb what she was suggesting. That the situation had reached a crisis stage. Sarah still pinched the document between two fingers. Her heavy breathing and peppermint breath filled the circle.

"I'll have you know, it happened again the very next day," Bev stammered, when Dar did not respond. Dar stared back in awe at the gall of the woman before her. Bev had waited all this time to share such vital news. "We've been doing the best we can with this mess," Bev defended.

Lily stammered forward, coming in tight beside her mother. Bev quickened her speech. "Once more, she called the police," she said, straightening her posture. "In the process of pacing about, Virginia tripped on a rug, fell, and passed out on the floor. Or so she says. The police had to break a pane of window glass to get in. Unconscious or just too scared, we will never know." Bev looked around at each face. "Yes, the truth is upon us. Virginia is something that shifts now, and there she might remain," she announced, as if all would, with that slow release of words, grasp the hard truth: the irreversible moment they had now entered as a family.

Dar cocked her head in disbelief.

"No one had been in the house, and the paramedics checked her for injuries," Sarah chimed in.

"Only a bump to the back of her head, and her blood alcohol level was way up," Bev added.

"Why didn't she call me? Why didn't you call me? She is my mother." Dar's tone was testing anger. Lily reached and squeezed her mother's hand.

"Your line was busy," Bev lied. "Police called me, as we sisters are close and have our phone numbers posted on the wall above our phones. Something you might have considered. But of course, you're too busy sorting out your life to think of that."

With her body clinched, Dar stepped up to within a foot Bev. "Of course, we did not want to worry you," Bev said. Gin and cold breath wafted into Dar. "Dar, honey, things are happening fast. Maybe you have too much going on. That's why your family is here to help."

"She peed on herself," Sarah blurted.

"Well, we thought you should know," Bev said.

"I live a quarter of an hour from the truth at all times, Bev," Dar said, seething. Bev turned away, made a tiny expulsion of air to express her frustration. Lily remained frozen behind. Dar had seen her mother several times over the prior week and Virginia had said nothing about this incident. That the event maybe slipped Virginia's mind made Dar start. She eyed Sarah, the one person she might trust. Sarah's munificent eyes, Dar thought, were trying to speak the truth.

Maybe, Dar mused, she had denied that Virginia's condition was worsening. Yes, she had forgotten to button up her blouse one day. Had, on another day, left the bathroom door ajar while peeing. Just kept right on talking to Dar in plain sight.

Dar bit her lip and eyed Bev. Bev stood triumphant. Dar looked out the window to the porch where she could see Tish and Virginia talking.

Sarah called out. "She is uninspired. That is not our Virginia."

Dar turned a challenging eye upon Bev, suspecting conspiracy. "Most of the time, Virginia is as on as the sun," Dar announced.

Bev flipped her gaze to Sarah, who responded like she had been pinched. "She has been irritable," Sarah announced. "Quick to judge the innocent, like the grocery delivery boy who forgot her milk. Didn't even tip him. Called him half-witted, also. To his face."

"She told me," Dar snapped. "The boy had forgotten something on the list for the third time. Can't blame her. Kid is twenty and can't remember what's on a piece of paper in his hand." Dar felt constricted, seeing all of them huddled in here while her mother played solitaire outside on the porch with Tish as guard. The sisters seemed hurried, the state of things on fire. Even if Virginia's mind was not quite up to standard on occasion, that was just part of the evolution of aging. Dar suspected this was all about getting hold of River Oaks and the tea plantation. This rush to get to panic was not in sympathy for Virginia but of a pattern of greed.

"There's no grace here, I can tell you, just sneakiness trying to riven a cleft for their own purpose," Dar said. She reached and snatched the paper out of Sarah's grasp. A police report of the second incident. Dar tossed the paper to the floor. "So what? It's a police report, not a diagnosis," she said. "Getting a bit slower is not a crime the last I checked." Lily moved forward, her clammy hand taking Dar's.

"Maybe there were noises in her house. Maybe there is a raccoon in the attic. Have any of you thought about that?" Dar asked. "Her legs, nor yours for that matter, work as well as they did. That is why she fell. Living alone can be scary."

Sarah, upon taking in the depth and sense of Dar's words, pursed her lips in a lemon-eating way. She cocked her head and looked with curiosity at Bev who had assured her that all was dire. Sarah looked frightened. "What if she starts blabbering?" she blurted, and then looked out the window at Virginia, who was chatting with Tish.

Bev eyed Sarah. "I don't know what you're talking about, sister," she fired.

Lily looked up and back at Dar. Dar squinted, trying to focus on if she had missed something. "Blabbering," Dar asked. "About what?"

"About nothing and everything. You know, about things that don't make sense," Sarah stuttered to say. "Getting everyone riled up and confused."

"We will keep you informed," Bev said. Pivoting, she nodded for Sarah to follow as she shuffled out the door to the porch.

"Hi gals, teatime. Plantation tea. Maybe the last," Bev called out for all ears.

"We will fight. And win," Dar whispered to Lily, patting her on the shoulder.

47

Looking to the Heart of the Marble

Dar visited Virginia to the point of pestering her. "She is her old self," Dar confirmed, on the second visit the following Friday. Virginia had just brought up the plantation, calling the prior tenants "vagrant scum," and adding with a cackle, "They can't even grow a tomato, the most venerable fruit in the South."

Sitting across from her, Dar laughed. "Lily and I would try to tackle that mess, but we've just bought a house and I need a real job, making real money. Besides, I want Lily focused on finishing high school. Maybe over the holidays. We'll get there soon enough." Dar looked hard at the petite and fragile face of her mother. Virginia bit into her tomato sandwich. After relishing every chew, she nodded. "Damn Bev came by this morning and started asking about paperwork and if I had met with any lawyers and such. About what, I asked. She went quiet, looked scared. Bev seems to savor my aging as well as wanting it quick and organized. That woman is confused," she said, as Dar sat back hard.

"Bev doesn't own a rubber stamp on anything," Virginia said. They finished their tea.

Shutting the door, Dar sucked in the scent from a gardenia shrub off the porch. During her long exhalation, she saw the tottering forms of Bev and Sarah coming up the sidewalk. Bev's shell looked hard. Sarah, in her wake, seemed unsure. To emphasize her faith in Virginia's longevity and for the preservation of all the places she loved, Dar stood ready.

"Looking as spry as ever, as pink as a summer rose," Dar said, nodding over her shoulder toward the house, even before they had greeted. The sisters, breathing heavily, topped the steps. Dar continued her defense. "There are three places she loves, each in their own way the only sanctuary she will ever need," Dar said. "Her home here, River Oaks, and the tea plantation. There is no order to children you love, just the fight to keep them happy and healthy." Dar flitted down the steps, enjoying the stiff silence behind her as much as anything in a long while.

Virginia's peril did not seem imminent, Dar thought, crossing her fingers. Her mother had her glow back on today.

48

Bird of Prey

The following Monday, on her way home from another temp job, Dar headed to her mother's. Potluck Monday. Dar had named the celebratory day, cooking an emergency shelter's worth of food over the weekend and freezing it for the days ahead. "Monday's a good day for everyone to get off the ground for the week," she told Virginia. "We must not impede the hum of life by being lazy," she added, with that new tradition in mind.

"No matter the voices of complaint, we must endure," Virginia, giddy, chimed back.

Dar parked. Standing under claps of thunder and the portico roof, she could just hear Bev's voice through the screen saying, "Time is not our friend," and then something being "parsed out," were the fragments Dar could hear through another rumble of thunder.

Coming hard through the door, Dar took in Bev and Sarah. Each was slack in jaw. Sarah ambled away. Turning, Bev pinched one rouged cheek and the other and checked her eyeliner in the reflection of a plate hanging on the wall.

"Always an anniversary of something in this family," Bev announced, with her back to Dar. "Maybe today will mark something to celebrate."

Dar closed in behind Bev when Virginia came in from the kitchen. She carried a tray with a bucket of ice, glasses, and a bottle of Old Crow bourbon. Dar whispered sideways to Bev, "Are you just stubborn or addled?" Dar then faced her mother with glee.

"Lookee here. Mother, you look as stately as the queen." In her periphery, she watched Bev shuffle away. "Always said that dress loved you," Dar added.

"Hey, who's ready for a drink?" Virginia asked, not appearing to register Dar's compliment. She was fidgety, for sure. Dar then knew it had to do with Bev and Sarah. They had of course arrived early, "to get the worm," as Bev liked to say.

Dar took a breath and tried to focus on the reasons they were all here tonight. This was Potluck Monday. Dar decided to concentrate on making it good for all.

Sarah came up next to Dar and gave up a thin smile. She had tried to make it more, maybe even make a stab of admiring the notion of a family potluck. Sarah, latched to her side, used Dar's arm to push off. She aimed toward the tray Virginia had placed down on the yellow wicker serving cart. Sarah's perfume smelled sour; old on old. Where the hell was Lily, Dar wondered.

"How do we go back?" Dar said under her breath. But then she wondered, go back to what and where? She tried to recall the smell of the coastal air of the plantation and then the muddy waters of River Oaks. She looked toward the sisters hovering over the drink cart like it was an old beau come to visit. Though they weren't, they looked so old, standing in a close circle around that cart. With the prosperous dispositions of chipping white statues, they were bored in their parks. It was an image that always came back to her. Dar started as the mantle clock began to chime. Six times, and no one moved, just counted. Bev looked at the clock with pure agitation. Dar wanted to announce the old cliché: You can't take time with you. Enjoy the good memories. In sight of these fraught women, Dar was happy for her current struggles. She then heard Bev's sing-song voice, proclaiming the godliness of her drink. She jingled her glass.

"Just standing there, sister?" Bev asked, chiding Sarah. "Get yourself a seat with a view."

"Leave her be," Virginia demanded. "Just like River Oaks, my house, my rules."

Bev laughed as if it that had been a joke. Suddenly, Dar had the view that Bev could die where she stood, and that all of them, after proprietary mourning, would be fine. It was a thought that should have been unpleasant. But then how long can a dog be beaten before it is filled with hatred and fear? Dar watched as Bev's glass went forward and clanked into Sarah's and then Virginia's. Her blue eyes were as bright as polished silver. She might outlive them all, Dar mused. Still, Dar knew, Bev feared death. At Bobby's funeral, she had shaken in holy fear when Bigbee walked over his grave. Bev knew Bigbee hated them both.

"Well, here's to...whomever. To making right decisions about our futures," Bev announced. Hooking her mouth over the rim of her glass, "To Potluck Monday," she muttered, eyeing Dar with a cynical look.

Virginia looked like she might slap Bev, but then Sarah spoke up. "To all we have been given." Sarah's words and tone were meant to be positive, and maybe to challenge Bev.

"To all the men we loved and who did not love us," Bev said, and cackled.

"Goddammit, Bev," Sarah said, and spun away.

"We are not toasting anything that does not shine positive on this night." Virginia's words were final.

Dar was at her end to know how to respond any longer. Let insanity just prevail, a voice inside told her. Let yourself live and walk away. She swallowed hard. Was plunged into a need to hold Lily and Virginia in a wide sweep of her arms. "Fuck it," Dar said, and all heard.

In the broad window facing the street there was movement. A huge white owl landed on a branch outside, its perch sagging under its weight. Rain poured over its bright feathers. The bird's eyes blinked and settled on the room, on Bev in particular, for what felt an eternity. The huge bird's eyes closed and opened on her. The owl then lifted and flew away. It was something that Dar would think about for years to come.

No one made a sound. Ice settled in the bucket on the cart. Peculiar to Dar was the timing of the owl's visit, close to when her mind was on Bev's eventual passing. There was certainty to that owl, its unflinching and almost predatory gaze on Bev. Like all was playing out as it must, as a necessary addendum to the chime of the clock minutes before. This was no accident. A white owl was a spokesman for the reaper. That is what the oldest of the old said.

"Dear God," Dar whispered.

The three sisters stood in a triangulation of fear, their eyes searching the others for confirmation. Sarah and Virginia each took in Bev in whole. She looked frightened. Sarah's hand went to her mouth. The room, Dar thought, carried a burden weighing more than the entire years of their lives. Bev looked to the floor, as she knew the owl had chosen her. Sarah's mouth moved in silent prayer and Virginia looked up the staircase and touched her breastbone. Remembering Bobby.

The passing of this moment was brief. It was like a twinkle of a distant star blotted out by a cloud. But that is what happened. Someone's future hung with that bird. The sisters looked fearful and in shame. In that shared expression of theirs, Dar's mind was flattened by something invisible. Something she did not want to know but knew was right in front of her.

Virginia moved in slow motion, dropping one cube then another into a glass. Bev called out, "pshaw," and waved a dismissive hand toward the window. If anything prophetic had transpired, she had swallowed and digested it as fallacy. Or pretended to.

"This was such a great idea," Sarah said, pleading. Like the night was already over.

Bev rolled her eyes at Dar like they were the only ones in the room with any sense.

Sarah stared at the window. "There is nothing we can do about it. That is God's messenger."

Bev turned to her. "That is a bird and nothing more. I oversee my own destiny, you twit."

"All of ours, it appears," Sarah muttered and shut her mouth.

Dar, still staring at Bev, had not paid much attention to the last thing Sarah said. Instead she concentrated on Bev's proclamation of her destiny. Here was something beyond playful antics, beyond Bev's closeted lesbianism, beyond men's seductions, and revenge on enemies. Bev's existence was negative, an atom without a nucleus. There was no cure, and no heart. Only time and hope of a better ending than what Dar's gut now told her Bev's closure would be.

Sarah shook her head as if to clear her vision. Dar wondered if Sarah would have plunged a whole life's worth of drugs into her mouth if she had them. "Wow," Dar whispered, and wondered if she too had lost her mind, as she had an image of her helping her shove them down.

Silence filled the space. Then the sisters began talking. No transaction, no word said, no apology. Something had flipped. In the severity of the moment an organism had mutated to survive. Awed, Dar had the image of three disparaging lizards turning the color of the background. Sarah went and turned on a lamp.

Dar stared, almost too tired to move. This act arose before her time. What the sisters had found was at the tip of their fingers. They had changed costumes and gone back to the past. Virginia put on a record. Dar watched. Sarah turned where she stood, flailed her arms just so, but it looked horribly awkward. Bev countered that by mouthing something which made the others laugh. By magic, Dar mused, gloom and poison were retracted by just ignoring the existence of dark. Virginia, though looking scared, turned in a circle, holding her cocktail to the top of her head. The hoop-dee-doo, she called it. Dar had seen it as a child, when she appeared happy. Now that dance felt like something else. Inexplicable by any word.

They were soon in what Dar termed old gal hysteria. Dar was confused, almost disturbed. She then realized that this was what they were. They needed rescue, needed to ignore what was wrong and make another reality. But how wrong was wrong, Dar wanted to know. And then not.

Dar looked to the front door for hope. Lily and Tish would be coming soon. The sisters were breathing heavily and converging toward the drink cart. They were desperate, Dar thought, moving against time, logic, and reality. Turning on the music, Virginia had turned up the glass for the sand to run. Dar caught Virginia's gaze. See, we are content, visibly filling up with relief. Dar's head swam. It was just a bird, she told herself. A weird incident in a nonconformist family, where nothing was ever served up normal.

From behind, Dar heard the door open and shut. Lily had arrived. Dar could feel relief pour into her chest and warmth fill her veins as Lily smiled from the door. Encouragement from the outer ranks. The changing of the guards. Dar beamed at her.

"How's it, Mother?" Lily asked, squinting. "Salt, sugar, or fat?" Lily asked, seeing she needed rescue.

"All of the above," Dar answered. "Welcome to Potluck Monday."

Lily surveyed the room with curiosity. Her posture was bent under the burden of a pot of stew, a bundle of flowers, and wet hair. Within the spotlight of Virginia's big grin, Lily determined that she had weathered these rooms a hundred times and could do so again. She leaned and set all she carried on the floor.

She looked beautiful, Dar thought. Look what I've brought into this world. Lily had said she wanted to make her own way here, had refused the ride Dar offered. Her independence, once like shiny metal, no longer needed to brag. It was now an easy thing.

Lily stepped forward, the polished floor squeaking from the water dripping off her. She waved and smiled, reddening, as everyone was staring with admiration. "Gosh, y'all, I'm a girl on a tear, not a neophyte," Lily said with slow, endearing confidence. "Potluck Monday, I love it," she added, then leaned on graceful legs and tugged off one rubber boot then the other.

Dar now felt safe. Lily had been reared safely, was happy, and had turned into a beautiful girl. Out of the womb of gangly angles onto the springboard above a shining river below, her daughter was, Just There.

Yes, seconds after a June rain. Or maybe the change had reflected from a window onto her. Might have been born during sleep or garnered from a smile of admiration from a stranger. Dar shook her head, with butterflies, knowing. The owl and the antics behind it slipped away.

"Lily Hooper Smith, hang up that wet jacket, and get over here and give me a squeeze," Virginia called out.

Lily's bright eyes shown on her granny as she wriggled and let the yellow slicker fall to the slate floor. Picking it up, she hung it on the coat tree behind. Her hair had continued to grow long, and it fell in front of her shoulders. She wore a black silk top that she could not wait to show off as she had purchased it with her own taste and money. Lily picked up all she had brought, and with her white skirt swaying, bounced into the room to greet everyone.

"That bike basket could have carried Bo along with everything else," Lily called out.

"Yes, that would be worth a gander," Virginia's voice chimed. Lily kissed her mother on the cheek. Dar smiled, taking the flowers she had asked Lily to pick up on the way.

Setting the stew pot down on the table, Lily kissed Virginia and looked over her grandmother's shoulder at all gathered there. At that moment, they looked like a happy bunch. Lily lifted her hand to wave to Bev, then to Sarah. Lily watched as her mother lifted the pot of beef stew and moved toward the kitchen. Dar paused beside Bev, hugging her with her free arm.

"Thanks for making the first Monday Potluck," Dar whispered into Bev's neck. "Wouldn't be the same without all three of you together," she added. Sidling away, she took in Bev's marbled blue eyes. Still ageless, still a wonder, despite the other parts.

Rattled by Dar's sincerity, Bev stepped backward, then like a boat, righted herself. She looked out across the room, finding Virginia. Raising her chin, Bev spoke, her words shaky. "Dar is right, sister, that dress does love you. But then you were always the prettiest of us all. I remember at a party once. Sam Green—before you shucked him down to his mealy corn—was eyeing you like a chrome fender. Said out of the side of his mouth to me that you would look good even in burlap." Bev stuck her finger in her drink, stirred nervously.

Virginia took this all in. Bev, despite her earlier claim to oversee her own destiny, was superstitious. Where there was never guilt over her many harmful indiscretions, Bev was fearful of the afterlife. Though she tried hard to believe in the abstract heaven, the kind in stained glass in church, she saw something darker. On the surface she tried to shun the link between good and evil. But Bev, drunk, had once shared her belief that people could be chosen by the devil at random or by boredom. Tonight, she must be wondering how random that owl was.

Virginia knew also that being in this house upended Bev. Bobby's pale blue body, his angry eyes, frozen from just before the plunge to death, spooked Bev. To her, Bobby was more harmful in death than in life, where he could be dealt with. Sarah was not much better, the first girl to scream over the Ouija board in youth. Several times tonight, Virginia had seen her sisters looking at the staircase. Virginia looked that way now, something she just did now and then.

Bev called out from across the room. "Lily dear, what you are witnessing here is the only thing that matters." Despite the odds, Bev was a fighter. "Play when the grass is green. If it is not, you can always pretend it is. My God, we did," Bev added.

Just then the door flew open and Tish raced in. She slipped on the wet floor. "Sorry I am late. Had a play date," she said, laughed, and then blushed. She placed her umbrella, still open, on the floor. Her white linen dress was spotted through with rain.

Sarah pointed to the open umbrella. "Bad luck," she said. "Hope it's not too late."

"You're here, thank goodness," Lily called out. Mickey and his wife were off at a convention. The boys at "summer camp for hellions," as Lily called it. Tish would be staying at Dar and Lily's for two days. She dropped her pink suitcase on the floor beside the coat rack.

Outside a horn blew twice, and Tish blushed once more. Lily looked forward to the dirt that Tish would share later on in bed.

After dinner, Sarah came back from the kitchen. She was nibbling on a cookie, her pointy lips working around the edges. She had stopped drinking, and whatever other elixir she had taken before she arrived had worn off. "Still love your kitchen, Virginia," she said. "Don't know about y'all, but the kitchen was my favorite room in the plantation. The warmth from those big stoves. Didn't even mind being drenched in sweat, as long as I could just sit there and listen to the kitchen help go on and on."

"Not sure this is a good subject right now," Bev said looking concerned.

"Remember our mother stirring up the help into rearing us by scaring the daylights out of us," Sarah continued. "Stories of the blue-gummed men from the swamps seeking out young wealthy white girls to take back to their huts to make them their wives."

"Until they grew tired of them and ate them," Virginia added. "Blue-gummed because they lived off berries between meals of flesh. That awful story was just to keep teenage girls at bay and around the premises."

Bev cleared her throat. "Enough of this frightening stuff," she said, rising for a drink.

"I can't wait to tell my children the history of that cool old place," Lily said.

Virginia smiled and nodded to Lily. "Goodness, yes, before we know it, children, just like we three sisters once, will be dancing in the sprinkler at the plantation. Makes my heart happy. Though, you two keep your clothes on," she added and laughed.

"Has something been decided?" Bev called out.

"What, Lily and Tish having children?" Virginia answered and laughed. "You silly girl, Bev, of course, Lily and Tish will maintain the family tree."

49

After the Rains, Into the Sparkle

Two days later, at Dar's house, there was a knock on the door. When Tish went to answer, a man stood with a bunch of flowers in a purple vase. Dar stood below the landing. "They are for you," Tish squealed, and dipped her head to smell the bouquet. "From a Chantelle."

Dar reddened, remembering that she had written to apologize for desecrating Chantelle's art card. Dar took the flowers and placed them on the dining room table. She left out through the kitchen to the yard with the note. Opening the card and reading, she was in disbelief. She turned the card over, as if by miracle it would say, "Only kidding kiddo." Chantelle's note said, in a few curt lines, that they should take a breather. Until Dar was "a more practiced lesbian." The note then mocked Dar for hanging on to the "goodness of the opposite sex." Three things struck Dar. One, Chantelle was principled in her hatred of men. Second, she herself felt like she had a one-night stand. And third, she had no intention of practicing anything in order to be taken back by someone she just realized she despised.

Dar came back into the house where Lily and Tish were talking about the flowers. With Dar's entrance, they went silent. "Tell all," their sweet, polite faces pleaded. Dar placed the note in Lily's hand and took the flowers out of the vase. In the kitchen, she opened the tall cupboard by the back door, dragged out the plastic trashcan, and threw in the bouquet of flowers. Dar plunged her leg into the bin, stomped a half dozen times, and walked out the back door.

Lily and Tish were eating ice cream from a container when Dar came back more than an hour later. Her hair was wet. "Went swimming in a pond," Dar said to the two curious faces. "Well, it was swamp, but the water moves a bit. Better than therapy. Got a spoon for me?"

Late in the day, they took Tish home. Upon returning, Lily and Dar stood in the front yard viewing their house. Not much had changed. Except there were curtains in the windows, the unruly hedge along the front was trimmed, and the shrubs Virginia had gifted them along the drive were browning and in need of water.

"No cicadas, at least," Lily said, thinking back to that day when her mother was at odds over how to sell a house to her that was already in the bag. "Seventeen years to wait for those bugs. Wonder where we will be then?" Dar stared up at the greening shingles of the house. Lily went to drag out the garden hose to water her granny's wilting shrubs.

Turning off the spigot, Lily pondered how to counsel her mother. She stepped out of the shrubs along the house. Dar had not moved from where Lily had left her. The language of her mother's body was cinched in many things. The therapy of the swim had worn off. Sadness, of course, ran through her. That, Lily understood. Dar took a step forward, took a trembling breath and looked Lily's way. Her gaze said that Lily could not possibly understand these things.

Lily had rescue in mind and moved in timid steps toward her. "Please don't touch me, or I will cry," Dar said. She then winced and held her guts.

Every association with Chantelle, like a knife, was tearing through her brain, Lily mused, feeling powerless. Watching her mother commit to taking all the pain at once was hard. Without making a sound, Dar bent back up and sucked air through the small round tube she had made of her mouth. Her face contorted in a piss-fit of anger. She flailed her arms wildly, killing everything in their path. Dar then let out a slow and high-pitched scream, setting the neighbor's dog to bark.

"That was just not a kind way of breaking up," Dar at last said, without looking at Lily. "You know this is not about just that woman," she added.

Lily guessed that meant many things, inclusive of her father. For Lily's part, she was thankful Chantelle had the note delivered. It made it easy to loathe her and think her weak-livered. And she was way dumb for sending flowers, as the occasion was not joyous.

Dar nodded, giving Lily consent to come close. From their front stoop, Lily and Dar took in the sun squashing down over the neighbor's roof. It was a therapeutic scene. Sprawling oaks cut that giant life-threatening ball into a hundred glowing pieces. "This is better than ice cream," Dar said, as two vultures skulking on the power lines froze to stare at them. Lily pointed, naming them Sarah and Bev. "Amen," Dar said.

Lily edged over and leaned against her bare shoulder. She rolled her head to look up into her mother's face. There in every taut curve was a banner expressing unfairness pulled along by a fury she had not a hundred percent doused. "Oh, what the hell," Dar at last said, but wasn't sure.

Lily pulled away. These things, Lily knew, just don't wash off. Had not for either of them with the divorce, with transition, and all their unsureness coming like waves of showers. Dar just then nudged Lily and stiffened her look of conviction that she had survived.

Chantelle had come and gone. She was a blip, Lily wanted to say, but could not. Lily had all along carried her mother's ailments over Chantelle, as they were part hers. Lily thought her mother had gone into Chantelle blind and needy. But maybe not. Chantelle might have been the test for the truth of her sexuality, and Lily was fine with that.

She nudged her mother back. Dar responded with a shrug of hope. Lily had an image of her as a horse stalled at a fence when its mates were running free. Running up and down that fence, just as Lily's father did, driving by in his car day after day when everything fell to cinders. He could not find a place to cross the river to move on, to heal, to be again with his kind. He would find that place to cross and so would her mother. "You are the best, Mother Dearest," Lily said, and Dar cried.

That night, settling in, Lily and Dar pattered about, saying little. Lily's father called out of the blue to say he was just thinking about them and wondered how Virginia was. Dar had told him, of course, because he always liked Virginia. Said once that she was, "a little flower on a spiny cactus. She will always protect what that flower means to her."

Lily listened and watched as they chatted on the phone. Her mother seemed inspired by hearing his voice, once even laughing at something he said. Lily knew she would keep everything Chantelle a secret from him. Dar's expression then faded to something between awe and eagerness. "Well that is news," she said and eyed Lily. "Yes, I'm sure she would love to talk to you," Dar looked perplexed when she passed Lily the phone. Before hanging up, Lily told him she would come by and tell him the whole sordid story of the reunion.

Lily kissed her mother on the cheek. "Goodnight," she said. "Just checked the forecast. Bad luck's been all used up."

"Your father has decided to not sell our old house. Says he will be moving back in."

Lily stared back, disbelieving this as kind of a slap down. She then saw what she wanted to find in the news and smiled. Her first thought was that she wished she had not thrown away her telescope. The one that had brought her to the stars from their old driveway.

Dar saw her enthusiasm. "He's just moving back in, Lily." Dar was sad, happy, and confused. They both turned and drifted to their rooms.

The next morning when Lily walked into the kitchen, Dar was dressed like a star. "I have a real interview. For a good job. Not taking any chances."

Dar got the job, as a clerk at the courthouse. After a few days, she claimed that she loved it. Said what was expected of her was beyond her experience, though the curve to answer those things was short. "Impressed both myself and my boss," Dar said. "Never been in a position to learn I am smart." Dar was gleaming. The next day she announced that she would start attending classes to be a stenographer. Her boss, an unselfish kind, told her she was way too quick between her mind and fingers to not give that a try and offered to pay for the course.

50

The Edge of the Marble

Virginia had another stroke. She had managed to call an ambulance and was now back at home. She had righted, but a murkiness had moved into her gaze, a permanent hollow in Virginia's light. Dar lied to Lily that it meant Virginia was just scared.

Dar and Lily sat cross-legged, facing one another on the end of Dar's bed. "It is in our genes, honey—both the desire for consuming alcohol and the shifting identity of who we will think we are in the end. Both are damaging and foolhardy. I believe Sage went the same way, though the family claims that with her being as near to a ghost as humanly possible that she was a tricky diagnosis. She expended all her boundless energy on earth and was just gone," Dar said, snapping her fingers. "Kind of gives me the willies to think when we visit any of her old haunts that she can watch everything we are doing. I mean everything." With that, Dar blushed deeply. She took a deep breath, squaring in on Lily. "Granny will bounce between the Virginia you know and the one you don't." "And then one day, Lily, it will be like she has become a child again. We will bear witness, dig in, and clean up the mess as it unfolds."

Lily squeezed her sight down. "So, you don't give me much reason to go on living. It's like you have guaranteed us all how we will perish. I think you are maybe misdiagnosing. Granny is just aging." Lily fell silent, picking at the skin around her toes.

Dar waited for Lily to come to her senses, for her to flinch. For a nod of agreement that families know when to hunker down, to take care of business, no matter the force and pain of the subject. Dar watched as Lily looked up, squinting. She then flipped back her hair.

"So, the monster is in the castle," Lily said, both asking and stating.

"Yes, and he will not be going away until he is done," Dar said, and then felt the coldness of that. "We will need each other's help to get through this."

In Lily's mind, the reunion, not so far behind, seemed unreal. Its arguments, fires, and bloodshed were nothing to complain about. "Comes on this fast? And to the wrong people?"

"There's just a million ways to die, Lily. Some crueler. Some soft, none having been picked with favorites in mind."

"Don't ever become a therapist for small children, Mother."

"As I said, her stroke pushed dementia to the front of the line," Dar continued, her chest constricting. "The sisters really put the pedal to the floor in their lives. And it shows. Sadly, disease is never fair when it chooses the wisest over the tasteless and insipid—Bev and Sarah." Dar's eyes began to water. Not having Virginia around was not a vision she was ready to endure.

In reaction to her mother's tears, Lily's gaze chromed over. "Granny's my girl," she pleaded. "Are there any pills to fix it?" she asked, tearing up as she heard the answer: a solemn stare from the face opposite her. Gulping air to abate tears, Lily wagged a finger at Dar.

Dar wriggled over the bed spread to hug her. Lily waved two quick hands putting up a barrier. She knew a bigger flow lay behind the puddle in her eyes and was afraid to break down that far.

Rising off the bed, Dar led the way out of the bedroom. Downstairs, Dar turned to Lily. "We will make it through this, Charlemagne."

"That is so queer," Lily exclaimed. "Charlemagne was a man."

"Oh," Dar said, embarrassed.

Lily paused and pointed to the room before her. "Charlemagne did not own this ugly, frayed orange shag carpet," she announced and stepped down. She wrinkled her nose with disgust at the forest of hard fiber under her bare feet. "The world has become really cool and we have this in our little museum. Faded to the color of orange pushup sticks."

Dar gazed at the carpet. The wide threads were pocked here and there with melted burns from cigarette ash and unidentifiable stains.

"Are we stuck to ride on this until we think it is wonderful?" Lily asked.

Dar thought of a response but declined to speak. She then pondered something grander. Dar started moving furniture. Lily caught on, and in moments they moved about in frantic waves, piling the sparse furnishings of the family room into the small kitchen. Then, without a word, they strode and kneeled at the curled-up end of the carpet. Each eyed the other.

"Go," Dar said. They rolled up the carpet, their knees grinding into the dirt underneath. Straining, they lifted the rug. With a drooping end, they pushed open the screen door and carried the rug to the curb. They wiped off the grit embedded in their red knees and hands. Walking back to the house arm-in-arm, Lily said something that startled Dar.

"Do you think we have enough time? You know, to learn all I need from her. My only reliable resource to our history. I kind of have a rough outline: tea, booze, and dead men." Her smile was sardonic. "How will I know what's the truth next time if her memory's failing?"

Dar, thinking all that a bit cold, considered a response. No, she thought, Lily was just being practical. They came up the concrete steps to the front door. The streetlights popped on. With that almost as a cue, sadness filled her, the predictability, the setting of life unalterable. Dar's mind flashed back to the first Potluck Monday. To the owl. She took a deep breath and raised her chin for Lily. "Better just get it done—the story, I mean," Dar said, holding her smile, until Lily perked up. "Write everything you know and see what happens. Imagine the rest and it might just be true. After all, you know the characters and their weaknesses."

Lily looked back to the heap of carpet by the road, turned and slapped her mother's open hand. "Writing it is," Lily said, and Dar headed in.

"Bath for me," Dar said.

Lily walked across the gritty pine floor and sank into the Chippendale chair, the only piece of furniture, as the rest was still piled in the kitchen. With the room so bare, she was struck with the image of moving on. It was an awful feeling, as they just got here. She patted the cushioned arm and called for Bo. A muffled radio in the bathroom, where her mother soaked in the tub, threw out a static opera. Bo jumped up in Lily's lap with tail tucked, sensing her reserve. She sank down, rendering the day.

Closing her eyes, Lily dozed and shook awake with the tattered ends of a dream. Of herself with wrung hands at her granny's bedside. Virginia's final story released through bloodless and cracked lips, her air coming out as a countdown. Lily did not want any of the truth in that last second, in such a manner. She had imagined and hoped for the moment of confession to come in a far more civil way, the whole family having buried all wars. The final secrets of their lives told and shared by one then the other around the dining room table at River Oaks. Virginia chiming in with lucid determination, leading the way. The old sisters giggling of a tale of sassy heroines and tea farmers. Of a ghost named Sage. And nothing sinister, as Lily sometimes imagined and sometimes knew as the truth. Stroking Bo, Lily heard again her mother's impervious logic. Follow the crumbs. Imagine and write. That will be the truth.

Dar slipped into bed without a stitch of clothing. It felt good, like swimming to the muddy bottom of a river. The soft cotton sheets, like the oil of earth against her body. She did not miss Chantelle, in fact pushed that ugly chapter away. Get on with the get on, Dar thought. Lily and I must be brave. There is always something waiting.

51

Letting Go of the Handlebars

The school year began and ran its course that fall. To her mother's surprise, Lily became a model student. In October, Lily had turned sixteen. In December, Lily pulled out the thin book of her near perfect school grades. "Please tell me this is not a 'What are we going to do with you, Lily?' moment," she said, as if to forewarn her mother.

Watching Dar's eyes wander over the gold embossed cover, Lily pretended the worst by looking down at the floor. She passed the book to her mother's waiting hand. Through one eye, covered by dark waves of hair, she saw her mother's lips widen with pleasure. In her gaze, not some dark cleavage in the future of her daughter, but the wide vista of brain cells shining.

Lily's head shot up from her lair. She grinned, her body swaying. "Yep, I've become a model citizen," she announced. "Gotta find some way to thwart those depraved genes of ours."

"This here is real business," Dar said, shaking the grade book in the air over her head. "You are a rare little gypsy," she added, as a piece of paper fell out of the book to the floor. Springing to the freezer, Dar out took two grape Popsicles. "Fewer visits to the principal about grades is something to celebrate," Dar said, handing Lily a Popsicle, while shoving the other in her mouth. "I jus wuv gwape," Dar muttered, sucking and grimacing through the cold. Lily leaned and picked up the scrap of paper and handed it to her mother.

Glancing at Lily's learner's permit, now three months old, Dar chuckled at the industry of Lily to place the permit alongside her shining grades. Lily tapped the book in Dar's hand. "Guess a little reward won't hurt."

By the end of the next quarter, Lily was near the top of her class. And she had been selected as "literary queen," though there was really no such classification until that ad-lib moment. She had written an essay on memory loss that was both gripping and tearful. Lily was asked to read her piece at the end of the quarter in the school gymnasium. That day upon them, Lily's creative writing mentor welcomed Lily to the podium. She was the eighth and final student to be honored for their excellence.

She was excited, had butterflies dancing in her eyes. She spotted Virginia sitting erect and poised. Lily had expressed trepidation over her presentation, considering that it was based on her granny's condition. Dar had convinced her that of anyone out there, Virginia was and would remain her biggest fan. "Besides, she has been sharp as a tack for a good spell."

Lily floated across the stage in a tight black dress, her figure cupped, petite, and perfect. Her head was up, her mouth sweet, pink and kissing the air with glee. She looked out across the sea of faces, realizing how few she recognized even after all these years. Yet, toward the front her family sat, most straight and neat as planted flowers. In the center of them was her mother, her ginger hair piled high in the hot gymnasium. She looked right and left, a beaming lighthouse telling all those about that "Yes, here is my daughter, not yours." Virginia looked about with similar gloating praise.

Dar began to shake as Lily read. Her daughter was poised in her glory of proving herself. She was beyond the reach of the judgment she had endured from her fellow classmates for years. The beauty that had been always present, but ignored, had arrived. Lily was stunning. And brilliant. Jealousy, admiration, and instant crushes formed in the sea below her. When Lily was through, Virginia clapped and yelped. Three chairs away, Tish let out a hoot that Lily would recognize anywhere.

"I am glad some of us Hoopers have all our brain cells in order," Virginia exclaimed to Dar over the noise of the auditorium. Dar looked sideways at her mother, relieved by the statement. Virginia's memory issues had remained stable since early fall. She had not had any further strokes and continued to endure Bev and Sarah's constant prying into her state of affairs. As for the plantation, Virginia had, with clear-minded decisiveness, arranged for the place to be painted and for the tea bushes restored back to health. "Until further notice," she replied to Bev and Sarah, ending their incessant questions of when she would stop spending money on what they argued was "a dying horse."

"Hey there, sweet stuff," Virginia, waving, called out over the clamor of the auditorium.

From the podium, Lily grinned. Even after people began to rise and stir, she remained to stare, suspecting she would have few moments to watch a room as this. She viewed her extended family, thinking them odd in nature though beautiful otherwise.

Next to Virginia, Bev wrung her hands after having, minutes before, bounced them together in a form of seal like clapping. She now looked stiff and untried as she was in a place where she had no control and where no one had an inkling to even notice her. Sarah, next to her, was what Snow White would look like in old age, a red carnation in her white lapel, her lips pale like she was poisoned. Lily looked once more at Dar, and her eyes welled up. Lily had never felt so proud. She closed her eyes and was lifted as they flooded.

Mickey had been there but hurried out as if he had to use the bathroom. He now came back through the big gym doors. Adjusting his belt, he spotted Lily, put a hand over his heart, and grinned. Lily shot him a peace sign. Mickey's wife had not joined him, and rumor was she might never. Marcel and Jessie sat next to Sarah. They looked dead in boredom with arms crossed. Lily refused in any more detail from that picture, then smiled, realizing how quick things could be summarized.

Afterward, they all went to brunch. It was like old times, if there were such a thing, Lily thought, smiling and finishing her granny's pecan pie. Virginia was sharp and witty. Bev and Sarah paid for brunch, which surprised all but Dar. Even Virginia's face relayed humorous suspicion of their ulterior motives. When Bev looked her way seeking praise for her generosity, Virginia propped up in her chair. The queen. Good graces should have begun years ago, Virginia thought, drilling that into Bev by winking. She then rose to go to the restroom.

Virginia was freshening her lipstick when her vision funneled down and the bright room about went to dull cotton. As she felt her balance going, Virginia grasped the sink. Her sight then cleared enough to make out details. The incident lasted a few minutes, after which Virginia returned to the table. She sat staring at her purse, trying to think what she was supposed to do with it. Dar was asking her something and Virginia took a stab at answering. "Yes," thinking that enough. Virginia then smiled. "Silly goose," she said to herself as her focus sharpened on the purse. She opened the pearl clasp and pulled out a beautiful topaz ring with a tiny bow tied to it and presented it to Lily. "This belonged to my mother. She would want you to have it," she said, refusing to register Bev's noises of protest from across the table.

52

Evoking Truth

A week to the day later, Virginia sat in a wingback chair talking with her mother. Her father came and went, commenting on this and that about a tea tasting. "While you can, do what's right," Sage murmured. Virginia loved the intoxication of her voice. Sage nodded her conviction that it was still a perfect world.

"I already have done what's right," Virginia said.

Winfield, who had drifted away, was drawn back to Sage's side. In reverence of that creature he always thought angelic, the corner of his mouth lifted to his favored daughter. His gaze asked her if she saw it, too. Your mother is as beautiful as ever. Taking her in, Virginia nodded. Sage's lips moved. "I always knew you would take care of things in the end." Sage's body flickered and edged into shadow then back. Virginia knew how hard it was for her to stay in one place too long, growing adventurous for other worlds, maybe to her gardens, maybe to make love with her husband. Sage shimmered in spectral light, as if she might will herself away.

"Please stay," Virginia pleaded. Sage smiled and held.

Virginia felt her eyes tearing but could not say if she was happy or sad. A sense of homesickness filled her. The smell of Sage was on her and coming from everything. From the grass, each raindrop though the screens, and overflowing the scent of flowers. Sage passed before her, running her hands over the oak table. "Bigbee needs to clean off this chicken blood." That name made Virginia want to cry. Attached was a sense of having fallen into a trap, where forgiveness and righteousness were perfectly equal and dark.

"Bigbee, that Godsend, is gone for good," Virginia said to her mother.

Sage smiled upon the room, her gaze cleansing Virginia's misgivings. Winfield and Sage's eyes met. Virginia felt jealous of their fortune and thought of her poor choices in men. Sage read her mind. "It was destiny, dear. But look what else you have," she said, and into Virginia's mind came the faces of Dar and Lily. Then River Oaks and the plantation.

Virginia wondered why it had gotten cold so fast. She heard her father speaking again. She could not see him, but his voice was all she needed. "The tea will always grow well. And the house never rots, so stop your worry." His jubilant voice echoed. "All the plantation needs is the love of a Hooper, darling. You know the one," he said.

"Yes, it's time," Sage said, maybe calling down the staircase. Waiting for Winfield to come love her. Virginia slept and woke within minutes. She felt light-headed and confused. Bigbee's name had made her unsettled. She thought she heard water running, then a shuffle on the upstairs boards, the creak on the steps from Bigbee's heavy footfalls.

"Hello, it's me, Granny," Lily said in a low voice, as to not startle her. She had come in the front door and heard Virginia talking. "You're alone? I thought you were here with someone."

"Well hello, my favorite granddaughter," Virginia reached back, wriggling her hand in the air in greeting. She strained over her shoulder to see Lily.

"Yum, chocolate cake," Lily said. "Let's break open this bad thing."

"Chocolate cherry," Virginia called back with glee. "Yes, let's. Bev and Sarah dropped it off."

Lily chuckled. "That cake will be loaded with bourbon," she said.

"Well, it was sweet of them to do it, and we had the most wonderful chat. Three young birds talking about our monkeyshines."

"Monkeyshines. I like it. Mind if I borrow that?"

"It would be my honor. Come and sit where I can see you. And bring me a piece of that cake," Virginia said, smacked her lips and patted the chair arm. Virginia then leaned forward and whispered to Lily. "Sage and Winfield came by for a visit."

53

Behold a Piece of Paper

Lily returned home from Virginia's. She had decided to keep what her granny said about Sage and Winfield's visit to herself.

"She asked me to give you this," Lily said to her mother, reaching onto her purse. She handed the envelope to Dar, who stood wide-eyed with curiosity.

Dar tore open the seal and took out an official looking document. Dar's mouth moved as she read in silence. She paused, looking over the top of the letter at Lily's taut expression.

"Okay, mystery lady, what does it say?" Lily asked.

"Can't tell you. In one week at Potluck Monday." Lily's mouth fell open with disapproval. "Wow," Dar said, folding up the letter and placing it back in the envelope.

On that scheduled day, after drinks and potluck, Virginia asked all to be quiet. She then stated that she knew something was wrong with her. With that admission, Bev, twirling the melting ice within her highball, sat up straight. Her gaze tunneled into Virginia, then went around the room. Her eyes twinkled. Hovering behind Bev, Mickey seemed mildly interested. He averted his sight from his mother, who was trying to get his attention.

Lily, seated next to Tish, took in her granny and mother's childlike buoyancy. In the back of the room, Marcel and Jessie were sticking bits of ham to their foreheads and thinking that was just about the funniest thing in the world. Sarah looked hard at Virginia, her little prayer hands resting on her midsection.

Virginia, dressed in a brand-new blue satin dress, sat by the fireplace. Looking from face to face, she continued. "But I am not yet incompetent. Seeing this unpleasant development months ago, I took steps to fulfill my wishes. That is what people do when they own property. What they do while they still can, if they are smart."

Dar moved beside the Victorian chair and draped an arm over the back, touching Virginia's shoulder. She watched Bev. Her smug expression, her beady eyes darting, questioning the validity of everything. Noticing the envelope in Virginia's lap, Bev began to rub the flat mole on the back of her right hand. The ground was coming up fast. Dar checked her desire to gloat.

"Let's see, where were we?" Virginia began again, looked up at Dar, and patted her hand. Bev's face lit up. Virginia was stumbling, her mind just not sharp enough to be at the helm any longer. Just like she said.

"Oh, sis," Bev crowed in sympathy.

Virginia smiled her way. It was a grin of fortitude and joy. Dar, knowing some of the document's contents and that her mother was as lucid tonight as ever, suspected Virginia was playing with Bev. After all, she had put up with her crap for a long time. Why not jiggle the line a bit?

Virginia held up her glass of iced tea and toasted the room. "Plantation tea. With mint from River Oaks," she called out, and took a deep and wondrous breath.

"I'm not sure this is a good idea," Bev announced, her voice loud, nervous, searching down for her old tenacious self. Virginia...."

Dar surveyed her failing structure. Bev looked anything but resilient. Her mouth and eyes had taken on an awkward shape, half eclipsed in wonder, maybe seeing her dreams broken. Yes, in front of Bev was a wall. Sarah, beside her, on the other hand, looked ready to accept anything. The gulf between those two had flipped.

Virginia looked at Bev and then back up at Dar. "Let's be gentle," she said. In that gesture, Dar realized something that made her feel sorry for Bev and Sarah. It was not just losing what little grip they had on River Oaks and the plantation, but the familiar administration of money to keep things going in their own paltry corners of life should Virginia up and die. Yes, Dar hoped the full extent of this document had enough juice in it to keep them going.

"I'll try," Dar whispered.

"Let's get on with what's already done," Virginia announced. Blood filled her face, the pallor of health glowing on her cheeks. She took the envelope and handed it to Dar.

Dar opened the envelope and read aloud. When she finished reading the clear and precise legal document the room was silent. Even the male cousins had quieted. Lily squealed and jumped up from her chair. With her hands spread over her cheeks, she made a complete circle where she stood. Tish got up and grasping her hands, jumped up and down.

River Oaks was willed to Lily and Dar. The tea plantation also went to them, with a small monthly compensation going to Mickey's family when the energetic team of Dar and Lily got it up and running again. Dar and Lily were to receive expenses and salaries for managing the plantation and for the upkeep of River Oaks until the plantation again found its rhythm. In those carefully worded lines were sentiments from Virginia that it would be to Mickey's benefit to chip in and help get the plantation back in order. He would be compensated, per directions in the will and per his contribution. Bev and Sarah were to receive an up-front sum of money that, if they were wise and frugal, would last their lifetimes. The other stipulation was more of a wish with consequences. The family was to continue the tradition of the family reunion at River Oaks. Her trust stated that if that tradition was not followed, the place was to be rented out to summer vacationers.

"These places along the river are in high demand," Virginia said, mocking what Bev had said this summer when she pressed selling the place.

Virginia rose from her chair and spread her arms to celebrate this hard-wrought decision. "Someone get me a big drink. We now have no more mystery. No more reason for theatre. We can go back to being something resembling a family. Oh, sweet Jesus," she said pressing her tiny palms together.

Bev mouthed a sequence of sounds making no sense. Her expression was one of irretraceable fear, disgust, and confusion. Short little burst of air erupted in lieu of words. "Bev is having a day terror," Dar whispered to Lily as she came up to hug her.

"Are you serious?" Bev called out. "We were making these decisions together."

"We did, Bev," Virginia said. "When I bought you and Sarah out. You were as happy as clams then," she said, and then took a swallow of the drink Tish handed her. "Bev, you, Sarah, and I have all we need. You have been taken care of. It's all legal. And generous, so how about some appreciation. Be sweet and all that."

Sarah had come to stand beside Bev. She nodded, her face showing relief, possibly satisfaction that on one level the stress might be coming to an end. She patted Bev on the shoulder. "It's going be just fine, dearie," she said. "You should sit."

"Wow," Dar said, awed by Sarah's accurate and sober spirit. Her grit so real.

"Oh, and Dar and Lily," Virginia called out. "Once the teaspoons are clanging again, you can go between living at the plantation or at River Oaks. You know it gets so hot on the coast in the summer. And, Lily honey, you're smart enough to decide if you want to go to college. Or you can just make tea your business. Tish, the same goes for you. I'm sure Lily would love to have you on board." Virginia sighted Mickey, who seemed complacent over the whole deal. "Mickey, your boys need to go to a good, strict Christian college. See where that takes them." Mickey stood with his arms crossed and conceded that with a gentle laugh.

An hour later, Dar and Lily sat at their tiny kitchen table at home. It was midnight, and in a decadent manner of celebration they had made root beer floats.

"Things suddenly seem so much bigger," Dar said, daydreaming. They spoke about changing the ugly chandelier in the kitchen at River Oaks and whether they would still sleep in their favorite rooms. Lily said she wanted a hammock on the porch at the plantation. "With one of those big, draping mosquito nets," she added, spooning the foamy remnants from the bottom her glass.

"I just have to pinch myself," Dar said. The duo fell into silence, each taking in the stubborn spaces in their minds slow to grasp that this was real.

Dar went to bed. Lily, too excited to sleep, remained in the kitchen. She began to think what this transformation would mean for her. To live on the plantation would mean that she would be breathing in its history. The family lore would be embellished by the environment and the ghosts around her. Maybe she would get a whiff of Sage, Lily thought. With the thought of being immersed in that place, secrets suddenly held no value. She knew enough, and to know more meant little, in light of all she would make of her own going forward. Yes, someday she would have her own secrets, and she would hold them because they were hers. She would finish the story, and for better or worse it would belong to the whole line of them, Sage and Winfield included. And all the ones who had sacrificed without having a say. She thought of Bigbee and all those who worked themselves to the bone for so little. Never to be added to the family tree. Lily would make amends and by her rigor consecrate the grounds of the plantation with their memory. She would never forget it wasn't just a dream that made it work. She could never erase bigotry and the insane idea of servitude. Lily knew that whatever she did would never be enough. It would take thousands of her and as many years to atone for those wrongs.

54

In the Cold Nest

From her bed, clutching the ashes of her mother, Bigbee thought of all things except her illness. She ignored the sensation of her inflamed and dying organ, unsubstantial against her tortured mind. She had given up on the voice inside telling her to live. She thought only of the THING starving her: the isolation from those she loved and the fact that for so long she had been lost to them. At the headwaters of her ailing soul and heart was the image of the beast that had torn her away from her island. The priest. He had controlled her fate and ruined the souls of all others there. That cruel man had stilled in her center, his hot breaths heaving alongside hers every moment since she fled. His racism laughed alongside her constant grief.

She could still see his venomous smile on the docks as he left. That look saying that bigotry can strike wherever it chooses and just walk away. Bigbee's revenge upon men as he had been symbolic, as it could never match the priest's wrath upon the ancestors of freed slaves. Bobby's death was a gesture against prejudice and cruelty. She had just done what God had too much time to do and had not.

Bigbee repositioned the urn of ashes between her biceps and the bed covers. She rolled her drenched head, took a labored breath, and looked around. Ten years in this tiny rundown house, she had let the place swallow her. In a house once shining, all was green and rotting. On the floor about her death raft, tin buckets collected water from the derelict roof over her. This was the home her mother had fled to. The place where she wore down her beloved Bible almost to pulp. And where Bigbee at last found her. In her final days, clutching that mangled book, she smiled, telling Bigbee that in death she would return those pages back to the church and lift the spell.

Bigbee pushed back to prop up. In the center of the window facing the sea was a splotch of colorless land sitting in the hazy distance. That island, home for a third of her life, had refused her when she returned, begging for forgiveness. There, Bigbee learned, she was cursed, her history revised, her goodness forgotten. She was a memory the island's core would not hold.

There had been a time when she had been a friend of all the people of her village. An apostle from heaven, her family said of her, their amazement in her capacity for love never abating. From child to adult she remained selfless. Children clamored to be under her sagging arms and the umbrella of her smile. Bigbee, back then, was evidence of the secure world.

On the island was a single church, a schoolhouse, and a cluster of brightly colored wooden houses. The church was well over a century old and built of ship's ballast stones and great slabs of granite from an inland source. For her people, the hard structure had symbolized the notion of permanence, that their inheritance was real. That slavery was dead. That church was where life moved in a rhythm of tranquility and fair play.

The people's fear of foreign men waned with the gift of the island the century before. The young grew up without being bullied with prejudice. Time passed in this manner and of course would forever. Opposite gears began to move with the death of the church's pastor. The village went without a replacement for six months while the church's counterpart on the mainland worked to find one. Everything changed with the arrival of the new priest, a man close to her age. His outward goodness was a guise for hatred and intolerance. With his entrance, the island's hard-won prosperity and harmony was set to fall.

Without notice, the new priest arrived on their dock. He was tall with smooth, almost porcelain skin, and had jet-black hair. Dressed in black, he wore his white collar loosened and carried a small traveling bag in his hand. The priest stood on the wharf with the air of a son coming home from war. His eyes, roaming the village, might have been reclaiming what he once knew and had missed. And then he looked to the sky and smiled broadly. A Godly man seeing his God, some guessed, that first day.

The priest walked heavily over the heat-twisted boards toward the shore. Behind, the boat that had delivered him chortled off in a blue cloud of fumes. Two men working on the dock nodded briskly. One man whisked his hat off his head, greeting the man. The second tried to hand him a fresh handkerchief to cover his face from the noxious fumes. The priest refused, looking past them toward the stone church. Then he turned back and smiled, his eyes brightening to show irises of different colors, one gray, one blue. Taking in the tiny bag, the man with the handkerchief joked, "Not planning on staying long, I see."

The priest put his hooked nose up to the sky and said, "We shall see. This parish is entrusted to me now." One fisherman smiled and said, "Don't know anything about a parish, but welcome to our island." The priest turned and eyed the man with stone-cold glare and then turned his attention back to the church, transfixed. After prolonged silence during which the two men waited in awkward silence, the priest took a deep breath and spoke again.

"My name is John Worthington, and I have come to guide my flock."

The islanders were slow to open up. This man was not like their old gregarious priest. Eventually, lured by his good voice and thoughtful sermons, they accepted him. The church hummed as before, the air filled with the wail of gospel and prayer. Then one day, John referred to their apocalypse being near, and that the islanders should count their blessings as fast as they could. This last mantra was hard to fathom for some, but as he had conveyed it with a smile, most assumed he meant for them to take nothing for granted.

Nineteen-year-old Bigbee fell hard for John. The attraction was instant and rare for her, but she kept her distance out of fear of such a forbidden thing. Her involvement in the choir and teaching at church brought her within breathing distance of him on a frequent basis. She tried to ignore her urges, saying this was impossible and dangerous. The priest, however, made himself available, charismatic, and attentive. She was drawn further in. His hypnotic voice, the way he let the children frolic at his side. The way he held her with those eyes, one gray, disseminating her weaknesses, one bright blue, happy and inviting her in. It took all her might to thwart his lure.

Then one afternoon, John Worthington came upon her alone. She packed up books from Wednesday's children's Bible study. His arms came around her body from behind, his mouth on her neck. She had no will to resist and let him kiss her. He apologized for being a sinner, made her pray with him, and granted them both freedom from God's judgment. After that, Bigbee never questioned the immediacy of his desires because they were equally hers.

Where Bigbee tried to keep the relationship quiet, one day John Worthington sold it as a hawker of goods. It was a Saturday, the lone street crowded with fisherman, wives, and their children. John took Bigbee's arm in his and would not let go even as she blushed and tried to pull away. Her friends watched, knowing this was wrong on many levels. Later, some singled her out to express their fears. Perhaps, they asked, she was smitten with an impossibility, and in her first real-life infatuation, had not considered that things would not end well. Bigbee did not know what to say, as her body and mind were tangled up. It was not long before many questioned the priest's soundness. His swagger was more that of a charlatan than a priest. He began to boast at the pulpit of God's one-way love for men as he. Lectured them to prepare, but for what, he did not say.

The real John Worthington rose to the surface. Bigbee knew she had erred. She should have known his ravenous ways did not fit the soul of a priest. The gluttonous way he drank wine and ate. The way he kissed. The way he never laughed anymore. The way she could not turn from under him, his strength so severe, and the cryptic things he hissed at her concerning fate.

The turn kept turning. Their new priest became hardened. He walked with hands folded behind his back, as a lord over his own land. He began to sing his gospels, no longer theirs. All was done in the manner of some storm building, his purpose yet to be revealed. This new priest was contradictory in every manner to their priest of old. He grew sharp toward what he called their petulance, telling them that they were sluggish and had wasted many years.

John relished their unease and turned his sermons upon them. Asked why the fishermen did not go out every day, why the women sang songs from a time that was lost. He suggested that they were thankless for the island, and suggested it was not theirs. He said they were servants of a God they did not know but would soon. When the numbers in the congregation dwindled to nothing, he did not seem to care. His ungodly mood bled out into the street, saying they would soon understand what righteousness meant. He began to drink publicly. The children would not come near him. The church became his chamber. There he slept and ate. And plotted.

When the elders of the village came to John and suggested he leave, he laughed. Surely, he could see he did not fit, they said. His eyes became playful and dangerous. "You think she is too good for me?" he asked. "You think you can borrow back what I own? Whose terrain is this anyway, whose bright shore?" he ranted as those men left.

And then, John went to Bigbee to confirm his sole purpose for being there. He began by chastising her, as he had the elders. "Who brought you here, my obese lover? Who has filled you and will watch you empty?" he asked, caressing Bigbee's cheek. "I can see it. In your eyes and glow, I have given you life, my big, black dumpling. And soon those small eyes looking back at you from your deflated belly will be mine." He informed her that he was not sterile, as he had bemoaned to her at the start of their bond; crying out to an unjust world leaving him barren of the seed of life. Bigbee now understood the cause of her recent nausea and fatigue. She was pregnant. Taking his hand from her face, he told Bigbee the dark truth of their church.

Bigbee walked out and collapsed in the middle of the road. Her mother and friends gathered about her. Through her sobs, she told them what the priest had shared. John Worthington stood in the church doors, that structure behind now ringing as a tomb to all in the street.

As he looked upon that stunned fray, he yelled, "I am a pilgrim of truth. Yes," he walked forward. "See this face. See my color. We brought order to this land. We taught the lessons against rebellion. It was a fool who left this to you. Now I take it from your heart and dreams." He looked at Bigbee crumpled in the road. "Raise our fair-skinned child well. He or she will be my heir to all of this. I leave this vestige to remind you all that you cannot hope to win in a country where you do not fit." John pointed to the church.

Beneath the floor of the church, lined in rows like crops, were buried one hundred and fifty adult slaves head-first. They had been set there alive more than a century before by his ancestors, the heavy stone slabs placed over them. Their children had been taken away to those who would ignore their hopes. Their parents had become rebellious and unthankful, John had told Bigbee. "God eats their filthy souls one by one."

In time, his ancestors bequeathed the island to a sea captain, to grow crops. They brought him new slaves. Ignorant of all that had occurred, that man ultimately left the island, freed his slaves, and bequeathed Bigbee's ancestors the island.

"Haven't you heard them singing in their everlasting suffocation?" John asked and pointed to the church. "And you thought it was God answering your prayers," he laughed. "He was a weak man, that captain, his mind betraying him into false guilt over the right to own a lesser being." The priest laughed again. "You have waxed the stone over those poor souls. The altar that you sang before, the effigies of all you were supposed to trust, were props mocking your ancestors. You are salient lemmings. Slaves, still."

"You are what feeds the devil," Bigbee's mother called out to him. "Why should we believe you? The devil knows no bounds for trickery."

"Just look inside the church to prove my claims," he said. "Right before your eyes. You have seen them, human figures engraved into the stone, their heads toward the floor."

Wails filled the street as all knew John was telling the truth. The former priest had said the carvings showed God's power, levitating men to trust and not falter while being held by his grace. In their frozen state along that wall, their legs were drawn together, and their arms extended down, their praying hands pointing to the floor. There were no eyes, their priest saying they must follow God blindly.

John left the next day. He had served his mission to reinstate to these islanders that there was no freedom. Taking Bigbee's flesh was not just for his pleasure, but for added insult. To leave them a child that would forever remind them of him and this day. The islanders were now isolated within his trap. Their harmony was forever lost.

No one would ever enter the church again. The superstition of the people grew into fear of Bigbee's presence. The prejudice against them seemed everlasting. She was left hollow, her strongest reserves gone. Someone tarred the stained-glass windows and sealed the church. Bigbee left. She worked the onion fields inland for weeks, until in a fit of sadness and anger, she took the child within her out with a wire. That mangled swath of boy was buried in the sands of coastal Georgia. A month later she showed up on the doorstep of the Hooper tea plantation, the voice of Sage inviting her in. Bigbee needed a home, and there she found it.

The goodness that Sage showed her made life tolerable. When Sage passed, Virginia took over and together she and Bigbee raised Dar and Marshall. When they lost that precious boy, they were hurled into the clutch of agony. For him to pass in such a way, and only a few years after Bigbee's own child, it showed them both life's cruel intention. Bigbee did not know it then, but reprisal had settled deep inside her.

55

The Tempest

The death of Marshall at age five cemented a lasting bond between Virginia and Bigbee. Virginia's husband took the tragedy of Marshall's death like it was only he who had lost. He did not see that his wife's open bleeding was from a ruptured heart, what it was for a mother to lose a child. He fled, calling it a respite and leaving the rest blank. Years passed. Husband two, an old beau, arrived as a cap over Virginia's aching soul. He rode in on his white convertible with all the acumen of a troubadour and savoir.

When Virginia and Dar at last left the plantation, succumbing to Bobby's wishes to move closer to the things he knew, Bigbee had gone with them. By then the plantation was foundering. Virginia's sister's having given up, Virginia could not hold it down on her own. Back in his territory, Bobby surrounded himself with the boisterous set. Having secured his prize and no longer able to hold onto the act of a gentlemen, Bobby became what Bobby was. An indifferent good old boy who ran Virginia down to hopelessness. A train of abuse and a vagrant womanizer. He was just like John Worthington. A killer of souls. A bigot.

Bobby was a burden that Virginia did not have the stamina to shed or defeat. And the timepiece kept ticking. Every second felt like crushing humidity. Virginia purchased two bars for Bobby to keep him busy and away. There his chauvinistic heart could pitter-patter alongside hellion friends and ladies who traded their self-respect for attention. Dar was sent off to boarding schools to grow up and later have a family of her own. God knows how Virginia passed the time.

Bigbee sighed, recalling the moment when reprisal against John Worthington was at hand. It was Sunday, and Virginia was out for the day with Dar and four-year-old Lily. Bobby came in drunk, ranting bigotry. He'd been out with good old boys who drove convertibles, threw empty whisky bottles out the back, and taunted a world they saw as inferior. Bobby goaded Bigbee, spewing claims that after all these years he owned her. Said if Virginia did not stand between them, he would teach her the way of the world. After verbally degrading her, he tried to force his way on her. She knocked him out with a cast iron skillet, forced a sleeping pill down his throat, and dragged him to the couch. Bigbee considered killing him, but she still held hope she could one day return to her island and be forgiven.

That sleeping pill was the beginning. Bigbee saw Bobby listless on that couch like a river coming to a stop. When he awoke, she gave him a cold rag for his head and a double bourbon with a second sleeping pill in it. Bobby threw back the drink in one swallow, asked her to forgive him, and lied that he remembered only pieces of the incident. He also asked her not to tell Virginia, though that request was laced with the threat that always resided in his voice. He could not risk the loss of Virginia. The reality was that without her money, Bobby would own no airy Cadillac, no open tabs anywhere, or swank with his fellow prestigious redneck friends. Bigbee silently spun her plan on the spot and lied when she told Bobby she would forgive him. Moments later, when he was passed out again, Bigbee stood over him. "Time to let out the dam, Bobby," she said, and spat in his face. "Bad men, even in sleep, are doing something wrong."

Except for a few bright stars in her life, Bigbee had grown accustomed to reticence toward mankind. She had become efficient in matters of the heart and had abandoned the power of compassion required by God. Empathy was for those she respected. Heinous men still fantasized about owning other men and regaled in instilling fear and stealing dignity. That she must rid the world of one worthless man was making room for a better one. Her tempest was to erase another John Worthington, that dark storm against beauty, against freedom. It was now clear why God had sent her into Sage and Virginia's life. She must free her soul and the souls of those for whom she cared. The plot over Bobby was akin to cooking a long, slow meal.

Bigbee had not meant for Virginia to know how things were going to go. At least not at first. She would need Bev and Sarah to help maintain the pretense of his failing health within the circles that might ask. It was more than fortunate that Bobby had just been to his doctor for a nasty cold and high fever. He was a pin cushion for disease. Bobby was an alcoholic, had uncontrolled diabetes, gout, and heart complications. Still, his doctor said he was a Sherman tank that could go on for years.

Convincing Bev and Sarah had not been as hard a task as she imagined. They had seen his wares firsthand and that he was draining Virginia's bank account. Sarah's hatred of Bobby was religious from the get-go. She despised his foul mouth, his bad temper, his irreverence for God and all creatures he could not eat. Her conviction that Virginia must get rid of him before he drove her to her death was longstanding. Sarah had begged her to divorce him, but Virginia was never ready to consider that. That confounded everyone who loved her.

Bev got on board by simply stating that Virginia was unhappy. No glitter or diatribe for her, which was unusual. Bev saw Bobby standing in the way of things she wanted, and Bigbee knew that. "Good money going through the pockets of a decadent man. Virginia would do the same for me, I'd like to think," Bev said, stirring her iced tea. She treated it like they were simply going to sell Bobby's golf clubs. "He will forever suffer with disease anyway. This way, he will just slow down and stop, kind of like an unattended watch. Is that right?" Bev had asked, pretending to be baffled by the concept being presented to her.

"There will be no mess in his death," Bigbee recalled confirming to Bev.

Paregoric and liquor first. Pills as a booster. That was the plan. "The drip of arsenic later, but not quite yet," Bigbee told Bev and Sarah, gathered on Virginia's patio. "He will become as complacent as an old chained dog." Bigbee informed them that she had already begun his treatment. "He's got enough booze and paregoric in him to see us all as saints." She remembered Sarah's fright with that confession. Bev was ready without further conscription. Bigbee sent her in with a flask of paregoric and bourbon to stick out of the mattress so anyone with suspicions might find that Bobby, just like with his affairs, hid his addiction. His buddies would come by and tell him to get off his fat ass. Some would bring liquor to toast him, impairing him further.

Virginia realized something was going on when Bobby missed work for a week. He had slept in over the weekend and Monday, saying he was not feeling well. And because he had not been moving about, his gout was acting up. The business was his, two highway bars run mostly by his employees. The bars were just a place for Bobby to act like a big shot. Virginia was happiest when he was there, and so was he. On Tuesday, Virginia had gone in to put a cold cloth on his head and to tell him she was calling the doctor. Crazed, he yelled at her, cursed the doctor as a crook and said she was no good for anything. "Even in sex. Never any good," he said, and grabbed Virginia by the wrist to pull her down. Bigbee had come in, wrenched his weak hand away, and slapped him.

The next day, Bigbee laid a finger on the bruise on Virginia's arm. That touch and Bigbee's hard silence looking deep into her eyes had sparked Virginia to look deeper. She realized she was already involved by his verbal slander and sometimes physical abuse. By the affairs she tried to ignore. She thought of her one affair with a man who truly loved her and how she had walked away, not wanting to be like Bobby. He had gone on to be with someone else, and that loss never subsided within her.

"Your blind patience, Virginia, is no different than making excuses for a dog that has bitten a hundred people. Besides, your heart emptied him long ago." Bigbee had hugged Virginia until she began to cry. For a good half-hour, Bigbee recalled.

"I'm not a murderer," Virginia said, when Bigbee revealed the plan.

"He is already way down that path, anyway," she told Virginia.

"I can divorce him," Virginia said, pleading.

"What, so he can abuse another? And what of the teens he follows around at the strip mall—what about the stories, Virginia? Those things you ignore because you are just worn out. You have become a reliable prisoner," she told her.

"There must be another way," Virginia said. "I can try harder to make our marriage work. I know what he likes. I can pretend to be compliant and still have my life." Anger had welled up in Bigbee. The image of slaves buried alive with the fierce glare of John Worthington standing over them bore down on her.

"Compliant? You mean you're going to be his slave? Bobby is the devil," she said to Virginia. "I don't want you to be the one dead, Virginia. Years go by, and they find your bones tied to a refrigerator at the bottom of a swamp. They would never catch Bobby, because the people he hangs with know how to take care of those things. This is his territory."

"It is not as dangerous as that," Virginia uttered.

"It is death while still breathing," Bigbee retorted.

Virginia paced for two days. On the third, she announced she would never enjoy a man being tortured but would accept this ending as preordained, if it was gentle.

Bigbee, at the helm of Bobby's madness, would not relent, even as he physically tossed in the devastation upon his mind and body. Bobby's river got muddier and deeper. The coils in his thoughts widened until there was nothing to recall. Bigbee told Virginia that they were now in the eye of the tempest. "We must be strong," she said. And even as the moral side of her stood awake, Virginia reminded herself of the whips of his prior voice and hands against her. Sometimes she cried when his white mouth seemed like that of a clown, moaning up from the pillows under his head.

But Virginia knew that one day that motor would stop. She would open the windows, and then all she would hear would be the whippoorwills, lawn mowers, and dogs barking. Coffee would smell glorious again. She would sip on air. The pain in her heart would remain, but she had accepted that cost. Inexpensive when compared to brutality, Bobby's blinding cynicism toward all women would vanish. She would call out to the sleepy street, "Virginia Hooper is a fine and good woman."

Bigbee sighed recalling those days and looked out at her island. She shivered. Even in summer, the chills came and went. The breeze from the window facing the island had a voice. A jeering sound filled the air, letting her know that she could never return to paradise. And though her heart said she might cry, there was nothing left.

56

Bigbee's Last Night at the Party

The three sisters sat huddled below. Bigbee went upstairs with a bowl of rice for Bobby. It was quiet until they heard water running. The sisters tilted their heads up to listen, to understand what the sound meant. Then a noise they could not describe crossed the ceiling. Following that, a loud thump, and maybe Bigbee's voice.

Bigbee carried Bobby's frail, bony body down the hall. She had grown impatient, and undressed him, placed him in the tub, and watched the water rise. He looked up at her with hatred, unable to retaliate, as she pressed his head under the cold water.

She came downstairs twenty minutes later without a word, just her heaving lungs and slow footfall on the treads. She wanted to say she saw the blue and gray eyes of a minister on Bobby's scared face. Wanted to say she saw the resurrection of the child she wired out of her own body the moment Bobby's eyes went still. Wanted to tell Virginia that Marshall was now a king in heaven.

Bigbee said instead, "There he lay, in his heap of ego, where I swear I saw dark throughout him. Lucky our creator is so forgiving." Then she said something that stunned them. The plan had changed, and it was going to take some adjustment to see how things worked in the end. Simply dying in bed was not good enough. A more violent thing had broken rank.

"In the end, he went to the water. Down, where he fell asleep," she said. In her hand, she held a small hand towel that she ran over her damp brow. The vision of Bigbee drowning Bobby swept the room. All the months of inching him toward his end seemed useless, as here Bigbee had thrashed him out like she had just shot him. "I came in. He was taking a bath, bless him. But it seems he had a heart attack. The owl, the bird of prey had come."

The sisters sat still as dust in a perfect half-circle, their tension and sacrifice so dry and infused. Their plan had been squeezed down to a frightening and violent alternative. And now they had to envision him, not with hands crossed over his crisp dry sheets, but his blue eyes looking up through the water at Bigbee's dark face as her strong arms pinned him down.

With a sagging wrist, Bigbee flipped on the ceiling light and took in the sisters cloistered in their deathwatch. Outside, sunlight clamored to squeeze through the edges of the closed shutters. The attic fan whirled a million miles away, sucking against the sisters' humid breathing and the waving curtains. Bigbee frowned. Beyond the movement of Bigbee's shoe, all remained quiet in the room.

A low droning sound began. It was Sarah humming, her paleness eerily illuminated from the ceiling light. Her eyes were closed so tight that she looked to be in pain. She had started sharing Bobby's paregoric to dull her senses. Virginia looked out as if there were no walls in her home. She was exhausted, her face gray, her curled hands in her lap. Bev began to tap her knee and watch Bigbee. She had orchestrated a hard and violent death, the same woman who looked over the kitchen at the plantation with such care, who Sage had worshiped, and who cried so hard when Marshall died. And stood by Virginia's side every moment since.

"It is done. That, what needed to be for him and you to have peace," Bigbee told Virginia. "I will call the coroner. You girls need to get up and move. Things are looking unnatural and dangerous here. I will be going home after he is buried. I need my own peace. Virginia, don't live on the memory of that man, cause there ain't none," Bigbee said, gently kicking her on the soles of her shoes. Virginia raised her eyes and nodded. To her right, Bev looked stunned but might have smiled just so. Sarah was waxen and a thin remnant of who she once was. A common truth then wound through each sister: Bigbee's calm, her face washed of any sin.

"That man was nothing but a slow killer," Bigbee said, looking down at Virginia. "I knew a man like him once. It's okay now. You and I can move on."

Virginia stared back at those words. Her disbelief went to understanding and she nodded. Bigbee's big brown eyes were callous and set on survival.

Virginia heard the fabric of Sarah's dress shift and her frail voice call out. "A family should hold no sorrow when they need to protect themselves. Daddy said that once. Right?"

"Right," Virginia said, sat for a few more minutes more, and then rose to end this.

Bigbee stood at Bobby's funeral with a heavy arm around Virginia, protecting her from all that had been done and all she would go through once she drifted away forever. She watched as Virginia stared at the hole in the ground, the casket nestled tight to the dirt. "A vessel keeping criminality from you for eternity," Bigbee whispered, looking down.

Virginia had looked around at those present, the distant relatives and friends from other parts of other lives. She wondered if the "plantation Hoopers" existed as an anomaly. Outside their circle of glass, were others burdened by this insanity? Did all this dysfunction come from their entitlement? In the South, spells had been cast by civil war, by voodoo, and by insensitivity, by the heat, by retribution with a sweet smile, by deathly slow and generous voices, by deceit that was "really not that, but because someone had just misunderstood?" Where all had a piece of the throne in that secret place, that place where laughter and death fell into the same sentences. And one could find the humor in the worst misfortune. And that was to keep it sane. Virginia looked down at Bobby's casket and knew, of course, that few would understand.

57

The Finest Hour

Lily and Dar sat together on bar stools at The Creeping Kudzu, a diner Lily had discovered and made her haunt. It was the first time Lily had invited her mother to join her there.

"Mother, when I write the family story, how do I align my conscience when some bad guys end up winning? Because the author doesn't know the whole truth. What kind of tale will it be without me pushing someone off the pinnacle?"

Dar eyed Lily and then her coffee. "I don't want to think any more about messes that I do not have to clean up," she said while pouring way too much sugar in her coffee. "Why do we drink this stuff, Lily?" Dar asked, pointing at her mug. "We are supposed to be pushing tea now that we own a tea plantation. Lily, we have won, and by God that's all you should require. We will have to just deal with what we are left with. As I once said, we are stuck on this marble we call family. It's a planet with its own gravity."

Lily sputtered. Placing her arm down, Dar leaned to mimic her vexation. "Damn," she exclaimed, lifting her hand. Syrup from her plate of French toast clung to her wrist.

Dar eyed Lily. "You can write your story in whatever way you please. Put bad noses on them, pluck off an arm, and all that. But I know you will leave the good ones intact. Right?"

Lily looked away, as Dar continued. "Our good fortunes make mincemeat out of things misunderstood about the past. If we understood it all, no more tale. No more good book."

Lily stabbed at her bacon to take a bite. It shattered to pieces, though she would not have her bacon cooked any other way. "Okay, then *you* put a mustache or udder on the clowns. I am gonna dress them in things crows like to eat." Lily pinched up a tiny crumble of bacon.

Dar's expression widened. "Wow, that is harsh. But I suppose justified, and it's your story." She swirled on her stool, faced Lily, and placed a hand on each of her shoulders. "In fact, you are the real story, Lily. You are blessed, and all in your path are brightened. What's behind has left us alone. We are on our own and cannot be judged by what happened in another time, in another family member's storm. Because, your... maybe even *my* goodness has changed the cycle, the direction of that storm's path. You know, the health of the offspring determines the direction."

Lily smiled. "That, Mother, was a decent effort. Philosophically beautiful for a crazy, red-haired stenographer."

They sat in silence. Lily looked at her plate where liquid sugar had hardened, and eggs turned an unnatural yellow in the air of the hot room. She looked past her mother to the window where bright yellow letters spelled the name of one of her favorite places on earth. For a second, she closed her eyes and gave silent thanks to the gods that hers was the story she had. As for the Hooper sisters, Lily would write what she knew thus far, and as her mother once said, follow the crumbs for the rest. The truth will be at the end.

After living half of his life in the South—including Tennessee, Georgia, Mississippi, South Carolina, and Texas—Jones graduated from the University of Georgia with a BBA in Marketing with a minor in Psychology and got a job in Dallas and Houston handling corporate accounts. To pursue his love for art, drawing, photography, and especially writing, he made a break from the business world and soon ran a small farm. Now, he and his wife live in Vermont, a wonderful place to raise children, and dig into one's dreams.